# Begotten Not Made

Cónal Creedon is a novelist, playwright and documentary filmmaker.

www.conalcreedon.com

# Begotten Not Made

WITH ILLUSTRATIONS BY THE AUTHOR

## Cónal Creedon

IRISHTOWN PRESS

# Begotten Not Made

*Acclaim and Reviews*

Nominated for The International Dublin Literary Award promoting excellence in world literature.

"It might open like a Frank O'Connor story – but goes to places O'Connor never did. Not surreal, exactly, more a different reality. This novel brings us characters and situations we almost never encounter in fiction anymore, but is definitely not a throwback. Beautifully written, with very funny dialogue and the author's own unique take on the world. No resume could do it justice – read it!"
*IDLA Book Award, Ireland.*

The Montaigne Award – USA. Finalist 2020.
"Most Thought Provoking Book — The author is a master at constructing

fluid, lush prose and developing deep characterization in this highly literary story about faith, doubt, love, regret and conviction. It is a tale about the choices we make in life and, ultimately, about the healing power of belief ... For those who appreciate a deeper plunge, this is a thought-provoking story about human nature and a reflection on the "what if?" questions we ask ourselves during difficult times."
*Judging Panel Comments*

The Montaigne Medal is awarded to the most thought-provoking book published during a given year [US Review of Books]. The award is dedicated to the memory of Michel Eyquem de Montaigne, Lord of Montaigne was one of the most significant philosophers of the French Renaissance, known for popularising the essay as a literary genre.

The Eric Hoffer Book Award – USA. Winner 2020.

 The award honours the memory of the American philosopher Eric Hoffer by highlighting salient writing, as well as independent spirit. Since its inception, the Hoffer Award has become one of the largest international book awards for academic and independent presses.

Next Generation Indie Book Awards – USA. Bronze Winner

 The Literary Fiction Category.
*Begotten Not Made* – Winner of Bronze Award.
*NGIB Book Awards USA.*

BOOK OF YEAR – Highlights of the Year.
Cónal Creedon's recently published novel *Begotten Not Made* is a beguiling tale of tragic Christian Brother who forsook a potential love affair for the cloth having met a young nun on the night Dana won the Eurovision Song Contest.
*Collette Sheridan – Highlights of the Year – Irish Examiner.*

Selection of – BEST BOOKS OF THE YEAR.
It's a delight to read. Cónal Creedon's *Begotten Not Made*. One of the most peculiar books I have read this year.
*Theo Dorgan – Liveline. RTÉ Radio 1*

READERS' FAVORITE BOOK AWARDS USA. ★ ★ ★ ★ ★

 This is a work of quirky and conceptual literary fiction. For readers who enjoy fully realized, unusual lead characters, look no further – Cónal Creedon has created what feels like a real person, on whose shoulders we sit as the narration takes us deep into his life and work, his philosophy and his sense of love in moments which are both moving, bizarre and very amusing at times. The harsh backdrop of Irish life clashes beautifully with concepts of heavenly and mortal love, miracles and strange appearances, painting a world which is ethereal in its fairy tale moments yet painfully recognizable and relatable too. I particularly enjoyed the dynamic dialogue, as its pacing really moves scenes along. Overall, *Begotten Not Made* is a highly recommended read for literary fiction fans searching for truly unusual books that keep you thinking long after the last page is turned.

*KC Flynn - Readers' Favorite Book Awards.*

US REVIEW OF BOOKS.

Caught between indulgence and renunciation, young Brother Scully exchanged thoughts with Sister Claire for only an awkward hour in December 1970, but their love inspired a daily ritual of flashing lamps at dawn between monastery and convent. When her lamp fails to flash from her window on Christmas Day near the fiftieth anniversary of their serendipitous meeting, "his mind is haunted by memories, twisting and turning and churning around his tormented brain … He laughs at the painful loss of his innocence, and the brutal consequences of a single embrace that set his life trundling off the edge into the big black with no way back." Brother Scully then relives that enchanting hour and the subsequent five decades of unconsummated love and rebellious scriptural analysis in a single day, revealing a tantalizing theory of the true paternity of Jesus Christ that turned his monastic vocation and his heart inside out.

Cónal Creedon, deals with biblical themes in previous writings, describes his novel as "a fairy-tale for the twenty-first century." This book spins a delicious yarn that tips nearly every sacred cow of Christianity—a timely sport in this era of diminished participation in monastic life and the laity's scathing criticism of the Church's sins and shortcomings—all the while spotlighting the archetypal unrequited romance made fresh in the monastic setting. In the backdrop is the soul of devout Irish Catholic culture and the lives of the working-class men and women of Cork who lend a down-to-earth stability to the tale as well as zest and color. As a bonus, the author includes his fanciful pen-and-ink drawings and tasty stories within the story, such as Sister Claire's retelling of a saga about Mossie the Gardener and his war hero pigeon, Dowcha-boy. This is a plot thread sure to tickle even the most obstinate funnybone, and it specifically lends a magical yet realistic aura to what could have been a far more level, self-conscious story.

Though many masterful novelists have eschewed punctuation of various types, including the indomitable James Joyce, the lack of quotation marks in the dialogue takes some getting used to. But this attribute also lends a lean and mean playscript or screenplay effect, and the novel certainly could and should inspire a lively and memorable film or stage production. Creedon's well-honed, multidimensional cast of characters, his vividly portrayed settings and interiors of 1970s and contemporary Cork, and his measured but lyrical prose nail every nuance of the story arc. The author has ripped open his Irish heart to spill this marvelous pastiche, a real-life creed that must be absorbed with one's heart open wide to the pathos and poignancy of love lost and found, life lived and unlived, and spirituality bound to blind faith or soaring on the wings of perception. Ultimately, Creedon's tour de force pays tribute to an end-of-life journey that paradoxically celebrates the winter of regret and the eye-opening gift of having nothing left to lose.

*Kate Robinson - US REVIEW of BOOKS*

I thoroughly enjoyed reading *Begotten Not Made* by Cónal Creedon - it maintains a Joycean flavour throughout the story. The writer's perspective in introducing the reverend brother's intellectual interpretation of authentic Biblical facts is so brilliant that it encourages you to fact check.

*Ronald Clifford - Irish American Examiner. New York.*

It's all there in *Begotten Not Made*, alongside the mysteries of the scripture, the alchemy of love, the pathos of life and the legend of a war hero racing pigeon: a picaresque epic that at times dips into the surreal.

*Donal O'Donoghue - Books, RTÉ Guide*

*Begotten Not Made* is incredibly nuanced in that sympathy. Brother Scully is developed far beyond the definitions of his profession, beyond the collar, he is intellectual, emotional, sensitive and troubled. Such nuance is explored intricately in Cónal's classic, conversational style, ranging from profound humour to tinges of sadness and airs of dark comedy. The humour of the novel is colourful in every sense of the word, which Cónal infuses to dramatize the life of Brother Scully's adolescence. These playful anecdotes are threaded throughout the novel giving the lives of the characters depth and sincerity. At the end, the book is really set in that one hour, a feature reminiscent of Joyce.

*Liz Hession – Motley Magazine.*

Cónal Creedon's new novel puts a magic-realist twist on the tale of a cleric's unrequited love for a nun. Brother Scully delves back through his analysis of scripture, which has led him to a unique and highly plausible theory regarding the true paternity of Jesus Christ. Inside the covers of *Begotten Not Made*, there unfolds a tale that's part poignant love story and part meditation on the phenomenon of faith, a uniquely Corkonian take on magical realism served up with Creedon's customary flair for colourful dialogue and tall tales – a fairy tale for the 21st Century.

*Ellie O'Byrne – ARTS, Irish Examiner.*

*Begotten Not Made* is rewarding, straddling a fine line between pathos and comedy. We see the disintegration of Brother Scully – between the torment of his unrealised love and his unique take on Catholicism, he doesn't believe in the divinity of Jesus and has a theory as to his real paternity. This is a troubled man, literally crumbling into a despairing heap as an elderly man. Brother Scully elicits sympathy despite his obnoxiousness – a hard man to like but Creedon's talent is to draw out the humanity of this demented individual. There is a lot more to this novel than sexual and spiritual frustration – It is funny and it has real charm. There are elements of magic realism here which give the novel an air of fairytale. *Begotten Not Made* is well written, strong on highly amusing dialogue and has a twist that is satisfying, well worth the wait. Like all good art, the local becomes universal with its truths and its understanding of human nature.

*Colette Sheridan – WEEKEND*

*Begotten Not Made*, a multi-faceted fairytale which gives a fresh twist to an ancient story – the life of Jesus. The book deftly presents an insight

into human frailty: through the complicated love that arose between Br. Scully and Sr. Claire on the night Dana won the Eurovision. Equal parts hilarious and poignant. The story unfolds as Br. Scully grapples with his existence and his sanity and his unique exploration of the nature of belief. The book is also resplendent with illustrations by the author.
*Aisling Meath - The Southern Star.*

Last night I finished Cónal Creedon's Begotten Not Made. It is multi-layered, funny and touching, at times madcap or magic realist, quintessential story-telling, and has a wonderful and satisfying ending. It's about the unrequited love between Brother Scully and Sister Claire, a novitiate in the convent across the valley from his monastery in Cork city. That spiritual affair began on the night in 1970 that Dana won the Eurovision Song Contest, and it lasts for almost fifty years – their correspondence continues: Scully and Claire send a signal to each other every morning at dawn by quickly switching their bedroom light off and on. That one single act of devotion gives Scully the courage to live out his chaste life. But not all is how it seems. And there is a sting in this tail.

There are several poignant moments in the novel, the most moving of which is when towards the end of their hour or two together in 1970, in the garden, Scully and Claire are faced with a crucial decision. And that predicament, upon which their fates turned, reminded me of that great Cavafy poem, Che fece... il gran rifiuto (The Great Refusal).
Cónal has drawn a number of fine pen and ink illustrations to accompany the story which lends a charmingly quaint feeling to the rich reading experience.
*Danny Morrison - [Novelist/Playwright] Chairperson of Féile an Phobail.*

What a rollicking good read it is. I have to confess that the Dowcha Boy pigeon business remained my favorite since it is so hilarious. But there were many such laugh out loud moments to be met with exclamation points in the margins. That whole Eurovision conceit was just brilliant. And coming round again and again to the flashing of the dawn lights. Loved the surreal moment when Scully walks off on the beam of light. And the great switcheroo of the ending was terrific. Wonderfully enjoyable book. Thanks a mill', Cónal!
*David Monagan - Jaywalking With The Irish.*

Published in 2018 by Irishtown Press

Irishtownpress@gmail.com

© Cónal Creedon 2018

The moral right of the author has been asserted.
A catalogue record for this book is available from the British Library.

ISBN 978-0-9557644-6-2 (print)
ISBN 978-0-9557644-7-9 (digital)

Book design (print and digital editions) by John Foley.
www.bitedesign.com

Set in Tala, designed by John Harrington.
www.shandontype.com

I dedicate this book with love to Fiona O'Toole — a very special woman who has a natural ability to laugh in the face of adversity and continue dancing long after the band has packed up and left the stage.

With special gratitude to John Foley, Lisa Sheridan, Tony McGrath, Eileen O'Connell, Conor O'Toole, Martin Lynch, Hugh Quillinan, Doireann Ní Ghríofa, Roz Edwards, Mary McCarthy, Rachel McGovern and The School of English UCC.

— • —

It's the darkest before dawn this Christmas Eve morn, and all the world is at peace. Not a soul scurrying through the streets, no movement along the quays, nothing stirring. The only sign of life is the odd flicker of light from the houses away up on the Northside.

In a monastery towering above the town an elderly brother leans forward in his chair and laughs. With a stretch of his arms he straightens the arthritic curve of his twisted spine, then clears the condensation from his bedroom window with the back of his gnarled and knuckled hand. He polishes his spectacles and looks out over the rooftops across the city. His eyes trawl from east to west, past darkened silhouettes of slate-clad buckled beams, half-cocked chimney pots, spires and towers, before finally fixing on the belfry of St Joseph's Convent. Then, scrolling down to a twelve-pane window, he sets his gaze on Sister Claire's bedroom. It is a private and secret ritual he has observed every single morning for almost fifty years and this Christmas Eve morn is no different.

    — Begotten not made, begottennotmade, begottennotmade begotten ...

He says it faster and faster until it becomes a mantra of garbled sound. Every now and then, his eyes dart away from Sister Claire's window and towards Mecca, all the way across Brewery Valley to the grand houses perched on the crest of Patrick's Hill. He sits there waiting for the dawn, watching for that moment when the first shaft of light of the rising sun will crack the horizon line along the rooftops. *The Changing Of The Guard,* he calls it.

He can never quite pinpoint the defining moment when his fascination for this daily ritual of observing the rising sun began, but he remembers that first morning when he awoke as a fully-fledged brother in this cell-like room. It dawned on him then that his life had changed and nothing would ever be the same again.

Space had always been scarce in the house where he was reared. But, that morning, for the first time in his life, he awoke to find he had a room to call his own. Everything within the four walls belonged to him. His bed. His chair. His lamp. His sink. The shoes by his locker were his shoes, not hand-me-downs, and hanging in his wardrobe was his crisp new black soutane. All that he surveyed belonged to him. He smiled when it occurred to him that a vow of poverty had made him a man of means overnight.

The glow of an opal moon drew him to his window like a moth to a flame. Looking out across the city, his eyes traced schoolboys' footsteps from street lamp to street lamp, down Peacock Lane, across Gerald Griffin Street, past Denny's slaughterhouse and all the way to the brewery. Then the steep climb, lamp post by lonely lamp post, up Fever Hospital Steps, past the stacked red-bricked terraces of Goldsmith's, Roche's and Sutton's Buildings until his view was blocked by the row of grand houses along the crest of Patrick's Hill. His mind carried him over the slates and chimney stacks, past the barracks and Glancatan, all the way to the little house in Barrack Buildings where he was born. His thoughts were of childhood, his family in the kitchen each morning, the scramble for school bags. Sister yelping as mother frantically tugged and plaited her hair. Father cursing and grappling with his bicycle, hopping it off every door, chair and table from the backyard all the way through the house and out the front door, making ready for the freewheel down to Ford's.

— Christ-dam-blasted-buckin-bike-an-blasted-buckin-door …

At the height of this spiralling chaos, mother would shift the drying clothes from the rail above the stove and, opening the oven door, a warm wave of freshly baked brown soda would embrace the house like the love of God. Then, cutting the crisp crackling crust, she would smother each slice in melting salty creamery butter, and all would be at peace in the world again.

When young Brother Scully looked out from his bedroom window that first morning all those decades ago, he swore he could smell his mother's freshly baked bread. It was a scent from childhood that had been buried deep in the memory of his senses. He clenched his eyes tightly shut hoping to hold onto the lingering aroma, but it was gone.

A strange thing happened that morning. Just at the very moment he opened his eyes, the first ray of dawn clipped the rooftops along Patrick's Hill. It was as if that golden stream of light was beaming out directly to him from the oven in his mother's kitchen. He sat there at his bedroom window watching the sun climb into the heavens and, like the power of the Holy Spirit, it drove the darkness from the city and the world. Something about the power of the dawn touched the young brother's soul. He placed his hands to his face and sighed. Brother Scully wept.

What began that morning as an expression of loneliness has developed over the decades from fascination to obsession, and every dawn since that very first morn, he has been at his post observing *The Changing Of The Guard.*

*  *  *

It's the stillness before dawn this Christmas Eve morn and Brother Scully is sitting at his window in darkness, in silence, waiting in anticipation of the inevitable morning glory of the rising sun. Over the years, those first shards of light have come to mean many different things. Sometimes at dusk, as if inspired by Isaiah, he sees Michael the Archangel showering spears of gold into the overpowering blackness of Lucifer. Then again at dawn, just when the fallen angels of Hell relax in the confidence of their supremacy of the heavens, Michael the Archangel creeps up behind Lucifer's Venus, lofting golden darts from behind the chimney stacks along Patrick's Hill, quenching the Morning Star. Other times it's the never-ending struggle between Yin and Yang, like the white and brown bulls of the Táin, with their horns locked in eternal equilibrium, and with each new dawn the battle between good and evil begins all over again.

Every single morning for almost five decades Brother Scully has looked out on the heavens, mesmerised by the pure power and mystery of the planets. His wonderment is a type of worship, more pagan than Christian, yet his confidence in his vocation to Jesus Christ has always remained steadfast.

But, as if attempting to reassure himself of his core belief in the divinity and deity of Jesus Christ, Brother Scully sometimes mutters the parting words of a young novice many decades ago. Brother Crowley was his name. He had arrived from the seminary just a short few months previously, but due to an alleged indiscretion the young Brother Crowley came under a cloud of suspicion. It was determined that he would be sent to the missions, where he would have time to reflect and refocus his vocation. But young Brother Crowley made an unexpected and unprecedented decision. On the morning of his extradition, he quit the monastery. Brother Crowley's departure was unsettling. It was the first time Brother Scully had witnessed one of the community just walk away from religious life. Ever since that morning, young Brother Crowley's parting words have remained locked in Brother Scully's brain.

— *Call It the sun. Call It the stars. Call It the moon.*
*Call It Vishnu. Call It Allah. Call It Jehovah.*
*Call It nature. Call It everlasting life.*
*Call It whatever you like. After all, what is in a name?*
*There is only one true God, with a humility that knows no bounds.*
*Call It what you like.*
*It will always answer as long as you call It with respect...*

Then young Brother Crowley turned and walked out of the monastery. The sound of his footsteps echoed around the corridors and faded into the distance. He was never seen or heard of again.

That night the whisperers who gathered in the cloisters agreed that there was something seriously contaminated, corrupt, if not evil in young Brother Crowley's soul. They agreed that the monastery was better off without him. They prayed for Brother Crowley. They prayed that God would have mercy on his soul.

* * *

Brother Scully sits back and enjoys nature's light show while meditating on the day that has been and the new day that is about to begin.

*The Changing Of The Guard* always brings its own unique, spectacular display, yet there is one constant to this daily ritual, one very special moment that is both personal and precious to Brother Scully. Every morning just before the break of dawn, his eyes travel from east to west, back across the city all the way to the belfry of St Joseph's Convent. He finds focus on that twelve-pane window, third from the left on the second floor, and he fixes his gaze on Sister Claire's bedroom.

Brother Scully met Sister Claire only once in his life. It was back in 1970 on the night Dana won the Eurovision Song Contest. Every single morning since their first and only encounter, with a flick of her light switch and the flash of a bulb, Sister Claire has beamed out a coded message of love from her bedroom window.

– Flash-flash, Flash Flash. – *Good morning, Brother Scully.*
And then with a click of his light switch Brother Scully has always replied,

– Flash-flash, Flash Flash. – *Good morning, Sister Claire.*
It is as simple as that. For almost fifty years they have not communicated in any other way except for their daily exchange of flashing bulbs. This coded greeting of flickering light, with its simple and secret message, has forged an unbreakable bond between the two. It is a bond that has endured through the decades. Brother Scully treasures this moment of shared intimacy.

This Christmas Eve morn, Brother Scully is uneasy. He sits by his window waiting. Sister Claire is late. It is almost seven-thirty and still no light has shone out from her bedroom over in St Joseph's Convent. He has been flicking his lamp on and off for the past half hour, but still no reply. Maybe something is wrong? Maybe something has happened to Sister Claire? A growing concern takes root in his mind. He begins to laugh.

He is distracted just for a moment as the first faint, pink glow of dawn begins to warm the slates beyond the eastern horizon. Brother Scully settles in for *The Changing Of The Guard.*

It begins like a diamond, dazzling bright, then one single crisp ray of sunlight pierces the ridge tiles on Patrick's Hill. Like a silver spear, it cuts straight through the ink-black sky and travels right across the city in a direct line towards Shandon steeple. Brother Scully watches, spellbound, as this shaft of light connects with the gilded fish weathervane on top of Shandon, causing it to shine out a full spectrum of gold. As if by the hand of God, the fish swivels on its pivot and relays the beam all the way to St Joseph's Convent. Like a flash of lightning, it transforms Sister Claire's bedroom window into a mirror of blinding gold.

— Well, Holy Mary, Mother of God ...

In all his years observing *The Changing Of The Guard* he has never seen anything like it, and because no greeting has yet shone out from Sister Claire, he assumes that this extraordinary first ray of dawn must have connected with her bedroom window at the very moment she flickered her light bulb. So, reaching for his switch, Brother Scully sends his reply.

— Flash-flash, Flash Flash. — *Good morning, Sister Claire.*

But a seed of uncertainty is planted in his brain. He has never known the first beam of the rising sun to connect with Sister Claire's window. For it to happen at the precise moment that she flashed her coded message defies belief. And though the phenomenon he has just witnessed is technically possible, as no law of physics has been broken, it crosses his mind that such a random act of nature stretches the principles of probability.

— Hmm? Most extraordinary and highly improbable, he mutters.

Doubt takes hold. Was it just a coincidence? Maybe Sister Claire did not flash her light? Was it just the reflection of the first stark ray of dawn on her window? Could it be one of those rare mysteries of the heavens? An overpowering fear grips Brother Scully. Maybe Sister Claire was unable to send her greeting this morning. Something may have happened to Sister Claire. Could there be something wrong? And what if something has happened to Sister Claire, what then? How would he ever know? How would he ever find out? A sense of panic begins to build inside his mind when he realises he has no one to turn to, no one with whom he can share his concerns. He knows better than to confide in any of the other brothers in the monastery. It would only confirm their long-held belief that his grip on reality had once again surrendered to the delusions of his insanity.

*Hmm? Most extraordinary and highly improbable...*

*Maybe I am mad...*

— And maybe I am mad, he mutters and suppresses an urge to giggle.

It crosses his mind that maybe his old friend Brother O'Connell would understand, but then dismisses that idea. Brother O'Connell is just too excitable to trust with such a delicate and confidential matter. How in the name of God could he even begin to explain that he has forged a relationship with a nun over in St Joseph's Convent spanning almost fifty years, a relationship that exists and thrives solely on the daily flick of a light switch.

The first flush of dawn sweeps across the rooftops, sending trickles of light down over slates, along gutters and seeping into the dark cracks and crevices of lanes and alleyways. Brother Scully fixes his eyes on Sister Claire's bedroom window, hoping for a glimmer of light or some sign of life. He flicks his light switch on and off, faster and faster, over and over again, but no reply. As the brightness of dawn drives out the darkness of night, an overwhelming feeling of desperation brings a smile to his face. He now knows he must wait until dusk casts a blanket of darkness over the city before he can attempt to make contact with Sister Claire again.

His thoughts become lost in a maze of memories twisting and turning in his tormented brain. So he sits there mumbling his mantra, eyes strained and set on Sister Claire's bedroom window.

— Begottennotmadebegottennotmadebegottennotmadebego ...

It's been a lifetime since Brother Scully stood at the head of a class-room. He was a lot younger back then, and maybe that's why he placed such importance in matters of so little consequence. He thrived on the feeling of power when he paced the classroom up and down between the desks. Back then he could sense weakness in a raised eyebrow, the twiddle of a pencil or the shifting of a shoe. He remembers those days with the sepia-toned sadness that nostalgia brings. Sometimes when he closes his eyes he still sees the boys' dirty faces peeping out at him from under ring-wormed bowl-cuts. Some faces he remembers, some names he forgets. Sometimes he recites them like a roll call or an ancient druidic chant.

— Buckley, Flynn, Perrott, O'Toole ...

Sometimes boys' names and faces haunt him. Like ghosts from the past they appear out of the darkness without warning.

— Right lads! Put away the books!

We're going to carry on from where we left off yesterday.

And, where did we leave off yesterday?

From the horn-rimmed corner of his glasses he sees the Parrot fluttering and spluttering on the edge of his desk.

— Brudder! Brudder! Brudder! Brudder! Brudder!

Jimmy Perrott was the Parrot, not because his name sounded like parrot, but because he was Brother Scully's parrot, always repeating Brother Scully word-for-word and finishing Brother Scully's sentences with a squawk.

He sees him now, the little beak on him, and he up and down, and out of his desk, with his hand flapping in the air, crowing out.

— Brudder! Brudder! Brudder! Brudder! Brudder!

— Well, Mister Perrott?

— The birth of Jesus, Brudder, squawked the Parrot.

— The birth of our Saviour Jesus Christ. Dead right, Mister Perrott.

So, why! Why did Mary and Joseph go to-oooo?

— Bethlehem, Brudder, chirped the Parrot.

— Right again, Mister Perrott.

So, why? Why did Mary and Joseph go to Bethlehem?

Brother Scully's eyeballs trawled the classroom, row-by-row, desk-by-desk, eventually finding anchor at Christy Buckley.

— Well, Buckley.

Come on, man! Come on! We did all this last week.

Why, man! Why!

— Why what, Brother?

Without missing a beat, he delivered one sharp jab of a pointed index knuckle into Christy Buckley's ribs.

— Yer asleep, man! Yer asleep!

Out b'the wall, Buckley! Out b'the wall! I'll deal with you in a minute! When they're offerin' you a day's work, ya won't hear that either, Buckley.

And why won't Christy Buckley hear the offer of a day's work?

— Brudder! Brudder! Brudder! Brudder!

— Well, Mister Perrott?

— 'Cause he'll be asleep, Brudder!

— Dead right, Mister Perrott. Christy Buckley will be asleep. Now, repeat the question for the benefit of those of us who were asleep!

— Why did Mary and Joseph go to Bethlehem, squawked the Parrot out the side of his beak and slid back onto his perch.

Brother Scully swooped on Nicky Flynn.

— So Mister Flynn? You've heard the question. Why? Why, from your vast knowledge of theology and all matters biblical, do you think, in the wide earthly world, did Joseph and Mary happen to venture to the little town of Bethlehem, all those years ago?

— Eh?

— Come on, Mister Flynn! Come on! We did all this last week!

— Mary and Joseph, eh, went to, eh?

— Now think about what you're sayin', Flynn. We're not dealing with any old village or crossroads here, ya know. We're talking about the town, the town where the Saviour, the Saviour Jesus Christ was born. The birth of civilisation.

Right, Mister Flynn! So why? Why did Joseph and Mary go to Bethlehem?

— Eh? Mary and Joseph went to Bethlehem, for, eh?

— Come on, Mister Flynn, we did all this last week!

— Mary and Joseph went to Bethlehem … for the Christmas, Brother?

— The what!

— The Christmas, Brother?

— Sur' Jesus Christ and his Holy Mother, there was no Christmas back then, man! That was the first Christmas!

Brother Scully grabbed Nicky Flynn by the scruff of the neck.

— We did all this last week! Come on, Flynn! Come on! Why did Mary and Joseph go to?

Then clicking his fingers he pointed to Christy Buckley.

— Eh? Bedlam, Brother!

— Bedlam? Bedlam? Did you say Bedlam, Buckley? Spell Bethlehem, Buckley?

Releasing his grip on Flynn's neck he lunged towards Buckley.

— Come on, Buckley! Spell it, man! Spell it!

— Eh? B-E-D-D?

— No, man! No! It's T, man! T!

— B-E-T-E?

— No! It's H, man! H!

Each letter was punctuated with a punch to Buckley's shoulder.

— B-E-T-H-E-L?

— Not E-L! It's L-E, man! L-E!

— B-E-T-H-L-E-M ...

— No Buckley! No! Yer not listening, man! Yer not listening! It's B-E-T-H-L-E-H! H, man! H!

Repeat after me!

B-E-T-H-L-E-H-E-M.

He signed off with a clatter to the back of Buckley's skull.

— B-E-T-H-L-E-H-E-M, Brother.

Then Brother Scully turned on Nicky Flynn.

— So, Mister Flynn? Why! Come on, man! Come on!

Why did Mary and Joseph go to Bethlehem? Why, man! Why?

Nicky Flynn's eyebrows knotted as the question contorted inside his brain. Brother Scully stood towering over him, eyes bulging and roaring.

— Why, man! Why! We did all this last week, Mister Flynn! Come on! Why did Joseph and Mary go to Bethlehem?

— Joseph was, eh? Joseph was lookin' for a job closer to home, Brother?

— A job? A job is it! Why would Joseph be lookin' for a job, and he a fully qualified, self-employed, car-pen-ter! Why, man! Why!

A clatter lifted Nicky Flynn clean out of his desk.

— Yer not listening, man! Not listening! Get out b'the wall, Mister Flynn! Go on, get out b'the wall and join yer friend Mister

Buckley! I'll deal with the two of ye in a minute ...

Right lads! I'll say it one more time and one time only.

Mary and Joseph went to Bethlehem to fill in a census for-um!

So why did they go?

And a room full of dirty faces sang out the reply,

- Mary and Joseph went to Bethlehem to fill in a census for-um!
- Why did they go!
- To fill in a census for-um!
- And one more time for Mister Buckley!
  Why did they go!
- To fill in a census for-um!
- Arís eile!
- To fill in a census for-um!

The chorus of shrill voices fades with the memory. Brother Scully's thoughts gradually return to the present ...

\* \* \*

It's the brightness after dawn this Christmas Eve morn. Brother Scully is still alone, still sitting at his bedroom window looking out across the city. His gaze locked on Sister Claire's window over in St Joseph's Convent, watching for a sign of life.

- Mary and Joseph went to Bethlehem to fill in a census for-um, he mumbles as his mind drifts. — A census for-um, acensusfor-um, acensusfor-umacensusfor-umacensusfor-um ...

He laughs at the insanity of it all. He questions why any man in his right mind would head off across the desert with a pregnant young girl on the back of a donkey just to fill in a census form. He laughs louder when the thought crosses his mind that the baby she was carrying wasn't even his.

- Jesus, some census form that turned out to be.

  *Father's Name: God Almighty.*

  *Father's Occupation: Creator of Heaven and Earth.*

Wiping the tears from his eyes, Brother Scully holds his hand to his mouth to restrain his guffaws of laughter.

*  *  *

Over the years Brother Scully's sudden outbursts of laughter have become accepted as normal around the monastery, but it wasn't always that way. In the early days, he prayed to God for divine assistance to control his hysterics. He remembers that time Deputy Head Brother Lynch cornered him and warned him that there would be serious consequences if he didn't restrain his wild swings of emotion.

— If ya don't cop onto yourself, maybe a few months in the missions would knock some of that foolishness out of you! D'ya hear me, Scully!

But that was a long time ago. These days Brother Scully is firm in his belief that it is better to laugh than to cry, so he just throws back his head and laughs whenever he takes the notion, mopping the tears streaming down his cheeks on the frayed cuffs of his soutane.

He remembers his first public uncontrolled surge of giddiness. A chill of embarrassment causes his shoulder blades to flinch.

It was one of those dark winter evenings in the chapel, sometime back in 1970. Deputy Head Brother Lynch was on the altar, his arms outstretched, his eyes cast towards heaven. He was reading from John's gospel in a deep and sanctimonious tone. Brother Scully was young and naïve, fresh from the seminary, yet he sat there baffled as to why he was listening to the old tale about a wedding that ran out of wine in a place called Cana almost two thousand years ago.

There was something farcical, something absolutely absurd about the way God in heaven, the supreme and eternal master of the universe, creator of heaven and earth, decided to unleash all his power and divine forces on mankind just to conjure up a few kegs of drink for a wedding that had run dry.

— Fairy tale!

Young Brother Scully didn't realise the words had slipped out of his mouth until Deputy Head Brother Lynch stopped reading mid-sentence and glared out over the lectern. Not a sound in the chapel as, one by one, every brother shuffled uncomfortably and turned in their seats, relaying the stare of condemnation from the altar all the way to Brother

Scully. But the stark silence in the chapel was shattered when Brother Scully's resolve dissolved under the mounting pressure and he erupted in wild roars of uncontrollable laughter.

— Take him out, roared Deputy Head Brother Lynch. — Remove him from this house of worship. Remove him from this house of God! This instant! Out! Out! Out! Get him out of here! He is possessed by evil spirits, maybe even the Devil himself!

— And you don't get much more evil than the Devil, whispered young Brother O'Connell with a hint of sarcasm.

The more Brother Scully struggled to suppress his laughter the louder it became. He hadn't eaten for a number of days, not since the night of the Eurovision Song Contest, so his escalating hysterics caused his empty stomach to convulse. This brought on such intense muscle spasms of empty retching that a mouthful of green bile and thick globules of saliva oozed and bubbled to his lips. Brother Ambrose, the theology master, leaned toward Brother Scully, examining his mouth.

— Jesus Christ, he whispered and blessed himself. — His mouth! His mouth! He's frothing at the mouth!

This only served to fuel Deputy Head Brother Lynch's outrage.

— Possessed! He's possessed! Possessed by demons, he roared. — Get him out of here! This is the house of God!

Rumours spread throughout the monastery that some evil spirit had invaded the young brother's soul and taken control of his mind. At first the others kept their distance for fear of contamination, but in time it became clear that he had only temporarily lost his grip on reality. Suspicion of madness can become a self-fulfilling prophecy, and in the days that followed, young Brother Scully's words, deeds and actions were scrutinised in every detail. Later that night the whisperers who gathered in the shadows of the cloisters agreed that all was not well in Brother Scully's mind, and feared that he was in danger of trundling off the edge of sanity.

* * *

When Brother Scully was a novice in the seminary, he spent his days devouring the well-thumbed pages of his bible, cross-referencing the various accounts with historical fact and established theological dogma. Though his research always led to more questions than answers, his belief remained steadfast and unwavering. Never, for one moment, did he doubt that the New Testament was anything but an honest and factual account of the life and times of Jesus Christ. But yet, there was something about the miracles in the holy texts that had always presented a problem for him.

Every Friday afternoon the young seminarians would gather in the Aula Maxima for an open debate on all matters theological and the fundamentals of Christian belief. Sparks would fly as they quoted chapter and verse, arguing their findings, as they attempted to impress the theology master Brother Ambrose. During one particularly fiery debate Brother Scully made a contentious declaration.

— As I see it, he said. — The early Church leaders inserted the miracles into the gospels as a crude device to convince primitive man of the power of God and the divinity of Jesus Christ.

This did not go down too well with Brother Ambrose.

— Do you suggest we dismiss the miracles altogether, he demanded.
— What I'm saying is that the miracles have served their purpose. But in these modern times the miracles in the Holy Scriptures are obsolete, and have become an obstacle between God and man. In these days of science and technology the miracles appear to be no more than elaborate parlour games and cheap magic tricks ...
— Cheap magic tricks?
— Speaking as an educated, modern man, Brother Scully continued. — I don't need such sideshow gimmicks or sleight of hand to convince me of the power of the Almighty.

A cautious whisper spread throughout the hall. Realising he was in too deep to withdraw, Brother Scully pressed his point home.

— Do we really need God to pull a rabbit from a hat, when the miracle of nature is plain for all to see? The miracle of nature is God, and, just like nature, God is everywhere. The miracle of God is the miracle of life itself. It is the flutter of a butterfly's wing. It is the grass seed as it bursts into life every spring. The miracle of God is life, not death. God is the planets and the universe. God is mankind in all our joy, heartbreak, illness, health, poverty and wealth. What is life but one incredible, mysterious and magical miracle, and through this miracle of life we proclaim that God is all-powerful and is alive and lives amongst us, and I don't need some second-rate, sideshow Houdini to convince me of that.

— Houdini, questioned Brother Ambrose.

— Look, what I'm saying is …

Brother Scully paused to gather his thoughts before he continued.

— The truth of the gospel is found in the dirt-under-the-fingernail gritty realism, and not the smoke and mirrors of magic surrealism. The credibility of the gospel is revealed in the detail and integrity of its reality, and not hidden in some conjuror's bag of tricks from the Shilling Stores.

Brother Ambrose was visibly challenged by the audacity of Brother Scully's questioning of core Christian beliefs, but as a theologian he was intrigued by the logic of the young seminarian's thesis.

— Maybe you would like to expand on that, he probed. — Do you contest the veracity of the gospels?

— Of course not, said Brother Scully. — The New Testament offers a true account of Jesus Christ's time among us. If proof ever be needed that the gospels are founded in reality, we need look no further than Matthew 27:32, Mark 15:21 or Luke 23:26.

— Please tell us more, Brother Scully.

— I refer to the passage where Simon of Cyrene was plucked by the Roman soldiers from the anonymity of the crowd to help Jesus carry his cross to Golgotha — the place of his ultimate crucifixion.

— How so?

— Well, as I see it, the inclusion of this seemingly inconsequential episode in the holy manuscripts is actually proof, if proof be needed, that Jesus walked among us, and the gospels are in fact a true account of Christ's time on earth, rather than an elaborate work of fiction.

— Interesting? Please explain?

— Think about it, he said.

Brother Scully hesitated to create a moment of dramatic effect before expanding on his theory.

- What self-respecting fiction writer would introduce a brand new character with the unlikely name of Simon of Cyrene so late in the plot, and at such a pivotal point in the story, to carry out such an important task?

A gasp of shock filtered from the back of the Aula Maxima at the implied suggestion that the gospels might be works of fiction. But Brother Scully forged ahead.

- The gospel comes to a heightened, dramatic moment when Jesus Christ was brought before the most powerful men of his time, Herod the Great, King of Judea, Pontius Pilate the Roman Consul and Caiaphas the Jewish High Priest, and they contrived to have him whipped, stripped and forced him to carry his own cross through the streets of Jerusalem to his place of execution.
- That's all in the gospel, said Brother Ambrose.
- Well, if the gospels were works of fiction, surely rather than introducing this previously unknown character, this Simon of Cyrene, plucked from the anonymity of the Greek Chorus and thrust centre stage to help Jesus carry his cross, any fiction writer of merit would have selected a character that had been previously established in the story. Surely a character with a vested interest in what was happening to Jesus would have been selected, and not some unknown...
- Simon of Cyrene was not totally unknown, Brother Scully. It is suggested that Rufus, one of the apostles mentioned in the Acts of the Apostles, was the son of Simon of Cyrene.
- Ah, yes. But the Acts of the Apostles happened many years after the crucifixion. But on that day of Jesus' crucifixion, Simon of Cyrene had never been heard of before...
- Point taken, said Brother Ambrose. — Please do carry on.
- If the gospels were works of fiction, it would have made more sense if one of Jesus' twelve loyal and trusted disciples had stepped forward from the crowd. Maybe James the Less, or James the brother of Jesus, or James the son of Zebedee.

Or what about John, the young and idealistic boy whom Jesus loved? We are told that the beloved disciple was with the Marys at the foot of the cross on the day of the crucifixion. It would make perfect sense if, in a mad fit of blind love or youthful indignation, John had broken away from the women and dashed out from the crowd to help his Lord.

Or what about Simon Peter, the one hand-picked by Jesus to be the rock on which the church would be built? It would have been a far better ending to the story if Peter had stepped forward saying something like,

*I have denied you three times before the cock crowed twice, my Lord. But now in your hour of need. I, Simon Peter, I will be your rock.*

— Interesting perspective, commented Brother Ambrose. — Although on a point of detail, the cock didn't actually crow twice, that's a mistranslation of Mark from the original Greek. The cock only crowed once.

Brother Ambrose said something about the Greek word *dis* meaning *again*,

— ...before the cock would crow *again*, implying the next day. But somewhere along the line the word *dis* meaning *again* was mistranslated by some ignoramus as *twice*, explained Brother Ambrose.

But Brother Scully did not stop to clarify what he considered to be a detail of little consequence.

— Or what about the villain of the piece, he said. — What about Judas Iscariot? What if, in a fit of remorse, he came barging through the Roman security cordon, begging for forgiveness. Just imagine if it was Judas who put his shoulder to the cross and helped the Son of God, and if Jesus turned to Judas and said something like,

— *All is forgiven, Judas. Future generations will know that your act of betrayal played a pre-destined role in the unfolding of this magical mystery play.*

Then again, maybe to re-introduce one of the twelve apostles into that cliffhanger moment would be too contrived an ending.

But that being the case, there's a whole array of secondary characters to choose from for this final, dramatic scene.

Imagine. Just imagine if the Samaritan woman stepped out from the crowd to repay Jesus' acts of kindness towards her and her race. Or what if Simon the Leper turned up to give him a hand.

A giggle of amusement trickled around the hall at Brother Scully's hackneyed gesture of a leper giving a hand.

— Or what about the groom from the wedding feast of Cana, what if he shot out from the crowd shouting,

— *You helped me when the wine ran out at the wedding, now I wish to repay your generosity. So, I will help you carry your cross.*

The obvious person to make a dramatic entrance at this point would have been Lazarus, the man Christ had raised from the dead just a week previously in the town of Bethany on the outskirts of Jerusalem. Just imagine if Lazarus stepped forward saying,

— *You brought me back to life, Jesus. Now I am willing to lay down my life for you.*

Or better still, what if, like a scene out of *Spartacus*, all those characters, Lazarus, the Samaritan, the groom from the wedding feast of Cana, Judas and the twelve apostles, the lepers, the cripples, the women of low virtue ... what if they all rushed out from the crowd, took the cross, then carried the Christ shoulder high to Golgotha, the place of his crucifixion, in full knowledge that he would rise again in three days in accordance with the scriptures, and they would all live happily ever after for eternity? That would be an amazing ending to the greatest story ever told! But alas, that did not happen. No. That did not happen because that would have been powerful fiction.

The hall was gripped in stunned silence, as young Brother Scully continued to present his case.

— The gospel writers were adamant that there was no such intervention in the grand finale, no glorious moment of redemption unfolded. No!

Instead the writers insisted that the only one who came to help the Lord was a previously unknown character, a poor misfortunate, innocent bystander who happened to be in town for the Passover Festival. They didn't even know his surname. They only knew he was from a place called Cyrene. Simon of Cyrene, that's what they called him. A man never heard of before or since, a man who decided to stop and take a look at this procession of the damned, while his wife was busy doing a spot of shopping. Next thing he knew, Simon of Cyrene was plucked from obscurity and ended up, slap-bang, in the middle of the most magnificent moment in the history of mankind.

And, having carried the cross of the Son of God to his place of execution, this Simon of Cyrene just stepped back into the crowd and vanished from the pages of history forever.

That one episode in the New Testament must surely be proof that it is a factual and biographical account of Jesus' life on earth and not some elaborate work of fiction.

Again Brother Scully paused for a moment or two as, one by one, he eyeballed his fellow seminarians. Then he continued,

— I put it to you, the reason this episode proves that the gospel is a true and factual account of Jesus' life on earth is because it does not make sense!

A whisper of confusion filled the silence.

— You see, my learned friends and colleagues ... that is the difference between fact and fiction, because unlike fact, fiction must always make sense.

The Aula Maxima erupted in spontaneous applause. The theology master, Brother Ambrose, with his flair for all things theatrical, got caught up in the moment, and, in a fit of flamboyance, he led a standing ovation with calls of,

— Bravo! Bravo! Bravo!

\* \* \*

Brother Scully began to earn a reputation for his commanding oratory skills, enquiring mind and incisive intellect. His leadership on the playing fields had not gone unnoticed, his charismatic personality and popularity amongst his peers had come to the attention of his superiors. Whispers circulated around the cloisters that one day he might become the youngest Head Brother since the founding of the Order. Brother Ambrose dared to suggest that, maybe sometime in the future, young Brother Scully might even hold the supreme office of Superior General.

Young Brother Scully's star was in the ascendant and burning bright. So impressed was Brother Ambrose with the young seminarian that he chose to give him extracurricular tuition in the fine detail of theology. Over time, a bond of familiarity replaced the barrier of formality that had existed between student and master.

— Brother Scully?
— Yes, Brother Ambrose?
— I have decided that from now on you can dispense with the formality of addressing me by the title Brother. So please feel free to address me as plain Ambrose.
— Ambrose? Ambrose without the Brother, Brother Ambrose?

Ambrose interrupted Brother Scully, saying,

— Here in the monastery and in the eyes of God we are all brothers. So from now on Ambrose will do just fine.
— Eh? Just plain Ambrose, said young Brother Scully cautiously.

It was a level of informality that was usually reserved for long-established friendships between more senior brothers. It was a familiarity that had to be earned over time, a familiarity that had withstood the test of friendship and the challenges of community life. But it wasn't long before Ambrose was to regret the concession he had granted to young Brother Scully.

* * *

It was around that time that Brother Scully set out on a quest to fully understand the living Christ. He studied the origins of this man they called Jesus. He set himself the challenge of separating the man from the myth. What was it about this illegitimate boy, born in a stable and raised by a carpenter that made mankind sit up and take notice? Brother Scully's voyage of discovery led directly to the heart of the ancient, holy texts. It became a journey that challenged his beliefs and shook his faith to its very foundations. Night after night he immersed himself in the writings of all the great philosophers, historians and holy men from the earliest of times right down through the ages.

In the works of Josephus he found a definitive historical context written from the Judean perspective, while the writings of Tacitus gave him the Roman point of view and an insight into the psychology of power politics. For an accurate first-hand account of the treatment of Christians under the Roman legal system he turned to Pliny the Younger. He referenced early Christian writings such as the gospel of James to bridge many of the gaps he found in the various accounts of the nativity and early childhood of Christ. And though Brother Scully always returned to the writings of the four evangelists — Matthew, Mark, Luke and John — as his primary source of reference, he was careful not to allow his research to become overly influenced by Christian, Jewish or gentile ideology.

As days became weeks, young Brother Scully's enthusiasm for his research intensified. He would be heard walking the corridors late into the night muttering to himself, teasing out anomalies he had uncovered in the scriptures. Every now and again he would shout out a spontaneous yelp of delight at the unravelling of some nugget of biblical contradiction, then he would scurry off and seek out Ambrose to discuss his latest revelation, sometimes ambushing him when least expected, like that time Ambrose was in the toilet, reading the newspaper.

By the sound of the creaking hinges and the whoosh of air as the doors swung shut Ambrose could tell that someone had entered the toilet block. The confident click-clacking of footsteps across the terrazzo floor left him in no doubt but that it was young Brother Scully.
> — Lord God, what is it this time, he muttered, and threw his eyes to heaven in silent prayer.

He craned his neck, and caught a glimpse of the polished toecaps of Brother Scully's shoes under the door as they made their way past the battery of sinks towards the urinals, until they finally stopped outside the cubicle.

— Jesus, is there no peace in this world, he whispered.

A knock on the door was followed by Brother Scully's voice.

    — Are you in there, Ambrose?

    — Yes, I'm in here, Brother Scully.

    — Ah good. Apologies for disrupting your privacy, but I'm looking for guidance.

*I'll give him guidance*, Ambrose thought to himself.

    — I was researching the Annunciation last night and it left me wondering why Luke's gospel tells us that the angel appeared to Mary to announce the Virgin Birth before she became pregnant, while in Matthew's gospel the angel came to tell Joseph a few months later, sometime after Mary became pregnant, shortly before the baby was due to be born ...

    — Eh? Excuse me, but I'm on the toilet here, Brother Scully. Can this wait?

The voice from inside the cubicle was measured and curt.

    — Oh by all means, Ambrose. By all means ...

Brother Scully stood back against the sinks tapping his foot, heel to toe, and when a respectable amount of time had passed he proceeded to ponder this latest inconsistency he had uncovered in the scripture.

    — It just makes me wonder, he said. — Was it the same angel that appeared to both Mary and to Joseph? If so, well surely it would have been far more practical if the angel had appeared to the both of them together. After all they were a young couple just about to set out in married life. You'd think that God would have called them both together to announce his plans for them, especially as they were going to give birth to his Son, Jesus.

Raising the Son of God as their own child would have had huge implications for the both of them, changed their lives forever, so it would. And they'd have needed time to come to terms with the whole Virgin Birth thing. A lot of explanation to be done there, not to mention the requirements of rearing the Son of God?

So it makes me wonder why God, in his wisdom, sent two angels down to earth a few months apart to deliver the same message. Do you think that maybe God got the timing wrong when he sent the first angel down from heaven to Mary? Or maybe Joseph wasn't around when the angel called? Or maybe the angel just forgot to tell Joseph the first time, and had to come down a second time? I guess we'll never know, but considering this was *the* most important and personal announcement made by God to any human being, the delivery of the message was fairly clumsy...

Don't you agree, Ambrose?

Ambrose? Ambrose? You still in there, Ambrose?

— Yes I'm still in here!

— Well as I was saying, why did God send down two angels to deliver one message. Unless? Unless? Unless Mary and Joseph weren't living in the same place at the time of the Annunciation? Like maybe Mary was living with her cousin Elizabeth and her husband Zachariah? The gospels tell us that Mary spent the early part of the pregnancy living with Elizabeth and Zachariah. So, maybe that's why the angel didn't appear to Mary and Joseph at the same time. What do you think, Ambrose?

With no response coming from inside the cubicle Brother Scully continued to expand on his conundrum.

— In fact, now that I think about it, in and around that same time God also sent another angel down to Elizabeth's husband Zachariah, to announce the birth of their child, John the Baptist. That's three angels sent down from heaven in a short few months. Quite amazing really, don't you think, Ambrose?

Eh? Ambrose?

Once again Ambrose remained silent.

— Ambrose? Ambrose? Are you in there, Ambrose?

— Christ! Of course I'm in here! Where else do you think I'd be?

— Well you were gone very quiet there...

Anyway, what I'm getting at is...

Considering Mary, Joseph, Elizabeth, Zachariah, and their unborn children, Jesus and John the Baptist, were all related and the two children were on a similar mission from God, you'd think it would have made a lot more sense if God gathered them all together into the one room and sent one angel with one straightforward, unambiguous message to the four of them. Told them exactly what was going to happen, let them know what to expect. It would have saved a lot of confusion. At least they'd all have been singing from the same hymn sheet, so to speak...

But not a word was heard from Ambrose.

   — ...when you think about how seldom angels come down to earth with personal messages from God, there seemed to be a whole flock of angels flying around with messages during those few months. Busy times, I guess? Busy times...

Don't you think, Ambrose?

Eh? Ambrose? You in there, Ambrose?

   — Yes, I'm in here, shouted Ambrose. — Jesus Christ, what does a man have to do to get some privacy in this world!

Ambrose flushed the toilet. With a click of the latch, the cubicle door opened and Ambrose stormed past Brother Scully.

There was that Sunday afternoon, when Ambrose was relaxing in the garden reading the sports pages, only to be interrupted by young Brother Scully.

   — Ah, Ambrose, there you are. Do you mind if I pick your brains with one quick question, he said.

   — Eh, can it wait?

   — It's only a little question, Ambrose. I just need a small bit of clarification...

Ambrose closed the newspaper.

   — Alright, he said. — If you must...

   — My question is... Why did God create the world?

   — Ah for God's sake! One little question! Sur' Jesus, that's the most complicated question known to mankind? I could be here 'til kingdom come to get to the bottom of that! Christ Almighty, man! Only for God having infinite wisdom, I'd say he'd have trouble answering that one himself...

   — But see, said Brother Scully. — If God is all-powerful and perfection personified, and if God lives in heaven, and heaven is eternal bliss...

Well you'd have to wonder, why in the name of God did he feel the need to create something as imperfect as the world? And why did he choose a life form so flawed as us human beings to inhabit it? Like the question I'm asking is, why did he create imperfection, when he could have created perfection? Or, do you think God was bored in the perfect bliss of heaven and needed a dark and devious challenge to spice up his life and occupy his mind?

— Are you trying to be smart, Brother Scully!

— No, Ambrose. It's an honest-to-God question. Like, we know from the Old Testament that God became disillusioned with his creation on a number of occasions. The Book of Genesis tells us how the wickedness of mankind drove God to wipe out the whole human race off the face of the earth, and that's why he instructed Noah to build the ark. And what about Sodom and Gomorrah? God killed every man, woman and child, except for Lot and his wife and family.

— Ah now, Brother Scully, you and I know that the Old Testament takes a certain amount of, how should I put it, artistic licence.

— Well, even if we do take the Old Testament with the proverbial grain of salt, no disrespect to Lot's wife, we can't deny that God sent his only Son, Jesus, to earth for the salvation of mankind. After all, that is the cornerstone of the New Testament?

— True. So what's your point, Brother Scully?

— Well, I'm wondering if it was the case that God saw some flaw in his creation? So, he sent his only Son down to earth to put things right?

— Look, it is not for us to question the will of God! Now, does that answer your question, Brother Scully?

And with a flick of his wrist Ambrose straightened his newspaper and returned to reading. Brother Scully was not satisfied with the answer.

— Well it's sort of a two-part question, he said. — You see, if we believe that God created the world and every aspect of the universe...

— Yes?

— And if God sent his only Son, Jesus Christ, down to earth for the salvation of mankind? Well then, that must mean that Jesus came to earth to save mankind from some aspect of God's creation?

— What are you talking about, man? Jesus came to earth for the salvation of mankind. End of story! Why are you trying to complicate matters?

— I'm not disagreeing with you, Ambrose. But to take that to its logical conclusion, it begs the obvious question. Did Jesus come to earth to save mankind from some flaw in God's creation? Was he sent down to fix one of God's mistakes?

Like, did God's creation go so badly wrong that he had to send his Son down to fix it? It raises the obvious question, is God in his infinite wisdom capable of making a mistake?

— Christ's sake, God does not make mistakes, Scully!

— But this is very confusing. See, if God is eternal and timeless, why did he send his Son down to do the job? Why didn't he come down and sort it out himself? Was it because the job required the strength of a younger man?

— You're just being facetious, Scully!

— No honestly, I'm not...

I just don't understand the logic behind God sending his Son down to earth to be tortured and tormented and crucified, so that in some cryptic way his horrific death would save mankind from some looming catastrophe of God's own making?

— Are you questioning God's logic, Scully?

— No, no, no, not at all. But when you put it that way, I suppose I am...

— Christ Almighty, man, there's no logic to God, shouted Ambrose.

— Really?

— Oh for God's sake, Brother Scully. Do we really need to get into this now? All I want is to sit and relax here in the garden and read the newspaper like I do every Sunday afternoon. Is that too much to ask? Is that too much to ask?

Young Brother Scully did not respond, he just stood there waiting.

— Right, said Ambrose. — To answer your question simply: Jesus came down to earth to be crucified for our sins, so that God

39

could resurrect him from the dead. The resurrection of his Son, Jesus Christ, was to be God's grand display of power to mankind.

— Ah now I get it, said Brother Scully.

— So if you don't mind, I'll get back to reading my newspaper, said Ambrose, and he turned sideways on the bench away from Brother Scully.

— But? But? But if the resurrection of Jesus was intended to be the greatest display of God's divine power, well, how come Jesus went and stole God's thunder a few days before the big event?

— What the hell are you talking about! How do you mean, Jesus stole God's thunder?

— Well just a week before God performed the resurrection of his Son, Jesus, as his greatest display of divine power, intended to make mankind sit up and take notice, Jesus arrived into the town of Bethany and, there, in front of every man, woman and child, didn't he go and resurrect Lazarus from the dead. Just like that, on a whim. Jesus stole the show. He went and pulled the rug out from under God's great display of power, and all because he was late for Lazarus' funeral.

And what's more, don't you think it's odd that God's great display of power to mankind was exercised so discreetly. After all, the whole of Jerusalem witnessed Jesus' death by crucifixion, and yet not one single person witnessed his resurrection.

The good book tells us that the boulder had been pushed aside from the tomb, and the corpse was missing. That's all we know. Even Jesus' own disciples believed someone had stolen the body. What was the point of that? You'd have to ask yerself, why would God's grand display of power to mankind, the resurrection of Jesus, be witnessed by no one.

Ambrose just folded his newspaper under his arm, got up from the bench and walked away.

And there was that time Ambrose was coming out of the refectory, and he noticed Brother Scully's shadow at the turn of the stairs, so he sidestepped into the library. But it was too late ...

— Ambrose! Ambrose!

Taking the stairs two at a time, Brother Scully called out his name again, then, quickening his pace, he chased after him into the library.

— Ambrose? You in here, Ambrose?

He found him crouched down behind a bookshelf.

— I have unearthed another inconsistency in the gospel, Ambrose.

— I'm sure you have, he said.

— At the time of Christ's death we are told that the sun went dark... Now, as you know, the historian Thallus is credited as the first chronicler to have recorded that the sky went dark. And Luke's gospel picks up on Thallus and reaffirms that the sun stopped shining between the sixth and the ninth hour on the day of the crucifixion...

— So your question is, Brother Scully?

— Well don't you think it's odd that the sun went dark on the day Christ was crucified?

— Why would it be odd? Christ's sake, man! It was a big day for mankind. Obviously important enough to be marked by a solar eclipse.

— See that's my point, said Brother Scully. — Jesus was crucified during the Jewish feast of the Passover. As you well know, the Passover celebrates the escape of the Jews from captivity. The Jews picked the night of the full moon for their exodus from Pharaoh.

— So what's your point, Brother Scully?

— My point is that it is an astrological anomaly to have a solar eclipse during the full moon phase of the Passover Festival. A solar eclipse happens during a new moon, but the Passover takes place during a full moon. It puts a serious question mark over the solar eclipse at the time of Christ's crucifixion...

— Well maybe it wasn't a solar eclipse! So what, snapped Ambrose. — So what!

— So what? So what?

The question is, what was it so, demanded Brother Scully, with an increased sense of urgency in his voice.

— Jesus, how am I supposed to know! Look Brother Scully, who cares if the sky went dark or not! Who cares if the sky went green with orange polka dots, for Christ's sake! What's important is that the Son of God died! He died for our sins! What more do you want!

— All I'm saying is that consistency in the detail of the gospel is important, argued Brother Scully. — We need to know, did the sun go dark or didn't it! Any question mark over the gospel, no matter how insignificant, puts a question mark over all of Christianity. And an eclipse of the sun during the full moon of the Passover is not a small technical inconsistency.

Brother Scully became more agitated as he proceeded to put his case.

— And what's more, even if by some freak of nature the planets did align and a solar eclipse did occur, well it would have only lasted for three minutes at the very most. Whoever heard of a solar eclipse lasting three hours? We really must get to the bottom of this, Ambrose. The credibility of Christendom is at stake. This contradiction may be the very rock on which Christianity will perish.

So Ambrose, he continued. — How do you explain the fact that the sky went black?

— Ah for God's sake, shouted Ambrose. — Maybe it was just a dark day in Jerusalem. It could have been an extremely dark cloud, for all I care!

Ambrose stormed out of the Library, leaving Brother Scully standing there.

— Yeah, but for three hours? Really, whispered Brother Scully. — Hmmm, interesting? Eh? Ambrose! Ambrose!

Once again young Brother Scully took off after the theology master.

— Ambrose! Ambrose!

He caught up with him by the common room door.

— What is it now...

— If a dark cloud over Jerusalem is not such a significant event, Ambrose, why was it recorded in the scripture?

And though Ambrose was mild-mannered by nature, his patience had been stretched to snapping point by Brother Scully's relentless questioning.

— Look, Brother Scully! I couldn't give a fiddler's fart if the sun bounced up and down and shot off across the sky like a flamin' rocket!

You need to get one thing into your head, Scully. This is your voyage of discovery. Not mine. This is your own personal journey to enlightenment and fulfilment. It's got nothing whatsoever to do with me!

Now I'm sick to death of you chasing me around the monastery like a hound after a hare, asking questions about this and that and every little titbit of biblical trivia you dig up.

I can take no more of it! Do you hear me? No more of it!

Brother Scully was not prepared for Ambrose's brutal honesty, and was surprised by the frustrated anger in his voice.

— I'm sorry Ambrose, I had no idea ...

— I don't want your apology, Brother Scully. I just want you to stay away from me. Just leave me alone.

— It won't happen again.

— Maybe I'm being a bit harsh with you. As you know I believe you are one of the special ones here in this seminary, but your behaviour is becoming more and more erratic.

— Erratic, Ambrose?

— Yes! You're beginning to act like a mad man.

— A mad man?

— Yes, and acting mad is madder than being mad. Your behaviour has come to the attention of your superiors. I'll tell you something for nothing, if you get pigeonholed as being a bit flaky or unstable while in the seminary, it's a label that will stick with you right throughout your religious life. Give a dog a bad name, sort of thing.

Now you're an intelligent young man, and I know all your running around in your search for the living Christ is probably just youthful exuberance. But you need to curb your enthusiasm.

This sort of euphoric behaviour and religious fervour happens to many of the new vocations in the seminary. They get carried away with the whole God thing. But a little information can be a dangerous thing, Brother Scully. You really need to keep a lid on it.

Ambrose explained that the seminary was a retreat from the pressures of modern life, and if Brother Scully put his time to proper use, it offered a great opportunity to a young novice for deep contemplation.

— ...a time for you to refine and define your vocation. A time of meditation and profound soul searching, he said. — But all this running around the seminary like a blue-arsed fly? You're doing yourself no favours. You see, Brother Scully, the secret to transcendental thought is to keep your ideas inside your head until they are fully formed.

— Hmm, never thought of it that way, Ambrose.

— And a word of advice. When you read the scripture, don't be blinded by the mystery of God. Keep your sights on the big picture. Don't become sidetracked by inconsistencies in the detail. But most of all, try to accept the gospels at face value.

— At face value, you say?

— Yes, Brother Scully. My advice to you is to go back to the very beginning. Read the gospels as if it's your first time. Abandon all preconceived learning. Take a step back from all Church teachings that may have shaped your perceptions. Make it a personal journey, and you will hear what God wishes to say to you, and you alone. And remember the only way you will hear the word of God is if you remain very quiet, very still, and listen. Then you will hear and all will be revealed.

You have been offered a wonderful opportunity to discover Jesus Christ, an opportunity to welcome the Son of God into your life. Don't waste it on facts and figures.

The gospel is not a history lesson of names, dates and times. No. It's a journey to the furthermost regions of your soul. It's a journey into time: the past, the present, the future and on into eternity ...

Ambrose's words were fire to young Brother Scully's soul, and that night, in the privacy of his room, he vowed to trace the living Christ from the cradle to the grave and beyond. But his newfound zeal floundered when he read the opening sentence of Luke's gospel. For some reason the words just lodged in his brain.

> — *When Herod was King of Judea, there was a Jewish priest named*
> *Zachariah and his wife Elizabeth ...*

Something about that simple statement of fact did not sit comfortably with Brother Scully. He couldn't understand why the gospel should begin by establishing a link between King Herod the Great and the Virgin Mary's cousin, Elizabeth. It just did not make sense. If anything, he believed the story of Christ should have opened with an exploration of the relationship between God the Father and the Virgin Mary. Brother Scully did not sleep that night, as the words twisted and turned inside his brain.

Early next morning he went to the chapel knowing he would find Ambrose there giving instruction to one or two of the new seminarians. Brother Scully lingered in the shadows until they had finished. Then just as Ambrose was about to leave the chapel, he stepped out from behind the statue of Our Lady of Good Counsel.

— Morning, Ambrose.

— Jesus, Brother Scully! You put the heart sideways in me! What did I say to you about creeping up on people?

— Sorry, Ambrose, sorry ...
  It's just that in my reading of the scripture last night, I hit a stumbling block, and I would really appreciate some guidance.

— Lord God, I thought we had been through all this yesterday! Remember yesterday? Do you? Remember? You agreed not to pester me anymore.
  This is ridiculous, Brother Scully! We agreed that from now on this would be your private and personal journey.

— Sorry, Ambrose. It's just that I'm having a problem with one little thing. Please, I promise I'll never bother you again after this ...

— Okay, go on! What's on your mind, and I'll see if I can set you

straight. But really this is ridiculous ...
— Thank you, Ambrose, Thank you ...
— Well?
— See here's the thing, Ambrose. King Herod the Great is the first person named in Luke's gospel.
— So what's your question?
— Surely the story of Jesus Christ the Son of God should begin by establishing the relationship between the Virgin Mary and God the Father?

Like, why, of all the barefooted maidens across the known world, did Almighty God select the Virgin Mary to be the surrogate mother for his Son. I mean, there must have been some sort of planning on God's part before he made such an important decision?

Now we know that through the Immaculate Conception, Mary was born without sin. Her role as the mother of Jesus was pre-ordained even before she was born. Yet there is no explanation in the gospel of why or how God picked Mary! Or why did he pick Mary's parents for the Immaculate Conception? Or who were Mary's parents? Because of the Immaculate Conception, clearly Mary's birth was also divinely engineered? Like, Mary must have been sent down from heaven just for the sole purpose of giving birth to Jesus? There must have been some reason why Mary was chosen as the mother of God. Like, it can't have been a simple case of, — *Eeney, Meeney, Miney, Mo?*

Surely God didn't pick the mother of his only child in a lucky dip, then rewind her life back to her birth and present her as having been born through Immaculate Conception? I mean the burning question in every Christian's mind must be, what selection process did God use to pick the Virgin Mary?

But, for some strange reason, this is all dismissed in the gospels and the story of Christ begins by establishing a connection between King Herod the Great and the Virgin Mary's cousin, Elizabeth, and her husband Zachariah.
— I don't understand your concern, Brother Scully. After all, as you

correctly point out, Elizabeth was the Virgin Mary's cousin, and the child Elizabeth was carrying grew up to be John the Baptist. So obviously the gospel writers were giving some of the background into Jesus' extended family.

— But that doesn't explain why the very first person mentioned in the story is King Herod the Great?

— Christ man! The story had to start somewhere!

— But don't you think it's odd, pressed Brother Scully. — The story of Jesus Christ beginning with King Herod the Great?

After all, Herod was the very man who tried to slaughter Jesus when he was an infant. He was the man who chased the Holy Family up and down the Holy Land. He was the man who had Elizabeth's husband, Zachariah, murdered. And then, thirty years later, Herod's son chopped the head off Jesus' cousin, John the Baptist. And if that wasn't bad enough, when he finally caught up with Jesus, he subjected him to the most horrific torture, mocked him, stripped him, whipped him, crowned him with thorns and then crucified him.

So it's odd, isn't it, Ambrose? Well isn't it? To begin the story with the man who spent his whole life trying to kill Jesus and exterminate his extended family? Don't you think so? After all, the gospel is supposed to be the story of God's relationship with us humans, through his Son, Jesus.

But for some reason the story of the Herod dynasty is an integral part of the story of Jesus Christ from the very beginning to the very end. It seems that, just like Jesus himself, Herod is the alpha to omega.

I mean, you'd have to ask yourself, why was Herod so vital to the story of Christ? Maybe the answer is obvious? But for the life of me I can't understand why two generations of the all powerful royal family of Herod became obsessed with killing, what was, on the face of it, a poor illegitimate boy, born in a stable to a barefooted serving girl and raised by a carpenter.

For once, Ambrose did not have all the answers. He just stood there looking slightly confused.

— What I'm getting at, Brother Scully continued. — Do you think that placing King Herod the Great as the first person named in the scripture is some sort of a message?

— A message?

— You know, a message that had been deliberately inserted into the text. Like a clue passed down through the millennia so that we might uncover some long-concealed revelation.

— Ah for God's sake, shouted Ambrose. — The gospels are not some sort of puzzle. They don't require decoding. Brother Scully, you are beginning to really get on my nerves now with all this cloak and dagger stuff.

— But there's something about it that doesn't sit right. Don't you think?

— Look, Brother Scully, there is no right or wrong in the gospel. It is what it is! It's just the story of Jesus Christ and make of it what you will. I really don't have the time or the energy to be putting up with you and your wild theories.

So here's what I suggest. You should read the New Testament and keep a journal. I guarantee you that all the inconsistences you find in the scripture will become self-solving when set against the context of the greater narrative.

— You're saying that I should step back from the detail and try to look at the big picture?

— Exactly! And this I promise you, Brother Scully. If you look for the mundane, the mystical will become apparent. Examine the obvious, and the abstract will be revealed. Search for the humanity of Christ, and it will lead you directly to the divinity of Jesus.

And so began Brother Scully's private and personal journey to discover the living Christ. Night after night he scoured the ancient texts, and each morning he would pace the corridors resisting the temptation to confront Ambrose with the latest contradictions and anomalies he had uncovered.

In his heart of hearts Brother Scully wished for nothing more than to tease out and debate his findings with Ambrose; after all, knowledge is a dead weight unless it is shared. But on Ambrose's instructions, Brother Scully kept himself to himself. He retreated deeper into his own private world of holy texts and manuscripts. There was something about the social isolation of solitary research that created an intensity all of its own. Young Brother Scully found himself drawn to the seclusion of monastic life.

The ascent of Brother Scully's rising star was as brief as it was bright, and, as weeks became months, it soon faltered and crashed down to earth, burnt out and lifeless, like a meteorite from the heavens. These days, Brother Scully finds some consolation in the belief that a light hidden beneath a bushel may not shine brightest but in all probability it would shine longest, and the brightest star in the heavens is often the last spark of a dying sun.

* * *

Brother Scully looks out over the city this Christmas Eve morn and wonders where the years have gone. All that running around the seminary was such a long time ago, half a century ago or so. Sometimes Brother Scully looks back on those early days and mutters,

— Where did it all go wrong, wherediditallgowrongwherediditallgo ...

He recites the catechism of his childhood, the simplicity of the theology indelibly imprinted on his brain.

*Who made the world? — God made the world.*

*Why did God make the world? — For his own glory.*

*How can you glorify God? — By loving him and doing what he commands.*

*Where is God? — God is everywhere.*

*Can you see God? — No. I cannot see God, but he always sees me.*

*Does God know all things? — Yes. Nothing can be hidden from God.*

The list goes on and on and on. He stops and whispers,

— Where did it all go wrong, allgowrongallgowrong, allgowrong ...

He was young back then, young and foolish. Many years were to pass before he realised that forces beyond his control were in control. In his innocence he had found himself caught up in a power struggle that had been escalating between Deputy Head Brother Lynch and Bossman Begley.

It all began when old Head Brother Xavier succumbed to a particularly virulent strain of Alzheimer's. Recognising Head Brother Xavier's incapacity as an opportunity, the ambitious Brother Lynch stepped into the power vacuum and assumed the role of acting Head of the monastery. Self-appointed and without official sanction from the Superior General of the Order, Brother Lynch ruled with a clenched fist of iron. An arch-conservative, he cast a long and dark shadow over all aspects of life around the monastery. He took a personal interest in every minute detail, from the enforcement of discipline to the planting of the flower beds. Brother Lynch's rule was absolute and went unchallenged, yet the whispered consensus that echoed around the cloisters was that Bossman Begley would be far better suited to the role of Head Brother.

Some men lead from the front, some men lead from behind, but Bossman was one of those rare individuals who led from the side. For the most part he just stood in the wings observing events unfold, he would only step in whenever he saw fit. Like a seasoned sea captain, Bossman could weather the most furious of storms with the lightest hand on the tiller. His experience and balanced approach to the future development of the Order, in the face of falling vocations and secularisation of religion in a rapidly changing world, made him the obvious successor to old Head Brother Xavier. But as long as there was still a pulse in Head Brother Xavier's veins, Bossman was quite content to step aside and look on at Brother Lynch with all his huffing and puffing, pushing and shoving and jack-booting around the monastery.

When old Head Brother Xavier eventually died, it came as no surprise that Brother Lynch was overlooked, and the position of Head Brother was officially conferred on Bossman Begley. Brother Lynch was furious. He spent days storming around, spitting fire and causing an ever-widening rift between the traditionalists and those who were more liberal-minded. His strongly worded letter of protest to the Superior General was unprecedented and further polarised the community. Fearing the dispute might escalate into another split, it was decided that a new position of Deputy Head Brother would be created specifically to calm Brother Lynch's fury and accommodate his ambitions.

From that day forward, Deputy Head Brother Lynch insisted on always being addressed by his full title, every single syllable of it. With his newly conferred title he became a constant thorn in Bossman Begley's side, and seized every opportunity to challenge and undermine his authority.

So when young Brother Scully arrived at the monastery, fresh from the seminary, he blindly stepped into the middle of the bitter war of attrition that had been raging between the recently appointed Head Brother and the Deputy. It was too late before Brother Scully fully understood the meaning of the old East African proverb: when two elephants go to war, it's the grass that gets trampled.

But all that was a lifetime ago, almost half a century ago, and all things change with time. Bossman Begley has long since passed to his eternal rest, and Deputy Head Brother Lynch may as well be dead, struck immobile in suspended animation ever since that stroke he suffered thirty years ago, or so.

Over the years, Brother Scully's personal dreams and aspirations have fallen by the wayside, but he takes some consolation in his belief that the wars of mighty men become no more than the squabbles of fishwives once the mighty men have fallen.
- All dead. All dead. All dead. All dead, all dead, all dead, all-deadalldeadalldeadalldeedlediddledum,
   deddle-diddle-diddle-didle-dum, diddle-didle-dum.
   Deddle-diddle-deddle-dum,
   Deddle-di-de-deedle-diddle-diddle-dum.
The rising sun has cleared the rooftops along Patrick's Hill this Christmas Eve morn, and the elderly Brother Scully is still sitting alone at his bedroom window, laughing hysterically and mumbling,

— How did it all go so terribly wrong, so terribly wrong, soterri-blyterriblyterriblywrong ...

\* \* \*

It is said that every rumour has a root lodged firmly in some grain of truth, so when young Brother Scully stepped down from his teaching duties back in 1970 the stories crept like wild Virginia right across the Northside, stories that became tangled and strangled by the weeds of gossip, hearsay and idle tittle-tattle.

Brother Scully's fall from grace gave wind to the sails of barroom bluffers, whispering women and chattering shawlies. Some said he lost his faith in God, others said he lost his faith in humanity. For a while it was doing the rounds that he had witnessed a vision of the Blessed Virgin and, ever since, had devoted his life to prayer. More claimed it was all about his plans for the school's Christmas concert that went badly wrong and it all became too much for his mind. But most had Brother Scully pegged as a plain and simple madman who had been driven demented by the burden of his vocation and had not been right in the head ever since.

Brother Scully seldom leaves his room. For decades he has lived in the shadows, choosing to remain on the fringes of community life. Day in, day out, year in, year out his yellowing face can be seen peering out across the city from his bedroom window. He sits there, always alone, and sometimes, when the wind is blowing from the north, the shrill sound of his laughter can be heard echoing around the school yard and out over the monastery walls. And so, the many rumours about Brother Scully live on to the present day, passed down through the generations from schoolboy to schoolboy like a baton in a relay race.

Sometimes on a rare hot summer's day, he leaves his room to walk the grounds and read from his bible. He notices the children and hears them say as they run away,

— Scatter! It's Screwball Scully!

Maybe he is insane? Maybe he is a genius? Maybe he is a fool? But one fact remains undisputed. In 1970 Brother Scully, the idealistic and promising young brother, became a recluse when his mind shattered and plunged down into the deepest and darkest depths of disillusion. That was the year Brother Scully withdrew from his teaching duties. It was the year the school's Christmas concert was cancelled. It was the year Dana won the Eurovision Song Contest.

\* \* \*

He is sitting at his bedroom window, looking out across the city, laughing at the absurdity of it all. He laughs at how the brightest and fittest of his generation picked up their vocations and charged blindly towards religious orders, just as earlier generations charged towards the guns in another insane and unholy crusade.

— Ours is not to reason why, oursisnottoreasonwhytoreasonwhy…
He sometimes wonders what in the name of Christ ever drew him to monastic life at such a young age. He believes in God, but not the Father Almighty. He no longer believes in a vengeful God, a God sitting on a throne, looking down from the heavens in judgement. He dismisses as pure and utter nonsense the concept of a human-like deity who created heaven and earth for his own glorification. He believes there are forces far more powerful than mankind in this universe, destructive and creative forces, forces in perpetual conflict, forces struggling for survival or supremacy. And Gods may come and Gods may go, but it has always been the way of the Gods that supremacy and survival amount to the same thing.

And yet his calling to religious life has always remained strong. Sometimes he wonders why? Maybe it's because his vocation matured as he matured, and it became his way of life. Like so many of his generation, his initial commitment was fuelled by cultural emotion rather than religious devotion. His vow was a sworn oath to everything and everyone he held dear: his parents, his family, his friends, his neighbours, his community. And from the very moment he took that vow, whether he believed in a supreme deity or not, Brother Scully became their representative, fighting their corner, at God's table.

He has witnessed many changes down through the decades. In recent years Brother Scully has seen countless younger, disillusioned men leave the Order. It all seems so simple now. Sometimes he wonders why he didn't walk away half a century ago.

> — But things were very different back then, very different back then, different back then, differentbackthendiffer ...

It was a time when social pressure and moral expectation exerted more power than God in heaven. To break his vow with the Almighty and walk away from the Church would be nothing short of eternal damnation. The dishonour and disgrace brought down on his family would be just too much to bear. But even if he could have endured the public humiliation and somehow found the strength to walk away, what life could a defrocked cleric expect beyond the monastery walls? Shunned like a leper. Turned away by his own. Who would ever trust a man tainted by the shadow of a broken covenant with God?

In recent years when he'd see young men leave the Order he would sometimes experience bitter regret, and resentment would fester. But, as if justifying his decision to remain true to his vows, Brother Scully would once again recite the catechism of his childhood.

> *Who made the world? — God made the world.*
> *Why did God make the world? — For his own glory.*
> *How can you glorify God? — By loving him and doing what he commands.*

Brother Scully closes his eyes and sighs, then smiles and whispers,

> — Where did it all go wrong, wherediditallgowrongwheredidit ...

He now knows that it all went wrong long before it had even begun. His destiny had been written on the wall before he was born. A fury surges up from the depths of his soul.

On the very morning he was baptised, his godparents rejected Satan on his behalf, and all trace of original sin and the ancestral curse of Adam and Eve was cleansed from his soul. Three days old and he was reborn, welcomed back into the fold, saved from an eternity of weeping in anguish with the lost souls of Limbo. And when those drops of holy water splashed on his infant skull, the Kingdom of Heaven was placed firmly within his mortal grasp. There was no going back, his destiny was preordained. He was on the road to the benchmark rites of passage: Confession, Communion and Confirmation. In time he would become a Soldier of Christ defending the way, the truth and the life.

Blinkered by a moral code set in place by the convenient contrivance of church and state marching towards One People, One Church, One God, he found himself being enticed forward by the expectations and ambitions of others.

From his first day at school he was immersed in the catechism of his faith. In a masterstroke of indoctrination, the most complicated theological concepts and fundamental truths were simplified into baby-sized questions and tailor-made answers designed to clarify any ambiguity in a child's mind. Endless lists of undisputed facts committed to memory by generations of the faithful, to be rattled out daily in every classroom up and down the country.

*Can you see God? — No. I cannot see God, but he always sees me.*
*Does God know all things? — Yes. Nothing can be hidden from God.*

He was on the road to becoming a strong and perfect Christian and it would only be a matter of time before he would learn to fear the Lord, and so began his introduction to all wisdom.

On the morning of his seventh birthday, having reached the official ecclesiastical age of reason, it was deemed that from that day forward he would know right from wrong. The first thing he learned was that temptation was everywhere, most often concealed in dainties and delights and all things sweet and nice. God was everywhere. The Devil was everywhere. And at every living moment of his childhood these two supreme beings fought in an eternal struggle for his soul. It was never-ending. Morning, noon and night, every turn of the day he was called to pray. Every ringing of a bell was a reminder to save his soul from the burning fires of Hell.

Sin was lurking behind every pleasant thought and deed. Guilt became his constant companion. There followed an intense period of instruction on how to examine his conscience so that he could root out those black marks of evil buried deeply within his soul. Then, every Saturday night, this seven-year-old boy would enter a darkened cubicle and kneel in front of a godly man to confess his inner most evil thoughts and temptations and beg forgiveness. Whispering a contrite act of contrition and a few short prayers of penance, the Almighty would wipe clean the slate, and once again his soul would be stainless as steel, ready to receive the body and blood of Christ in the sacrament of Holy Communion at Sunday Mass.

Religious instruction was the focus of all formal education. And beyond the school gates, every festival and holiday was marked by some feast or holy day, and again the faithful would gather to pray and listen to a man proclaiming what God had to say.

At the ripe old age of eleven, now a discerning adult, he exercised his first act of free will. He joined his peers from every school across the city and paraded through the streets, two-by-two, all the way to the cathedral. They marched as one, to accept the sacrament of Confirmation and re-establish the covenant with God that had been made on their behalf at Baptism. They rejected Satan and welcomed into their hearts the Holy Trinity: Father, Son and Holy Spirit. Sealed with the invisible yet invincible gifts of the Holy Spirit, a new generation was finally initiated into the Church ready to step forward to fight the good fight.

And so, year in year out, the enticement intensified. And all lessons, classes and homework would be cancelled for a week, when a well-polished visiting cleric would invite the class on retreat. He was slick and suave, well-heeled with cufflinks peeping through on each wrist. He knew all the answers and spoke of the depth of their souls, the transience of the mortal coil, the endlessness of eternity and the magical mysteries of monastic life. And, like a recruiting sergeant selling the thrills of trench warfare, he instinctively recognised a glimmer of interest in a young boy's eyes. And, one-by-one, he would invite them forward to join the fray.

Brother Scully remembers his mother, scurrying up and down to the church, lighting candles. He'd see her on her knees offering novenas. He'd hear her whispering at the church door while loosening her purse strings. Like every other mother from right across the Northside, she knew of no greater honour than the prestige of having her boy grow up to become a man of the cloth. And when the nod was given, and the word came down from the monastery to Barrack

Buildings, that, like the fishermen who had cast their nets along the shores of the Galilee, her son was a chosen one, it was the talk of the town and she was cock of the walk.

And maybe minor complicating factors such as chastity, abstinence and the loneliness of self-denial were not priorities in the mind of a fourteen-year-old boy, but any doubts that crept in would be blamed on the temptations of Satan and sin. All devious thoughts could be washed away by a sprinkling of holy water, or concealed behind a smoke screen of sweet-smelling incense; washed away to be dealt with at a later date, when it was all too late.

Brother Scully now concedes that times were different back then, and like so many boys and girls who went before him, his vocation had been set in motion by those who knew best, long before the sap of puberty could raise its ugly head to seduce him away from his life of celibate prayer. And still he wonders,

— Where did it all go wrong,wherediditallgowrongwhere ...

There was power in poverty, and for the people from the lanes, the monastery was that hub of power. It was a place where politicians came on bended knee promising the sun, moon and stars for the block-vote. It was a place where the *Merchant Princes* donated generously in the hope of a short remission from purgatory or a last minute fire escape from the burning flames of Hell.

But that was a long time ago and all that has changed. These days the monastery is but an empty shell, and only a few brothers remain.

— Most too senile to know their names, the rest too feeble to care.
   Most too senile to know their names, the rest too feeble to care.
   Most too senile to ...

Brother Scully repeats it over and over again like a nursery rhyme.

Downstairs, the common room, where once the leading lights of his generation held sway over the City Fathers, is now the resting place for the remnants of what was a mighty and powerful religious order. There, like the last of a dying breed, or a near extinct species, a handful of elderly brothers gather around a wide-screen television. Stretched out on their lazy-boys, mumbling to themselves or muttering to each other, they sit there watching some book-thumping evangelist beamed in from the heavens via satellite from somewhere below the bible belt.

Brother Scully laughs out loud when he remembers the commotion that erupted when the first colour television came to the monastery. He remembers it well.

\* \* \*

The rising tension between Bossman and the Deputy had the whole community on a knife-edge. When Bossman was appointed Head Brother, Deputy Head Brother Lynch was convinced his rightful position and ambition had been scuttled by an insidious slander campaign orchestrated by his arch-rival. He viewed Bossman's assignment as an indictment of all that was wrong with the Church since Vatican II. It was an affront to everything the Church stood for, a victory for the liberals and a crushing defeat to all those loyal and true to conservative, core Catholic values. So when Bossman announced his plans to rent a colour television for the Eurovision Song Contest, it sparked an explosive reaction from his Deputy.

— Colour television! Colour television! The Devil's disciple! Bring that contraption into this monastery and it will be the beginning of the end. I warn you, Brother Begley! No good has ever come from television. Bad enough in black and white, but in colour! Broadcast from pagan England! It will corrupt the minds of the young novices. There are ideas and notions inside that thing, and once they get out they will infect the minds of the youth. It will have disastrous consequences.

Television first attacks the brain, then the conscience and finally it devours the soul. And once the Devil is released from that box, there will be no way of getting the Devil back into the blasted thing!

— You need to calm down, Brother Lynch, said Bossman.

— It's Deputy-Head-Brother-Lynch, he snapped. — And if you insist in bringing that contraption of evil into this monastery, on your head be it! Do you hear me? On your head!

The Deputy stormed out of the office and slammed the door behind him.

Brother Scully looks back on that time with the clarity of hindsight. He sometimes wonders if maybe there was a truth in the Deputy's warning of the evils of television. It had been ten years since Vatican II set the winds of change blowing at gale force across Christendom and the world had become gripped by the fear that mankind was on the eve of destruction. Television had stealthily crept into every little homestead, first black and white, then in colour. Night after night, happy families turned from their firesides and gathered around the box in the corner, to watch the free-fall disintegration of civilisation. Unimaginable images from the four corners of the globe were beamed into the homes of a people who had never known life beyond the crossroads outside their home village.

With the flick of a switch everything had changed. No longer were tales of ancient battles won or lost handed down from generation to generation at the flickering flame of a fireside. From the comfort and safety of the couch they watched the Tet Offensive unfold in black and white like some serialised *Peyton Place*. Holy Catholic Ireland looked on in horror as their man at the centre of the universe was cut down on the streets of Dallas. For the first time in the history of humanity, the real-life hoary, gory atrocities of war were played out every evening in full living colour in every living room right across the land. And just when they thought they had seen it all there was always something more enticing coming down the tube to excite and disturb.

— Man walking on the moon, roared the Deputy. — Ho Chi Minh! Soviet threat! Viet Cong! Communist Russia! Berlin Wall! Cold War! What next! I mean, Lord God Almighty! Students rioting on city streets, from Paris to Prague to the holy city of Rome. And now they're talking about banning corporal punishment in the schools? Corporal punishment? Is it any wonder they're acting like corner-boys? Spare the rod and spoil the child! A good boot up the hole is what they need! That's what I say!
Students! Bloody-well students!
Like some perversion of Moses on Mount Nebo, it was as if the Deputy caught a glimpse of the *Promised Land*. He had a vision of the future,

but what he saw was not good. He wondered if television was the new Messiah or a messenger from Hades, bringing with it all the horrors of the netherworld, creating an insatiable hunger for all things wicked and evil. And every evening after the Angelus bells rang out, the latest news of man's inhumanity to his fellow man was beamed into every home and hovel across Christendom. From the very moment colour television crossed the threshold of the monastery, life as they knew it was turned on and tuned in, all had changed and changed utterly.

* * *

Brother Scully sits alone in his room; the stark light of day picking out the detail of the sparse furnishings, his desk, his wardrobe, his bed.

— Then again, not a lot has changed. Not a lot, notalotnotalot... His mind drifts to that night when the colour television arrived into the monastery.

* * *

Saturday, 21st March 1970

The monastery was a beehive that day. A special dispensation had been sought from above, and permission was granted for a colour television to be rented from Madden's TV Shop.

That night, a young Catholic girl from Derry in the North of Ireland, would be taking to the stage in Amsterdam, to represent the Republic in the Eurovision Song Contest. There was something about that seemingly inconsequential moment of popular music history that fed directly into the very life-blood, soul and marrow of every brother in the monastery.

For generations the brothers had beaten the drum of long dead Irish patriots and martyrs for the Catholic faith. They had sung the *March of Brian Ború*, recited Emmet's speech from the dock, championed hurling as the ancient Irish sport of the Gods. They had guarded the flame of Celtic, Catholic culture, the language, the music and traditions. They had inspired each new generation of young Gaels to learn the steps of the secret war dances. Dances deemed so subversive that they were banned by the English colonists; the *Bridge of Athlone*, the

*Siege of Ennis* and the *Walls of Limerick*; dance steps that concealed a history and chronicled hundreds of years of oppression by the Saxon invader.

But above all, the brothers eulogised the heroic rebels of 1916. They venerated the Irish Volunteers like they were Gods of War. In their hearts they held special reverence for the heroic guerrilla leaders of 1920; men like Dan Breen, Liam Lynch and Sean Moylan. They immortalised the escapades of Tom Barry's IRA Flying Column, and celebrated how he had led the British Black and Tans on a merry dance around the hills of West Cork before driving them into the sea and away from our shores forever, like Saint Patrick drove out the vermin.

But songs of past glories are easily sung. Over the previous twelve months, news filtered down from north of the border, news of religious persecution, civil rights denied and Catholics manning the barricades around Free Derry Corner. And when the stone-throwing Catholic youths stood up against the might of the British Empire, just as Father Murphy stood up to the Yeomen at Vinegar Hill, or David stood up to Goliath in the Valley of Elah, the brothers agreed it was nothing short of biblical. Word travelled through every townland and village that once again British soldiers were patrolling the streets of Ireland, but the Catholics were holding their ground at the Battle of the Bogside. Yet, after generations of flag waving, drum beating and singing ribald, rabble-rousing rebel songs, no pikes were taken from the thatch. The brothers could do nothing but shelter behind the walls of the monastery and look northward hopelessly, helplessly, in fear, praying that the border would hold.

But then, right from the heart of all this strife was heard the lone voice of a young schoolgirl. She was singing out her sweet song of hope. A song that rose up from behind the barricades, cutting clean through the rhetoric, sabre rattling and bloody racket of conflict. And the more the English claimed she was British, the more the fire of Irish nationalism was stoked, and when they insisted that she was from Londonderry rather than Derry, it only heightened the awareness that Derry was an ancient Gaelic name meaning oak wood, and the very notion of coupling it with the word London as a symbol of dominion was as farcical as it was futile, and only served to further erase a pencil line on a map.

She was Dana. She was from Derry. When they asked what sort of a name was Dana, they were told it was a Gaelic name, a name that meant bold, fearless and brave. And when Dana, along with her Mammy and Granny, were invited to receive a blessing from the Catholic Bishop of Derry before setting out for Amsterdam, it was a sign, a sign that declared loud and proud to every brother in the monastery that Dana was singing for Ireland, a united Ireland, a united, holy and Catholic Ireland where civil rights would be enshrined, and she had God on her side.

So, on the night of Saturday 21st March 1970, that young girl would walk in the footsteps of the great warrior Queen Maeve and brave Gráinne Mhaol, and every Irishman and Irishwoman who held freedom in their heart believed that somehow she had the power to deliver an enslaved people from captivity.

When news reached the sisters of St Joseph's Convent that the monastery had rented a colour television for the Eurovision Song Contest, Reverend Mother phoned Bossman, enquiring if she and three of her community could visit the monastery to witness the great event in colour. In the spirit of Vatican II, Bossman was delighted to oblige. He assigned young Brother Scully to the task of attending to the needs of the visiting sisters. Brother Scully was presented with a checklist of the schedule for the evening and briefed on his duties by the Deputy.

- Now, get this right, Scully! You'll be meeting the visiting sisters at the gate. Then you'll escort them up the avenue to the monastery. Then bring 'em to the library to be formally introduced by our full titles: Head Brother Begley, Brother Dempsey the Trainer of the Hurling Team, Brother Ambrose the Theology Master. You got that straight, Scully! By our full titles!
- Will you be here on the night to watch the Eurovision, Brother Lynch?
- I have to be here, don't I! But I won't enjoy it, he said. — And it's

Deputy-Head-Brother Lynch! Do you hear me, Scully! That's Deputy-Head-Brother!

— Apologies, Deputy Head Brother Lynch. My apologies.

— ...Christ no, I won't enjoy it! That blasted Devil's toolbox! But as House Master it's my responsibility to make sure that the whole evening works like clockwork. You got that into your skull, Scully!

— I do, Deputy Head Brother.

— So after escorting and introducing the visitors from the convent, you'll offer them tea and biscuits, maybe a glass of sherry or wine. After the refreshments, you will lead them to the refectory where four chairs of the padded variety will be reserved in the middle of the front row.

Then, win or lose, when the contest ends, you will serve tea and biscuits in the refectory to the community and guests. And after all that, you will serve a nightcap to the visiting sisters in the library before they return home to St Joseph's Convent. Have you got that, Scully!

— Yes, Deputy Head Brother.

— I want this done right. I was against this whole thing from the very beginning. But now that it's happening, we need it done right! Do you understand, Scully!

— I do.

— I do? I do? I do what?

— Eh? I do, Deputy Head Brother.

— That's more like it, Scully!

\* \* \*

A cold eastern wind cut across the city that night. When Brother Scully arrived at the monastery gates to welcome the guests, he found the four holy women huddled together for warmth. Without small talk or formality he directed them up the avenue towards the monastery. They scurried along, backs bent and shoulders arched to the bitter breeze, muttering their aspirations and cursing the cold as they went.

- Sweet Mother of Divine Jesus! 'Tis freezing ...
- Oh, Sacred heart of Jesus! Cut through you, so it would ...
- Oh, Jesus, Mary and Joseph! To the bone ...
- Lord save us from all harm! Perished I am! Perished with the cold ...

Young Brother Scully escorted them into the library where Bossman and the welcoming committee had gathered a few hours earlier. They were glowing with expectation, and the inviting warmth of the blazing fire set the tone for the evening. Reverend Mother said she'd have a glass of sherry to warm her bones. Sister Michael, the Head of the Secondary School and Sister Veronica, the Head of the Primary School opted for good strong cups of tea. The young novice, Sister Claire, who was *aide de camp* to Reverend Mother for the evening, declined the offer of refreshments, but instead assisted Brother Scully.

While Brother Scully served the tea, Sister Claire topped up Reverend Mother's sherry glass with increasing regularity, and after forty-five minutes of small talk and short drinks, Brother Scully announced that the Eurovision Song Contest was about to commence and they should make their way to the colour television. He then led the way to the refectory, followed by the others in decreasing order of superiority, with young Sister Claire and the bottle of sherry following behind.

Brother Lee the Physics Master and Brother McGrath the Geography Teacher were busy realigning the orientation of the aerial, trying to pick up the colour transmission broadcast by the BBC. The signal faded in and out, as a string of brothers, stretching from the refectory through the kitchen, past the pantry, along the hall, from the vestibule into the porch, out the front door across the car park and all the way to the water feature on the front lawn, relayed Brother McGrath's precise calculation of the location of London to Brother Lee. Brother Lee had climbed up onto the roof and was battling the biting wind while hanging onto the chimney stack for dear life. He slowly rotated the aerial ever so slightly away from Mullaghanish and towards the general direction of England.

- Back a bit! Back a bit! A little bit more! To the left! To the left!

Hold it! You have it! You have it! Ah! Back a bit! Back a bit! Hold it! Hold it! Ah! Back a bit! Back a bit! Stop! Stop! Stop! You have it! You have it!

And then he had it, tuned in, picture locked square and sound perfect.

The usual Saturday night sessions of confessions had been brought forward by an hour to accommodate the broadcast, all penance had been reduced to a standard three Hail Marys. As the time drew closer, Father Kelly left the confession box and asked the five brothers still waiting in the queue,

— Have any of ye any mortal sins, or impure thoughts to confess, lads?

They shook their heads in silent denial.

– Good, said Father Kelly. — Say three Hail Marys.

Then closing his eyes he muttered a splattering of Latin and granted a general absolution before rushing off to the refectory where an armchair had been reserved for him, strategically placed between Head Brother Begley and Reverend Mother.

At thirteen minutes to eight, thirty-three brothers, four nuns and a priest had gathered in the refectory, seated in rows in front of the television. Elderly, feeble-minded members of the community, confused by all the commotion, wondered if another war had broken out, while the more inquisitive and scientific-minded gathered at the rear of the television, investigating how the thing worked. They spoke of cathode ray tubes, anodes, coils, resistors and electrostatic charge, but for all that they knew, they might as well have been looking into a hole in the ground.

The babble of banter faded as they settled down, took their places and sat there, transfixed by the marvels of colour television and modern technology. Deputy Head Brother Lynch had taken up position at the back of the refectory casting a cynical, mistrusting eye over the proceedings, while far away in Amsterdam the minutes counted down as the nations of Europe prepared to send forward their champions to do battle.

Young Brother Scully made his way to the kitchen because, win or lose, when all the songs had been sung and the votes counted, there would be an immediate and urgent demand for tea and biscuits for the post mortem. He estimated that each individual would probably drink two cups of tea, and calculating that eighty cups of tea at approximately quarter of a pint per cup, he would need two gallons of boiling water, with an extra half gallon at the ready just in case. So he began filling the Burco boiler.

Outside in the refectory the din of debate swamped the chatter of excitement as ancient alliances were evoked in an attempt to anticipate the voting patterns of the judges across Europe.

- The French will throw a vote the Irish way. Remember Killala and 1798.
- I wouldn't be holding out for too many favours from the French. Who can forget the Vichy Regime during the last war?
- Dammed collaborators, roared old Brother O'Hegarty.
- Well, we can always count on the Catholic Italians...
- Christ! The Italians are likely to change sides halfway through the chorus.
- The Spaniards are the lads. They were there for us in 1601, and we were there for them during the Spanish Civil War...
- Well, technically, we fought on both sides of the Spanish Civil War...
- Maybe we'll get an aul' guilt vote from the Nordics.
- The Nordics! The Nordics! Sur' Norway, Sweden and Finland have boycotted this year's contest.
- Boycotted?
- 'Twas all over the news, something to do about fair play and the scandal of last year's voting...
- The Nordics are some shower to talk about fair play! Them and all their aul' plundering and pillaging of us back in the ninth century...

And so the analysis deepened, but there was no mention of the old enemy. Not a word was spoken about Royaumne-Uni, Great Britain, United Kingdom, England, Mary Hopkin or her song, *Knock! Knock! Who's There?* The silence was an indictment of the contempt with which those assembled held the colonialists. Although the history master, Brother Cummins, did say,

— I can tell you one country the Germans won't be voting for,
    particularly after what they did to Dresden...
And old Brother O'Hegarty was heard to mutter the words,
— Come out ye Black and bloody Tans!
    Come out and fight me like a man!
But then again, there was nothing out of the ordinary in that. In his
own doddering mind, old Brother O'Hegarty was still fighting the War
of Independence.


Tension had been mounting right across the Continent ever since the
voting fiasco of the previous year left the contest without an outright
winner. And with victory shared, in a four-way tie between France,
Spain, Netherlands and the United Kingdom, these warlike, colonial
nations had no understanding of how to deal with the concept of a
shared victory.

Long before the days of myth and folklore, Europe had been at war
with itself. Staunch allies had slit each other's throats, treaties of peace
had been treacherously broken and the soil was soiled by the entrails
of generations of young men. Walls had been built only to be knocked
down again, and borders had been drawn and re-drawn across the map
in blood-red ink. For millennia the most powerful armies of Europe had
faced each other across some farmer's field in a wet and boggy lowland
to do battle, land of such low yield it would keep neither snipe nor
grouse. Yet, battle-hardened men stood their ground and fought to the
bitter end of total annihilation with no quarter given, no quarter
sought. And after generations of bloodletting and treachery, the lines
of loyalty between the nations of Europe had become so confused that
the age-old sentinel salutation, — *Who goes there, friend or foe,* could
never expect a clear and simple answer.

The men of Europe were born to fight, and fight to the death. Victory
by compromise was an insult, because victory, just like defeat, had to
be total and absolute. So, when the Eurovision Song Contest ended the
previous year without an outright winner and a four-way tie was
declared, old wounds were opened and the scabs on the sores of unset-
tled scores were picked raw. By the time the curtain went up in
Amsterdam that Saturday night in March 1970, Norway, Sweden,

Finland and Portugal had boycotted the competition and left the field of battle.

With a reduced number of combatants the United Kingdom's entry was championed as the hot favourite to win. In the days leading up to the contest the newspapers had been full of it and, true to form, the British used every trick in the book to secure a victory. But when, on the eve of the contest, their song was released on a record label owned by a popular band of the day called The Beatles, it was seen as a low blow by all fair-minded people right across the Continent.

Brother Campbell, the Music Teacher, shook his head in disgust,

— It is nothing but a shameless ploy by the Brits to seduce a floating vote or two from the wishy-washy Europeans.
— To hell with Europe, roared old Brother O'Hegarty. — Sinn Féin! Ourselves alone!

Young Brother Scully was busy in the kitchen, relaying saucepan after saucepan from sink to Burco when the swish of the swing doors interrupted him, and there stood Sister Claire.

— Ah, Sister Claire, he said, surprised to see the young nun standing there.
— I was wondering, do you need any help, she asked.
— No thanks. I'm just filling the boiler for the tea.
— I can put out a few plates of biscuits if you'd like?
— Actually, that would be great. The plates are up there and the biscuits are in that thing there ...

Brother Scully nodded in the direction of the big earthenware jar on the worktop with the word *BISCUITS* printed in bold letters on its side. Sister Claire reached towards the press saying,

— How many plates do you think we'll need?
— Ten with about a dozen biscuits on each plate. Or on second thoughts, maybe, a dozen plates with ten biscuits on each might be better. And extra chocolate biscuits for the front row ...

Maybe it was because they were so deeply engaged with the task in hand, or maybe it was because the monastery had been overcome by a sense of excitement that night and the usual strict enforcement of the *rule* seemed to have been relaxed. Whatever the reason, Brother Scully and Sister Claire chatted with ease like brother and sister. When Sister Claire realised that they both shared the same birth sign, she slapped her palm on the back of Brother Scully's hand.

— Snap, she laughed.

The tingling sensation sent a wave of warmth through his body and stirred up feelings and emotions in Brother Scully that had been dormant, concealed beneath an impenetrable robe of piety since puberty. It occurred to Brother Scully that for the first time in his life he was in the company of a girl his own age. They were unsupervised, and that subtle feeling of freedom was new and exhilarating. Pain never being too far from pleasure, and pleasure never being too far from guilt, their laughter petered out to an awkward silence. But they were alone and enjoying each other's company, and there was no real sin in that. It wasn't long before their chatter was back on track. The conversation was free and easy between them as they proceeded to arrange the teacups and saucers along the counter top, stopping occasionally to count and re-count the plates and biscuits.

\* \* \*

The sound of the clitter-clatter of cups and saucers fades with the memory of that fateful night, and once again the elderly Brother Scully finds himself alone in silence, still looking out over the city from his bedroom.

The cold light of day brings with it a clarity of thought. He is increasingly worried that no greeting light had beamed out from Sister Claire's window this Christmas Eve morn, and with each passing hour his concern for her deepens. Now that the sun has taken its dominant position in the sky, he knows it is pointless to attempt to make contact with her, yet he can't resist the urge to continue flicking his light switch in the futile hope that it might stir some response.

— Where do the years go, where do the years go, wheredothe-
    yearsgo ...

He repeats it over and over again until his jumble of sound is interrupted by another wave of uncontrollable laughter.

A lifetime has come and gone since that night back in 1970 when he met Sister Claire, yet it seems like only yesterday. Whenever he closes his eyes he still hears the sound of her voice, every single syllable she uttered that evening in the kitchen still indelibly etched, word for word in his brain. He remembers how he wallowed in her company, transfixed by her very being, entranced by every movement of her lips, mesmerised by the sight of the moist pale-pink tip of her tongue peeping out between pearly teeth. He became lost in the carefree sound of Sister Claire's voice as she spoke about this and that and nothing at all.

Sister Claire told how she first realised she had a vocation when she was brought to see the film, *A Song for Bernadette.*

— ...and what age were you then?
— It was the year of my Confirmation.
— Your Confirmation?
— Yes. And when Our Lady appeared to Saint Bernadette in the film that was the moment I knew I had a vocation. I made up my mind that very day that I too wanted to be in the presence of Our Lady, if not in this life, well then in the next. I decided there and then to offer my life to God and join the convent.
— The year of your Confirmation? But sur' you were only a child.
— I was around eleven or twelve. I was so inspired by that film that when it comes time to take my final vows I have decided to take Bernadette as my religious name.
— So you won't be known as Sister Claire?
— No, she said. — I was baptised Claire when I was born. As a postulant the sisters call me Sister Claire. But when I take my vows, I will be Sister Bernadette, after Saint Bernadette.
— Sister Bernadette? Sister Bernadette? Nice ring to that ...
— I know this might sound silly, but after seeing Our Lady appear to Saint Bernadette in the film, I've been praying for a divine apparition of my own ever since.
— And do you really think you might someday be visited by a saint from heaven, maybe even Our Lady herself, he asked.
— If I did I wouldn't be telling you.
— Why not?

Sister Claire stopped and stood back from the biscuit jar, and just like that the mood changed in the kitchen. Sister Claire answered in a hushed voice.

— Well you have to promise to keep what I'm going to tell you a secret.

Discretion was fundamental to religious life. But secrecy? Secrecy was irresistible. Brother Scully was intrigued.

— I promise.

Sister Claire leaned towards the door and glanced into the refectory just to make sure they were alone.

— Well you've heard about Sister Francesca, she whispered.

— Who?

— Sister Francesca Of The Birds?

— Oh, Francesca Of The Birds? The old nun that was curing the animals? The one that died?

— That's right, said Sister Claire. — She passed on to her eternal rest a few weeks ago. But before she died, something amazing happened...

— Something amazing?

— Shhhhh!

Again Sister Claire's eyes darted towards the refectory door, and placing her finger to her lips she checked that it was safe to continue.

— Well, as you know, back around the time of the First World War, when Sister Francesca was a young nun, she cured a famous racing pigeon.

— A racing pigeon?

— You must have heard that story?

— Well I know she cured birds, said Brother Scully. — Isn't that why people call her Sister Francesca Of The Birds?

— Well yes, but this racing pigeon was the bird that set the ball rolling, so to speak. Dowcha-boy? Does that name ring a bell?

— Dowcha-who, he said.

— Dowcha-boy, the pigeon?

— Eh, no, never heard of him...

— I'm surprised you never heard the story of Dowcha-boy. See,

Sister Francesca actually began curing animals long before she famously cured Dowcha-boy. But Dowcha-boy is the big miracle she's remembered for.

— A miracle? Really, said Brother Scully.

Young Sister Claire told how the history teacher, Sister Agnes, was the only nun in the convent old enough to remember the early days when Sister Francesca first began curing animals.

> — ... and Sister Agnes The History Teacher told us that, back in 1914, when Sister Francesca was a novice she was given a gift from God through the intercession of Saint Francis, and ever since God has answered her petitions for the curing of sick animals. A legend in her own lifetime. Some say she was a living saint ...

Sister Claire explained that one day, while out walking in the garden, the young Sister Francesca came across a small bird with a broken wing.

> — Now, Sister Agnes The History Teacher told us that the caretaker in the convent at that time was a young lad called Mossie The Gardener, and because of an accident at birth, Mossie was born with one leg shorter than the other, so he walked with a very pronounced limp. Employers at the time couldn't see beyond his limp, so that's why Mossie The Gardener ended up working around the convent as an odd-job man.
>
> But it was as if God had compensated for the limp by giving Mossie the most powerful upper body strength. It was said that he once raised a garden bench above his head with two sisters sitting on it. I'm not sure if I actually believe that, but that's what they say ...
>
> Anyway, when young Sister Francesca found the injured bird she brought the creature to Mossie The Gardener who identified it as a robin. He suggested that the most humane thing to do would be to administer one swift slice of the sharpened blade of his spade down on the crippled bird's neck ...

— *Put the creature out of its agony,* Mossie said.

Sister Francesca couldn't bear the thought of such a brutal end for one of God's creations, so she smuggled the bird into the convent where she kept it in a box under her bed and fed it with crumbs from the kitchen.

Every night at bedtime, she said a special prayer to Saint Francis, the patron saint of animals, and first thing every morning Mossie The Gardener would ask for the latest news on the health of the bird. After two weeks of prayer and care, that little robin was well on the road to recovery. So one morning she brought the creature to the garden to stretch its wings. Mossie The Gardener lit a Woodbine and leaned on his rake. It was a signal to the world, and anyone else who might be watching, that he was taking a break and would not be returning to work until that cigarette had been smoked right down to the twist of the butt.

Sister Francesca carefully opened the box. Out skipped the robin and hopped onto her shoulder. The bird then walked the full length of the young nun's arm and perched on her finger.

— Well now isn't that something, said Mossie The Gardener. — And isn't she the neat little birdeen.

Sister Francesca puckered her lips and made a bird sound.

— Cheep! Cheep!

— Cheep, the robin replied.

The robin spread her wings, unfurling her feathers, and with a glint in her beady eye, she rose gracefully from Sister Francesca's outstretched palm and flew the short distance to the blooming cherry tree. With her confidence restored, the little bird glided from shrub to bush to tree around the garden, full of the joys of flight. The gardener and the young nun stood beaming with delight as the robin swooped and swirled and soared skywards way above their heads and vanished into the blue. The young nun's heart fluttered a beat and flittered between fear and exhilaration as she imagined what it would be like to rise above it all, to be free of the gravity of this earth, free of the gravity of life.

She stood there, eyes closed in silence, her arms outstretched like a bird on the wing, her mind and soul travelling to lofty heights until, eventually, she was brought back down to earth when the robin came to land on the open palm of her left hand.

— It's a miracle, whispered Mossie The Gardener.

— No, not a miracle, said Sister Francesca.

She was annoyed that Mossie would suggest that God the Father, creator of heaven and earth, would concern himself with something as trivial as curing a small bird's broken wing. She was adamant that no miracle had been procured, and insisted that the bird's recovery had been nothing more than a combination of care and the power of prayer.

Gardening can be thirsty work, and sometimes gardeners drink more than they should. That evening on his way home from work, young Mossie The Gardener dropped into the Shandon Arms for a pint or two. Word of the robin's miraculous recovery spread along the bar counter like ink on a blotter, through the snug, past the card players in the corner and out into the lanes around Dominick Street and Eason's Hill, then right across the city from the northern tip to the southern tip of the butterfly wings, from the laneways at the top of Shandon Street, all the way down into the bowels of the town, across two rivers, past mirror images of breweries, bridges and undertakers. Then shopkeepers and shawlies contrived to whisper and gossip from the North Gate Bridge, the full length of the North Main Street, and down along the South Main Street, all the way to the South Gate Bridge. The word travelled cheek by jowl up the steep climb of Barrack Street and swept into the maze of little houses that is Greenmount.

Later that evening, when Johnny the Echo-boy poked his head into Tom Barry's snug and said,

— Ladies? Did ye hear about the young nun up in the Northside? The news was there before him. They turned from their jugs and spoke as one.

— About the miracle, is it?

By the following morning the whole town was talking about the young nun up in the convent who was performing miracles and curing birds. It stirred up a trickle of curiosity, and a few requests for prayers for the odd sick parrot, hen, finch and budgie arrived to the convent.

— ...but nothing could have prepared them for the deluge of petitions for prayers after the miraculous cure of Dowcha-boy, the most famous racing pigeon of them all, said Sister Claire. — But I suppose you're not really interested in the story of Dowcha-boy, are you?

— I am! I am!

Young Brother Scully had no particular interest in stories of a nun curing pigeons back at the time of the First World War, but there was something irresistible about the sweet girlish tones of Sister Claire's voice. So he folded his arms and leaned against the bubbling Burco listening to the sounds that tripped from her lips.

— Please, I'd love to hear it, he encouraged.

— Well this is the story exactly as Sister Agnes The History Teacher told us.

And so Sister Claire began to tell the story of Dowcha-boy, the most famous racing pigeon ever to have hatched on the Northside of the city. She said that Dowcha-boy was a cock-pigeon among cock-pigeons, hand reared from the egg.

— ...and on the night Dowcha-boy hatched from his shell, Mossie The Gardener knew there was something stirring in the loft, so he sat there by the nesting box until the...

Sister Claire was interrupted by a bang, a crash and a gush of wind, when young Brother O'Connell burst into the kitchen through the refectory door frantic with excitement; eyes popping out of his skull, his brush-cut of copper coloured curls swaying on his head.

— Lads! Lads! 'Tis started! 'Tis started! Ah lads, ye're gonna miss it! Come on, ye're missing de Eurovision! 'Tis just started! Absolutely brill-unt! Amsterdam looks amazin', the whole city fil-umed from an aeroplane, absolutely brill-unt...

— Nearly ready here, said Brother Scully. — Just organising the tea and biscuits, we'll be out in a minute.

— The Dutch song is class. 'Tis on now, ye'll miss it, lads! Three little black girls! Triplets, I think? Or sisters at least? The head off a' each other! In colour! Eatin' fish they are! 'Tis amazin'! Ye're missin' it lads, ye're missin' it! 'Tis absolutely brill-unt...

And with a swooooch of the swing doors Brother O'Connell vanished back out into the refectory. Sister Claire stood back surprised, amused and slightly confused.

— What was that?
— Only Brother O'Connell. He's a little on the excitable side ...
— Excitable? Is that what they call it, she said and laughed.
— Ah, he's harmless. He's all good intentions ...

Sister Claire stepped towards the refectory, followed by Brother Scully. Peering through the little glass porthole in the door they could see rows of holy men and holy women sitting there seduced by the multi-coloured glow shining out of the box. And just as Brother O'Connell described, three girls, black girls, sisters if not triplets, walking across a bridge in Amsterdam, and then by the magic of television they arrived on stage.

— Do you think we should join the others, she asked.
— I'm happy enough to stay in here listening to your story about the pigeon, Doochieee?
— Dowcha-boy?
— Dowcha-boy. That's it. Dowcha-boy, said Brother Scully.

Sister Claire smiled and took a few moments to regain her thoughts.

— Now you must remember this happened a long time ago, back around the time of the First World War. Old Sister Francesca was a young nun back then.

Anyway, as I was saying, on the night Dowcha-boy hatched from his shell, Mossie The Gardener knew there was something stirring in the loft, so he sat there by the hatching box into the early hours of the morning ...

Sister Claire told how every now and then the young gardener raised a candle to the egg, hoping for a sound or a sign of life, but there wasn't as much as a scratch. Then just as dawn was about to break he heard a gentle tapping noise. It was faint but determined and regular, like the rhythm of a blacksmith's hammer on an anvil, and when his little beak eventually chipped through the shell, Mossie The Gardener whispered,

— *I never doubted ya, boy. Doubt ya, boy!*
— ...and that's how the pigeon got the name Dowcha-boy, she said.

— Ah, right, said Brother Scully.
— And that night when Dowcha-boy poked his little face out of his shell into this world, the first living soul he saw was Mossie The Gardener. From that moment on an inseparable bond was formed between boy and bird.

The little chick was so frail that the glow of the moonlight shone right through his featherless wings. But Mossie The Gardener saw a spark in his eye, and there was no doubt in his mind but that scrawny little hatchling would grow up to be a special bird.

Maybe it was because he was hand reared by Mossie, and Mossie had built a special little nest for him by the fireside in his kitchen, whatever the reason, Dowcha-boy grew up to be a home bird, and that made him a natural-born racer. Come race day, once that latch was sprung, the hatch opened and the birds released, Dowcha-boy would not stop for drink, rest or food. He would flap his wings with every beat of his heart all the way home to Mossie The Gardener's fireside.

Word soon spread across the city from Montenotte and Mayfield all the way to Blarney Street and Sunday's Well, that in accordance with the ancient Legend Of The Northside, a pigeon had been hatched up on Fairhill, a pigeon that would be a saviour, a pigeon that would bring fame and fortune to the people. And there is something about the power of belief, because by the time Dowcha-boy was three months old, the people of the Northside believed he was that chosen one.

Every Saturday morning crowds gathered on the hills above the city at Gurranabraher just to watch Dowcha-boy train. They would stand there gazing skywards, mesmerised by the majestic display of his rainbow-tinted breast plumage flashing in the sun. He'd soar away above the flock, and wherever Dowcha-boy led the other birds followed.

— ...that's what made him king among pigeons, explained Sister Claire. — He was a born leader, and Sister Agnes The History Teacher told us that Dowcha-boy would have made a top-grade racing pigeon at the highest international level, except for a minor interruption to his racing career.
— A minor interruption, asked Brother Scully.

— World War One, she said. — Mossie The Gardener called a halt
  to the racing at the outbreak of war.
— Did he enlist?
— He did. And what's more, when the war was over he returned
  home a hero, said Sister Claire.
— Really! Old Mossie The Gardener was a war hero? Who'd ever
  think it?
— No! Not Mossie The Gardener. It was Dowcha-boy! Dowcha-boy
  was the war hero.
— The pigeon, shrieked Brother Scully.
— Shhhhh!

Again she glanced cautiously through the porthole into the refectory.
On the screen, a young man was singing and walking around the
ancient Coliseum in Rome. They sat there gazing at the box of moving
pictures, hypnotised by the power of television. Sister Claire withdrew
out of sight when she noticed Deputy Head Brother Lynch standing at
the end of the room, his arms folded, his chin gripped between thumb
and index finger, glaring disapprovingly at the ungodly colourful wiz-
ardry beaming out across the refectory.

Sister Claire hesitated for a moment or two until she was sure it was
safe to continue.

— Yes, it's true. The pigeon was a war hero, she whispered. — But
  Sister Agnes The History Teacher told us that Mossie The
  Gardener was no slacker. He tried to enlist in the Royal Irish
  Regiment but he was too young, and born with one leg shorter
  than the other didn't help matters.

She told how Mossie The Gardener nailed half-inch heels onto his
boots to give him a bit of height, and put an extra two-inch lift on his
right boot to compensate for his limp. He rubbed soot into the pores of
his face to look like he was old enough to shave, he even forged his birth
certificate, but nothing could hide the fact that he was a fifteen-year-old
cripple, and a small fifteen-year-old cripple at that.

— ...to make matters worse, Mossie The Gardener's older brother,
  Liam, had heard the call to arms and was out in the trenches
  fighting. Sister Agnes The History Teacher told us that, every

week, Mossie's brother, Liam, sent a letter home from the Front telling stories of courage and heroism, and how a thin green line of Irishmen was saving Europe from the curse of the Kaiser.

Each letter home from the trenches, with tales of derring-do, only strengthened Mossie The Gardener's resolve to do his part for the war effort. But when a letter arrived telling how his brother Liam had walked out through the blood and the guts and the death of No Man's Land, singing the *Boys Of Fairhill*, and saved the little drummer boy from certain death or a fate much worse, it all became too much for young Mossie The Gardener.

The following morning he went up to the barracks and demanded to see the Recruiting Sergeant. But once again the Recruiting Sergeant rejected his application, saying that he was too young. That's when Mossie, in a display of physical strength, walked out onto the barrack square and overturned a gun carriage, tossing it to one side like it was made of matchwood.

— I'm as strong as any two men, he roared.

But still the Recruiting Sergeant insisted he was too young and suggested that Mossie should come back the following year.

— But sur' the war will be over by Christmas, pleaded Mossie.

— Maybe so, maybe not, said the Recruiting Sergeant. — But there are more ways of beating the Hun than carrying a gun ...

The Recruiting Sergeant spoke for a while, teasing out the various options open to Mossie. After drinking pints of black tea, Mossie The Gardener came to the conclusion that the best way he could help the men at the Front was to volunteer the services of Dowcha-boy.

— The pigeon?

— Exactly, said Sister Claire.

The Recruiting Sergeant explained that there was a shortage of good messenger pigeons in the army. And making no bones about it, he told Mossie The Gardener that the mortality rate in the carrier pigeon corps was the highest of any regiment in the army. Mossie decided to go home and sleep on it. The following Friday morning, he arrived up to the barrack gates with Dowcha-boy in a basket.

- The pigeon joined the army?
- Yes, she said. – The pigeon enlisted.

Sister Claire laughed when Brother Scully clicked his heels, snapped to attention saying,

- Private Dowcha-boy, reporting for duty, Sir!
- Sister Agnes The History Teacher told us that Dowcha-boy was the bravest pigeon of them all. He was even awarded the Dickin Medal of Valour ...
- The Dickin Medal of Valour?
- That's right, she said. – Dowcha-boy was awarded the Dickin Medal of Valour posthumously. *For acts of conspicuous gallantry and devotion to duty*, that's what was written on the citation.
  And Sister Agnes The History Teacher told us that the Dickin Medal for a pigeon is the same as the Victoria Cross for a human.
- And what conspicuous act of gallantry could a pigeon do, asked Brother Scully.
- He saved the lives of three young boys from the Northside of this very town.
- Really? The pigeon?
- Yes, the pigeon, she said. – You've heard of the Battle of Guillemont?
- Eh, Guillemont? Eh no?
- A little village, not far from the River Somme ...

Sister Claire considered for a moment if she should tell the long version or the short version.

- Best begin at the beginning, she said. – Well, Sister Agnes The History Teacher told us that the world had never known horrors like the horrors of trench warfare during the Great War ...

\* \* \*

It all began one cold September night when Mossie The Gardener's older brother, Liam, was out on a nighttime reconnaissance patrol near the village of Guillemont.

- Reconnaissance patrol?
- That's right, she said. – Out in No Man's Land snooping around

the German lines with two other lads from the Northside...

— Really?

— Yes, she said. — The Lawless brothers, Dinzer and Danzer Lawless. And as Sister Agnes The History Teacher put it, they were Lawless by name and lawless by nature.

So there they were, the three of them groping around in the dark, and they knew that if they were caught, they could expect nothing but a belly full of German hot lead. Well that's how Sister Agnes The History Teacher put it.

What those three young boys witnessed that night was more than any grown man should see in a lifetime...

Sister Claire told how the two greatest armies ever known to mankind had lined up across from each other in a field in France. They had been slogging it out for months. Salvo after salvo, attack after counter-attack, both sides gaining and losing men and ground in equal measure.

— ...months of carnage, death and destruction, but still no budge in the line, not as much as an inch.

It was the blackest night of September in nineteen-hundred-and-sixteen when the three lads from the Northside slinked out from their blood-drenched, vermin-infested trench and into the jaws of hell. Crawling on their bellies, they made their way across No Man's Land, not stopping to pray for the dead, or give ease to the dying. The stench of putrefying flesh was thick in the air as they grappled their way over rotting carcasses of animals and the mangled bodies of friend and foe strung out along miles of blood-stained barbed wire, tangled in death for eternity.

Eyes peeled, watching, listening, the three scurried from shell-hole to bloody shell-hole, all the time moving towards the German line.

— Ah Jesus lads, whispered Liam. — Something's wrong here...

— Something wrong, asked Dinzer.

— We've been here already.

— Been where already?

— We've been in this shell-hole already.

— You sayin' we've been going round in circles, asked Dinzer.

— I think Liam's right, said Danzer. — I recognise that dead horse.

— For Christ's sake, hissed Dinzer. — All dead horses look the same.

— But I recognise that one by his front legs.

Dinzer pushed Danzer aside.

— Here show us? Front legs? Show us? Jesus Christ, that horse has no front legs, he said.

— That's how I recognise him, said Danzer.

— Danzer's right, said Liam. — We've definitely been in this shell-hole already.

— Fuck's sake!

— This is your fault!

— My fault? How do you mean my fault!

— I was following you!

— You were following me? Well I was following him!

— I never asked nobody to fuckin' follow me!

They bickered until they finally agreed that it didn't matter who was following who, or who was to blame. The problem facing them was that they had been crawling around No Man's Land in circles in the dark for hours and were hopelessly lost. That's when Liam decided that they should cancel the mission and head back to the relative safety of their trenches before the sun came up. So, to find his bearings, he laid on the flat of his back and studied the starry heavens, searching for some recognisable point of reference.

— I think that's the North Star there, he whispered.

— Think? You think! This is the fella who had us wandering around in circles...

— You'd want to do better than think.

— So which way is home?

— Well, I think it's that way, Liam pointed.

— You think!

— See if that is the North Star, well then our lines should be that-a-way.

— And if it's not the North Star, snapped Danzer.

The three sat there in silence, eyeballing each other, contemplating the disastrous consequences of a slight miscalculation of direction.

— It'd be a fuckin' nightmare, whispered Dinzer.

Unsure what direction was home, they decided to bed down for the night and wait until dawn's first light.

That night in that shell-hole with only the rotting remains of a two-legged horse for company, Dinzer and Danzer Lawless, and Mossie The Gardener's brother, Liam, huddled together for warmth. They talked about home, crubeens, tripe and drisheen. All three agreed that Murphy's Stout had the edge on Beamish ...

— I'm not saying Murphy's is better than Beamish, but I know in my heart and soul that the spring water from Our Lady's Well gives Murphy's that creaminess that Beamish don't have.

— It's got nothing to do with Our Lady's Well, argued Dinzer. — Murphy's will always bate Beamish hands down, and do you know why? I'll tell you why! It's from the Northside, that's why!

And so the three nattered on about this and that and a far away place called home.

Maybe it was sheer exhaustion, maybe it was the relief to be out of the death traps of trenches, or maybe they found comfort in the silent calmness of the corpses that surrounded them? Whatever the reason, one by one they drifted off into deep sleep. As always, Dinzer had the last word.

— Tell you this much, he said. — I've seen enough of Europe for one lifetime. You can keep yer Chomp-a-Leesay, Noter Dam and the I-fell Tower. Give me Patrick's Street, the North Chapel and the bells of Shandon any day ...

It was bright morning when Liam awoke. His mind was still far away in a place where it is always springtime, and the tree-lined boulevards of the Grand Parade and South Mall are carpeted pink with fallen cherry blossom petals, a place where everyone is rosy-cheeked and speaking in a sing-song lilt, up and down like the rolling hills of his hometown. He was snapped back to the horrific reality of his surroundings by the sight of the Lawless brothers snuggled like suckling children into the fly-infested carcass of the mutilated dead horse.

— Jesus, he whispered. — Dinzer! Danzer! Wake up, will ye!

He shook the brothers.

— Wha'? Wha'?
— Where are we?
— Huh? Jesus Christ!
— Wha' time is it? Huh?

The clarity of dawn's light brought the reality of their billet of muck and blood and rotting flesh into sharp focus. Removing their helmets, they peeped out over the ridge of the bowl-like shell-hole.

— Something's wrong here, whispered Liam.
— Jeezus, hissed Danzer.
— What the fuck, said Dinzer.

There, in plain view, about a mile behind them, stood the bombed-out church spire of the village of Guillemont, not two miles ahead of them where it should have been.

— The place is crawling with Germans, whispered Danzer and he ducked down into the shell-hole.

Gradually it dawned on them that somehow in the darkness they managed to make their way three miles behind enemy lines. The first thing that crossed Liam's mind was that they had found a gaping hole in the German defences.

— A gap in the German defences! Brilliant, he whispered, and shook his fist in defiance. — Fuckin' brilliant. Information like this could end the war! We'll get a medal when we get back to HQ with this information.

Liam's celebration was cut short by Dinzer,

— That's all fine and dandy, but how in the name of Christ are we going to get back to HQ without getting killed?

The silence of fear descended on the shell-hole. That's when Liam came up with a plan. Sometimes the simplest plans are the most effective, and Liam's plan was the simplest plan of all. He decided he would take his chances, and put his life in the lap of the Gods. He would run the three miles back past the enemy lines, right through the German-infested village of Guillemont, then across the bombed-out barbed wire of No Man's Land, and all the way back to his own trenches to report the gap in the German line.

— Are you off yer fuckin' chuck, snapped Danzer.

— I'll run zigzag.

— Zigzag, me hole!

— My mind's made up, and when my mind's made up, my mind's made up, he said.

— Off yer fuckin' chuck!

— No seriously, he said. — I've the fastest pair of legs in the Northside.

— Well you're not in the Northside now, said Danzer.

— Whatever about the fastest legs, but if you ask me, you've the thickest brain in the Northside, added Dinzer.

— Look, I'd bate any of the two of ye in runnin'. And at least it's a plan! Do either of ye have a plan?

The Lawless brothers exchanged a glance and shrugged their shoulders.

— No! Ye don't, he said. — So shut the fuck up!
See, I'll strip down to my long johns. And without me uniform and greatcoat to slow me down, I'd have a good chance of making it across there before the Germans even realise what's happening. And if I run zigzag there's a good chance that ...

— And that's your plan, said Danzer. — Strip down to your underpants, and do a bit of zigzag running! Jesus Christ Al-fuckin'-mighty!

— Some fuckin' plan that is, said Dinzer. — And even if you do get past the German lines, what makes you think that our own lads won't shoot the head off ya, when they see this half naked lunatic running towards them across No Man's Land ...

Young Brother Scully stood there spellbound, leaning against the Burco as Sister Claire became more and more animated.

— Now Mossie The Gardener's brother Liam's plan wasn't a great plan, said Sister Claire. — But it was the only plan they had. So, there and then in the little shell-hole, three miles behind the

German lines, Liam began stripping down to his undergarments, getting ready for his great cross-country run to victory …

— But, Sister Claire, Brother Scully interrupted.

— Yes, Brother Scully?

— I thought you were telling me about Sister Francesca Of The Birds and her miraculous cure of the pigeon Dowcha-boy, he said.

— Sorry, I almost forgot about Dowcha-boy, but it's all connected, said Sister Claire. — You see, while all this was happening out in that shell-hole at the far side of the enemy lines, back at the far side of No Man's Land Dowcha-boy was kicking-up a commotion in the pigeon loft at the Signal Corps HQ, banging his beak against the grill, flapping his wings and cooing at the top of his lungs.

The officer in command assumed it was battle fatigue, or maybe the early stages of shell shock so he summoned a medic to sedate Dowcha-boy. But the moment the medic opened the door of the loft, the pigeon shot out like a scalded cat, and took off straight for the enemy lines in the direction of Guillemont.

— What! Are you trying to tell me that Dowcha-boy knew that Mossie The Gardener's brother Liam was in trouble, so he flew out to save him?

— Exactly, she said.

— You're joking!

— No, I'm not joking. This is exactly the story as Sister Agnes The History Teacher told us …

So there they were in a shell-hole, three miles behind enemy lines. Mossie The Gardener's brother Liam was stripped down to his long johns, and Dinzer and Danzer were saying their last farewells to their pal and comrade-in-arms.

But just as he was about to climb out of the shell-hole and charge headlong into the pages of history, who came in to land?

— Dowcha-boy? The pigeon?

— You said it, Brother Scully! Well you can only imagine the relief. I mean, you must remember those lads knew Dowcha-boy since he was a hatchling. They had watched him train from the hills of Gurranabraher. Just imagine the pride Liam must have felt, when the pigeon, hand-reared by his own brother Mossie, risked life and wing to fly three miles behind enemy lines to save them.

— That's all very heroic I'm sure, said Brother Scully. — But how in the name of God could a pigeon save three grown men trapped in a shell hole, miles behind enemy lines?

— Well Sister Agnes The History Teacher told us that Mossie The Gardener's brother Liam drew a microscopic map on a cigarette paper, showing exactly where the gap in the German defences was. He then scribbled a short note on the back of it to inform HQ that the three of them were still alive and well. He signed it — *The Boys of Fairhill.*

Mossie's brother, Liam, held Dowcha-boy in his hands. He knew his life and the lives of the Lawless brothers, maybe even the outcome of the whole war, rested fairly and squarely on the shoulders of that pigeon. So, looking deeply into Dowcha-boy's eyes, he whispered,

— Fly, Dowcha-boy! Fly like the wind! But remember, from the moment you take to the sky, every German gun will open up on you. So whatever you do, keep low to the ground and don't break the horizon line.

He kissed the pigeon on the beak and gently released him to his destiny. Dowcha-boy circled above their heads as if reassuring them that he would do his best, for what more could a pigeon do but his best. Then unfurling his wings in one broad sweep, he took off like a swift, skimming not six inches above the blood-drenched earth. Dinzer, Danzer and Mossie The Gardener's brother, Liam, watched as their only hope of survival made a beeline for home.

— ...and that pigeon was no daw, said Sister Claire. — He must have known he hadn't a hope of surviving a flight over a town so heavily fortified by the enemy. So, at the village of Guillemont, Dowcha-boy did the most amazing thing.
You'll never guess what he did? Will I tell you what he did?

— Do. Please do, said Brother Scully.

*Fly, Dowcha-boy! Fly like the wind!*

— You're not going to believe this, she said. — But Dowcha-boy came in to land at the outskirts of the village and decided to walk.

— Did I hear you right? The pigeon walked?

— Well that's what Sister Agnes The History Teacher told us. She said that, rather than risk being shot down by the enemy, Dowcha-boy decided to blend in, act like a local pigeon.

And that's what he did. He walked from one end of the village to the other, past the dugouts, bunkers and sentry boxes, past the German High Command and armoured divisions. Sauntered right through the village, so he did, with his wings folded behind his back, as bold as brass, with nerves of steel, chirping a tune like a local French pigeon from Picardie.

Sister Agnes The History Teacher told us that Dowcha-boy was so confident of his deception he even stopped for a snack at a little café in the market square. Skipped up onto a German Officer's table and pecked a few crumbs of his croissant, so he did. Cool as a cucumber...

— And did he get back to HQ with the message?

— I'm getting to it! I'm getting to it, she said. — Just as he reached the far side of the village, a German sentry became suspicious when the note Liam had tied to Dowcha-boy's leg came loose and fell to the ground.

By all accounts the sentry shouted, — *Halt! Das Englisch brieftauben!*

That's the German for, — *Stop that English carrier pigeon!*

But see, Dowcha-boy didn't realise the sentry was shouting at him. After all he was an Irish pigeon, not an English pigeon. But when the Germans opened up with a hail of gunfire pinging and skimming the cobblestones around his claws he wasn't long realising his mistake.

Well, you don't need me to tell you, Dowcha-boy didn't waste time trying to explain to the German sentry the difference between an English pigeon and an Irish pigeon. Oh no, he scrambled airborne as fast as his two wings could carry him.

The Germans threw everything that they had at him, every sort of bomb, bullet and ballistic, blasting away at that little feathered target. Dowcha-boy ducking and diving, soaring and swerving...

And just when he thought he had managed to out-fly the range of the German guns ...

Bang! A sniper's bullet got him just there!

Sister Claire prodded Brother Scully's arm at the place where the bullet hit the bird's wing. The sensation of her finger penetrating deep into his biceps sent a jolt, like a bolt of lightning to Brother Scully's spine.

- In there, she said. — Into his right wing, they got him. Dowcha-boy hit the ground like a sack of potatoes. Up went a roar of victory from the German line.
- Was that the end of Dowcha-boy, asked Brother Scully.
- Wait for it, wait for it ...

Now, all this commotion attracted the attention of Dowcha-boy's comrades in the Irish Guards at the far side of No Man's Land. But they were helpless. They could do nothing but watch as Dowcha-boy fell to his doom, still clutching the note in his beak.

But then, just when they thought it was all over, one of the sentries saw a slight movement. He wasn't quite sure, maybe it was the wind ruffling the dead bird's feathers.

- *Sergeant,* the sentry shouted. — *It's Dowcha-boy! I think he's still alive, sir.*

Well let me tell you, when the news wound its way down along those muddy, bloody, twisted and vermin-infested trenches, a thousand pairs of Irish-helmeted eyes peeped above the sand bags, watching as Dowcha-boy clawed his way back onto his feet. Then, slowly, he gathered every ounce of strength in every muscle, bone and sinew and managed to get one leg in front of the other. He continued his journey home, limping and staggering across the death, and the bombed-out, blood-drenched barbed wire of No Man's Land, still clutching the note firmly in his beak.

Again the Germans opened fire, sending dirt and muck splattering around that gallant little bird. Then a huge explosion sent Dowcha-boy spinning. Dazed, bewildered and disorientated by the blast, he set off, staggering in the opposite direction, towards enemy lines.

All his comrades began shouting and roaring,

— *Turn around Dowcha-boy! This way, Dowcha-boy! This way!*

Eventually the confused pigeon found his bearings when his natural homing instinct kicked in. He turned the full one hundred and eighty degrees and once again continued his trudge towards home.

Then, bang! Another puff of feathers. Dowcha-boy was knocked tail over beak, and he vanished out of sight into a shell-hole.

Sister Claire placed her hand flat on Brother Scully's leg just above his knee, and firmly probed her middle finger deep into his thigh muscle.

— Right in there, she said.

Sister Claire's finger set Brother Scully's heart racing, stirring up emotions he never knew he possessed. He had never experienced such intense feelings of intimacy with another living soul.

— But it'd take more than two slugs of German lead to put that bird down, she said. — And make no mistake about it, he was down, but just as the Bugle Boy of Company B was about to play the Last Post and chorus, in honour of their brave, feathered comrade, didn't Dowcha-boy appear up over the side of the shell-hole, the note still clutched in his beak.

— Dowcha-boy was still alive?

— You better believe it, Brother Scully. Then slowly, with determination, that heroic bird put one foot in front of the other and staggered.

He staggered the last few yards across No Man's Land and into the arms of his comrades. And if that wasn't a conspicuous act of gallantry and devotion to duty, well I don't know what is.

And when Dowcha-boy delivered the note, showing the gaping hole in their defences, the Germans knew it marked the turning point of the war. But even so, they couldn't contain their admiration for that bird's bravery. And do you know what they did?

— Eh, no? What did they do?

— Well Sister Agnes The History Teacher told us that the Germans climbed up out of their trenches and gave three cheers for Dowcha-boy. Then they fired a volley of shots into the air as a mark of respect for the bravery of that bird.

You see, those young men had stared into the eyes of death more than once, and they knew a heroic act of conspicuous bravery when they saw one. And a heroic deed is a heroic deed, no matter if it was carried out by friend or foe, man or bird ...

Well, that's what Sister Agnes The History Teacher told us.

And the rest, as they say, is history ...

— That's an amazing story, said Brother Scully. — Absolutely amazing.

— Sister Agnes The History Teacher told us that Dowcha-boy served in the army to the bitter end of the war, and returned home to a hero's welcome.

Thousands lined the headlands with tar barrels blazing from Fort Carlisle right around the harbour to Fort Camden. And when the troopship docked at Horgan's Wharf the whole city turned out to welcome home their heroic bird. They carried Dowcha-boy shoulder high in a torch-lit procession all the way to Mossie The Gardener's house up in Fairhill.

— I suppose because of his war wounds Dowcha-boy never raced again?

— Interesting you should ask, she said.

Sister Claire told how Mossie The Gardener decided to give the old bird one last day in the sun, and though Dowcha-boy was not as young as he used to be, and was weighed down by the two German bullets inside him, Mossie threw down the gauntlet and challenged the Southside Racing Pigeon Federation to one last race. It was to be a one-on-one, their best bird against Dowcha-boy.

The Southside breeders scoffed and mocked when they heard that the ageing and battle-torn Dowcha-boy was to be pitched against their finest and fittest bird. But the more the Southsiders sneered, the more the pride of the Northside was stirred, and when the Southside bookies went and offered outrageous odds against their own bird, fifty-to-one down on the beak for Dowcha-boy to win, it was an insult too far.

Some said the pride of the Northside was at stake, others said the pride of the Northside was stoked, but most agreed that unrealistic odds are always an attractive proposition to a desperate people. Whatever the reason, the Northsiders believed in the dream. Dowcha-boy had saved the Lawless boys and Mossie The Gardener's brother, Liam, from the jaws of death. And there was no doubt in anyone's mind but that this bird was the Saviour. In fulfilment of the ancient Legend Of The Northside, Dowcha-boy was the chosen one, and had come to deliver them. So, maintaining their dignity, they chose to accept the Southsiders' wager as a challenge rather than an insult.

Mossie The Gardener may have been blinded by pride, or maybe his judgement was skewed by the arrogance of youth, but the ink was barely dry on the race agreement when the impossible reality of the challenge that faced Dowcha-boy dawned on him. That evening, as he tucked the old bird in for the night, he could tell his war wounds were acting up, even the slightest movement caused his feathers to ruffle as he winced in pain.

> — ...that's when Mossie knew that his elderly and tattered pigeon had little hope of getting airborne, not to mention finishing the race, and as far as beating the finest and fittest bird on the Southside, he may as well have been trying to get Dowcha-boy to swim backwards underwater across the River Lee, said Sister Claire.

Panic set in when Mossie The Gardener realised that the people of the Northside had risen to the challenge of the wager, and had bet money they could ill-afford on Dowcha-boy's victory. In desperation, the young gardener went to his friend, the young nun, Sister Francesca. He found her in the garden sitting by the fountain near the statue of Our Lady of Good Hope.

> — I don't know what I'm gonna do. I mean all I wanted was a friendly race, give the old bird one last day on the wing. But when the Southsiders laughed at Dowcha-boy I just couldn't let

it off. And now my poor bird is in a race he don't have a snow-ball's hope in Hell of even finishing. They'll all be laughing at him. Dowcha-boy don't deserve to be the laughing stock of the town, not at this stage of his life.

— It seems to me your pride got the better of your good sense, Mossie, said Sister Francesca.

— So what if it did! Haven't I a lot to be proud of. That pigeon saved the lives of my brother, Liam, and the two Lawless boys out in the trenches. That bird gave up a great career as a racing pigeon to go and fight in the war. That bird risked life and wing for the freedom of small nations, so he did. Came home a war hero. Haven't I every right to be proud of him. Dowcha-boy is like the son I never had, Sister Francesca ...

The young gardener was close to tears. Sister Francesca listened as he poured his heart out for over half and hour. Then she said,

— Leave it with me, Mossie. Leave it with me ...

Sister Francesca prayed for three days and nights. So intense was her meditation, it was said that beads of perspiration dripped from her brow and fell to the floor as drops of blood. The laneways and alleyways were alive with the rumours that Sister Francesca Of The Birds was praying for Dowcha-boy's victory. And so, neither rents, nor money-lenders were paid that week right across the Northside, and every man, woman and child went into hock for everything they held of value. They gathered every last penny they could together. And with all their hopes and aspirations bolstered by their confidence in Sister Francesca's miraculous powers, they placed all that they had, fair and square, down on the beak of the old bird to win.

But something extraordinary happened in the convent during those three days and nights. On the morning of the race when the latch snapped back, the basket sprung open and the birds were released, Dowcha-boy took off like a swift. Soaring and banking with the agility of a yearling, and while the Southside bird struggled to find its bear-ings, Dowcha-boy had set his flight line direct for Mossie The Gardener's house. Without veering left or right, it was all the way home to

Gurranabraher and Fairhill. It was said that Dowcha-boy was back home and snuggled up in his nest by Mossie The Gardener's fireside while the Southside bird was last seen out by the Blackstone Bridge heading in the wrong direction towards Donoughmore.

The moment the news hit the town that Dowcha-boy had made it home in record time, the people of the Northside came out onto the streets and danced.

> — ...and Sister Agnes The History Teacher said that they danced and danced and danced 'til dawn ...

But tragedy cast its shadow over the great victory. The following morning, when Mossie The Gardener went to bring Dowcha-boy his breakfast, he found the old bird stretched out in the straw, dead in his nest.

The news that Dowcha-boy had not made it through the night was passed from street corner to street corner in hushed tones with heads bowed in dignity. By noon of that day the city had come to a standstill, and for the first time in living memory the bells of both Catholic and Protestant cathedrals rang out in harmony.

Dowcha-boy was buried with full military honours in the garden of St Joseph's Convent. They came from far and wide to pay their respects, even the Southside Racing Pigeon Federation sent a most magnificent wreath. And as they lowered the old bird's body into the grave, the Butter Exchange Band struck up and played *The Lark In The Clear Air*. Mossie The Gardener stood there at the opened grave with the young Sister Francesca Of The Birds by his side, tears streaming down their cheeks, lips quivering as they mouthed the lyrics.

> *Dear thoughts are in my mind and my soul soars enchanted.*
> *As I hear the sweet lark sing in the clear air of the day.*

When they came to the line, *For a tender beaming smile,* Mossie The Gardener felt young Sister Francesca's hand clutch his arm and her fingers wrap around his muscular biceps. He glanced into the young nun's eyes, she smiled through the tears.

*For a tender beaming smile to my hope has been granted.*
*And tomorrow she shall hear all my fond heart would say.*

And that summer's day in the convent garden back in 1919, when the young nun stood there gripping the young gardener's arm tightly, something changed between them that neither man nor God could ever take away.

*I shall tell her all my love and my soul's adoration.*
*It is this that gives my soul all its joyous elation.*
*As I hear the sweet lark sing in the clear air of the day.*

The Butter Exchange Band stood down their instruments, and the sound of woodwind and brass faded. Mossie The Gardener stepped forward, then, clearing his throat, he addressed those assembled at the graveside.

— Dowcha-boy did not belong to me. No cage, no loft did keep him. He was a free bird. Free to come and go as he pleased, and I'm just grateful he chose to stay. Grateful and honoured he chose to make his bed by my fireside.

A force of nature, a born survivor and a fighter to the last, Dowcha-boy flew his heart out in that race. He gave it his all for the Northside, and that's the way he would want to be remembered. So let there be no more tears for Dowcha-boy. We will not mourn his death. Today we celebrate his life. The greatest tribute I can pay him is to say that Dowcha-boy lived as he died, for the honour of the Northside.

And no! Dowcha-boy did not belong to me. We were friends. He was the kind of friend I could open my heart to, the kind of friend I knew I could always turn to. The kind of friend that would listen without judgement. A true friend. And today I'm sad, because today I say goodbye to my friend.

Mossie The Gardener broke down in tears, and falling to his knees he began to backfill the small grave with handfuls of earth. He then patted it down at the edges, like a mother tenderly tucking a blanket around a slumbering infant. When he had finished, Sister Francesca helped him to his feet.

The Butter Exchange Band struck up the *Dead March from Saul* and led the mourners from the garden. At the convent gate Sister Francesca released her grip on Mossie's arm and, looking deeply into his tear-filled eyes, she softly said,

—  Now that Dowcha-boy is gone, if you ever need a friend, Mossie, I'll be here for you...

Dowcha-boy's funeral marked the first day of a lifelong friendship that blossomed between the gardener and the nun. It was a friendship that survived two world wars and some earth-stopping events, from the first transatlantic flight, to man walking on the moon.


Young Brother Scully stood there listening to Sister Claire, his mind, body and soul lost in the misty-eyed world of the epic tale. She told how the Southside bookies honoured their betting slips directly after the funeral.

—  An orderly queue formed outside Quinlan's pub, she said. — A queue that wound its way along Gerald Griffin Street, the full length of Great William O'Brien Street and down to Blackpool Church, around by Tomás McCurtain's shop and all the way to the foot of Dublin Hill. The Southside bookies paid out a small fortune that day, every last penny of it in cash.

And the people of the Northside? Well Sister Agnes The History Teacher told us that the people of the Northside sang and danced for a week after that...

In the days that followed Dowcha-boy's great victory, the city was alive with the news that a young nun up in St Joseph's Convent had a special hotline to St Francis and was miraculously curing animals. What began as a trickle of curiosity became a raging torrent of activity as more and more sick animals were paraded up and down to the young Sister Francesca Of The Birds. But the more she protested that no miracle had been procured, the more convinced they were of her saintly humility.

—  But if she was curing animals, what did it matter if it was miraculous or not, asked Brother Scully.

—  Well, there's a big difference.

Sister Claire explained that Sister Francesca Of The Birds had always insisted that the power of prayer should not be confused with the mystery of miracles. She was concerned that the demands put on her through constant praying for sick animals interfered with her other duties around the convent. So, she asked the then Reverend Mother for guidance. Reverend Mother would have been conscious of the many offerings of gratitude bringing so much relief to the cash-strapped coffers of the convent, but she did not allow something as vulgar as monetary gain to influence her judgement. So they prayed on the matter, and, following a brief period of reflection, Reverend Mother said, — *Who are we to question the will of God.*

That very day Sister Francesca was relieved of all her teaching duties to concentrate full-time on praying for sick animals. That was back in 1919, and for over fifty years until her death, Sister Francesca Of The Birds, with Mossie The Gardener by her side, continued to cure sick animals through the intercession of St Francis, and the offerings and donations continued to pour into the convent.

  — So what do you think, asked Brother Scully. — Do you think it really was a miracle? I mean, you said it yourself. Dowcha-boy was old, war-torn and wounded. It's incredible that the old bird was able to fly at all, not to mind win the race …
  — Of course it was a miracle!
  — I'm not sure I believe in miracles, he said.
  — Well, everybody said it was a miracle, said Sister Claire. - Mind you, you'll always have the few cynics who will tell you that just before the race Mossie The Gardener switched Dowcha-boy with a young cock pigeon that had spent the previous two weeks in a cage next to a most attractive yearling hen pigeon with only the thinnest gauze separating the two love birds …
  — Separated by a thin gauze? What was that all about?
  — The theory being that when the love-struck two-year-old was released on the day of the race, nothing was going to get between him and that attractive yearling hen back in Mossie's loft. So it would be full speed all the way …
  — So that's it, said Brother Scully and clicked his fingers. — They

switched the birds? That's how they did it. Brilliant!
- How d'you mean, that's how they did it?
- Mossie must have switched the birds, how else could that old pigeon at death's door have won the race …
- Switched, repeated Sister Claire. – You think Mossie The Gardener switched the birds?

And maybe Sister Claire didn't believe that the saintly Sister Francesca Of The Birds would have become involved in switching the pigeons for the sole purpose of winning a bet, but for the first time she felt compelled to at least consider the possibility that Mossie The Gardener had switched Dowcha-boy for a young two-year-old lovesick pigeon.

Sister Claire became visibly upset when Brother Scully insisted that there had been nothing miraculous about Dowcha-boy's great victory. She couldn't accept that the whole escapade had been an elaborate betting swindle, and the decades of deep devotion and dedication to the saintly Sister Francesca Of The Birds had been based on nothing but a rigged pigeon race. She stood there, biscuit jar in hand, battling the internal conflict that raged inside her mind. For over fifty years, the faithful had brought their sick animals up to the convent seeking a cure from Sister Francesca Of The Birds. It was a devotion built on the belief that Dowcha-boy had a miraculous recovery and went on to be victorious in a pigeon race he never even flew. The very thought of Sister Francesca Of The Birds sweating blood praying for a miracle, when all the time it was just a cheap betting scam, was too painful to contemplate.
- Do you think Sister Francesca spent her life praying for sick animals, unaware that Mossie The Gardener had switched pigeons, she whispered.

Brother Scully did not reply, instead he just shrugged his shoulders and cast his eyes towards heaven. Sister Claire refused to accept the obvious conclusion that Sister Francesca had been complicit in the deception from the very beginning.
- Sister Francesca Of The Birds devoted her whole life to prayer, she said. – She sweated blood, for God's sake. She was a living saint! I can't believe she was involved in a betting fraud.

And what about all the people down through the decades who faithfully brought their sick animals to the convent to be cured? What about all the poverty-stricken people of the Northside who gave donations and offerings to the convent because they believed? And all the time it was just a sham, a fraud! Nothing but a lie...

Sister Claire was close to tears. And just like that everything changed. The light-hearted atmosphere and fun they had shared together just seemed to disappear. Brother Scully attempted to turn the mood around.

— Look, he said. — Even if it was a scam, the whole Northside must have been in on it. They must have known that Dowcha-boy would be switched. I mean, give them some credit! Do you really think they would put all their money on the old bird to win, unless they knew it was a sure bet?

Do you think they would be stupid enough to go into hock, and put every penny they had on a pigeon, not to mind an old pigeon that had been shot twice.

No disrespect to Sister Francesca Of The Birds, but the people of the Northside wouldn't gamble their hard-earned money on something as unpredictable as the prayers of a young nun or the intervention of God. I mean come on, like? They're not total fools! You can be sure they knew the race was rigged. They knew it was a sure bet...

— If everyone knew, why then did each successive new Reverend Mother to the convent make special provisions for Sister Francesca's vocation to pray for sick animals, argued Sister Claire. — If all the time it was a lie! A fraud!

— So, Sister Francesca spent her life praying for sick animals, what's wrong with that? Surely prayer is fundamental to religious life. Anyway, if praying for sick animals brought badly needed funds into the convent, why would any Reverend Mother kill the golden goose?

— But the deception?

— What deception, he interrupted. — From the very beginning

Sister Francesca Of The Birds always insisted that there had been no miracle. You said it yourself! She denied it from the very beginning. She always claimed that the cures were all down to care and the power of prayer. Never once did she claim a miracle! Did she? Well, did she?

— But what about all those people who believed?

— Look, people will be people, Brother Scully reasoned. — And people will believe what they want to believe. Tell you the God's honest truth, it wouldn't surprise me if Sister Francesca Of The Birds was in on the whole scam herself, from the very beginning.

The thought that the saintly Sister Francesca Of The Birds would have been involved in a betting swindle brought an uneasy smile to Sister Claire's face.

— Sister Francesca was in on it, she questioned.

— Ah well, God acts in mysterious ways, he said.

— Do you really think that God would involve himself in betting fraud?

— Well if it served his purposes he would, said Brother Scully. — Put it another way, do you really think God would answer a nun's prayers for divine intervention to cure an injured pigeon just to win a race?

The absurdity of Brother Scully's question made young Sister Claire laugh. Her laughter faded to silence. She contemplated the possibility that the whole story of Dowcha-boy was no more than a modern-day fairy tale.

But there was magic in the telling of this fairy tale, a magic that nurtured intimacy between them. They stood there face to face, Brother Scully resisting his desire to reach out and hold her in his arms. Their eyes met. Sister Claire raised her lips towards his. She closed her eyes. Brother Scully leaned towards her. But the magic of the moment was shattered when, once again, the refectory door crashed open and young Brother O'Connell burst into the kitchen.

— Ah lads ye're missing it! Ye're missing it! Knock-Knock, Who's There! Mary Hopkin! The UK entry! Ye're missing it! Very catchy! She's only nineteen! A Welsh girl! Ah lads! Brother O'Hegarty's

roaring at the telly! Ye gotta come out and see this! Ye're missing
it, lads! In colour! Ye're missing it!

He ran a full circuit of the kitchen, grabbed a few biscuits and
then vanished back into the refectory before the door had time to
swing shut.

Brother Scully glanced towards the refectory door, then back to
Sister Claire again. But the moment was lost. In that split second of
hesitation, it was as if they both instinctively chose not to be led into
temptation. So, with an uneasy shuffling of feet, they stepped back and
stood a respectable distance apart. Sister Claire once again began
counting biscuits and Brother Scully returned to filling the Burco.

Sister Claire broke the silence.

— Will she do it, she asked.

— Will who do what?

— Dana! Will she do it? Win the Eurovision, like? Have you heard
the song?

— 'Course I have, he said. — It's on the radio morning, noon and
night ever since she won the National...

Sister Claire turned to face Brother Scully.

— You know in the lyrics of the song, where she sings the words,
— *All kinds of everything remind me of you.*

— Eh? Yeah?

— Well who is the, *you,* she's referring to?

— How d'you mean, he asked.

— Like, when Dana uses the word, *you,* in the song, who is the *you*
she's referring to?
Do you think she's referring to God, or is she referring to a
person?

— Eh? I never really thought about it. Why? What do you think?

— Well when I first heard the song a few weeks ago when she won
the National Song Contest, I assumed she was talking about
God. Y'know, *All kinds of everything remind me of God,* sort
of thing. But now I'm coming around to the idea that she's
singing about her love for another person. Like a boy she loves.
Y'know like?

*All kinds of everything remind me of you?*
— Reminds you of me, gasped Brother Scully.
— No. I'm not talking about me and you, silly! I'm talking about the words of the song...

The suggestion that Brother Scully was the object of her affection brought the flush of a blush to Sister Claire's cheeks, like she had stepped through some invisible barrier that had been keeping them apart. Again their eyes connected in a flash of intimacy, and there was something irresistibly seductive in that. They stood there in confused silence, each one hoping the other would do, or at least say, something. But not a word was spoken. Every ounce of emotion that had been locked away and buried deep since they had first decided to take religious orders seemed to rise up to the surface like frayed nerve endings exposed, tingling and sparking, ready to erupt in a frenzy of passion.

Brother Scully attempted to suppress his feelings by closing his eyes, counting to five and changing the subject.
— So, you figure Sister Francesca Of The Birds was the brains behind the great racing pigeon betting swindle, he said and laughed.

Sister Claire slapped him on the arm.
— Don't be so bold, she said. — I never said any such thing! Anyway the story about Dowcha-boy is just the background to the story I want to tell you about old Sister Francesca.

Again Brother Scully laughed. It was a considered laugh of indifference. It was a forced laugh, a laugh of convenience intended to dissipate the escalating intensity of intimacy.
— I don't know if I should tell you now, she said. — You won't take it seriously, you'll only laugh...
— Ah, go on, go on...
— Okay, but this is serious and you have to promise not to laugh.
— I promise, I promise...
— Well a few weeks ago, just before old Sister Francesca Of The Birds died, a most amazing thing happened...

Unsure if she should continue, Sister Claire waited for Brother Scully to settle down.

- Now seriously, she said. — You'll have to promise to keep it a
  secret.
- I promise! I promise!
- Well, a few weeks ago, just before she died, Sister Francesca had
  a...
- She had a what?
- You promise you'll keep it a secret?
- Ah, for God's sake, I promise! Cross my heart!
- Swear to God?
- Yes! Yes! I swear to God and hope to die, he said and sealed his
  word with a dismissive sign of the cross.

Sister Claire leaned close to Brother Scully and said in a low voice,
- An apparition...
- An apparition!
- Shhhh!

The young nun put her finger to Brother Scully's lips, and cast a sharp
glance towards the refectory door. The touch of her fingertip sent a
shudder through his body.

Sister Claire stood rigid and silent until the sound of excitement
from the Eurovision Song Contest outside the refectory reassured her
that it was safe to proceed.
- It's true, she whispered. — Old Sister Francesca Of The Birds
  had an apparition from heaven, shortly before she died.

Sister Claire described how, just a few weeks earlier, the whole convent
was awoken from their sleep by the wild wailing of the elderly Sister
Francesca as she ran along the corridors in her nightgown, screaming
that she had been blessed with a miraculous visitation from heaven.
- You're joking?
- No, it's the gospel truth!
- And who appeared to her? Was it the Virgin Mary, asked Brother
  Scully.
- Well that's the strange thing, you'd expect it to be the Virgin
  Mary. After all, Our Lady does most of the appearing. But it was
  not Our Lady who came to visit Sister Francesca that night, said
  Sister Claire. — It was...

— Who?
— You're not going to believe it, but...
— Who, pleaded Brother Scully.
— It was Saint Joseph.
— Saint Joseph? Jesus' stepfather?
— Yes!
— Jesus, Mary and Joseph, he whispered.
— I know it sounds mad, Brother Scully. But it's true. Over in our convent just a few months ago Saint Joseph appeared to Sister Francesca Of The Birds, just before she died.
— Ah, for Christ's sake? Saint Joseph? Who ever heard of Saint Joseph appearing to anyone?
— Well that's exactly what Reverend Mother said and that's why she doesn't want word of it to get out, whispered Sister Claire. — But there's something very sad about the whole thing, don't you think?
— Sad? Nuts if you ask me!
— No seriously? Just imagine, said Sister Claire. — For almost sixty years Sister Francesca Of The Birds had been curing animals, and everybody claiming she was performing miracles. Yet right throughout those years she always insisted that she had no miraculous powers, and that divine intervention had no hand act or part in the cures.
— And what's so sad about that, asked Brother Scully.
— Well, it just seems so unfair that after all these years, she now claims to have had a divine encounter with Saint Joseph and nobody believed her. And what's worse, everyone is saying that she was after losing her mind.
— But Saint Joseph, said Brother Scully. — Who ever heard of Saint Joseph appearing to anyone?
— I know it's a bit of a stretch of the imagination, she said. — But everything about Christianity is a stretch of the imagination. Christianity is all about believing the unbelievable ...
— God curing a racing pigeon is one thing, but Saint Joseph appearing to an old nun! I mean, come on!

— Well you don't have to believe me if you don't want to, she said. Young Sister Claire insisted that Brother Scully would not speak one word of Saint Joseph's apparition to another living soul.

- It is very sensitive, she said. — There is a lot of scepticism around the whole thing.
- I'm not surprised.
- An around-the-clock vigil was kept on Sister Francesca even while she slept. Reverend Mother didn't think it was safe to leave the elderly nun alone, just in case Saint Joseph decided to call again. The Bishop and the Vatican have been informed and there's a full investigation going on.
- The Bishop and the Vatican? But this is 1970, not the middle ages, said Brother Scully. — I mean like, apparitions from heaven and voices from the sky? That's all from another time. We don't really get apparitions in this modern day and age.
- You're wrong there, she said. — Lucia Marto, the girl who saw Our Lady in Fatima, is still very much alive. I mean that's right up-to-the-minute modern day. How modern day do you want? In our convent library we even have a book with photographs of the crowds in Fatima looking at the *Miracle Of The Sun*. Photographs! Is that modern enough for you? Surely that's proof.
- Ah well, a photograph of crowds looking at a miracle is not the same as a photograph of a miracle, he said.
- Look, I don't care if you believe me or not, she said. — But there is a ring of truth about Sister Francesca Of The Birds' visitation from Saint Joseph. It has all the hallmarks of a genuine apparition.
- Ah, I don't know. Like why would Saint Joseph be appearing to an elderly nun up here on the Northside?
- Be that as it may, said Sister Claire. — But like most other authenticated apparitions, Saint Joseph came bearing three messages. And three seems to be the magic number.
- Messages? You didn't mention messages. Messages about what? Armageddon? The salvation of mankind? The second coming?
- Well that's the odd thing, said Sister Claire. — The messages

from heaven were more of a personal nature.

— Personal nature? Personal messages from God?

Sister Claire told how she had sat by Sister Francesca's bedside each night while she slept in the weeks before she died.

— I would just sit there watching her sleep. Sometimes she would wake in the middle of the night and we would pray together. But one particular night old Sister Francesca sat up in the bed, totally lucid and told me that she would like to talk. She wanted to talk about what happened on the night Saint Joseph appeared.

— Really?

— Yes, really! She told me she felt no fear whatsoever when she saw Saint Joseph standing at the foot of her bed. On the contrary, it was the most beautiful experience of her life.

It was just past midnight when the elderly Sister Francesca Of The Birds awoke that night. The first thing she noticed was a strange smell, then she felt a presence in her room. That's when she saw Saint Joseph standing at the end of her bed in the darkness.

— ...and these are the words of Saint Joseph, exactly as Sister Francesca told me, said Sister Claire.

— *Who's there, asked old Sister Francesca.*

— *Don't be afraid, came the reply. — I have something to tell you.*

— *Something to tell me?*

— *Yes, he said. — Now, I don't have much time. So, listen to what I have to say.*
  *You must tell Reverend Mother that she needs to check the joists in the attic of the convent. They're riddled with woodworm and there's a touch of dry rot in the apex. She must do something about it straight away. And secondly, you must also tell her to take a look at the fascia board on the western gable of the chapel as it needs to be weatherproofed in the spring.*

— You're joking me, said Brother Scully. — Those were the messages from heaven! Woodworm and dry rot.

— Well, that's when old Sister Francesca realised it was Saint

Joseph standing there, said Sister Claire. — It had to be Saint Joseph, after all, he was a carpenter, and woodworm and dry rot are the sort of things that would concern a carpenter.

— So did Reverend Mother check the joists in the attic and the fascia board?

— Yes she did.

— And?

— Believe it or not, but Saint Joseph was right, said Sister Claire. — The woodwork needed attention.

— So it was Saint Joseph, he said.

— Well he was right about the woodwork. And Saint Joseph is the only carpenter who also happens to be a saint.

— Hmmm, interesting, but that's only two messages. What about the third message?

— The third message? Now that's where the whole thing got a bit strange, said Sister Claire.

— Strange? How stranger could it get?

— Well, Sister Francesca told me that just as Saint Joseph turned to leave, he stopped and these are the exact words he spoke to her.

— *You should never have become a nun, Francesca. You should have married and had children. You would have been a most wonderful mother. The world needs wonderful mothers bringing new life into the world more than it needs holy sisters curing animals.*

Saint Joseph stepped into the light. The elderly nun strained her eyes, bringing his hazy outline into focus. He was elderly, stooped and slightly unsteady on his feet. There was a glint of tears in Saint Joseph's eyes, and something familiar about the aromatic blending of Woodbines and alcohol that filled the room.

— *You should have come away with me, Saint Joseph continued. — The two of us against the world, my beautiful Francesca ...*

As the moonlight picked up the detail of his features, it occurred to Sister Francesca that Saint Joseph had an uncanny resemblance to her lifelong friend, Mossie The Gardener. Sister Francesca reached out her hand, but before she could utter a word Saint Joseph vanished into the darkness.

Veiled whispers swept the corridors of the convent, whispers that echoed around the halls of the Bishop's Palace and all the way to Rome, whispers that it had been Mossie The Gardener and not Saint Joseph who visited Sister Francesca that night.

The physical demands of gardening over the years had taken their toll on old Mossie, and the previous week he had reluctantly been persuaded to retire from his duties around the convent. Someone said he had been seen wandering aimlessly in the garden earlier that afternoon, and although it may have been unrelated, a half bottle of wine had been reported missing from the sacristy that particular day. It was suggested that the missing wine might just have been what Mossie The Gardener needed to pluck up the courage to visit Sister Francesca's room. But right up to her dying day Sister Francesca insisted it had been Saint Joseph who visited her bedroom that night. She would be heard repeating over and over.

— It was Saint Joseph, it was Saint Joseph, it was Saint Joseph...

When Sister Francesca Of The Birds departed this world, her final hours were fraught with anxiety and distress. She lay there in her candlelit, cell-like room, her community of sisters gathered around her bed. These brides of Christ who chose to come together in cloistered life stood as one, in solemnity, reciting the mantra of the Rosary.

*Hail, holy Queen, Mother of Mercy.*
*Hail, our life, our sweetness and our hope.*
*To thee do we cry, poor banished children of Eve.*
*To thee do we send up our sighs,*
*mourning and weeping in this valley of tears.*

The dying nun cried out in anguish, begging Saint Francis for assistance and God for forgiveness. Young Sister Claire held her hand gently but firmly, easing her pain and comforting her distress. Reverend Mother drove on the prayers louder and louder, drowning out Sister

Francesca's torment. But then, in an instant, there was silence.

Some said that Sister Francesca had a saintly countenance, and a visible glow emanated from her bed. Young Sister Claire relaxed her grip. The elderly nun raised her head, her eyes fixed in a glazed stare toward the foot of the bed, and she calmly whispered,

— He is here. He is here among us. I knew he would come…

And like the Red Sea of old, the gathered community of holy women parted. Sister after sister stepped aside creating an avenue of nuns that gradually made its way from the end of the bed all the way to the door, and as the last one stepped aside, there in the hallway stood Mossie The Gardener crying uncontrollably, cap in hand.

— I knew you would come, she whispered.

What happened next may have been a sin, and, if not a sin, it most certainly broke with protocol. Mossie The Gardener, slowly and with uncertainty, inched his way through the parting of sisters and stood at Sister Francesca's bedside. The old man took the dying nun by the hand and kissed her fingers. Then, kneeling by her bedside, he gently said,

— Me and Francesca would like to be alone.

And, for some unknown reason, Reverend Mother nodded her head and consented to the privacy he requested.

One by one the sisters filed from the room and lined the hallway in silent meditation. Mossie The Gardener sat on the side of the bed and cradled Sister Francesca in his arms. Then, leaning closer to her, he whispered,

— My Francesca. My beautiful Francesca.

All these years and I standing alongside you, and you curing the animals, all I ever wanted was to be with you. But many years ago, I realised that the only way I could spend my life with you was if I was willing to share you with God. And if being with you meant playing second fiddle to God, well so be it.

Maybe I should have been content to have you all to myself every minute of every day. But I'm a jealous man, because I wanted you all to myself for every minute of every night too. Was that too much to ask? Ah but, it wasn't to be, it wasn't to be…

God must be more jealous than me. Because I only wanted you

for a short lifetime, but he has you all to himself for eternity.
The only consolation I can take from this life is that we did grow old together, my beautiful Francesca. Every moment we spent together in the convent garden was ours and ours alone. And no one, neither God nor man, can ever take that away from us.
You've always known it. You've always known that I worship the ground you walk on. And maybe I should have said these words a long time ago. So I'm going to say them now.
I love you Francesca. I love you now as I've always loved you.
My beautiful Francesca ...

They spoke in hushed tones of a life shared and a love less ordinary. They spoke of the daily wonders of nature they had witnessed in that little walled convent garden. They spoke of the gentility of death and the brutality of life. And when Mossie The Gardener said,

— Do you remember Dowcha-boy, Francesca? My racing pigeon Dowcha-boy? D'ya remember him?

— Do I remember, she whispered and smiled. — Will I ever forget! You're a divil, Mossie. That's what you are, a divil. If I had known what you were up to with that pigeon ...

The elderly couple remained wrapped in each other's arms and spoke for over an hour, sometimes giggling like young lovers. It is said that the last words from her lips were,

— ...and I love you too, Mossie.

The old gardener held Sister Francesca close. He wrapped the blanket around her shoulders and, leaning towards her, he tenderly kissed her cheek, then gently lowered her head to the pillow.

A silence filled the room and permeated the halls and stony cold corridors of the convent. It was a silence that remained intact until the mournful sound of a lone harrier hound cried out in the distance. Then, one by one, every dog right across the Northside began to howl. From doorway to doorway and street to street, from the Northside across two rivers to the Southside, they howled out a lament that echoed around the five hills, like they were saying goodbye to a dear friend, goodbye to one of their own ...

* * *

— One of their own, oneoftheirown, oneoftheirownoneoftheir ...
Brother Scully says it over and over and over again.

The noonday bell has come and gone, and by the clock on Shandon
it's a few minutes to one. Old Brother Scully has not moved from his
bedroom window since before dawn this Christmas Eve morn, still
hoping upon hope for a flash of light or some glimmer of life from Sister
Claire's bedroom window across in St Joseph's Convent.

Thoughts of the lifelong, unspoken love shared by Mossie The
Gardener and Sister Francesca Of The Birds consume his mind. He
wonders if their love had been forbidden by God or forbidden by man.
It was an exceptional love, a love denied but yet thrived 'til death did
them part.

— But what is love?
Mossie The Gardener and Sister Francesca Of The Birds had spent
every single day together in the garden. They shared a fascination for
the marvels of nature and a passion for all of creation. Their lives
entwined like ivy, through the enthusiasm of youth, the idealism
of maturity and the complacency that old age brings. And maybe that
is love.

— But what is love, he says it again.
Mossie The Gardener was her window to the world beyond the convent
walls. Through his eyes she saw two world wars, boom and bust, men
walking on the moon and all the other earth-shattering events she had
vowed to leave behind. Some would call that love.

— But what is love ...
A lifetime ago when Sister Francesca was an innocent young novice,
and Mossie a fit young labourer, maybe back then, fuelled by the rising
sap of spring and a lust for life that youth can bring, maybe back then
she harboured feelings for the young gardener.

— But what is love ...
And maybe at nighttime, when her soft cotton nightdress brushed
against her untouched skin, did she sense a hollow pain of loneliness
in her heart? Was there a stark chill of emptiness in her bed? Did she
battle the temptations of her intimate venial thoughts? Did she ever

*A silence that remained intact until the mournful sound of a*
*lone harrier hound cried out in the distance...*

give in, and if she did, maybe some would call that love. But is that love?

— But what is love, whatislove, whatisloveisloveislove ...

Over the years Brother Scully's sadness has turned to bitter resentment when he thinks of love's opportunity wasted. Mossie The Gardener and Sister Francesca spent a lifetime together in the garden, and in all that time their love for each other remained unspoken. A rage builds up inside Brother Scully when he thinks of the futility of it all.

— What is love? What a waste! What-a-waste!

Whatawastewhatawastewhata ...

He thinks of his own love for Sister Claire, a lifetime of devoted yet isolated love, and he imagines what it would be like to have spent just one day in a garden with her. One day, one hour, or even one minute? He would proclaim his love for her over and over until the sands of time ran out. He would tell her that he loved God, but he loved her more. He would take her by the hand and sit beneath the falling blossoms of a cherry tree, he would look deeply into her eyes and tell her that he had seen a glimpse of heaven, but would willingly sell his soul for eternity if he could share the rest of his living days with her.

But it was not to be. Brother Scully and Sister Claire were born into a time when a vocation was for life. Their unrealised love became their cross and so they were destined to live in total separation, their only communication restricted to the flashing of light bulbs over and back from convent to monastery. Yet he finds some comfort knowing that with every bolt of light from his bedroom window, he has proclaimed his undying love for Sister Claire every single morning of every single day, down through the decades.

For almost fifty years Brother Scully has contemplated every aspect of love. Like an alchemist of old, he has searched for the Philosopher's Stone of true love. He has come to the conclusion that love is much like God. Love is elusive and powerful, cruel and vengeful, and yet all happiness and light. Love is many things to many people, and all things to all people. But yet, just like God, there is only one true love.

Ever since dawn this Christmas Eve morn he has sat anxiously, staring across at Sister Claire's bedroom window. The one o'clock gong for lunch now reverberates around the monastery, but Brother Scully has not yet been to the refectory to break his fast. He usually starts his day with a cup of sweet, milky Barry's best, but not today.

There is a jar of Bovril and an electric kettle stashed away beneath his sink for days such as this. He fills the kettle, plugs it in and waits for it to boil. He remembers back to that time, in the days after Dana's great victory over Europe, when his world collapsed and his friend Brother O'Connell called to his room and placed a jar of Bovril and an electric kettle at the end of the bed.

— *You might need it for days such as this, he said.*
That was a long time ago, but Brother O'Connell's single act of kindness was enough to carry Brother Scully through the darkest days of his life, and ever since, whenever harsh reality becomes too difficult to face, he turns to Bovril.

His arthritically-buckled fingers grip the lid of the Bovril jar, and he struggles to open it. Eventually perseverance wins. The sound of the kettle simmering reminds him of the old Burco boiler bubbling that night in the kitchen all those years ago.

Brother Scully fills his mug with boiling water and stirs in two heaped spoons of Bovril. The tinkle-tinkle of stainless steel on china transports him right back to the refectory on the night of Dana's Eurovision glory.

* * *

There was something in the air that night, like a sprinkling of stardust had cast a spell of enchantment over the entire monastery. Sister Claire was humming along to the sound of music filtering through from the colour television outside in the refectory. His eyes were drawn to the shape of her body swaying beneath her robe as she moved around the kitchen. Young Brother Scully had never experienced such profound feelings of attraction. He wanted to reach out, to touch, to hold, to embrace, but struggled to control his desires. So, he decided to talk instead.

— I was never quite sure what a vocation was, he said. — But from the first morning I woke up in my room here in this monastery,

I knew I had made the right choice.

— So have you ever doubted your vocation, she asked.

He paused before answering.

— Well you know the way you hear so much about God's great gift of free will to mankind? But it seems to me that with every step I took towards religious life, like every step I took closer to God, the more my free will was taken from me. Until eventually all choice was lost and there was only one way forward.

— God's way?

— Maybe God's way? Or maybe it's man's way. Like sometimes I think ever since I was born and baptised my road to religious life was paved by other people's ambitions and expectations.

— Other people?

— Like all the time being drawn forward on a conveyor belt of encouragement from family, neighbours, school. Next thing I know I'm in a monastery wearing a soutane. Sometimes it feels like I was enticed into a lobster pot. No way back.

I'm not complaining. My vocation is as strong as ever. Or should I say, my vocation to Jesus Christ is as strong as ever.

— Your vocation to Jesus Christ? Is there a difference?

— I don't know if I should tell you this, he said. — But to be honest with you, I'm not sure if I really believe in God...

— What!

— Shhh!

Brother Scully's eyes darted towards the refectory door.

— That's ridiculous, she whispered. — You must believe in God! God was Jesus' father! Without God there would be no Jesus, and without Jesus there'd be no Christianity!

— Ah well, God, Jesus and Christianity are three totally different things, he said. — You don't have to believe in all three of them to believe in one of them. There are billions of people all over the world who believe in God but don't believe in Jesus Christ. I'm just one who believes in Jesus Christ but not in God ...

— Ah, you're winding me up! How can you not believe in God!

— The whole concept of God seems all a bit, well you know ...

— Concept! Since when did God become a concept, she snapped.
— A white-bearded giant in a toga, sitting on a throne up in the sky, looking down on his creation in judgement, like some cross-mutation between Santa Claus and the bogeyman? I mean stop the lights!

There followed an awkward quietness as Sister Claire took a few moments to consider the notion of a universe without God. Brother Scully filled the silence and continued talking.

— ...tell you the truth, I've always had a problem with the miracles, he said. — Don't get me wrong, the miracle of nature is there for all to see. Nature has been hard at work long before man walked this earth, and nature will be hard at work long after man becomes extinct.

Call it God, call it what you like, but as I see it, nature is the eternal creator of heaven and earth, and so long as you treat nature with respect, everything will be fine, and nature will provide.

— You're just using the word *nature* instead of the word *God*, she said.

— Well, no. That's not exactly true. Nature is very different from God. Nature doesn't judge. Nature doesn't require ritualistic sacrifice or adoration. Nature doesn't demand money for favours. Nature doesn't need palaces of marble and gold. Nature doesn't want to hear my sins in a confession box every Saturday night. Nature doesn't demand celibacy. And at the end of the day, nature doesn't really respond to men dressed up in funny costumes and headgear, rattling bones and spouting mumbo-jumbo.

And when it comes to all the bell ringing and incense burning? I mean what's that all about!

I suppose what I'm saying is, there's no human-imposed morality or immorality in nature. There's no pomp and ceremony in nature. Nature just is.

And maybe every so often the vulnerability of humanity is exposed by the awesome power of nature when we're hit by some natural disaster like a cyclone, drought or earthquake, but, unlike God, nature does not use its power to threaten or control mankind.

Anyway, enough of this! I'd rather not dampen the mood with my stuffy theory about God and creation ...

— It's not dampening the mood. I find it very interesting, Brother Scully, she said.

— Really?

— Yes, really! But I've one question about your theory that nature created the universe?

— Go on, try me.

— Well, if nature created the universe, who created nature?

— That's my very point. Nature is eternal, explained Brother Scully.
— As I see it, nature was there long before God. Maybe the real question should be, who created God? And I disagree with those who say that God created man in his likeness. It was the other way around, it was man who created God, and in true human vanity, we created God in our likeness.

— What are you sayin'! Man created God!

— See, when I read all that aul' guff about Jesus walking on water, turning water into wine, the loaves and fishes, raising fellas from the dead, I mean come on, like? Abracadabra! Ala-kazam! Hocus-pocus! Gobbledegook!

What are the miracles but man's attempt at controlling mankind by claiming to control nature. Think about it, a miracle is by definition something that defies nature ...

If anything, the miracles are acts of anti-nature, or more to the point, acts of anti-God.

The way I see it, the miracles were inserted into the gospels by the early Church leaders to put the fear of God into primitive man. But these days we're far too sophisticated for that sort of carry on. I mean, look around you. Colour television. This is 1970. This is a modern age, the age of science and technology. Do we really need some God up in the sky to convince us of the great miracle of nature?

But enough of all this God and nature talk. This is getting far too serious.

Brother Scully attempted to steer the conversation away from his challenging theories on God and creation. He was anxious to get back on track with more light-hearted chat, but Sister Claire was intrigued by his direct challenge to her beliefs so she enticed Brother Scully with an open-ended challenge to his theory.

— It's not for us to question God's will, she said.

— *Not for us to question God's will*, is trotted out as the universal answer to all nonsense.

— God is a matter of faith! Faith and belief!

— Belief? What is belief? I'll tell you what belief is, he said. — Belief is the acceptance of something that, on the face of it, is blatantly untrue. That's what belief is. And there's none that believe like those who want to believe.

Belief only comes into the equation when there is no proof. For over a thousand years we Christians believed the earth was flat, and the sun rotated around the earth! That's belief!

And this whole malarkey of God sending his son down to earth two thousand years ago with a message for mankind? A message that was so ambiguous, so cryptic, that to this very day the whole world is at war with itself trying to work out what the message was in the first place. And as for the resurrection? I mean, come on like?

— But you can't deny the resurrection happened. It's the cornerstone of our faith?

— The cornerstone of *your* faith maybe, he said. — Did you ever ask yourself why God's great display of power to mankind was exercised so discreetly? Think about it. The whole of Jerusalem witnessed Jesus' death, and yet not one single person witnessed his resurrection.

The way I see it, his resurrection should have been more public than his crucifixion. If Jesus had risen from the dead he should have paraded through the streets of Jerusalem.

Just imagine Jesus striding down along the Via Dolorosa as

proud as punch with the scars of his execution exposed and for all to see. That's what the Jesus I believe in would have done, if he had risen from the dead ...

He would have walked straight up to King Herod's temple and overturned the moneychangers' tables for a second time. And if they crucified him a second time, he'd have come back and done it a third time, and a fourth time, and a fifth time, over and over again until there'd be no doubt in anyone's mind that he was the Son of God, he was invincible, he was eternal, and he had risen. But no! For some reason God decided that no one would witness his grand display of power to mankind.

An extreme case of preaching to the converted, don't you think? Does that set off any alarm bells in your head?

— Eh? No-oh, she said defiantly. — But if you don't believe in the resurrection, why did you take Holy Orders!

The mood in the kitchen had changed.

— I took Holy Orders because I believe in Jesus Christ. That's why!

— Oh yeah?

— Yeah! I'm a Christian in the purest sense of the word. I believe in the man, his message, his way of life ...
And that's enough for me. Whether he is the Son of God or not is of no concern to me.

— That's a cop out, she said. — And what about the Virgin Birth? I suppose you don't believe in that either?

— Well now that you mention it ...

— Ah, for God's sake! Sur' if Jesus was not the Son of God, whose son was he?

Brother Scully paused and stepped back in an attempt to calm the tension that had crept into the conversation. He could have told Sister Claire exactly who Jesus' father was but he chose to remain tight-lipped.

He had spent the previous two years researching the living Christ. It had been a long and lonely personal journey of the soul, a journey that led him to the darkest of conclusions, a journey where the intensity of his study had isolated him from his fellow brothers in the community. And ever since Brother Ambrose had instructed him to keep his findings to himself, young Brother Scully had not revealed the details of his discovery to another living soul. For over two years, the contradictions, anomalies and truths he had uncovered in the Holy Scripture had been indexed, tagged, filed and stockpiled inside his head, just begging for someone to come along and ask the question. And that night in the monastery kitchen, the young Sister Claire stood in front of him, and once again she asked the question.

— If Jesus was not the Son of God, whose son was he?
Brother Scully did not answer.

All the banter of heroic pigeons, miraculous cures, late-night apparitions from heaven and the romantic tale of a lifelong love affair between the crippled gardener and saintly Sister Francesca Of The Birds seemed to have been set aside, only to be replaced by something far deeper and darker.

Sister Claire's eyes begged him to continue, but still he hesitated. In his heart of hearts he knew it was neither the time nor the place to reveal his faith-shattering discoveries. To do so would fan the flames of creeping hostility, and kill the light and airy feelings of mutual attraction and intimacy that had taken root between them.

— Ah ha! There now, she said and clicked her fingers. — If Jesus was not the Son of God, well whose son was he? You don't know do you? You can't answer that one, can ya?
Well can ya?
— I have a theory, he said quietly.
— Oh, so you have a theory, have you? Tell me more.
— I don't think this is the proper time or place.
— Try me.
— I don't think you're going to like what I have to say. It might shock you.
— Don't be so patronising. I'm a big girl now.
Still concerned that his interpretation of the gospels might be too controversial for Sister Claire to accept, young Brother Scully paused for a moment or two, unsure if he should continue.
— Go on, try me, she said it again.

— Are you sure you really want to know?

— Yes, I am.

— Okay, he said. — The true story of the Christ is there for all to see, plain as day. It all makes total and perfect sense, if you read the gospels straight up and take them at face value.

— Take the gospels at face value, she repeated. — I always take the gospels at face value.

— You think you do, he said. – You think you do.

See, first you got to cut through all the bizarre and weird stuff. Y'know, the angels appearing out of nowhere, the voices from the sky and all that Aladdin and his magic lamp stuff.

— Well, are you going to tell me or aren't you?

Unable to resist Sister Claire's persistent probing, young Brother Scully began by outlining his findings in the simplest of terms.

— I'll go back to the beginning. At a very basic level, the gospels tell the story of a young maiden called Mary. She had a cousin Elizabeth, and Elizabeth was married to an elderly priest called Zachariah.

— Go on, I know all that.

— Well next thing Mary gets pregnant and she tells her cousin, Elizabeth, that she is the handmaid of the Lord, and the Lord had made her pregnant.

— Okay, that's all fine.

— But here's the odd thing. Her cousin, Elizabeth, had also become pregnant a few months prior to that...

— I know that, said Sister Claire. — Elizabeth's baby grew up to be John the Baptist...

— Exactly! And Elizabeth was also claiming that she had become pregnant by the power of the Lord.

— That's all fair enough, said Sister Claire. — That's all in the gospels.

— So, we're supposed to believe that there was total silence from God since the days of the Old Testament, then out of the blue, God, the creator of heaven and earth and the universe, in all his wisdom, decides to make direct contact with mankind, so he zaps down from heaven and makes two cousins pregnant.

   — Eh? Yes. That's what the gospel tells us ...

Sister Claire sounded slightly unsure.

   — For God's sake, that's outrageous, snapped Brother Scully. — What did this all-powerful, all-loving God, the creator of heaven and earth set out to achieve when he decided to make those two girls pregnant? The salvation of mankind! What sort of a misguided megalomaniac would come up with an insane plan like that?

   — Careful, she said. — This is God you're talking about.

   — Ah for Christ's sake, if God wanted to send his Son down to earth with a message for mankind, surely it would have been a lot easier for all concerned if the surrogate mother God selected for this momentous job had been Caesar's daughter, or Pontius Pilate's daughter, or maybe even King Herod the Great's daughter ...

But no. Instead he decided to make a young, innocent serving girl pregnant! I mean, think about it?

What hope did an illegitimate child, born in a stable to a serving girl and raised by a carpenter have of getting God's message through to mankind?

   — Well you've answered your own question, she said. — Because obviously, against all the odds, God's plan worked! Here we are, two thousand years later, and Jesus' message is still coming through loud and clear all over the world.

Sister Claire's sharp and incisive answer brought a smile to Brother Scully's lips.

   — Touché, he said.

Maybe Sister Claire's understanding of theology was not as deep and detailed as Brother Scully's, but he could tell she was enjoying the verbal jousting.

   — Right, he said. — Well just for argument's sake, if Mary and her cousin, Elizabeth, became pregnant through the divine intervention of the Holy Spirit, as we are led to believe, that would make their two children half-brothers in the Holy Spirit.

— Well I suppose a case could be made for your argument, she said.

— So how come Mary's child, Jesus, is recognised as the all-powerful, all-knowledgeable Son of God, yet her cousin Elizabeth's child, who had also been divinely engineered, is given no divine status, and is not recognised as the Son of God. Instead he grew up to be John the Baptist, the wild man, spending his days raving and roving around the desert with nothing but a camel skin to cover his modesty.

— Look, she said. — All I know is that God sent his only Son, Jesus, down to earth for the salvation of mankind. And that's all I need to know.

— Salvation from who! Who was Jesus supposed to save us from? The Jews? The Romans? Save us from ourselves?

If God created the universe and every aspect of creation, well then Jesus must have come to earth to save mankind from some flaw in God's creation? In other words, Jesus was sent down to fix one of God's mistakes.

Sister Claire looked on in amusement as Brother Scully threw the tea towel to the counter top, shook his head and stood back defiantly.

— You're just twisting words now, Brother Scully!

And though his interpretation of the gospel was irreverent, there was something captivating about his boyish enthusiasm. The skewed and unsettling logic in Brother Scully's argument was disarming and alluring. Gradually, she found herself irresistibly drawn into the cut and thrust of the ever-deepening debate.

— You still haven't answered my question. If God was not Jesus' father, who was, she said.

— I really don't know if I should go any further with this.

— Look, your theory will either stand up or fall on its own merits.

— Okay, said Brother Scully. — Put it this way. In the scripture we are told that Mary was the handmaid of the Lord. And the Lord made her pregnant.

— Yes! Yes! Yes! We are in agreement, she said.

— Exactly, he said. — So Jesus is the Son of the Lord.

— Yes!

- But the obvious question is, who was the Lord?

Sister Claire was confused by Brother Scully's twisting of the question.

- The Lord? The Lord is God the Father, she said.

Brother Scully said nothing for a moment or two, he just stood there with a raised eyebrow and set a patronising, enquiring gaze on Sister Claire.

- I really don't know if you are ready for this, he said.
- Ready for what?
- Ready for what I'm about to tell you.
- Try me, she said.
- But are you really ready?
- Yes, she said. — I am!
- Well I'll tell you who the Lord was at that time ...

Brother Scully hesitated, aware that what he was about to reveal would most likely set what remained of their time together spinning off down a path of no return.

- So are you going to tell me?

Brother Scully glanced towards the refectory door, making sure that they were alone.

- Right, he said. — I'll tell you. But then we draw a line under this conversation and get back to lighter stuff and the fun we were having earlier ...
- Go on, just tell me.
- Okay! I'll tell you who the Lord was, he said. — King Herod the Great, Lord of Judea, that's who!
- What are you saying?
- I'm saying King Herod the Great was Jesus' father...
- What!
- Shhhh!

Brother Scully leaned over and again he checked the refectory door.

- Honestly, I have no doubt in my mind, he said. — Jesus Christ was the illegitimate son of King Herod the Great.
- You are insane, she whispered.
- Seriously, I've been researching this for some time now, and the truth is there for all to see. Jesus is without a shadow of a doubt

the illegitimate son of King Herod the Great. In fact I wouldn't be surprised if King Herod the Great got Mary's cousin, Elizabeth, pregnant too.

— Are you nuts!
You're saying that King Herod the Great was the father of Jesus Christ and John the Baptist? You are, she said. — You are absolutely nuts!

— Think of it this way. At its very basic level the gospel is the story of the Holy Family: Jesus, his mother Mary and his stepfather Joseph. Right?

— Eh? Right...

— And not forgetting Mary's extended family, her cousin, Elizabeth, and her husband, the High Priest Zachariah, and their child, John, John the Baptist.

— I know all that, she said. — But what has that to do with Herod making the Virgin Mary and Elizabeth pregnant.

— See, what most people don't realise is that the gospel is a tale of two families.

— Two families?

— Yes! And the second family are every bit as important to the story, and every bit as present in the story as the Holy Family.

— The second family? You mean, Elizabeth, Zachariah and their child, John the Baptist?

— No! No! They are part of Jesus' extended Holy Family.
The second family I'm talking about is the royal family of Herod. Think about it? The very first person mentioned in St Luke's gospel is Herod the Great, King of Judea.

Every minute detail of Brother Scully's lonely research that had been filed away in his brain seemed to surge forward, unstoppable, like floodwater crashing through a dam.

— Look, he said. — Everything I'm saying is there in black and white. See, if you read the scripture from the point of view of the Herod family, rather than the Holy Family, it tells a very different story.
The gospel is one big game of cat and mouse. From the very

moment Herod the Great sent out his men to slaughter Jesus when he was born, the game was on. The Herod royal family hunted the poverty-stricken Holy Family up and down Judea and in and out of Egypt for over thirty years, with the sole purpose of killing that illegitimate boy-child.

They murdered Zachariah, Elizabeth's husband, they arrested and murdered Jesus' cousin, John the Baptist. They ridiculed him and then cut his head off, so they did. I could give you a list as long as my arm of the many times the Herod family crop up right throughout Jesus' life, from the beginning to the bitter end. And finally, after thirty-three years of hunting him down, they eventually caught Jesus. They publicly mocked him, tortured him and then they crucified him. And that's it. That's the story of the gospel in a nutshell.

You see, the story of Christ is not a power struggle within the Jewish faith. It was a battle between two half-brothers for the right to be King of the Jews ...

— King of the Jews? And what about Christianity?
— Christianity came into existence after Jesus' death. First and foremost, Jesus was a Jew. Some say he was a child born to be King of the Jews.

But King of Christianity was what he had to settle for after the Herod family saw off his challenge to be King of the Jews.
— Mother of God, she whispered and blessed herself in the sign of the cross with a darting index finger. — I think you need to be careful about what you're saying, Brother Scully.
— Did you ever stop and wonder why two successive generations of the Herod royal family wanted Jesus dead from the very moment he was born? Why would the most powerful family in the land have bothered their barney with this illegitimate child, born in a stable and raised by a carpenter? The answer is obvious. It's been staring all of us in the face for over two thousand years. Read Matthew, it's there in black and white. Herod sent out his men to find the infant who would be the King of the Jews. He didn't send out his men looking for the Son of God. It's all about

the paternity of Jesus. That is what the gospel is all about.

— You're treading on very thin ice here, Brother Scully. You can't just dismiss two thousand years of Christian belief on some half-baked theory.

— Consider the facts, he said. — The gospels tell us that High Priest, Zachariah, was struck dumb when he realised his wife, Elizabeth, was pregnant. Not one word passed his lips. Think about it? Why would a powerful man like Zachariah keep his mouth shut? Well I'll tell you why! The reason is very clear...

If I was Zachariah, and King Herod made my wife pregnant I'd keep my mouth shut too. That's why! Herod was a lunatic! He'd slit yer throat if you as much as looked sideways at him, so he would.

And it wouldn't have been the first time Herod went slinking around the temple looking for a woman. His third wife, Mariamne, was the daughter of a High Priest called Simon...

— Really?

— Absolutely!

Brother Scully began by explaining that Herod the Great, King of Judea, was one of the most powerful rulers of his age, and, as he approached the end of his life, he became obsessed with his legacy and the stability of the royal dynasty after his death. Weighing heavily on Herod's mind was that he had lived a decadent life, entertaining numerous mistresses and engaging in countless illicit affairs.

— ...he was married as many as nine or ten times. Once to his own cousin, and another of his wives was his niece. And along the way Herod had fathered more children than you could shake a stick at.

To put it in layman's language, there were a lot of loose ends around the place, and Herod decided to clean up his lineage before he died.

Brother Scully then went on to list members of Herod's own family that he had put to death as a crude but effective way of consolidating his bloodline and ensuring the stability of the Herod dynasty.

— ...then he murdered his wife, Mariamne, and his mother-in-law,

Alexandra, and his brother-in-law, Kostobar, and two of his own sons, Alexander and Aristobulus. The man was crazy, he accused his oldest son, Antipater, of attempted regicide and had him executed, and then he ...

— Hold it! Hold it! Hold it, right there, said Sister Claire. — I'm totally confused.

— Sorry, sorry. I got a bit carried away. Look, put it this way, Herod the Great didn't think twice about killing members of his own family, a bit like pruning the branches of a tree to make the trunk grow stronger, if you know what I mean? So after all this blood-letting and slaughter, throat slitting and execution, the only members of the Herod family we need concern ourselves with are the man himself, King Herod the Great, and two of his sons, Archelaus and Antipas.

— Archelaus and Antipas?

— That's right, he said. — Herod's sons, Herod Archelaus and Herod Antipas!

See, as I see it, the story of Jesus begins with Herod the Great and Mary's cousin, Elizabeth ...

And there in the monastery kitchen, with the faint sound of the Eurovision Song Contest seeping through from the refectory, Brother Scully began to conjure up an intriguing tale of conspiracy and the decadent excesses of Herod's royal court.

There was something repulsively challenging about King Herod's seduction of Mary's cousin, Elizabeth. Sister Claire's mind flooded with images of wild passion that sent a tingling sense of guilt to her soul, but yet she found the unfolding tale of decadence of Herod's royal household sensually alluring.

She imagined Elizabeth, starved of emotion, trapped in a marriage to the elderly High Priest, Zachariah. She understood the humiliation Elizabeth must have suffered when the whispers of the chattering classes around the court speculated as to why they had not been blessed with children. Old Zachariah's manly virility never came into question. It was Elizabeth alone who bore the burden of shame for their barren marriage. Did Elizabeth live her life under this burden of guilt? Had she counted the years, the months, the weeks, as day after day the sands of time slipped through the hourglass and her dream of motherhood faded? Could it be that Elizabeth's deepening sense of desperation and isolation in a loveless marriage fuelled her lust, and enticed her to look beyond the confines of her nuptial bed to fulfil her passionate desires? And maybe Zachariah was a kind and God-fearing man, a man who gave Elizabeth the stability and social standing that her ambition craved. But many years had passed and now he was old, and any spark of excitement or sensuality he had once lit in Elizabeth had long since burned out and faded behind a brittle veneer of sanctimonious respectability.

As the wife of a High Priest, Elizabeth enjoyed a prominent position of privilege in the royal court. Was she a woman who wanted for nothing, but yet needed so much more? Was it loneliness or boredom that drove her to hunger for the taste of forbidden fruit? And, like all the other, much younger women who flaunted themselves around the royal court, did Elizabeth fantasise about her Lord Herod's arms wrapped around her? Would she encourage or reject the advances of a King? Did she wilfully step into a double life of secrecy and become a concubine to the great King Herod? Did she willingly offer herself up as plaything to the most powerful man in her world?

And what of Herod? What did he find so alluring about Elizabeth? Had he grown tired of plundering the virginity of young serving girls brought to his court from far off provinces and paraded in front of him for his pleasure? Maybe Herod sought a challenge? What greater challenge than the seduction of this attractive, mature, sophisticated, well-groomed and cultured wife of a High Priest. Did he thrill when his courtiers whispered of the scandal? Did the great King Herod revel in the gossip sweeping his palace that the only reason he had taken Zachariah's wife was just to prove that he could?

And each Sabbath and holy day, when Zachariah was busy with temple duties, did Elizabeth accentuate her eyes with layers of the thickest black kohl? Did her heart pound inside her breast as she scurried along darkened secret passageways that led to the private chambers of her lord and master? Did she fasten her veil tight to her face to hide her identity and conceal the slightly visible age lines in her skin? And when she found herself in the arms of her lord and master did she perform acts of servitude that she had only ever dared to imagine in those darkest places of her mind? Did Elizabeth become wild and young again during those lost afternoons of white-hot lust?

The feelings of unbridled passion that surged up inside Sister Claire came crashing down to earth when Brother Scully told of Elizabeth's fear and Herod's fury when he heard she was carrying his child. Did Elizabeth's powers of seduction become repulsive to her royal lover? Did Herod cast her aside? Did she degrade herself, and beg for his affection? Did she throw herself at his feet and cry out in anguish, pleading for compassion from the man whom she believed shared her love?

    — How can you do this to me? What will I tell my husband?
Herod's response was as sharp as it was blunt.

    — Tell him it was I, your Lord willed it! Now get out of my sight, he
      roared. — Go home to your old priest, and bring your unborn
      bastard child with you!

But maybe? Maybe Herod did harbour some genuine feelings for the High Priest's wife? Or maybe he feared a Jewish backlash. Could the impregnation of the High Priest's wife be a scandal too far? Would the conservative Jewish leaders petition Rome to have him removed from his position of power? Would they insist that this debauched man was unfit to sit on the throne of Judea? Maybe that's why Herod sent a messenger to old Zachariah. This messenger of the Lord was not the Angel Gabriel nor heaven sent. He found the elderly High Priest in the temple preparing incense.

The first thing old Zachariah felt was the full force of a muscular forearm to the back of his neck that drove him face first to the ground. Then the cold edge of a blade pressed to the soft flesh beneath his ear, enough to put the fear of God into the terrified High Priest.

    — Th-th-this is a house of God, pleaded Zachariah. — There is no
      money here!

    — I don't want your money, holy man!

I will only say this once, so listen and listen well, the voice hissed in his ear.

The sharp tip of the blade pierced old Zachariah's skin, drawing a pin-prick of blood.

— Your wife is with child.
— What? How?
— Shut up and listen!
— Who's the father?
— I said, shut up and listen!
— But what will I say when I'm asked?
— Shut up and listen!
— I am a High Priest. People will talk ...
— Tell them the father is God Almighty for all I care!
— But, but, but ...
— Now a word of warning, holy man. If you value your life and the life of your wife, you will keep your mouth shut! No questions asked, no questions answered.

The messenger of the Lord vanished as mysteriously as he arrived, but the message was received loud and clear. Zachariah never opened his mouth, never uttered a single word, like he had been struck dumb, until long after the child was born. The child's seed and breed was never questioned or mentioned again, because the fear of God Almighty is one thing, but the fear of Herod, the most powerful man in Judea, is quite another thing entirely.

Young Sister Claire imagined the pain of Elizabeth's isolation when she was shunned, excommunicated, ridiculed by the ladies of the court, cut off from the power and the physical brutish force of her lord and master Herod, the man she craved. As her belly swelled with her indiscretion, did she again attempt to curry favour with the great man in one last desperate throw of the dice? Is it possible that, in an act of tormented despair, Elizabeth decided to groom her young cousin Mary to be the handmaid of the most powerful man in the land? Was this her final and futile attempt at retrieving her privileged position in the royal court?

But Elizabeth's new-found favour was short-lived. Her delicately woven web of intrigue unravelled within months, when her young cousin, the maiden, Mary, also fell pregnant and she too was banished from the court and sent back to her home town.

— Nazareth, whispered Sister Claire.

— Well, experts differ, explained Brother Scully. — Some say Mary's home town was Sepphoris, others say Probatica. I doubt very much if it was Nazareth, after all that's the town the Holy Family moved to long after Jesus was born. But regardless of that, the fact remains, that the young maiden, Mary, was three months pregnant and back living at home.

She was actively telling anyone who'd listen that she had been the handmaid of the Lord and the child she was carrying was the Lord's child. And then to top it all, a short few months later her cousin, Elizabeth, gave birth to John the Baptist. And just like Mary, Elizabeth was telling the same story, that she too had conceived by the power of the Lord.

And so began the greatest story ever told ...

Brother Scully had become so preoccupied with expanding his grand theory, referencing and cross-referencing the minute details of his research, that he did not notice the subtle change that had come over Sister Claire. By the time Brother Scully realised he had been listening to the uninterrupted sound of his own voice for over five full minutes, it was too late. Sister Claire stood there trance-like, mouth opened, eyes locked in an intense and vacant gaze, staring into space, as one by one her beliefs had been held up to the light.

— Sister Claire? Sister Claire? Are you alright, Sister Claire?

Seduced by the tales of conspiracy and sexual intrigue, Sister Claire battled to hold faith in her belief. Ever since she had joined the novitiate she had been warned that Satan would come in many guises to challenge and undermine her faith. Deep in her heart and soul she was confident that young Brother Scully was not in league with the Devil, but she had only met him for the first time that evening, and was not about to surrender her beliefs and lifelong vocation to his wild theory on the paternity of Jesus Christ. And yes, it was fascinating, challenging and thought-provoking, but it was irreverent and sacrilegious, and Sister Claire had become increasingly uncomfortable with the direction in which it was taking her thoughts.

  — Look, she said. — I understand everything you are saying, and it all seems credible in a far-fetched sort of way, but really Brother Scully, this is blasphemy.

  — Blasphemy? What is blasphemy but a charge levelled at anyone who challenges the prevailing understanding of God. Jesus himself was branded a blasphemer in his own time ...

  — I really think we need to stop. We shouldn't be talking about this sort of thing, she said.

  — Fair enough, he said. — I'm only asking the question.
    Maybe millions of Christians are comfortable with the notion of God making two cousins pregnant, but I'm not.

Then he laughed, as if dismissing everything that he had said.

  — You think it's all some sort of big joke, she said.

  — No, he said. — It's all some sort of a bad joke.
    I've spent a long time researching this. I have devoted my life to Jesus Christ. It's only right that I ask the difficult questions. And for the life of me, I can't understand how an all-powerful, all-loving God could leave a young girl barefoot and pregnant, to fend for herself with no means of support, to rear his child on her own. I mean is that consistent with the message of Christian love? Does that sound like the actions of a benevolent God of creation? Well does it? Is that the basis of Christianity? Well is it?

Brother Scully held his silence for a time, allowing Sister Claire the opportunity to consider all that he had said. Then he continued,

  — But consider this scenario. Take God out of the equation and just consider this ...
    What if? What if Elizabeth and her young cousin were made pregnant by a man and not by a God, well then there is a certain logic to the whole thing. And if that man was an all-powerful, unscrupulous man, a man like King Herod the Great, for example, a man heartless enough to make two girls pregnant

and then cast them aside, well then the whole thing makes perfect sense.

If there's one thing I know about power, power always leads to an abuse of power, and it's a sad fact of human nature but power corrupts and absolute power corrupts absolutely. Look, the fundamental essence of God is belief. And I honestly can't see the hand of a benevolent divine God in the birth of either Jesus or John the Baptist...

Well not any God that I'd want to believe in.

Sister Claire, attempting to change the subject, pointed toward the teacups and said,

— Are you finished? The Eurovision Song Contest will be over soon.
— Well, this is exactly the point where Jesus comes into the story, he said. — Would you like me to carry on?

Sister Claire did not reply, she stared at him and goaded him to continue.

— Right, picture the scene, he said. — An illegitimate child is born in a stable on the outskirts of town. Word on the street has it that King Herod is the father. Now, this wouldn't be the first child Herod had out of wedlock, so it's no big deal. But next thing, the three kings arrive from the east...
— The Three Wise Men?
— Precisely, said Brother Scully. — And when the Three Wise Men claim that this illegitimate child is the fruit of King Herod's loins, the rumours echo around the halls of Herod's own court that this illegitimate child has a legitimate claim to the throne of Judea. And one day this child would grow up and come knocking on the palace door looking for what was rightfully his. As the old Christmas carol goes,
— *Born is the King of Israel* ...
Well you can guess what happened next?
— Herod went berserk, whispered Sister Claire.
— Dead right, he went berserk! He ordered that every male child in the district be slaughtered.
— The Slaughter of the Innocents?

— Bingo! And he did, he killed every last one of 'em! That should have been the end of it. And as far as Herod was concerned it was the end of it. Except Joseph was tipped off, most probably by Mary's cousin, Elizabeth, and he escaped with Mary and the baby.

— The Flight into Egypt?

— Exactly! And the rumour gets out that this illegitimate child with a claim to the throne of Judea has escaped and is still alive and well and living in Egypt.

Then thirty years later King Herod the Great dies, and his son Herod Archelaus takes over.

— Herod Archelaus?

— Remember I was telling you about Herod's two sons, Archelaus and Antipas?

— Well I know about Herod Antipas, she said. — Herod Antipas is the one who sent Jesus for crucifixion. But to be honest with you I never heard of Archelaus ...

— It's not surprising you haven't heard of Archelaus. His reign was so short, blink and you'd miss it. But if you really, really want to get to the bottom of the story of Jesus Christ, you need to know about an incident that happened during Herod's son, Archelaus' short reign.

Skip ahead thirty years. Jesus is now a grown man, and a few years before he stepped into the limelight there was a bit of a commotion in Jerusalem. A commotion that was blown out of all proportion at the time, but was later edited out of the scripture. It started as a relatively minor disturbance, but it set in motion a chain of events that would change the world forever.

— Really?

— Absolutely, he said. — You see Herod the Great spent over forty years building a magnificent temple in Jerusalem on the site of Solomon's Temple. And on top of this temple he mounted a golden eagle. I suppose as a mark of respect to the Romans. After all, it was the Romans who appointed Herod as King of Judea, so it was in his interest to keep the Romans sweet. As you can guess, the religious, conservative and militant nationalist Jews weren't happy about this golden eagle at all because it represented the foreign colonial power of Rome. So, shortly before King Herod the Great died and his throne passed to his son Archelaus, a group of idealistic young religious scholars...

Brother Scully was stopped in his tracks, when once again the refectory door crashed open. It was young Brother O'Connell, babbling with excitement. This time he barely stepped over the threshold, he just shouted into the kitchen.

> — She's on now! Dana! She's on now! Come on quick! You'll miss
> it! She's on! Dana! She's on now! Now! Dana! Come on, will ye!

The door swung shut as Brother O'Connell's head darted back into the refectory.

Brother Scully and Sister Claire slowly made their way across the kitchen and, standing in the doorway, their eyes were drawn to the magic of moving colour images. The power of television was undeniable. There in the refectory, men and women who had vowed their lives to God, sat entranced like they were sedated, held spellbound, staring blindly at the garish images beaming out at them from the box in the corner. There was something about viewing the present with such intensity that made Brother Scully wonder if he was in fact staring into the future.

And there she was, centre stage, in life-like colour, Dana. Like a little angel of God, sitting on a high stool, dressed in the purest of Irish white báinín, detailed in dark green knots of Celtic needle-work; ancient knots that had been handed down through the generations from Cú Chulainn himself...

*Snowdrops and daffodils, butterflies and bees.*
*Sailboats and fishermen, things of the sea.*
*Wishing wells, wedding bells, early morning dew...*
*All kinds of everything, remind me of you.*

No wild outburst of euphoric emotion nor rebel yells of nationalism engulfed the refectory as the final note played and her angelic voice faded. It was not the time for such vainglorious triumphalism. Dana had given it her all. There was something in the purity of her voice that touched every living soul who witnessed her performance. Like some Celtic warrior queen of old, she had stepped up to the line, toe to toe against the mightiest nations of the earth, and the destiny of the Republic balanced on the verdict of the jury. Dana stood there commanding the centre stage of Europe, like Mother Ireland, with the green flag wrapped around her, and the heart of a nation pulsating in her outstretched hand. Slowly a thunderous applause infectiously spread throughout the refectory, as one by one they all rose to their feet in dignified respect, all except the Deputy, who was still standing at the back of the room scowling.

    — Who's he, whispered Sister Claire.

    — Deputy Head Brother Lynch, said Brother Scully.

    — And what's his problem?

    — It's a long story...

Brother Scully and Sister Claire withdrew to the kitchen unnoticed, back to the sanctuary of the bubbling Burco, confident that they would not be interrupted until the Eurovision Song Contest was over and all the votes had been cast and counted.

    — So, said Sister Claire. — You were saying?

    — Ah, I think I've said enough, said Brother Scully and he tried to change the subject. — So, what did you think of Dana's performance?

    — Don't mind Dana's performance! What about the golden eagle? You can't just leave it hanging there like that...

    — Ah enough about that, he said. — We were having so much fun earlier, before I got into that heavy stuff about Jesus and Herod and all that...

    — Just finish what you were saying about the golden eagle, and that disturbance that was edited out of the gospels...

    — What disturbance?

    — Y'know! The one in Jerusalem you were talking about before we were interrupted. The Jewish scholars. The golden eagle on Herod's temple. Herod's son Archelaus, and the thing that happened during his short reign that was to change the world forever...

— So, you were listening to me?

— Of course I'm listening to you...

Sister Claire stood there, her eyes sparkling in anticipation, and though Brother Scully was still unsure if he should proceed or not, he took a deep intake of breath and continued with the story, picking it up exactly at the point where he had been interrupted by Brother O'Connell.

— Right, he said. — You see, shortly before King Herod the Great died, this band of young, idealistic religious students went and toppled the golden eagle from the top of Herod's temple. In fact I have the sneaking suspicion that Jesus may have been the mastermind behind the desecration of that golden eagle.

— Jesus involved! No way! I have to stop you there, Brother Scully. You're way off the mark, she protested. — Everyone knows that Jesus was a pacifist. Turn the other cheek was always his way. Now you're trying to say he was some sort of a revolutionary.

— No, I'm not saying he was a revolutionary. What I am saying is that he was a pacifist, but he was also subversive, an extremist, a seditionist...

— How do you mean?

— Pacifism is the most lethal weapon in the arsenal of any subversive, he explained. — Pacifism was the strategy used by Ghandi. Even Terence MacSwiney said it and he dying on hunger strike in Brixton Prison,

*It's not those who can inflict the most pain, but those who can suffer the most who will conquer.*

So no, I'm not saying Jesus was a revolutionary in a militant sense, but he was a militant in a pacifist sense. Jesus was an extreme pacifist, and passive-aggression was his battle plan, *turn the other cheek* was his battle cry.

You see, pacifism as a strategy only works in times of war. There's no point in being a pacifist in peacetime. What's the point in turning the other cheek when there is no aggressor? And that's

why I believe Jesus was one of the backroom boys who instigated the toppling of the golden eagle off Herod's Temple. It was his way of inciting the authorities to react. So that he could put his pacifist strategy of turn-the-other-cheek into action ...
And by Christ, did they react!

Brother Scully explained that Herod's reaction to the toppling of the golden eagle was brutal in the extreme, exactly as the pacifists had planned. The people of Jerusalem were horrified when Herod arrested forty of the young students and two of their teachers and had them publicly burnt alive.

— But here's the thing, continued Brother Scully. — Very soon after this extreme response to what was a fairly trivial matter, Herod the Great died and it was left to his inexperienced son, Herod Archelaus, to deal with the public outrage, an outrage that was being fuelled by the pacifists.

Day after day, crowds gathered at the temple to protest at the brutality of the multiple executions. It was a peaceful protest, well, it was *peaceful* in inverted commas. This non-violent public outcry was organised by the pacifists, the turn-the-other-cheek gang. Do you see where I'm going now, Sister Claire?

— I think so ...

— ... and just as the pacifists anticipated, the protest escalated. It was only a matter of time before violent clashes erupted with Herod's forces of law and order. This was all playing right into the hands of the turn-the-other-cheek gang. The timing couldn't have been better.

Archelaus, the heir in waiting, was under pressure, trying to keep his nose clean until official sanction came from Rome confirming that he would inherit his father's crown, making him the next King of Judea. Meanwhile, reports were filtering back to Rome that the young and inexperienced Archelaus wasn't up to the job. He wasn't even able to control a protest in his own temple, a protest that was gaining momentum and threatening to spill out onto the streets of Jerusalem.

Brother Scully told how, day after day, the peaceful protest continued to escalate, all the while being fuelled by the pacifists, who were calling on the public to join the protest. And with the feast of the Passover coming up, Herod Archelaus feared that the crowds coming into the city for the festival would become a flashpoint for street violence. So he ordered his troops to clear the streets. But Herod Archelaus' determination to clear the streets was only equalled by the pacifists' resolve to resist all aggression and turn the other cheek. The city of Jerusalem swelled with more and more people joining this *peaceful* protest.

> — So you can see where this is all leading, he said. — It wasn't going to have a happy-ever-after ending. All you have to do is look at the student riots across Europe at the moment or, even closer to home, the Civil Rights marches happening up the North, and you'll see what I mean. There's nothing like peaceful protest to stir up civil unrest.

He explained how stone-throwing youths paved the way for an escalation of violence, further frustrating Archelaus' troops, who were beginning to lose control of the streets.

> — Law and order was breaking down and Jerusalem became a powder keg set to explode. And explode it did. It was a blood bath. Fully armed soldiers ran amock in the streets. Over three thousand civilians were massacred. And if that wasn't bad enough, to add insult to injury, fearing an extreme Jewish backlash, and worried that he would not be able to control the crowds coming into the city, Herod Archelaus cancelled the feast of the Passover.
>
> I mean cancelling the Passover for the Jews would be like cancelling Christmas for us Christians ...

Brother Scully outlined how a high-powered delegation of Jewish leaders went to Rome and petitioned Caesar, insisting that young Herod Archelaus was incompetent as a ruler of Judea. And so it came to pass that Caesar Augustus ordered that Herod Archelaus would not inherit his father, Herod The Great's, crown after all.

> — The downfall of Archelaus was short, sharp and sweet. It was a coup brought about by sheer people power. The turn-the-other-

cheek gang had won the day.

It might be near impossible to prove that Jesus was the mastermind behind that whole campaign, but I believe he was. Well at the very least, the downfall of Archelaus that Passover set a precedent for Jesus' own attempt at seizing power. Because believe you me, when Jesus decided to make his stand a few years later, it was no coincidence that he chose the city of Jerusalem during the Passover as his battle ground...

— I've never read any of this in the gospels...

— Ah well, you won't find it in the gospels, as presented to us in the New Testament.

— So you are only making all this stuff up?

— No, you'll find every detail of what I'm saying and more, much more, in the writings of people like Flavius Josephus...

— Who?

— You see if you want to learn about Jesus, the Devil is in the detail. The story of Jesus Christ as presented to us has been so highly polished over the centuries that the defining detail has been wiped clean...

— Are you sure you're not making this up?

— No, honestly, it's all there in black and white. Read Josephus! So Herod Archelaus stepped down, and his brother Herod Antipas is now the main man in the Herod royal family. And guess what Herod Antipas did?

— He went after Jesus, said Sister Claire, stating the obvious.

— Well yes. But no. But yes...

See Herod Antipas did go after Jesus, but he got the wrong man. He arrested Jesus' cousin, John the Baptist, by mistake. Chopped his head off, so he did. You see, Herod Antipas assumed John the Baptist was that illegitimate child who had escaped his father's Slaughter of the Innocents thirty years earlier. He assumed John the Baptist was Jesus, the child born to be king...

— That's a big assumption you're making there, Brother Scully. Are you sure you're not just joining the dots? Like putting two and two together and getting twenty-two?

— Not at all, he said. — It was an easy mistake for Herod Antipas to confuse John the Baptist for Jesus.

Think about it, John and Jesus were both conceived around the same time in mysterious circumstances, and, by my reckoning, they were both sired by Herod Antipas' father, Herod the Great. They were both cousins, born within months of each other. Their mothers lived under the same roof during their pregnancies. Not to mention the fact that John the Baptist had been roaming around the countryside for years, telling anyone who'd listen that there was going to be a new Kingdom and a new King of Judea ...

And here's a little known fact,

Brother Scully hesitated for a moment making sure he had Sister Claire's full attention.

— Remember the Slaughter of the Innocents?
— 'Course I do?
— Well, here's an interesting detail. Of all those murdered during the Slaughter of the Innocents, the name of only one of the victims is actually on record. Just imagine, thousands of children slaughtered by Herod's men, and in all the holy texts and historical documents the name of only one of the victims is recorded. And you'll never guess who that named victim was?
— I haven't a clue?
— The only victim of the Slaughter of the Innocents whose name is actually on record is John the Baptist's father, High Priest Zachariah. The husband of Mary's cousin, Elizabeth.
— But I thought it was only children were killed ...
— Well that was the plan, but when Herod's men came for the infant, John the Baptist, they murdered old Zachariah because he wouldn't hand over the child. That might explain why John spent his whole life hiding out in the wilderness and cursing Herod ...

So think about it? It would have been a very obvious mistake for Herod Antipas to think John the Baptist was the child that his father had tried to kill.

I mean, thirty years had passed, Herod the Great was dead, and so he wasn't around to identify the child or the mother. It was a time before photographs. It would have been a very simple and obvious mistake for Herod Antipas to confuse John the Baptist for his cousin Jesus. And you can be damned sure that John the Baptist was in no doubt that Herod Antipas' father had butchered old Zachariah at the time of the Slaughter of the Innocents...

So if you follow my theory, that both Mary and Elizabeth became pregnant by Herod the Great, well, that would make Jesus, John the Baptist, Herod Archelaus and Herod Antipas half-brothers, and all four of them had a valid claim to the throne.

When Herod Antipas arrested John the Baptist, he was convinced he had the right man. And you can dress it up anyway you want, blame it on the temptress with tales of dancing Salome, but make no mistake about it, Herod Antipas wanted John the Baptist dead.

— I can see where you're coming from, she agreed. — But it's all too much to take in. It all seems so far-fetched.

— Far-fetched! Far-fetched? Everything about Christianity is far-fetched. Walking on water, rising from the dead, Immaculate Conception? Don't talk to me about far-fetched, said Brother Scully. — But there's nothing far-fetched about brothers and half-brothers fighting over their inheritance.

Read the gospels again, and ask yourself what the parable of the Prodigal Son was all about, or the story of the shepherd who had lost his sheep? It's as plain as the nose on your face that Jesus spent his life crying out for his Father's acceptance. He spent his life telling anyone who'd listen that his father was the king. The king who could forgive all, and there was only one man back then who could forgive all, and that was Herod the Great, King of Judea.

Even in his dying moments, persecuted, blood-drenched, gasping for breath, crucified on the cross, what does Jesus do? He looks down to his mother, Mary, and cries out for his father. Can you imagine how Mary felt? She had given up her life for

Jesus, and in his dying breath on the cross, there he was calling out for his father.

There's no mystery in the story of Christ, it's all about paternity, inheritance and family. It's all about a father who had rejected his son at birth, and a son's lifelong struggle for his father's acceptance. It's all about an illegitimate boy's struggle to regain his birthright.

A change came over Sister Claire, as if the pieces of the jigsaw had fallen into place and the greater picture began to emerge.

— Just hear me out, said Brother Scully. — Between the jigs and the reels, Herod Antipas cuts John the Baptist's head off, and as far as he was concerned that was the end of the story. But no sooner had John the Baptist been executed, who steps out of the shadows up in Galilee only Jesus, John the Baptist's cousin or half-brother depending on which way you look at it, and he's proclaiming to the world,

— *I'm the son of the father! My father is the king who is in heaven...*

Can you imagine what went through the mind of Herod Antipas when he realised that the man he had killed was actually the mad cousin of the man he intended to kill?

— You're saying that when Herod killed John the Baptist he thought he was after killing Jesus?

— It's all in the scripture. Read the gospel of Matthew 14:2 or Mark 6:14. It's all there, when John the Baptist was executed and Jesus stepped out of the shadows and made his mission public, Herod Antipas was shocked, he couldn't believe he had killed the wrong man. In fact, when he was told about this man called Jesus who was claiming to be the son of the king in heaven, the first thing Herod Antipas said was,

— *It's John the Baptist, back from the dead!*

And to make matters worse, the people were openly rallying behind Jesus, and publicly proclaiming him to be the new King of the Jews. Chanting everywhere he went,

— *Hail, Jesus! King of the Jews!*

And the game was on, Jesus had thrown down the gauntlet and

stepped forward to publicly challenge his half brother, Antipas.

— I've read the bible from cover to cover, and this is all news to me, she said.

— Well maybe you need to read the bible again, but this time with your eyes open, rather than with your mind shut.

— How dare you, she said indignantly. — My mind and eyes are fully open!

— Think about it, it's as plain as day! It took three years. Three full years before Jesus built up enough support to go to Jerusalem to face his half-brother Antipas down.

When Jesus came to Jerusalem that Passover, he was coming with intent. He was coming to settle a lot of old scores, and Antipas knew he was gunning for him. The Herod family had chased the Holy Family up and down the Holy Land since his birth. They had chopped the head off his half-brother, John the Baptist. They had butchered old Zachariah. The scene was set for a confrontation of biblical proportions between Jesus Christ and his half-brother, Herod Antipas.

Young Brother Scully conjured up an image of the bustling streets of Jerusalem buzzing with the news that Jesus Christ was the boy-child they could not kill. The King of the Jews had returned a grown man and set up camp in the town of Bethany just a few miles outside town. The people flocked out of the city in their thousands to hear what he had to say, and he wasn't holding back. He was shouting from the hilltops and his message was clear: tear down the old, bring in the new. Like every revolutionary, before or since, he promised a new regime built on social justice, where the weak, the meek, the poor and the sick would be looked after. He promised to take from the rich and give to the poor. He pledged a workers' revolution that would redistribute wealth and dismantle the corruption of power.

Then, at nighttime around the campfire, he entertained his followers with stories of life in this new kingdom after the regime change. This new kingdom would be a place where the rich man always got his comeuppance, and the poor always had the last laugh. Like every military leader on the eve of battle, Jesus swore that he had God on his side. The poor and disenfranchised lapped it up.

— I think you're just lining up the facts to support your theory that Jesus was a revolutionary.

— I have no desire to change or challenge your beliefs, Sister Claire. I'm only telling you what I believe. I have never shared my findings with another living soul. Maybe I shouldn't have burdened you with all this.

But make no mistake about it, Jesus might have had heavenly notions, but he had earthly ambitions.

— Earthly ambitions?

— Jesus revealed his earthly ambitions when he guaranteed the loyalty of his captains by promising them a share in the spoils of war after the revolution.

— I think this has all gone a bit too far, she said.

— Read Matthew. Just read Matthew. On the eve of Jesus' triumphant march into Jerusalem, he gathered his twelve top men around him and this is the exact promise he made to them.

— *At the renewal of all things, when the Son of Man sits on his glorious throne, you who have followed me will also sit on twelve thrones, judging the twelve tribes of Israel.*

If that's not a promise of a share in the spoils of war, what is? He was promising royal power and favour to his twelve most loyal, trusted and true, once he got his throne back.

And Jesus was no fool, he was careful not to upset the Romans. He was not calling for a new world order. No, he stated very publicly and put it on the record that he would give to Caesar what was due to Caesar. He made it clear that Rome was not the enemy. This was not an attack on law and order. He was calling for a renewal, a regime change, not a revolution. It was to be a bloodless coup that would topple his half-brother, Herod Antipas, just as Herod Archelaus had been overthrown before him ...

But Sister Claire was still not convinced.

— Look, she said. — I know what you are saying seems to make

some sort of sense. But it's just too much for me. I really can't
take all of this in. I think I've heard enough ...

— Please, please, just close your eyes for a moment. Just close your
  eyes, and put yourself in Jerusalem. Just imagine ...

And though Sister Claire had never contemplated such wild and challenging ideas, her imagination was both ripe and fertile. Every word
spoken by Brother Scully created living colour images in her mind. She
could sense the excitement in Jerusalem as the rumour spread like a
virus, from street corner to street corner and right into the heart of
Herod's court, that in the town of Bethany, just a few miles from
Jerusalem, Jesus had raised Lazarus from the dead. The whole city was
alive with the news. Over in the Roman palace, Pontius Pilate's wife
and the ladies of Rome spoke of nothing but this new King of the Jews
with his special powers.

— Special powers, said Pilate's wife. — Really? Tell me more ...

She raised her eyebrows seductively, stirring up a chorus of anything
but ladylike cackling from her ladies-in-waiting. One said she had
heard tell of his attractive looks, another said that women and men
alike fell under the spell of the irresistible and mystical aura emanating
from his penetrating eyes.

— Penetrating eyes, said Pilate's wife, then swayed her hips pro-
  vocatively and laughed.

Meanwhile on the far side of Jerusalem, Caiaphas, the High Priest was
preparing to address the Sanhedrin. He had spent days in the library
feverishly scouring ancient texts, preparing for all eventualities in the
aftermath of the impending showdown between the two half-brothers.
He searched for context and precedence, and was secretly preparing
the case that Herod's bloodline confirmed him an Edomite from the
House of Esau, and even though Rome had sanctioned Herod and his
successors to be rulers of Judea, the fact remained that observant Jews
could never accept an Edomite as a legitimate King of the Jews.
Whereas this new man, this Jesus of Nazareth, with a little adjustment
of his lineage, the case could be made that he was connected to the
House of David on his maternal line. A little bending of the facts and
he could be made to fulfil what had been written in the sacred scrip-

tures, giving him some loose legitimacy as King of the Jews.

And when it came to convincing the Romans that Jesus was a legitimate King of Judea, well, even the dogs in the street were in no doubt that this man, Jesus, also known as the Christ, was fruit of the loins of the Great King Herod himself.

But like all power brokers in times of revolution, the Roman authorities and the Jewish leaders were not for putting their own heads on the block by prematurely placing a crown on the head of either Jesus or Antipas. Instead they chose to bide their time and stand back. They would wait to see how the events played out before showing their hand and swearing allegiance to the victor.

— Can you imagine what was going through Jesus' head in the days before his triumphant march into Jerusalem? Crowds pouring out of Jerusalem and cramming into the little town of Bethany. I mean, the place was so packed they even had to lower a cripple in from a roof on his stretcher, and all the time the sound of the crowds chanting,

— *Hail Jesus, King of the Jews!*

And he was. He was a king in everything but a crown. And it suited Jesus to be slumming it, rubbing shoulders with the poor and the sick. He was a working-class hero, and they were his people. There he was, staying in the house of Simon the Leper, feasting and drinking, surrounded by sinners. And the whole town chanting,

— *Hail Jesus, King of the Jews!*

He must have felt totally invincible ...

But see, that's where I think the whole thing began to unravel for him. That's when he started to make mistakes. Maybe it was pride, maybe it was vanity, or maybe it was because the prize was finally within his grasp. Whatever the reason, that's when Jesus made some bad judgement calls.

His first mistake was that night in Simon the Leper's house, when Mary Magdalene anointed him with a full bottle of scented oil worth three hundred denarii. Three hundred denarii? I mean that was like blowing a full year's wages on a bottle of aftershave.

You'll hear a lot of bad things about Judas Iscariot, but it was Judas who challenged Jesus about his excessive and extravagant behaviour. In fairness, Judas was the only one to stand up and speak out about the hypocrisy of wasting the expensive oil ...

— Really?

— Yes really! Judas was furious. He criticised Jesus at the dinner table in front of everyone. He basically called him a hypocrite saying he was way out of order, and that the oil should have been sold and the money used to help the poor.

— And what did Jesus do?

— I'll tell you what he did. Jesus put Judas in his place, that's what he did. He humiliated Judas and dismissed the whole thing by saying,

   — *The poor will always be with us!*

The poor will always be with us? That was some cop out! If you ask me, that was the start of the rot! There was Jesus preaching that they should abandon all material goods and give to the poor, but he didn't practise what he preached.

Look at it from Judas' point of view? Judas Iscariot had given up everything to follow Jesus, and that night in the town of Bethany with victory in sight, everything changed. Just like Orwell's *Animal Farm*, there was a slight bending of the rules here and there, a minor re-interpretation of the core values, a readjustment of principles, and everything changed. That was the moment Judas saw the hypocrisy in action, and for the first time he caught a glimpse of what life might be like if Jesus came to power.

If you ask me, that was the moment Judas realised that, just like any other power-hungry man, Jesus would promise the sun, the moon and the stars just to get on the throne.

I mean, you must remember, on Jesus' previous visit to that same town, a woman rubbed perfume into and kissed Jesus' feet, then dried them with her hair. That was shocking enough, and was still fresh in Judas Iscariot's mind.

But that night when Jesus uttered those immortal words, — *The poor will always be with us,* and he sitting there surrounded by his hard men, feasting and drinking and they all nodding their heads in smug agreement, and this woman massaging his head with expensive oil, I mean, come on like ...

That was the last straw. That was the moment that God became man. That was the very moment Judas got the measure of Jesus. It all fell into place. For the first time Judas truly understood what Jesus meant when he spoke of, − *my father the King in heaven.* There was no ambiguity in the message anymore. Jesus' father was King Herod the Great, dead and gone to heaven. And all the stories of prodigal sons and shepherds who had lost their sheep were no more than metaphors for this illegitimate boy's struggle to regain his birthright, his lifelong dream to be welcomed back into the family fold and to take his rightful place at his father's side.

That was when Judas Iscariot realised that Jesus Christ was exactly what he had always claimed to be, he was the son of man, and that man was King Herod the Great. And like every Herod before him, he had the same lust for power in his genes. He was a man who would be seduced by excess, a man who would become drunk on power, a man who would fall to flattery.

− Are you saying that's why Judas betrayed Jesus?

− The question I will ask you, Sister Claire ...

Did Judas Iscariot betray Jesus, or was it the other way around? Did Jesus betray Judas? That is the question.

Brother Scully's relentless reinterpretation of the New Testament rendered Sister Claire incapable of presenting a coherent answer. All she managed to say was,

− I think you've said enough, Brother Scully.

She stood there, her mind swamped by sacrilegious images and thoughts, but yet, for the first time in her life, it was as if she could see a glimmer of light shining bright. It did not hurt her eyes. And maybe Brother Scully had been reticent to share his theory to begin with, but now he was in full flow and there was no holding back.

— ...because believe you me, he continued. — There was nothing passive about that Passover. When Jesus stood there on the outskirts of Jerusalem that morning, looking in on the magnificent temple that had been built by his father who had rejected him from birth, he knew the day of reckoning had come.
There was no ambiguity in the mind of the chanting masses,
— *Hail Jesus! King of the Jews!*
For the first time in his life Jesus Herod the Christ was going to stand his ground and face his half-brother, Herod Antipas down.
— Jesus H. Christ, she whispered.
— Bingo! You hit the nail on the head! And if some archaeologist ever dug up the original census form that was signed by Joseph in Bethlehem on that first Christmas, I guarantee you, there in black and white you'd find the name Jesus H!
The H of Herod, and that H was the root of all his trouble. It was do or die time. Put up or shut up. And Jesus was back in town to reclaim the H of his birth.
Just imagine what was going through Herod Antipas' head, and he looking out from his stronghold on the Temple Mount, and he sees his half-brother, Jesus, with the crowds calling out his name. Just as the Three Wise Men had foreseen over thirty years earlier, there he was at the gates of Jerusalem calling out for what was rightfully his.
And when Jesus vowed that he would personally demolish the temple that had taken his father forty years to build, he knew exactly what he was saying. He was playing to the crowd, stirring up the still raw and painful memory of those forty young students who had been burnt to death a few years earlier for tearing the golden eagle off the parapet. He was speaking directly to the families of the three thousand citizens murdered by Herod's forces of law and order during the ensuing peaceful protest. Make no mistake about it, Jesus was calling out to the militant hardliners.
Standing at the gates of Jerusalem, he was speaking directly to

the families, the friends and the neighbours of all those who had died and suffered under the Herod regime. He was promising a new kingdom. And that day when he declared that he would level the temple to the ground, the message went out loud and clear that he would root out the rot, the time for turning the other cheek was long gone.

There was no mystery, no burning bushes, no angels popping up with some coded message from God. This was the real deal. It was high noon in Jerusalem, and Jesus was coming to town. And you know what happened next? Don't you?

Before Sister Claire could reply, Brother Scully answered his own question.

— Palm Sunday, he said. — That's what happened next. Jesus marched into Jerusalem like a victorious king. Thousands of people following him and lining the route cheering and chanting, — *Hail Jesus! King of the Jews!*

He marched right into Jerusalem he did, right into the lion's den, his whole life flashing before his eyes, and he was angry. You better believe he was angry. He was furious! A lifetime of pain coiled around in his brain like a fuse primed, set and ready to explode in a blind rage of fury. And what did he do?

— What did he do, she echoed.

— He exploded! That's what he did, said Brother Scully. — He marched straight up to the temple, the temple built by his father, King Herod the Great, and exploded!

Whipped the traders and moneychangers out of the place, roaring at them to get out of his father's house. That's exactly what he called Herod the Great's Temple, — *My father's house!*

I mean, Herod's temple was a royal fortress, the most impressive building in the known world. Forty years in construction? It would put the pyramids in the shade. Built on the site of Solomon's Temple. And there was Jesus, the illegitimate son of Herod the Great, stomping around the place in full view, staking his claim, whipping people and roaring, — *Get out of my father's house! And get out, now!*

I mean, God Almighty! You couldn't make this stuff up! And you
sure as hell don't need miracles to spice it up!

Sister Claire's lips trembled as if she had something to say, but still no
words came.

— But you know, he said. — If you ask me, that was Jesus' second
mistake. He lost control. I'm in no doubt that if he had kept his
cool, he could have toppled his half-brother, Herod Antipas,
just by the sheer strength of people power. He had the moral
high ground. He had the people eating out of his hand. He had
his half-brother, Herod Antipas on the back foot. He had it in
his grasp. But when he overturned the moneychangers' tables?
That was a big mistake.

You see power is all about money. Is now, was then and ever
shall be all about money. And in that one miscalculated act of
blind rage, not only did Jesus challenge Herod Antipas, but he
also took on the Romans who were the tax collectors, and the
Jewish High Priests who were guardians of the temple and were
taking a handy percentage off the top. Basically he bit off more
than he could chew.

Yep, he bit off more than he could possibly chew, and I think it
was too late when he realised it.

Sister Claire stood there in stunned silence as her whole belief system
was turned on its head, her blind faith rendered valueless. Brother
Scully had presented her with a credible creed based on logic, a creed
that required neither faith nor interpretation, and there was something liberating but terrifying in that.

— I've often wondered, he said, — what went through Jesus' mind
when he was arrested and brought before his half-brother,
Herod Antipas?

Can you imagine? It was the first time he had actually set foot
inside the walls of his father's house. Imagine how that felt.
There he was, stripped to the waist, naked to the navel, blood-
drenched, whipped and scourged, and all around him the royal
splendour and grandeur of his birthright.

Just close your eyes for a moment, Sister Claire. Just close your
eyes and imagine the atmosphere in Herod's palace that day?

Sister Claire closed her eyes. Brother Scully's words filled her mind with images. Images of lords and ladies, jostling to catch a glimpse of this man of mystical powers; this man who had walked on water, cured the lepers, given sight to the blind; this man who only a few days earlier had breathed life into a dead man.

Some of the older ones exchanged knowing glances when they remembered Jesus' mother, Mary, as a young serving girl in the court over thirty years earlier, others whispered of the scandal surrounding her cousin, Elizabeth, the adulterous wife of the old High Priest Zachariah, and how she had disgraced herself and humiliated her husband around the court. Some recalled the prophecy of the three kings from the east, when they foretold that this illegitimate child would grow up to be King of the Jews and would come back to claim what was rightfully his. More just shook their heads in disgust when they remembered the needless Slaughter of the Innocents.

Of course they all remembered old Zachariah, a God-fearing holy man who held his tongue, yet died at the hands of Herod the Great's thugs. And a knowing smile came to their faces when they thought of Jesus' cousin, the wild-man, John the Baptist, who only three years earlier had entertained them around the court with his mad antics until Herod grew tired of his jesting, and ordered John's head to be severed from his body and served up on a plate.

The unspoken question on everybody's lips right across Jerusalem had to be,

- *Is this man, Jesus, the one they call the Christ, truly King of the Jews?*

But that day when he was dragged unceremoniously before them in chains, the lords and ladies of the royal court of Herod Antipas were in no doubt but that he was neither king nor god, he was just another illegitimate son of Herod the Great.

- One thing's for sure, whispered Brother Scully. — They gathered that day to be entertained, and they were not disappointed. There they were, in all their finery and gowns of exotic fabric, wondering what would happen next, wondering if their Lord Antipas would reach out the hand of welcome to his half-brother, Jesus.

Just imagine the chatter around the royal court subsiding to a barely audible murmur and then a sweeping hush as he was led into the court. Then silence.

After thirty years of cat and mouse, finally the two half-brothers stood face-to-face, eyeball-to-eyeball, studying every blemish and birthmark, searching for some shared, inherited feature. The resemblance between the two was undeniable. Maybe it was the shape of the forehead, or the hook of the nose, or the dimple on the chin, or the high cheekbones, or something about the eyes.

Brother Scully paused, allowing just enough time for Sister Claire to grasp the gritty reality of such a monumental moment in history.

— Herod Antipas must have known that Jesus was no longer a threat to him or his throne, explained Brother Scully. — What threat could this physically and emotionally broken man, with a one-way ticket to his own execution be? So what did Antipas do? Well, just as he had previously entertained the court by serving John the Baptist's head on a platter, once again he rose to the occasion and subjected his half-brother to one final act of humiliation. He mockingly gave Jesus the respect he had always craved.

He dressed Jesus in a royal purple robe, and put a crown of thorns on his head, then placed a reed in his hand like a royal sceptre, and said,

— *I bow down before you, King of the Jews!*

Then he spat into his face, and paraded him through the streets of Jerusalem to be crucified. And in one final insult, a sign was nailed on the cross above his head in big bold capitals:

INRI, *Iesus Nazarenus Rex Iudaeorum.*

Jesus of Nazareth. King of the Jews.

Make no mistake about it, but that day Herod Antipas sent a message loud and clear to any other of his father's loose ends and indiscretions that might be out there, not to go getting notions above their station. There would be no welcome for them at the Herod family fireside.

— Holy Mary mother of God, whispered Sister Claire.

— But here's the thing. Jesus always said his kingdom would live on forever, and maybe he never made it as King of the Jews. But you know what, said Brother Scully. — As you already pointed out, Sister Claire, there's something I never really considered in all my research ...

The two of us, you and me, as members of the Christian clergy, are living proof that he was King of the Christians, and his kingdom still lives on, and thrives to this very day. Funny when you think about it, but the Kingdom of Christianity must be the only royal dynasty where inheritance is not dictated by bloodline.

Then again, I suppose it makes sense that bloodlines should not take precedence in the Kingdom of Christianity, especially when you consider that each new pope to sit on the throne since Peter, is a direct successor to that illegitimate son of Herod the Great. And maybe it explains why we clerics vow to remain celibate? The Church is only too aware of the trouble caused by children fighting for their inheritance rights.

But here's the irony of the whole thing. When we think of the most powerful men in Jesus' time, men like the Great King Herod, or Pontius Pilate, or Caiaphas, the Jewish High Priest, all those powermongers who contrived to put Jesus to death, well they would all be lost and forgotten to the pages of history, except for the fact that they live on only as footnotes in the life of that illegitimate boy, born in a stable and raised by a carpenter.

And that, Sister Claire, that is the true power of Jesus Christ. And you don't need walking on water, resurrections, immaculate conceptions or any of that sort of voodoo ...

As I see it, the gospel tells the true story of a dysfunctional family, no more, no less. But you can't deny it's the greatest story ever told.

She stood there, mouth open yet speechless, like she was battling some challenging internal conflict.

The sound of cheering from the refectory signalled that the Eurovision Song Contest would soon be over. The enthusiasm in Brother Scully's voice faded when he realised his time with Sister Claire was almost at an end.

— Maybe I've said too much, he said. — Maybe I should have kept my big mouth shut. I just got a bit carried away, that's all. Maybe Brother Ambrose was right. Some thoughts are best kept inside the head. I mean, Jesus, he warned me to say nothing, I should have listened to him.

Brother Scully attempted to change the subject and salvage what remained of their precious time together.

— It's only a theory, he said. — If word of my mad theory ever got out, the world as we know it would never be the same again. Like, what would Bossman Begley say? Or worse, imagine what the Pope would say? I can see it now, a banner headline across the Times,

*Breaking News*
*Jesus Proclaimed The Illegitimate Son Of King Herod The Great.*
*Vatican closes up shop.*
*Pope Resigns From Vatican And Gets Job As Taxi Driver.*

Brother Scully's laugh was hollow, it did not bring the anticipated smile to Sister Claire's face. She just stood there looking painfully confused.

— I hope I haven't upset you, he said. — I have! Have I? I hope I haven't, have I? Have I? Have I?
I have ...

Sister Claire placed her finger to her lips and whispered,

— Shhh! Just shhhh ...
— Honestly, it's only a theory, he pleaded. — A stupid theory, that's all.
— Shhh!

— I should have kept my big mouth shut...

She then placed her finger to his lips. The intimacy of her touch stopped Brother Scully mid-sentence. Sister Claire closed her eyes, and having gathered her thoughts she said,

> — I have always lived my life under a question mark, always had one big shadow of doubt hanging over the whole thing. But like the good Christian that I am, I always chose to ignore my doubts. Always placed my trust in faith...

She paused for a moment, as if delving into deep thought, then she continued,

> — But now...
>
> Now for the first time in my life, I suddenly realise that faith is just one big mind control game imposed on humans by men. Faith is the obstacle that stands between us and the magical power of nature's creation...
>
> — Well that wasn't exactly what I was saying, said Brother Scully.
> — See what I was saying is that if you look at the gospel in a certain way...

But Brother Scully's attempt to clarify his position was cut short by Sister Claire.

> — Shhh!

Then raising her voice she said,

> — Two thousand years of theological debate, inquisition, martyrdom, persecution, sectarian strife and war, and for what? For what!

Realising he had unlocked some dark, cavernous place in her mind, Brother Scully tried to diffuse the situation.

> — Ah, well sometimes the most difficult questions have the simplest answers...

But the change that had come over Sister Claire set her mind racing down a path of no return.

> — I'll tell you for what, she snapped, her voice sharpened by a frustrated anger. — For the priests and bishops and cardinals and popes! That's for what! It's an old boys' club, a hierarchy of men, with their funny hats, fancy dress, keeping women in their place.

A divine empire built on misogyny. Jesus, even in the eyes of God women are no more than a subspecies. For what? For what!

These are the very same men who would be the first in the queue to crucify the Christ if he were to turn up in the world today...

— Ah, well, maybe you're being a bit harsh there, Sister Claire...

Brother Scully hadn't anticipated Sister Claire's anger. Again he tried to calm her, but her fury seemed to escalate with every word that passed her lips.

— I'll tell you for what, she said. — For them to live in their ivory towers and palaces, drinking fine wines from diamond-encrusted, golden goblets and eating food served on the finest silverware, indulging in a life of pomp and ceremony, with their ermine-trimmed robes...

And, and, and their housekeepers! Housekeepers! For Christ's sake! Making their beds, washing their clothes, ironing their shirts, pairing their socks! Housekeepers! Christ's sake! 'Tis far from housekeepers they were reared! When have you ever heard of a nun with a houseboy or a butler? I'll tell you when. Never! Next they'll be having their feet washed with perfume and some young one drying them with her hair! Judas Iscariot was right! It's all a shameless hypocrisy! And vow of poverty! Don't make me laugh!

Shame on the lot of them and they claiming to have a direct line to the all-powerful God and creator. It's all a bloody circus. A circus of conspiracy contrived to deceive the people, deceive the honest-to-God, hard-working decent people who wait on them hand and foot, on bended knee, kissing their ring and keeping them in a lifestyle and comfort they've grown accustomed to!

As Sister Claire spewed out fury against the blind faith that had been instilled in her since birth, young Brother Scully realised he had unleashed a demon that had been buried deep inside her. It frightened him. What if she reneged on her vocation and decided to walk away from convent life? Could he shoulder the burden of that responsibility?

Then, as if in a flash of light, he experienced a moment of startling

clarity. It occurred to him that Sister Claire's outrage was the only logical conclusion to his theory on the true paternity of Jesus. If Jesus
Christ was the progeny of Herod the Great and a young serving girl,
well that would be the end of Christianity. And standing there in the
kitchen that night, Brother Scully realised how ludicrous it was that
two young people, a boy and a girl, fit and in their prime would vow to
live lives of celibacy, in honour of a God of creation. A God of procrea-
tion. A God who had sent his only Son down to earth to be humiliated
and tortured and crucified on a cross by mere mortals? A God who had
committed his only Son to death so that humans could live eternally. A
God of contradiction.

— It's all a farce, he whispered.
And it crossed his mind that he and Sister Claire should run away
together. What if they ran away that very night? That's when his well-
tuned, guilt-laden conscience demanded an answer to the direct question: Was this the voice of Satan taunting, seducing? Could it be that
Sister Claire was a temptress, was she Satan in one of his many cunning guises?

Only a short time earlier he had been making tea for the community
and all was well in his world. But then, as if by a flip of a coin, he found
himself contemplating the unthinkable, his mind flooding with
thoughts of abandoning religious life and taking this young nun with
him. Attempting to rationalise the irrational, he somehow came to the
conclusion that with Sister Claire by his side he had some hope in the
big, bad world, some hope that as two they might survive. But he was
crippled by fear of what lay in wait for them beyond the monastery
walls. What future could a defrocked brother and a runaway nun ever
expect? Cast out by their own. And what about the shame and the damnation it would bring down on their families. What future?

Up to that point, Brother Scully's homespun theory on the paternity of Jesus Christ had been a one-way theological debate conducted
within the confines of his own mind. It had been an intellectual stream
of consciousness, a clever new take on the traditional understanding
of the gospel, a rhetorical exercise, a hypothesis explored. But never
once during his two long years of research had he viewed his

controversial theory as a threat to his own vocation. He had not contemplated the full implications of his theory once released to the greater world. Brother Scully realised that thoughts and ideas are all fine, but once exposed to the world they can become a dangerous, seditious force, and maybe this was one such idea he should have kept firmly under lock and key.

Everything had changed. As Brother Scully stood there listening to the young Sister Claire in full flight, he battled against an overpowering desire to reach out and hold her in his arms.

— ...and as for celibacy! I could tell you a thing or two about priestly celibacy!

Jesus, it's like the Wizard of Oz, and we're the Munchkins, and bigger fools to let them get away with it!

A deafening roar of victory from the refectory distracted Sister Claire, and again Brother O'Connell burst through the swing doors babbling nonsense.

— Nine votes! Nine votes! Nine votes! Belgium has just given us nine votes! The Brits haven't a hope! Nine votes! Only five more juries to go! Unstoppable! 20 − 11, the Brits can't catch us now...

And though Brother Scully and Sister Claire were preoccupied with a conflict far more critical than the results of a song contest in far away Amsterdam, they managed to feign interest with a half-hearted cheer of, — *Hurray!*

Young Brother O'Connell was too excited to notice their cold indifference as he disappeared back into the refectory shouting,

— Nine votes! Nine votes! Nine votes!

Sister Claire followed Brother Scully towards the refectory door. Maybe they hoped the interruption would somehow rewind the clock, back to a time earlier that evening when all was fun and light. But the past was another place, and the clock was not for turning. They had witnessed a dark and painful truth, a truth that could not be denied.

The hysteria in the refectory was like one of the nine circles of Hell in Dante's Inferno, like Satan had the heart and soul of the monastery clutched in the grip of demonic ecstasy and was squeezing the blood out of the living Christ, drop by sacred drop. Sisters and brothers hugging each other, young and old alike leaping up and down with arms held high above their heads. They were howling and bellowing and baying like wild animals. Father Kelly had climbed onto the chair, his tightly clenched fists punching the air, shouting,

   — I-ur-land! I-ur-land! I-ur-land!

Reverend Mother and Sister Michael had their robes hitched above their ankles and were dancing a type of free-style jig, and old Brother O'Hegarty was on his feet and shaking his walking stick at the television, roaring at the top of his lungs,

   — Come out now! Ye Black and Tan bastards!

And there was the Deputy, standing stone-like at the back of the room, unmoved, leering judgmentally, casting a glance of contempt towards Bossman Begley, who was calling for order, with his hands outstretched like Christ calming the waters of Galilee.

   — Order! Order! Order! Order!

     For Christ's sake! Order, will ye!


The sensation of Sister Claire's moist breath on the back of Brother Scully's neck sent a tingling ripple across his shoulder blades. He turned to find her standing closer to him than she should have been, and yet he wished she was standing even closer. He noticed the gentle tapping of her fingertips on his forearm, then with a flash of her eyes, Sister Claire gestured that they should return to the sanctuary of the kitchen. The swish of the swing doors closing behind them dampened the sound of the uproar in the refectory, muffling Bossman Begley's shouting, — Order! Order! Order!

   She stood there, her gaze fixed like she was looking directly into Brother Scully's soul.

   — Look, he said. — The Eurovision is nearly over, and that will be the end of our time together. So can we just get back to where we were earlier this evening. Back to when it was all a bit lighthearted. Back to when we were having a bit of a laugh and enjoying each other's company. Can we just move on and forget all my aul' theology guff about Jesus being the son of King Herod.

Please! Can we just get back to the way things were, before I put the kibosh on the whole evening with my big mouth and heavy notions. Heavy notions that's all it was, heavy notions. I should have kept my mouth shut! The last thing you needed to hear was my half-baked theory on Jesus being the son of Herod.

It was just an academic thesis. A hypothesis. Really. I was just teasing out the question, *what if?* No more. No less. I should have kept my big mouth shut!

So, go on, please Sister Claire, tell me something funny. Tell me about the pigeon. Tell me a story about Sister Francesca Of The Birds. Tell me about Mossie The Gardener...

But Sister Claire's reply was slow and calculated.

— There was nothing funny about Sister Francesca Of The Birds or Mossie The Gardener, she whispered. — That was a tragedy of two lives lost to love.

— Well it seemed funny when you told it earlier.

— A lot of things seemed funny earlier.

— Please, he begged. — Go on, tell me some mad story about Dowcha-boy, the pigeon. Tell me something, please, anything...

Brother Scully attempted to reclaim the evening, but Sister Claire's eyes had been opened. She had seen the light. It was the light of truth, and she wanted more. She had been given a glimpse of another world and had no intention of returning to a life of teacups and biscuit counting. She stood there face-to-face with Brother Scully, craving the intensity of intimacy. Again Brother Scully attempted to divert his over-powering feelings of attraction.

— There was a lot more poverty in my life before I took my vow of poverty, he said and smiled.

Sister Claire laughed but it was a knowing laugh, a laugh tinged with cynicism, a laugh devoid of all traces of girlish innocence. Gradually Brother Scully had to concede that, not only had a change come over Sister Claire, but something had also changed in him. He found himself standing ever closer to the young novice, looking deeply into her eyes, and for the first time, as if stripped of all denial, he realised he was in the presence of a real-life, flesh and blood woman, a young woman, a terrifyingly attractive young woman. He battled with all his might to resist his overwhelming desire to reach out and hold her. She stood there like some vestal virgin, concealed from head to foot behind the coarse weave of her robe, yet all her lust for life, her human frailties and passions were exposed in the sparkling of her eyes. Her breathing was deep and rhythmical. Her every gesture was seductive. And again Brother Scully resisted his all-consuming thoughts.

  — No honestly, 'tis true. These days I even have a room of my own, that's something I never had before I became a brother, he blurted out.

  — So do I, she said calmly, and moving towards the window she pointed in the direction of St Joseph's Convent. — You can see my room from here.

Brother Scully leaned closer to the window.

  — Which one is it, he asked.

  — There, she said.

  — Which one?

Sister Claire gently took Brother Scully by the hand and cradling his outstretched finger she pointed into the darkness across the valley in the direction of St Joseph's Convent.

  — That window there, she said. — When I get back to the convent tonight, I'll flicker the light in my room so that you'll see it.

Her hand on his, flesh on flesh, created a bridge for their emotions to flow one to the other. His warm and comforting fingers entwined with hers, generating wave after wave of passion from fingertip to fingertip like fire to the soul. Without a word passing between them, they stood there lost in each other's eyes. It was as if some invisible and invincible force drew them together. Brother Scully wrapped his arms around her. He held her so close their bodies became one.

  — Sister Claire, he whispered her name.

  — Bernadette, she corrected him, then rising to her tippy-toes she closed her eyes.

And there in the monastery kitchen on the night of Dana's historic victory, Brother Scully and Sister Claire embraced. Their lips touched and for that eternal moment, like Adam and Eve in the Garden of Eden, their true emotions were stripped bare in the eyes of God.

When the tea and biscuits had been served, and all the excitement in the refectory had died down, the colour television was unplugged, the chairs and tables were stacked and put away and calm was restored to the monastery. Reverend Mother and the visiting sisters joined Bossman Begley in the library for a nightcap and a final analysis of Ireland's great triumph over Europe.

Brother Scully and Sister Claire stepped discreetly through the French doors out to the library garden. An inner warmth protected them from the biting east wind. They sat in silence on a bench beneath a budding cherry blossom tree, overcome by a most painful feeling of happiness. It was the pain of love, a love more intense than their love for God or any other living thing. They sat there silently in the agonising acceptance that their time together was almost at an end. Brother Scully had so much he wanted to say but was unable to find the words. Then, pointing towards St Joseph's Convent he said,

— So, that's your bedroom window there.

— That's it, she said. — Keep an eye out tonight for my light.

Sister Claire took his hand in hers and raising it up, she gently touched his fingertips with her lips, then firmly pressed his hand to her breast. The feeling was safe and warm. They sat there in silence, praying that the moment could last forever, not a word passing between them. Maybe there was magic in the moonlight and how it filtered and flitted through the mottled shade of the old cherry blossom tree, but her veil-framed face became the most beautiful vision he had ever seen. Tears began to flow.

Inside the library, beyond the fogged-up glass of the French doors, Reverend Mother and the visiting sisters were making ready to return to St Joseph's Convent. Sister Claire turned to Brother Scully, the strained urgency in her voice shattering the spell of silence.

— If you have something to say, say it now!

Brother Scully did have something to say. He wanted to tell her that he loved Jesus but he loved her more. He wanted to say that he would gladly abandon eternity in the presence of God, if he could spend the rest of his living days with her, but the words just would not come.

— Please, she whispered. — Just say something! For God's sake, please ...

He wanted to tell her that he could not live his life without her by his side.

— I beg you, Brother Scully, just say it ...

He wanted to tell her that he never knew what love was until he first set eyes on her.

— Just say it! Please! I beg you, just say it, she pleaded.

Most of all he wanted to say,

— *I love you.*

But something prevented him from uttering the words. In his heart and soul he did not have the courage of his conviction. He had stepped over the line of his vocation and now wanted nothing more than to step back again. And maybe his vocation had been tested and dented, but it still remained intact. Brother Scully knew he could not bear the responsibility of enticing the young nun away from religious life. And though he shared her pain, her love and her hopes for what might be, he prayed that it would pass and time would heal all. So he just sat there in silence staring off into the distance.

The sound of Reverend Mother tapping the glass with her keys broke the tense solitude. Sister Claire leaned towards Brother Scully and whispered frantically,

— Please, please I beg you. I must go. For God's sake! If you have something to say, say it now ...

The attraction he felt for her was like nothing he had ever experienced in his life. But, paralysed by the fear of the consequences of exposing his true emotions, Brother Scully did not say a word.

He slowly got to his feet and led the way into the library. The visiting sisters were preparing to leave. They were exchanging long goodbyes, and insisting that they should do it again sometime.

— Sooner rather than later, said Reverend Mother. — Sooner rather than later ...

— Maybe for the All-Ireland Final, said Bossman.

— Ah, we'll do it sooner than that ...

*For God's sake! If you have something to say, say it now...*

—  We will indeed, agreed Bossman.

—  And the next time, you and some of your brothers must come to visit us over in St Joseph's, insisted Reverend Mother. — Maybe for election night, or something like that ...

—  We'd be delighted, Reverend Mother. Absolutely delighted.

Young Brother Scully escorted the mumbling mass of holy women along the dimly-lit corridor. At the monastery door, they bade their final farewells.

—  It's been a most wonderful evening, a glorious day to be Irish, said Reverend Mother.

—  True for you, Reverend Mother, echoed Bossman. — Dana did us proud tonight, so she did ...

Then, led on by Brother Scully, the visiting sisters headed down the avenue and disappeared into the darkness.

With a bitter and biting east wind blowing, they did not delay at the monastery gate. Like four black swans gliding across a mill-pond, the holy sisters huddled together and set off towards St Joseph's Convent. As the latch snapped shut behind them, Sister Claire stopped and turned to face Brother Scully one last time. The light of the street lamp picked up the silver stream of tears running down her cheeks, and maybe it was the shadow cast by the old elm tree that arched the monastery gates, but Brother Scully swore he saw her lips move, like she was saying,

—  I love you, Brother Scully ...

She then turned, and quickening her pace to catch up with the others, she vanished into the night.


Brother Scully did not sleep that night. He sat by his bedroom window looking out over the city, and something about the darkness and that feeling of love lost made his sad heart lonely. He questioned if he had made the right decision when he denied his passion for Sister Claire. He came to the conclusion that their unrequited love would be the cross that he would bear.

But then, just before dawn, it happened. A beam of light shone out from St Joseph's Convent.

— Flash-flash, Flash Flash. — *Good morning, Brother Scully.*
He grappled for his light switch.
    — Flash-flash, Flash Flash. — *Good morning, Sister Claire.*
Then a second coded message came from the convent.
    — Flash-flash-flash, Flash Flash. — *I love you, Brother Scully.*
    — Flash-flash-flash-flash. — *I love you too.*

* * *

That was a long time ago, forty or fifty years ago or so, and every single morning since that fateful night back in 1970, when Dana won the Eurovision Song Contest, Sister Claire has beamed out her coded message of love to Brother Scully from St Joseph's Convent.

But this Christmas Eve morn no light has shone from her bedroom window, and as afternoon stretches towards evening, Brother Scully's worry for Sister Claire turns to anxiety. He sits there hopelessly helpless, looking out over the city, his gaze fixed on her bedroom window, waiting for the darkness of dusk to descend before he can attempt to make contact with her.

His gnarled fingers grip the life-giving, lukewarm mug of Bovril and his mind wanders back to those hellish days following Dana's victory over Europe. He remembers with clarity his mounting obsession, and how he became overwhelmed by thoughts of Sister Claire. He remembers the excitement of each new dawn, and the flickering lights carrying secret messages of love over and back between convent and monastery. Every bolt beamed out from her bedroom window sent a surge of energy coursing through his veins, like it was connecting directly with his soul. He remembers the nighttime torment of hell-sent dreams conjuring up visions of Sister Claire, her beautiful veil-framed face, her lips, her eyes, the sound of her voice, her carefree girlish laugh, the delicate touch of her finger tips. Brother Scully's mind became infected by thoughts of the soft, flesh-toned curves concealed beneath her robe. And maybe Brother Scully did not believe in God, but deep in his heart and soul he was convinced it was the seductive voice of Satan whispering in his ear, reminding him of that moment when she took his hand in hers and placed it firmly against the fullness of her breast.

With no one else to turn to, young Brother Scully reverted to his faith and went down on his knees and begged God Almighty to save him from his thoughts, and when God didn't answer, he cried out to Jesus Christ for salvation, and when all else failed he prayed to the Virgin Mary to cleanse him of his ungodly cravings. But no answer came from above.

Then, as if inspired by the Holy Spirit, it came to him that maybe the voice in his head was not that of Lucifer whispering, taunting and tempting. Maybe it was the voice of the Almighty offering encouragement and answering his prayers. Could it be that his cravings were heaven-sent, all beauty and light and fuelled by love. Brother Scully reasoned that if God is love, then surely to love another human being was to look into the face of God. God had brought Sister Claire to him, and with God's will he would be with Sister Claire again, hand in hand, lips on lips, body on body.

   — ...and surely be to Christ there is no sin in that, he whispered in
      his prayers.


That first night was like a journey through a tunnel of endless darkness. The only comfort Brother Scully could find to ease his pain was to sit by his window and cry. Right through until the early hours of morning, the sad and lonely sound of his weeping echoed around the cold, tiled corridors of the monastery. The following morning the Deputy called to his room.

   — Eh-hem, he cleared his throat. — It's come to my attention that
      you were heard crying last night, Brother Scully. Crying like a
      baby! Is that right, Brother Scully? Crying for your mammy is
      that what it is!
      Well let me tell you something for nothing, there's no room for
      mammy's boys in this monastery! Do you hear me?
   — Yes, Deputy Head Brother.
   — You're a grown man! No room for homesickness, this is your
      home now. A monastery is no place for emotions! So you'll just
      have to snap out of it, man. Do you hear me! Snap out of it!
   — I'll try, Deputy Head Brother.

— There's no, *I'll try*, about it! It's all about state of mind in a place like this! Attitude, man! Attitude! Positive attitude! You will snap out of it, and snap out of it now!

— I will.

— I will what?

— I will, Deputy Head Brother...

— That's more like it. So there'll be no more of that aul' sobbing out of you, will there?

— No, Deputy Head Brother.

— That's what I like to hear. Good man, good man.

See, that sort of carry-on can become an epidemic in a place like this. No, a monastery is no place for emotions...

Take a tip from a man who's been around the block once or twice. It's all about happiness. And happiness is a state of mind. So, if you act happy, you will be happy. It's as simple as that.

No doubt you'll hear a lot of aul' guff from these modern-day head-doctors and quacks coming out of America about being true to your emotions, finding your inner child and all that sort of aul' rubbish! But don't believe a word of it. Let the Americans have their therapists and psychologists, we don't need that rubbish. We have confession. Confession! Confession and denial.

You see, Brother Scully, denial is the most highly evolved coping mechanism known to the human mind. Denial is the most powerful weapon we have against all adversity.

Denial! It's what separates us from the beasts of the field. I mean Jesus, it took millions of years for the human mind to develop denial to such a high level of sophistication, that we can now deal with anything life throws at us. But then, along come these shrinks telling us to give up denial and face our demons. Christ Almighty, if we didn't have denial to turn to, most of us would go and throw ourselves into the flamin' river!

Maybe young Brother Scully did not fully understand what the Deputy had said, but he learned one thing that morning. He learned that crying would never heal his pain and tears of laughter would be far more acceptable than tears of sorrow.

Later that night he sat by his bedroom window looking across to St Joseph's Convent, tormented by the realisation that he would never see Sister Claire again, so he placed his hands to his face and began to laugh. Right through the night the sound of his manic laughter echoed around the hollow halls of the monastery.

Next morning, still in the depths of darkest despair, Brother Scully made his way to class, all chuckles and smiles. Turning the corner by the library he walked straight into the Deputy who greeted him saying,

— Well now, you're very happy in yourself this morning, Brother Scully.
— Ah sur', sometimes you just gotta laugh, Deputy Head Brother, you just gotta laugh...
— Good man, good man! That's what I like to hear...

Brother Scully continued along his way to class giggling sadly. He knew that laughter was no cure for loneliness. He would never find inner peace as long as the pain of love lost tortured his heart and temptations of the flesh tormented his mind. He knew that his life would not be worth living without Sister Claire by his side. So that morning, as he approached the classroom, young Brother Scully began to devise a plan to meet Sister Claire. There was something about his decision to take control of his suffering that brought him peace of mind and gave him the strength to carry on.


The door swung open and Brother Scully took the classroom in full stride.

— Right lads, put away the books!
  Now who can tell me what happened in Amsterdam last Saturday night?
— Brudder! Brudder! Brudder! Brudder!

As always he ignored the Parrot's hand flapping and fluttering under his nose.

— Anybody?
— Brudder! Brudder! Brudder! Brudder!
— Anybody?
— Brudder! Brudder! Brudder! Brudder!
— Well, Mister Perrott?

— Dana won the Eurovision for Ireland, Brudder.

— Dead right, Mister Perrott. And what was the name of the song she sang?

— Brudder! Brudder! Brudder! Brudder!

— Anybody?

— Brudder! Brudder! Brudder! Brudder!

— Well, Mister Perrott?

— All Kinds of Everything, Brudder.

— All Kinds of Everything, right again, Mister Perrott. And do any of ye know the words of the song?

— Brudder! Brudder! Brudder!

— Right, Mister Perrott, let's hear it...

Up you get! Up here and sing the song...

The Parrot made his way to the top of the room then turned to face the class. Brother Scully took his place by the blackboard, a fresh stick of chalk at the ready.

— Right, Mr Perrott! And away you go.

And as the Parrot began to sing, Brother Scully feverishly wrote the lyrics, word for word on the blackboard, sending a flurry of chalk like a snowstorm into the air. As the last words of the song faded and the chalk dust settled, Brother Scully marched the full length of the class-room, opening every window as he went.

— Okay, Mr Perrott, you stay where you are there, and we'll give it one more go...

Right, lads! On yer feet! On yer feet! All of ye, on yer feet!

La-la-la-la-la!

Brother Scully seemed to be a little more excited than usual. Confused eyes darted from desk to desk, baffled by Brother Scully's energy, an energy that seemed to reach new heights as he searched for a pitch, scale and key.

— After me lads! La-la-la-la-la!

One more time! La-la-la-la-la!

On a count of three! La-la-la-la-la!

Right, lads! One-two! And a-one-two-three!

And a room full of dirty-faced schoolboys filled their lungs and sang out as one,

> *Snowdrops and daffodils, butterflies and bees.*
> *Sailboats and fishermen, things of the sea.*
> *Wishing wells, wedding bells, early morning dew ...*
> *All kinds of everything, remind me of you.*

— One more time, lads!

Like a human metronome, Brother Scully hammered out a rhythm on the blackboard keeping pace.

— Out loud, lads!
> *Ear-lee Morning dew-u-u ...*
> *All kinds of everything remind me of you ...*

— One more time, lads!

Driven on by Brother Scully banging out the beat and roaring, they sang it verse after verse, again and again ...

— Louder, lads! Louder!
Come on, lads! Louder!
I want them to hear this over in St Joseph's Convent!
Come on, lads! Louder!
Lift the roof with this one!

The glazed glare in Brother Scully's eyes intensified, as ideas and notions and plans and schemes, that would one day bring him face to face with Sister Claire, began to germinate inside his brain.

— One more time, lads!

Over and over and over again, Brother Scully drove them on, verse after verse, chorus after chorus.

— Louder, lads! Louder!
One more time!
This one's for Sister Claire, he roared above the discord and racket.

Brother Scully spiralled higher and higher, sweat pouring from his every pore, veins popping in his neck, eyes bulging and roaring,

— Louder, lads! Louder!

One more time ...

All morning long they sang it, Brother Scully hammering the board and shouting encouragement. With each verse, plans of how he would contrive to meet Sister Claire again gradually began to take shape in Brother Scully's mind.

— One more time!

One more time!

As the clock struck noon, Brother Scully collapsed down onto his chair in ecstatic exhaustion. An uneasy silence descended on the class as one by one the voices petered out in awkward disarray.

When class ended that day, Brother Scully went directly to his bedroom. He did not come down to the refectory for tea or supper and was absent for evening prayer. He worked right through the night hatching a plan that would reunite him with Sister Claire. Maybe it was innocence or maybe it was insanity, maybe he was just weak and delirious from lack of sleep, whatever the reason, thoughts and images of St Francis flooded Brother Scully's mind.

There was something about the strength bestowed on St Francis, when he stripped himself of all his worldly goods, that inspired the young Brother Scully to stand naked at his bedroom window the following morning. He stood there in the darkness of dawn, his arms outstretched like Christ on the cross, praying that he might harness the power of *The Changing Of The Guard*. But just before dawn cracked the horizon, a flickering bulb shone out across the valley from Sister Claire's bedroom. Each flash of light sent a charge of energy coursing around his body, each surge of power brought a disorienting confusion to his mind.

A full hour passed before Brother Scully found himself semi-conscious, every nerve and neuron inside his cranium frayed and sparking like a short circuit to his brain. He lay there naked on his bedroom floor unable to move, his eyelids flickering, every muscle twitching in pain, his mind struggling to keep pace with the many elaborate ideas darting around inside his head.

In the days that followed, he wore a crease along the carpet of Bossman Begley's office, parading in and out, pitching his plans as they flashed one after the other in front of his mind. His schemes were as diverse as they were plentiful.

He suggested the monastery and St Joseph's Convent could combine their resources and build a swimming pool.

— For the youth of the Northside, he said. — If for no other good reason, they'd get a wash.

He had rough costs worked out, and calculated that, in co-operation with St Joseph's Convent, they would easily raise enough money to build the facility.

— ...and if we opened it to the public at weekends it would be a nice little earner for the monastery.

Later that day he was back into Bossman, proposing that the two schools should set up a language laboratory.

— I'm confident the Department of Education would support a joint proposal. It's only a matter of time before Ireland joins the French Common Market, it's important that the youth of this area will be able to speak French. Sur' we'll all be speaking French before the end of the century.

— French? French, said Bossman. — What about Irish!

— Irish is like Latin, the language of culture. But French will be the language of commerce, Head Brother.

And again that evening he cornered Bossman in the refectory suggesting that a two-week, intensive cookery course should be introduced for the younger boys doing the Group Certificate.

— Cookery for boys, repeated Bossman. — What use would boys have for cookery? Won't they have wives at home to cook for them?

— Ah, but the times they are a changing, Head Brother...

— Well they're not changing that much. I really can't see any use a cookery class would be to our lads...

— Vital, said Brother Scully. — It would be vital! They leave school at fourteen years of age and take the boat to England to dig holes. Most of 'em couldn't boil an egg for you. Cookery would be more useful to them than being able to conjugate some irregular Latin verb ...

— Do you have a problem with Latin, Brother Scully?

— No, Head Brother. Not at all.

— Latin is the language of the Church!

— I know, Head Brother. All I'm saying is that a basic knowledge of nutrition and cookery would be a vital part of their survival skills.

— Survival skills? Survival skills! Jesus, 'tis out looking for work they'll be, not heading off into the flamin' jungles of darkest Africa.

— Think about it, Head Brother ...

— Well I will think about it, but survival skills seems a bit extreme.

— We could do it at little or no expense.

— No expense you say?

— We could do it in co-operation with the domestic science class over in St Joseph's Convent ...

Then, later that night, he ambushed Bossman as he was coming out of the chapel, and made a strong case for converting the old playing fields behind the monastery into a market garden. He insisted that the whole project could be run and supervised by the boys and girls from the two schools.

— ... it would be self-financing, if not a profitable venture, he argued. — Invaluable from the point of view of teaching them the ways of nature and the basic principles of profit and loss economics. It would get them out in the fresh air and away from street corners. It could only be a good thing, Head Brother?

The following morning, Brother Scully was waiting outside Bossman's office.

— Ah there you are, Head Brother, he said.

— Of course I'm here, said Bossman. — This is my office! Where else would I be?

— I was reading the projected demographic trends for the Northside and they predicted a declining population ...

— I'm sure that's all very interesting, Brother Scully. Now if you'll excuse me, I must go to the ...

— See, Head Brother, with the predicted decline in numbers, I was thinking that maybe the monastery should open its doors to girls from the convent. Sharing of resources between the two schools would eliminate much of the duplication and cut overheads. The monastery could move into co-education ...

— Co-education? How do you mean co-education, asked Bossman.

— Co-education. Boys and girls together.

— In the same classroom! Are you off your flamin' head, Scully!

— It's the way of the future. They've been doing it in America for years, Head Brother.

— Just because they've been doing it in America doesn't make it a good thing! They've been doing lots of things in America that, quite frankly, any God-fearing man of moral fibre would not want any hand, act or part in.

— Well it was just a thought, Head Brother. But before I go, one other little idea that's been running around in my mind. Maybe we could start adult education classes?

— Adult education, repeated Bossman.

— For the parents.

— What! The parents going to school? Naw, it would never catch on. We have enough trouble trying to get the young lads into the classrooms, not to mind their parents as well ...

— But this would be different, Head Brother. See the parents would want to go to school.

— You must be joking! Didn't I teach most of them myself when they were youngsters. They couldn't leave school fast enough! What makes you think they'd have any notion of coming back to school now? Anyway you couldn't have the boys and their parents sitting in the same classroom, it would never work ...
An interesting idea, Brother Scully, but it would never work ...

— See I don't think you actually grasp the concept of adult education, Head Brother.

— Grasp the concept? What concept, Brother Scully?

- I'm talking about evening classes.
- Evening classes? And who would pay the teachers to come up here of an evening?
- The parents would pay an enrolment fee, Head Brother.
- An enrolment fee? God bless yer innocence, Brother Scully. They spend all their money on drink! How in the name of God would you entice the parents out of the pubs of an evening, and into a classroom, and then ask them to pay for the pleasure of it!
- This is 1970, Head Brother. Ireland is a changing place. Believe me, people are crying out for an alternative to the pub.

  Honestly, Head Brother. I can see a time when parents will be doing night courses instead of going to the pub. It would be more social than educational.
- More social than educational? There's nothing social about education.

  Evening Classes? Well Lord God, I've heard it all now. An enrolment fee, Bossman laughed.
- But this wouldn't be like school, Head Brother. It would be more about life skills.
- Life skills? Jesus, a few days back it was survival skills, today it's life skills. What in the world are life skills?

  Look, leave it with me, Brother Scully. We'll see, we'll see. But to be honest with you, parents going to school? I can't see it catching on. But, leave it with me. Leave it with me.

  Life skills you say, Bossman laughed again and walked away.

By the Wednesday following Dana's epic victory in Europe, Brother Scully's manic behaviour had become the main topic among the whisperers who gathered around the cloisters each evening. When rumours of his deteriorating mental health reached the Deputy, he marched straight to the office and, leaning across the desk, he went nose to nose with Bossman.
- What are you going to do about Brother Scully, he demanded.
- Why? What's wrong with Brother Scully?
- There is growing concern among the community for the state of his mental health. And it's your responsibility!

— My responsibility, Brother Lynch?
— Well if it's not your responsibility, it's your fault! And it's Deputy-Head-Brother Lynch!
— My apologies, Deputy-Head-Brother Lynch, said Bossman. — But what's all this talk of fault? He's not gone and done anything wrong, has he?
— Not yet!
— It's just the exuberance of youth. It's all positive energy.
— With all due respect, interrupted the Deputy. — One man's positive energy is another man's insanity. You know as well as I do, he's running around the corridors of this monastery day and night like a madman. He's drawing up plans for a new language laboratory, and hare-brained schemes like co-education. I mean, boys and girls in the same classroom! What planet is he on? Then he's talking about adult education classes. Parents going to school? Who ever heard such tripe!
Yesterday he was up the old playing fields marking out plots for some screwball idea of setting up a School's Co-operative Market Garden in collaboration with St Joseph's Convent. For Christ's sake!
...and just now I saw him in the library, and do you know what he's doing? Do you!
— No, but I'm sure you'll tell me.
— He's composing a new school song!
— Where's the harm in that?
— An all-inclusive new school song to include both the monastery and St Joseph's Convent, and wait for it, wait for it. The lyrics are tetra-lingual!
— Tetra-what?
— Tetra-lingual, four languages, Irish, English, Latin and French. French! For Christ's sake! The man's not well.
— Well, maybe he's been a bit enthusiastic lately, said Bossman.
— Enthusiastic! Is that what you call it! Insane! If you ask me ...
— No doubt he has a track worn in and out of this office every day with some new plan, all good plans I might add, but I must admit the sheer volume has me bamboozled!

— So we're in agreement, snapped the Deputy.

— In agreement about what?

— That something must be done ...

— And what do you suggest we do about it!

— We? We! What's this *we* business. You're the Head Brother, this is your problem. You sort it out!

He's running around like a lunatic. It's unsettling the novices and unless somebody reins him in, God knows where all this will end. He needs focus in his life. Somebody needs to sit him down and calm him down. I've seen it before.

— You've seen it before?

— Yes, I've seen it before!

— You've seen what before?

— When I was up in Limerick a few years back, one of the younger brothers went off his game and it spread like a virus through the monastery. Next thing you know half the monastery were acting like lunatics.

— Don't be ridiculous, Deputy Head Brother! Mental illness is not contagious!

— Mental illness may not be contagious, Head Brother. But acting mad is! And if Brother Scully doesn't get some focus in his life, he's gonna fly right off the flamin' planet, and that will infect the whole monastery. I mean Lord God in heaven, even the school-boys have a new nickname for him.

— Nickname?

— Screwball Scully they're calling him!

Screwball Scully! And they're right! The man is a screwball!

Deputy Head Brother Lynch paused for a few seconds, then he refocused his attack.

— 'Tis! 'Tis! 'Tis you! You and that blasted colour television, I blame, he shouted. — I was against it from the start! But would you listen to me? Oh, no! Ever since you brought that yolk into this monastery ...

The Deputy's fury was interrupted by a knock at the door.

— Come in, said Bossman.

182

The door opened and in walked young Brother Scully. He seemed excited. The Deputy cast a withering look and a curled lip towards Bossman.

— Ah, Brother Scully, said Bossman. — Come in, come in. How can I help you?

— I've just had a brainwave, he said.

— A brainwave, the Deputy echoed cynically.

— Well it crossed my mind ...

— Your mind, repeated the Deputy, his words tinged with sarcasm.

— Yes! It crossed my mind that I'd like to organise the School Christmas Concert this year.

— And I suppose you'll manage to squeeze in this Christmas Concert with all the other projects you're planning?

Young Brother Scully was too deeply engaged in the moment to detect the Deputy's patronising tone, so he proceeded to lay out a schedule for his various proposed collaborations with St Joseph's Convent.

— ...then the adult education classes would be held on Tuesday and Thursday nights, and with the growing season coming to an end around September, the work on the market garden should be slowing down.

I'd hold the language laboratory on Saturday mornings, that would give me plenty of time to rehearse the Christmas play on Monday, Wednesday and Saturday afternoons, and sur' the charity walk to raise funds for the sod-turning ceremony for the swimming pool would realistically only take up one, maybe two or three weeks to organise, then of course we could have the ...

The Deputy turned towards Bossman and rolled his eyes to heaven. That's when Bossman shouted,

— Enough! Stop! Stop! Stop!

He grabbed Brother Scully by the shoulders, firmly manoeuvred him onto a chair and held him there.

— Stop! Stop! Stop! Hold it right there, Brother Scully! Just hold it right there!

— Something I said, Head Brother, asked Brother Scully.

— Look, Brother Scully, you've come up with many wonderful and progressive ideas, but you'll just have to slow down. I don't know what's gotten into you! You're running around the monastery like you've ants in yer pants. In and out every day, with this plan and that plan, and it just has to stop. So here's my ruling on it. You must focus on one project, and one project only. The monastery has neither the time nor the resources to tackle so many different undertakings ...

— But, Head Brother?

— That's my final word on it! So what project do you wish to do?

— Eh? Let me think ...

Brother Scully considered the matter deeply for over half a second.

— The language laboratory! Or no! Maybe I'll do the adult education classes! No! The, ehm? Maybe the market garden! Eh? One second, one second, let me think? Eh, No! I'd like to do the concert, the School Christmas Concert.

— Are you sure?

— Ehm? Yes, I am. I'm sure!

— You're certain?

— Certain!

— Right, said Bossman. — The School Christmas Concert it is! From now on it's your sole responsibility. We'll see how you get on with that. This is all about focus! I don't want to hear another word about any other ideas you happen to have knocking around that head of yours. And if and when the School Christmas Concert is a success, and I'm confident it will be a glowing success, you can then come to me with another project.

— Thank you, Head Brother. Thank you.

— Is that fair enough?

— It is, Head Brother. Thank you.

— Now, I don't want to hear about anything else, only the School Christmas Concert. Is that clear?

— Yes, Head Brother. Thank you.

— Now, go on! Let that be the end of it!

— Thank you, Head Brother, I will, Head Brother. Thank you, Head Brother. I won't let you down, Head Brother ...

Brother Scully reversed out of the office, genuflecting as he went with a stream of grovelling gratitude trailing behind him. Bossman turned to the Deputy, who was standing there scowling,

— Well, said Bossman. — I think that's that sorted.

— I hope so, but I'm of the opinion that...

Another knock on the door interrupted the Deputy mid-sentence.

— Enter!

The office door opened, and in stepped Brother Scully again.

— Ah for Christ's sake, whispered the Deputy.

— You forgot something, Brother Scully?

— No, Head Brother, I've just had an idea.

— Another idea, said the Deputy, and shook his head in despair.

— Does it concern the School Christmas Concert, demanded Bossman.

— Yes, Head Brother, it does.

— Continue.

— Well, I just had an idea, wouldn't it be wonderful if the School Christmas Concert, was a combined production between us here in the monastery and St Joseph's Convent?

— A combined production you say?

While Bossman pondered the logistics, Brother Scully presented his case.

— It will be the first time in the history of the two schools that a joint venture such as this would be produced. It will be in the spirit of Vatican II, Head Brother. Just imagine the combined talent of the two schools. Imagine the power of a combined choir.

— Combined, Brother Scully?

— Boys and girls together, Head Brother...

— I don't know if I like the sound of boys and girls combined?

— Eh? Not so much combined, Head Brother, it would be more like a collaboration...

— A collaboration, you say?

— Yes, Head Brother. A collaboration that would send out a message loud and clear that we the brothers are a forward and progressive Order. This collaboration would announce to the city and to the world that the brothers are relevant in modern Ireland. The success of this collaboration might even give a much-needed boost to new vocations.

Having considered Brother Scully's latest proposal for another few moments Bossman smiled.

— Brother Scully, that's a wonderful idea. I'll draft a letter to Reverend Mother straight away.

— Thanks, Head Brother. Thanks...

— Now go! Myself and Deputy Head Brother Lynch have important business to discuss...

Once again, Brother Scully backed his way out of the office and closed the door behind him. Bossman turned to the Deputy and said,

— He's young and enthusiastic, young and enthusiastic, that's all...

But no sooner had the words passed his lips, than once again there was a knock on the door.

— What is it this time, Brother Scully, roared the Deputy.

— Sorry, Sorry, but it just crossed my mind, that maybe we could have a rendition of Dana's Eurovision Song Contest winner, as the grand finale.

— What are you on about, man, the Deputy slammed his fist down on Bossman's desk.

— All Kinds of Every...

— Just go, Brother Scully, shouted Bossman. — Go now, before I change my mind! Just go!

Brother Scully retreated from the office, and as the door clicked shut behind him, the Deputy shrugged his shoulders and said,

— What did I tell you? That man is a screwball...

Bossman just shook his head and whispered,

— Screwball Scully...

They shared a confused glance, and for the first time in a long time the Head Brother and the Deputy laughed together as one.

Brother Scully was too excited to sleep that night. He needed to share with Sister Claire his plans for the Combined Schools' Christmas

Concert. He wanted to tell her the good news, that Bossman had accepted his grand scheme. It would only be a matter of time before full permission would be granted, soon they would be together. Again and again his mind conjured up images of that moment when he would see her again, the sparkle in her eyes, the soft touch of her fingertips, the sensation of her hand on his, pressing firmly against her breast.

All night long, the young brother sat by his window feverishly flicking his light switch.

— Flash Flash! Flash Flash! — *Sister Claire! Sister Claire!*
Every few minutes he transmitted his call,

— Flash Flash! Flash Flash! — *Sister Claire! Sister Claire!*
Right through the night,

— Flash Flash! Flash Flash! — *Sister Claire! Sister Claire!*
Over and over,

— Flash Flash! Flash Flash! — *Sister Claire! Sister Claire!*
Faster and faster,

— Flash Flash! Flash Flash! — *Sister Claire! Sister Claire!*
Throughout the night,

— Flash Flash! Flash Flash! — *Sister Claire! Sister Claire!*
Until just before dawn, at precisely eighteen minutes to six a flickering beam of light shone out from her bedroom window.

— Flash-flash, Flash Flash. — *Good morning, Brother Scully.*
With a click of his light switch he responded, but the message he wished to convey was far too complicated for a vocabulary limited to the flashing of a light bulb, so he settled for something short and to the point.

— Flash-flash-flash, Flash Flash. — *I love you, Sister Claire.*
— Flash-flash-flash-flash. — *I love you too,* she replied.

\* \* \*

With a spring in his step and a swish of his soutane, there was a certain swagger to Brother Scully as he arrived into the classroom that morning.

— Right lads! Put away the books! I have an important announcement to make.

For the first time in the history of this school, our Christmas Concert this year will be in collaboration with Sister Claire's class over in St Joseph's Convent. It will be a Combined Schools' Christmas Concert. And who can tell me the meaning of the word collaboration?

Co-llab-or-ation, he said it again.

— Brudder! Brudder! Brudder! Brudder! Brudder!

His eyes trawled the classroom, ignoring the Parrot.

— Brudder! Brudder! Brudder! Brudder! Brudder!

Brother Scully clicked his fingers and pointed,

— Christy Buckley! The meaning of co-llab-or-ation?
— Eh? Would it be? Would it be? Ehm? Is it a German spy, Brother?
— A German spy! What in the name of all that's good and holy would a German spy be doing over in St Joseph's Convent?
— I saw it in a fil-um, Brother. Collaborators were German spies, Brother.
— Context, man! Context!
  Now in fairness to you, I can see where yer coming from, Buckley. The Vichy in France collaborated with the Germans in the war. But that's not the answer I'm looking for. Context man! Context! Think about the context! Anybody else? The meaning of co-llab-or-ation?
— Brudder! Brudder! Brudder! Brudder! Brudder! Brudder! Brudder!

The Parrot still squawking and fluttering up and down off his perch.

— Well, Mr Perrott? Collaboration?
— Collaboration is when people work together in co-operation, Brudder.
— Right first time, Mr Perrott. Collaboration is all about co-operation. And this year our Christmas Concert will be in collaboration with Sister Claire from St Joseph's Convent.
  Spell collaboration!
— C-O-L-L-A-B-O-R-A-T-I-O-N, collaboration, chirped the Parrot.
— Good man, Mister Perrott. Good man ...

Young Brother Scully moved towards the window. There was fire in his eyes as he gazed across the city, eventually focusing on St Joseph's Convent. He struggled to banish her from his mind, but as if trapped in an endless loop, he couldn't stem the flow of images of her veil-framed face lit up by the moonlight, the sparkle in her eyes, the soft touch of her finger tips, the sensation of her hand on his ...

— Jesus, he whispered, and his thighs tensed as he pressed toward the radiator and, leaning there against the warmth, his mind filled with the most beautiful, vile thoughts imaginable.

He slowly turned to face the class.

— That's right, he said. — It will be a collaboration with Sister Claire. And after much deliberation, I've decided that the concert will be a music and dance extravaganza, inspired by the birth of Our Lord, Jesus Christ. A nativity musical, so to speak. And what was the name of the town where Our Saviour was born?

— Brudder! Brudder! Brudder! Brudder!

Brother Scully snapped his fingers and pointed to Nicky Flynn.

— Well, Mr Flynn?

— Bethlehem, Brother.

— Very good, Mr Flynn. Very good. And why did Mary and Joseph go to the little town of Bethlehem?

Again the Parrot's hand was flapping up and down under Brother Scully's nose.

— Brudder! Brudder! Brudder! Brudder!

And again Brother Scully chose to ignore him.

— Christy Buckley!

— To fill in a census form, Brother.

— Ah, that's more like it, now we're getting places! Spell Bethlehem, Mr Perrott!

— B-E-T-H-L-E-H-E-M. Bethlehem, Brother!

— Now we're sucking diesel!

Brother Scully was in full flight. He moved around the classroom in fits and starts, like he was lost in his own private reality, clicking his fingers, rattling out questions one after the other in rapid fire succession. Then he stopped, stopped dead, his eyes staring into space. Hands outstretched demanding silence. Then leaning forward he announced in a conspiratorial whisper from the side of his mouth that he was planning a show-stopping grand finale. A tableau, he called it.

— A tableau! That's what it will be.

His eyes darted from side to side in his head, as if worried the details of his creative genius might be stolen, then, gathering the boys around him in a huddle, he said,

— It will be a tableau featuring the girls from St Joseph's Convent and you lads here in the monastery. A grand finale tableau that will end in a crashing crescendo.

Wait for it! Wait for it!

Just imagine, Dana's Eurovision winning song, *All Kinds Of Everything*, performed solo by one young girl from Sister Claire's class?

He then yelled,

– Ah ha!

Brother Scully jumped back as if surprised by the brilliance of his own idea.

— No one will expect it! *All Kinds Of Everything*! Dana! Brilliant! Who would think it! Dana! *All Kinds Of Everything ...*

Ye gotta picture the scene, lads! A girl from Sister Claire's First Holy Communion class made up to look like Dana, down to the last detail of the Celtic embroidery on her báinín frock.

Picture the scene, lads. Picture the scene ...

The stage in total blackout, except for one pinpoint spotlight illuminating a single high stool. Then, just like Dana did in the Eurovision, the young girl will enter stage left and make her way centre stage. She will sit up on the stool and sing, *All Kinds Of Everything*.

Pure brilliance! No frills. It will be a pure re-enactment of Dana's moment of glory. Simple, clean, pure. Believe me lads, it will steal the hearts of every man, woman and child in the audience. A total showstopper.

But then at the end of the first verse, just when they least expect it ...

Bang! The stage will flood with light, revealing all you lads togged-out in full school uniform, hair combed, shoes polished... And ye'll join in for the second verse in full harmony. Beautiful. Ab-so-lute-ly beautiful...

And then, just as the last words of the song float gently from the stage, and the audience are entranced and transposed to another place, just at that point of pure perfection...

Bang! The fire door will crash open at the back of the hall. In will march two columns of drummers from the Technical School, flanked by a guard of honour of standard bearers made up of the camogie team from St Joseph's Convent on the right flank, and the hurling team from here in the monastery on the left. Full kit, hurleys, the works! Each one of 'em carrying a hurley in the one hand and a flag in the other. They will march into the hall with the full thirty-two flags of each and every county of Ireland, North and South held high. United!

And out in front will be a colour party bearing the flags of the four provinces and the tricolour of the republic. Two columns marching military style to the beating of drums will form up in two ranks in front of the stage.

Bang! The combined accordion and flute bands of St Joseph's Convent and the monastery, marching in from the two side doors of the gym to the beat of a military tattoo. And at the very moment the band hits the first note, the full choir of sixty boys and girls, all in full school uniform, will launch into a rousing rendition of, *A Nation Once Again.*

Can ye see it, lads! Can ye see it! Can ye!

By Christ, we'll raise rafters, boys! We'll blow 'em outa' their seats! We'll bring the audience to their feet! Not a dry eye in the house. We're gonna shake up this town! They'll be talking about our Christmas Concert long into the future!

Long after I'm dead, you'll be telling yer children that you were part of this, the first Combined Schools' Christmas Concert. And your children will be telling their children long after we're all dead, so they will...

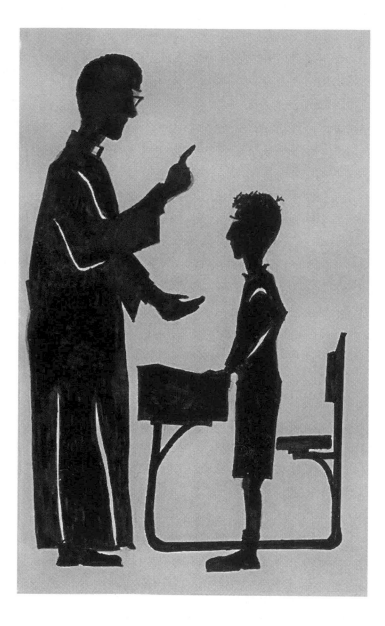

*Any true Irishman would be proud to step into Dana's shoes...*

Brother Scully paused as he attempted to harness the creative surge storming around inside his brain.

— Now, he said. — I'm still waiting to get the official go-ahead from Reverend Mother over in St Joseph's Convent, but that's only a matter of formality. So while we're waiting for the official green light, I say we get started ...

Right! No time to waste! Mister Perrott, you can be Dana!

— Dana, Brudder?

— Yes! Dana! Do you have a problem with that, Mister Perrott?

— But Dana is a girl, Brudder ...

A nervous giggle rippled from desk to desk around the classroom.

— What! What! Something funny about that? Something funny about Dana's great victory in Europe? I don't think you lads understand the historical significance of all this!

The Romans tried it, Attila the Hun tried it, Alexander the Great tried it, Hannibal tried it, Napoleon tried it, God in heaven, didn't the Germans try it twice in the last fifty-five years. But they all failed!

It took the Irish ...

The Irish in the form of Dana, one young girl from Derry, to step forward and make all of Europe bow down at our feet. And when we re-enact Dana's night of glory in our Combined Schools' Christmas Concert, it will bring the house down!

Do you have a problem with that, Mister Perrott? Do you? Well, do you?

— Eh? No, Brudder.

— Dammed right you don't! Any true Irishman would be proud to step into Dana's shoes ...

Do you have a problem with that? Do you? Do you? Well, do you?

— Eh? No, Brudder.

— Right! It's settled then!

Until we get official confirmation from St Joseph's Convent you'll be Dana, and no more about it! Up to the top of the class like a good man.

Okay lads. Get the air into yer lungs. Come on, on yer feet! On yer

feet! All of ye, on yer feet! On yer feet! Sing after me! La-la-la-
la-la!

Everybody! La-la-la-la-la!

Come on, lads, blow out them cobwebs!

After me, lads! La-la-la-la-la!

One more time! La-la-la-la-la!

Now Mr Perrot, off you go with the first verse on your own!

We'll all join in the chorus. Have ye got that, lads!

Have ye got that, lads, he roared again.

— Yes, Brother!

— Right! I want ye to raise the rafters with this ...

La-la-la-la-la! On a count of three! La-la-la-la-la!

Ready, Mr Perrott! Ready!

A–one! A–two! And, a-one-two-three!

And so the Parrot began to sing the opening verse.

— *Snowdrops and daffodils, butterflies and bees.*

*Sailboats and fishermen, things of the sea.*

Ready, lads, wait for it! Wait for it! All-to-geth-er now!

And right on cue they all joined in the chorus.

— *Wishing wells, wedding bells,*

*Louder, lads! Louder!*

*Ear-lee Morning dew-u-u ...*

*All kinds of everything remind me of you ...*

One more time, lads! All together now!

And so the madness began again, and with each repeated verse of the
song the manic stare in Brother Scully's eyes intensified.

— Louder, lads! Louder! Come on lads! Louder!

Lift the roof with this one!

One more time for Sister Claire!

\* \* \*

In the days that followed, young Brother Scully stepped over the thin
line of acceptable behaviour and wandered into the wide-open plains
of pure lunacy. Like that morning he was found standing on the ledge
outside his bedroom window, three floors up. It was just after dawn
when Brother O'Connell saw him up there.

It all began for Brother Scully when he awoke to find a footbridge outside his window spanning directly from the monastery all the way across the valley to St Joseph's Convent. Not a regular footbridge made of timber, steel or stone, but a single beam of light stretching from his bedroom window, right over the town to Sister Claire's window.

A voice of authority whispered in his ear, reassuring him that the pathway of light would hold his weight. So, opening the window, he carefully stepped out. Standing there, three floors above the ground, he was surprised to find it was solid and sturdy underfoot. Slowly and cautiously he stepped forward, one foot in front of the other and, just like Jesus when he walked upon the water, Brother Scully placed his trust in nature and he set off across the light-bridge towards St Joseph's Convent.

Midway along his trek he relaxed in the confidence that he was safe, protected by the invisible forces of nature. He hunkered down and, sitting there, he took in the panoramic view. From high up in the sky, he looked down on the town. It was a vista he had never seen before, a sight to behold, all beauty and delight. He marvelled at the strings of street lamps like rosary beads wound around the warren of dark lanes and alleyways. He saw royal splendour in labourers' cottages stacked up like a house of cards and the mystical misty blue-grey early morning smoke rising up from chimney pots.

This was a wonderful town of steps and steeples, more steps and steep hills, and there, set against the rolling terraces of Bell's Field, the Plots and Our Lady's Holy Well, vapours of cold pressed stout and mashed malt from Murphy's Stack signalled a new brew for a new day. Across to his right, the old fort of Shandon, standing staunch and loyal to a long forgotten royalty, crowned by a fickle fish of gold that changed direction with every call in the wind. His mind drifted to the court-house, the jail and the college, with their different types of knowledge ...

The sound of a harrier hound distracted his attention, and there in the distance, skimming the rooftops along Cathedral Road, Michael Crane's pigeons soared and swooped, like they were challenging the birds in Gerry Dalton's loft to come out and race them if they dared. Mary Aikenhead Place, Wolfe Tone Street, St Vincent's Avenue, there was something magical about this slumbering town, all tucked up in a comforting blanket of coal smoke. The beauty of all that he surveyed fired up a euphoric feeling from deep inside his soul.

    — My God, Brother Scully whispered, at the magnificence of it all.
    — My God ...

For the first time in his lifetime he saw the natural symmetry of this place. From Shandon steeple all the way to the turret over on Tower Street, the Northside and the Southside were almost carbon copies of one another, like butterfly wings fanned out on the rolling hills either side of the river, from the ribcage of narrow lanes along the backbone of Washington Street.

    Brother Scully's elation was dangerously interrupted when a seagull swooped, nearly knocking him off his beam. So he got to his feet and continued his wondrous journey across the bridge of light all the way to St Joseph's Convent and Sister Claire's bedroom window.

    There she was all snuggled up in bed sound asleep. Not wishing to startle her, he gently tapped on the windowpane, and whispered her name.

    — Sister Claire, Sister Claire ...

But she did not stir. So he called out a little louder. He was tempted to knock more forcefully but she looked so peaceful and angelic he couldn't bring himself to disturb her slumber. So he just stood there on the sill outside her bedroom window looking in at this beautiful sight.

    That's when something strange caught his eye, a slight movement, like a serpentine wave, gently rhythmically undulating beneath the blankets. His eyes followed the rippling motion across the bedclothes as it wound its way around towards the edge of the bed. And there, creeping out from under the sheets he saw it, a scaled and scabby, black and bristled tail of a beast, coiling and uncoiling with every breath she took.

    — Oh Jesus, he whispered.

A feeling of disgust made his knees buckle with weakness. Consumed by revulsion, he could do nothing but grip the window frame, as his mind battled to make some sense of what his eyes were seeing. He opened his mouth to scream, but no sound did flow.

    That's when he noticed the first faint glow of dawn warming the eastern horizon. Panic set in when it realised that his bridge of light would fade and disappear with the brightness of the rising sun. Brother Scully scrambled a hasty retreat across the causeway, all the way back over the city towards the monastery, the beam of light fading behind him with each step. Fear-struck and breathless he managed to get to his bedroom window ledge just as the rising sun washed away the foot-bridge in a deluge of dazzling bright light ...

That's where he was when young Brother O'Connell saw him that morning, standing on his windowsill three floors up. Brother Scully was still traumatised by the sight of the coiling satanic tail he had seen in Sister Claire's bed, so he just stood there, heart palpitating, a cold sweat formed on his furnace-hot brow.

Below him on the lawn, the whole community of brothers had gathered. They were frantically shouting at him to stay calm, imploring him not to jump.

— Don't jump, Brother Scully! Don't jump!
— Why would I jump, he roared. — Do you think I'm mad or something!

After much coaxing, cajoling and confusion, Brother Scully was eventually persuaded to step back inside to the safety of his bedroom, where the Deputy was waiting.

— Jesus Christ! Are you totally insane, Scully, he shouted the obvious. — What's gotten into you, man! What in the name of Christ were you doing out there!

Brother Scully knew it was more prudent to remain tight-lipped. He knew it was best not to even attempt to explain the inexplicable. So he said nothing. Later that day the doctor came. In his opinion Brother Scully didn't require hospitalisation, but he prescribed tablets that would calm him down, control his delirious ravings and stabilise his wild mood swings. Brother Scully slept soundly for a day and a half.

Brother Burke of the Technical School screwed his bedroom window shut. Four six-inch brass screws, two each top and bottom, and just in case young Brother Scully took the notion to go walkabout again, he nailed a steel plate to the base.

In the days that followed, Brother Scully's tormented mind was calmed but confused by a selection box of prescription drugs. But his dreams and every lucid waking moment became consumed by thoughts of Sister Claire. He planned in the finest detail every word he would say if he ever had the opportunity to be with her again.

He would tell her that he loved Jesus Christ, but he loved her more. He would ask her straight to her face if she would abandon God and her soul for eternity, to spend the rest of her living days with him. He would ask Sister Claire to put her hand in his, and run away with him because God in all his wisdom would provide. He would ask her to trust that love is a Godly thing and heaven sent. But until confirmation came from Reverend Mother, he could do nothing but sit by his window each morning, waiting for the light of love to shine out from Sister Claire's bedroom, and every morning just before dawn it would happen.

— Flash-flash, Flash Flash. — *Good morning, Brother Scully.*
Each flicker like a lightening bolt to his chest, enough to stop his heart momentarily, only to set it pounding faster and stronger than ever.

— Flash-flash-flash, Flash Flash. — *I love you, Sister Claire.*

\* \* \*

Holy Thursday, 27th March 1970.
Five short days had passed since Dana won the Eurovision Song Contest, five short days since Brother Scully met Sister Claire, five short days and his vocation to religious life had been turned on its head. Brother Scully counted down the minutes waiting for Reverend Mother's response to Bossman's request for a Combined Schools' Christmas Concert, and those five short days became the longest five days of his life.

Bossman Begley took a phone call from Reverend Mother that morning. She began by thanking him for his hospitality the previous Saturday night, adding how much she and her sisters enjoyed the Eurovision Song Contest. She then said she welcomed his proposed plan for the Combined Schools' Christmas Concert.

— ...a wonderful idea, Head Brother. Simply wonderful.

198

But right now, I am phoning you on a more pressing and urgent matter, she said.

Bossman listened as Reverend Mother told of her plans to petition the Vatican to bestow sainthood on the recently deceased elderly nun, Sister Francesca.

— You remember Sister Francesca, she said.

— Eh, I think so ...

— Ah, you do! You do! She had been curing animals here at the convent for donkeys' years, since before the First World War.

— Oh, that Sister Francesca, said Bossman. — Sister Francesca Of The Animals, isn't it?

— Of The Birds, Reverend Mother corrected him. — Sister Francesca Of The Birds ...

— Oh, right, Of The Birds, my apologies. I knew it was, of the dogs, or of the cats, or of the animals or something like that ...

— Well, said Reverend Mother. — As you know Sister Francesca passed on to her eternal reward recently, and even though protocol dictates that she should be deceased for at least five years before we officially petition Rome to consider her for canonisation, we have started the ball rolling and have entered into preliminary discussions with the Bishop.

— Canonisation?

— That's right, she said. — And the Bishop is confident that the Vatican will grant Sister Francesca a *Nihil Obstat*. If that happens it should only be a formality to have her declared *Venerable*. It's only a small hop, skip and a jump from *Venerable* to *Blessed*, and at that point, it would be like pushing an open door to have her *Canonised* to full sainthood ...

The whole process will take decades, maybe even a hundred years. It will be well into the next century before we see any results.

— Neither you nor I will be around to see that day, Reverend Mother.

— True. But you can rest assured when that great day comes we will be remembered as the ones who instigated the canonisation of Sister Francesca Of The Birds. Just imagine a saint in our very own parish.

— That sounds absolutely amazing, Reverend Mother, said Bossman.

— Well, fingers crossed. But there are still a few bits and pieces to be tidied up. We have the required two documented and verified miracles in place. Well, more or less.

— Miracles?

— As you know, Sister Francesca has been credited with numerous miraculous cures of animals down through the years. And of course, we have the trump card of Sister Francesca's well-documented divine visitation from Saint Joseph a few months back, shortly before she died.

— So yer well on the road, Reverend Mother, he said.

— But we have a problem ...

— Problem?

— You see, last Saturday night when we visited your monastery to watch the Eurovision Song Contest, one of your new arrivals from the seminary, a Brother Scully ...

— Oh, Jesus, that flute, muttered Bossman.

— Pardon?

— Oh, nothing, nothing. It's just that whatever way I turn these days, there's someone giving out about young Brother Scully. What's he done this time?

— Well it seems Brother Scully inadvertently convinced Sister Claire, one of our young and more impressionable postulants, that the saintly Sister Francesca Of The Birds had masterminded a betting scam with the convent gardener involving racing pigeons back in 1918.

— What! You're joking me! That's brilliant!

— Brilliant? What's brilliant about it! It's preposterous, she said.
— How in the name of all that's good and holy can we petition the Holy Father in Rome to canonise Sister Francesca Of The Birds, if it's doing the rounds that she was involved in rigging pigeon races.

- Oh sorry, Reverend Mother. You're right. It's absolutely preposterous.

Bossman concealed his laughter with a few loud coughs.

- Now I'm sure it's all just some small misunderstanding, she continued. — But you don't need me to explain to you the confusion that might arise from such a misunderstanding. It could spell disaster for our petition to the Vatican for the *Nihil Obstat*.
- Absolutely, he agreed.
- As you well know, any question mark over Sister Francesca's integrity and her miraculous curing of the animals would put a question mark over the credibility of Saint Joseph's apparition ... Do you understand my point, Head Brother Begley?
- I do indeed, he said. — To tell you the truth, Brother Scully has been acting very strange this past while. I'll summon him to the office straight away.
  Don't you worry, Reverend Mother, I'll give him a good tongue-lashing. Mark my words, I'll soften his cough. You can rest assured, and he'll issue a full retraction to your young Sister whatever-her-name-is. That should put an end to it. That sort of loose talk needs to be stamped out, and stamped out firmly!
- Well rather than chastise the young brother, Reverend Mother cautioned. — Maybe it would serve our purpose better if we were to entice him on side. After all we're not seeking retribution. What we are seeking is a result.
- How do you mean, Reverend Mother?
- Well slowly, slowly catchy monkey, Head Brother.
- Slowly, slowly catchy what-ee?
- Monkey! Head Brother. Monkey!
- What monkey?
- Catchy monkey?
- You've lost me, Reverend Mother ...
- What I am saying is, I believe the gentle approach would be more effective and would accomplish our objectives.
- How do you mean gentle approach?
- Well, maybe we could arrange for your young Brother Scully to meet with Sister Claire sometime this coming weekend. And,

how should I put this, eh? With your guidance ...

Yes, under your guidance, Brother Scully might explain the misunderstanding to Sister Claire and clear up any confusion surrounding the matter in a more, how should I say it, a more cordial, a more naturalistic, uncontrived and social setting, rather than some sort of grand inquisition. The last thing we need is some big formal retraction.

This must be dealt with calmly and discreetly, with as little fuss as possible. Do you see what I'm getting at, Head Brother?

— Eh? Yes, Reverend Mother, eh? I think so ...

— In certain situations, it is far better to fight fire with water, before one resorts to fighting fire with fire. I believe this situation calls for a good dose of water first. Cool it down, and we'll see where we go from there.

You see, this is really only a minor matter. But minor matters have an uncanny knack of becoming serious issues. And if rumours spread beyond the walls of the convent that Sister Francesca Of The Birds had been involved in a betting scam ...

It could jeopardise our whole drive for canonisation, and I'm sure you'll agree, having a saint in the neighbourhood would be beneficial to all of us ...

— So what do you suggest, Reverend Mother?

— Well maybe we could arrange a meeting between Brother Scully and Sister Claire this coming weekend with a view to discussing the proposed Christmas Concert. In the meantime, maybe you could have a gentle chat with Brother Scully, highlighting the implications of this misunderstanding. Then it would only be a matter of Brother Scully setting Sister Claire straight regarding Sister Francesca Of The Birds' involvement in the pigeon race ...

— A great idea, Reverend Mother. I will speak with Brother Scully this afternoon. And don't worry, I'll keep in mind what you said about, slowly, slowly catchy donkey.

— Not donkey! Monkey!

— Monkey? Donkey? Whatever ...

I will deal with it tactfully. Leave it with me, Reverend Mother. Leave it with me.

— In the meantime, Head Brother, I am absolutely delighted about
   your suggestion for a Combined Schools' Christmas Concert,
   and we look forward to working closely with you in the future ...

Word circulated around the monastery that an important phone call
had come from Reverend Mother of St Joseph's Convent that Holy
Thursday morning, so when Brother Scully was summoned to Bossman
Begley's office he assumed the permission for the Christmas Concert
had been granted, it would only be a matter of time before he would be
with Sister Claire again.

He bounded along the corridor, quarter-iron tipped heels hammering out a click-clack-clatter on the well-worn teak block flooring. He
paused for a moment outside the office to adjust his soutane, straighten
his sash, and with a firm rat-tat-tat-tat on the door he entered. Bossman
was seated behind his desk. Standing to his right hand side was the
Deputy who looked like a cat ready to pounce on a mouse.

— Ah, Head Brother Begley? Deputy Head Brother Lynch ...
They did not respond. By the look on their faces he knew all was not
quite right. Then Bossman got to his feet.

— The news is good, he said. — Reverend Mother has agreed to
   your proposed Combined Schools' Christmas Concert.
— Really? That's great, said Brother Scully attempting to control
   his enthusiasm.
Bossman stood there for a moment or two before he continued,
— But, we have a problem.
— Problem, echoed Brother Scully.
— I think you should take a seat ...
Brother Scully fumbled for a chair and repeated,
— Problem, Head Brother?
— Don't you act the innocent, snapped the Deputy.
— Innocent?
— You know dammed well there's a problem! And the problem is
   you, boy!
— Problem?
— Christ Almighty, man! Is there an echo in this room or what,
   roared the Deputy. — Yes! A problem!

— Please, Deputy Head Brother! Your anger is counterproductive, said Bossman.

Bossman's attempt at calming the situation seemed to aggravate the Deputy's fury.

— Counterproductive, snapped the Deputy.

Confused by the Deputy's rage, Brother Scully struggled to understand where the problem lay.

— So, he said. — The Schools' Combined Christmas Concert will go ahead, but there is a problem, Head Brother?

The Deputy rounded the desk and assuming the role of chief inquisitor, stared directly into Brother Scully's eyes,

— Does the name Sister Claire, mean anything to you?

— Ehmmm? Sister Claire? Sister Claire? Sister Claire?

Brother Scully repeated her name a number of times as if trying to recollect where he had heard it.

— Oh, Sister Claire, he said and clicked his fingers as if her name suddenly rang a faint bell of recognition. — Ah yes, the young postulant from St. Joseph's ...

— Ah, for God's sake, man! Don't insult our intelligence. You know exactly who we're talking about!

The Deputy slammed the desk with his fist.

With Reverend Mother's insistence on a gentle approach still fresh in his mind, once again Bossman attempted to calm the Deputy.

— Easy, Deputy Head Brother Lynch. Easy ...

But his call for calm was ignored. The Deputy had little control over his anger even at the best of times, but in matters concerning young Brother Scully, his natural disposition of anger tended towards blind rage.

— You know exactly who and what I am talking about, he roared. — Or do you want me to spell it out for you! I'm talking about you! You and the young nun from St Joseph's Convent in the kitchen here last Saturday night during the Eurovision Song Contest.

— I can explain, pleaded Brother Scully. — I can explain. Honestly, I can explain ...

— Explain? Explain, shouted the Deputy. — What's there to explain! That impressionable young novice told Reverend Mother everything. And Reverend Mother phoned the monastery this morning totally furious. She said that you, you, you, you ...

— Please, Deputy Head Brother Lynch. Please, let Brother Scully explain, said Bossman.

— Christ's sake, how can this thunderin' idiot explain anything!

— Calm, Deputy Head Brother! Calm! I must insist you allow Brother Scully explain ...

Now, Brother Scully, do please proceed. I'm sure there is a perfectly reasonable explanation ...

In truth, Bossman Begley was not overly concerned if the recently deceased Sister Francesca Of The Dogs or The Cats or The Rats, or whatever her name was, had been involved in some two-bit pigeon racing scam back around the time of the First World War. It was all just a big fuss about nothing, a storm in a teacup that was being blown out of proportion by a fretful Reverend Mother who had worked herself up into a tizzy. A pigeon race? What of it? Even if the saintly Sister Francesca had masterminded the greatest pigeon betting swindle of all time, who cared? Who really cared? Did the Vatican care? Did the Pope care? And the Bishop, did he care? It was a crisis of nothing. It would all be resolved as a simple misunderstanding, and everything would go back to normal, and Reverend Mother could proceed with her petition for the *Nihil Obstat*. Bossman was simply going through the motions and playing out his role of authority. So he stood erect with folded arms, looking stern and authoritative, just waiting to be entertained by young Brother Scully's blundering excuse, whatever that might be.

— Please, Brother Scully. Please do proceed ...

The Deputy was not so philosophical. He was ready for battle, his shoulders hunched forward on the desk, waiting to attack. The perspiration forming on young Brother Scully's upper lip was an indication of the intense pressure mounting inside his brain.

— Honestly, Head Brother, said Brother Scully. — You must believe

me. Sister Claire and me ...
Well, we only embraced.
— Em-braced? Em-braced, Bossman said it again. — Embraced
  what?
— We embraced each other, whispered Brother Scully.
Bossman was confused. He swayed left to right like he was disorien-
tated as his brain attempted to make some logical connection between
Brother Scully embracing a young nun in the monastery kitchen and a
racing pigeon scam that was rigged back around the time of the First
World War.
— Embraced?
— Yes, Head Brother. But it was all very innocent, Head Brother.
  Look, I'll be totally honest with you. Our lips did meet, but you
  couldn't really call it a kiss ...
Bossman leaned back on the desk as if his legs were about to give way
from under him.
— A what! A what, roared the Deputy.
— Okay, okay, I admit it! We kissed. We did kiss, and I placed my
  hand on her breast, but ...
— Jesus! You what, gasped Bossman.
— Christ Almighty, what is he talking about!
— ... well I only touched her breast on the outside of her robe. I
  didn't actually feel her flesh ...
  Swear to God, Head Brother. I didn't feel her flesh ...
— Feel-her-flesh? Jesus Christ, man. What are you saying? You
  what!
Stunned into silence by young Brother Scully's confession to his molestation of the young nun, all concerns regarding the great pigeon racing
scam of 1919 came into sharp perspective and faded to insignificance.
Bossman slowly worked his way along the desk, leaning hand over
hand as he went, like he was about to collapse in a weakness. He then
slumped down onto his leather chair and looked helplessly towards the
Deputy, who, for once, was speechless.
   Dazed and confused, and still unaware that he had revealed far too
much damning information, Brother Scully continued to explain what

had happened in the kitchen during the Eurovision Song Contest.

— You see, said Brother Scully. — We were in the kitchen preparing the tea and biscuits. Next thing Brother O'Connell came charging in, and you know how excitable he can be.

Anyway, in he charged shouting that Belgium had given Ireland nine votes. — *Nine votes! Nine votes!* He was shouting. Saying that we were way ahead of England, and I suppose with the excitement and the heat of the moment myself and Sister Claire...

— Heat! Heat-of-the-mo-ment?

So preoccupied was Brother Scully with presenting his case that he didn't notice the look of horror on the faces of his superiors.

— ...and yes I admit it. We embraced. Our lips met. We kissed. But, but, but that's all.

— What are you talking about, man!

— Myself and Sister Claire in the kitchen on the night of the Eurovision Song Con...

— Are you saying that you kissed and embraced that innocent young nun?

— I'm just trying to explain how it happened, said Brother Scully.

The blood drained from Bossman's face, but he managed to whisper,

— You embraced? Embraced and kissed? Jeeezus!

Maybe it was the anxious and confused glances exchanged between Bossman and the Deputy, or maybe it was the sight of Bossman clutching his chest and struggling for breath, or the fury in the Deputy's bulging, bloodshot eyes, but at that moment Brother Scully realised that he had revealed far more information than he should have.

— Ehm? Just trying to clear up the misunderstanding you mentioned about me and Sister Claire in the kitchen last Saturday night. Maybe our lines are a bit crossed here.

Young Brother Scully then attempted to change the subject.

— Silly me, he said. — Ah now I get it. The problem. Ah yes. The problem. I think I now know why you summoned me here. It's not because of that eh, innocent embrace I shared with Sister Claire. Reverend Mother phoned you because of what I told Sister Claire?

— Exactly! But after what you've just admitted ...

— Well I can explain what I said to Sister Claire ...

The Deputy had lost all interest in the racing pigeon scam, as his fury found sharp focus on Brother Scully's molestation of the young postulant. But young Brother Scully persisted in presenting his new defence.

— I can easily explain exactly what I said to Sister Claire, he said.

— You see, my theory that Jesus is the illegitimate son of King Herod the Great, and not the Son of God, comes from a number of years of research.

Now it's only a theory, mind ...

See if you read the gospel at face value ...

— What are you saying, man, Bossman roared, then looked helplessly to the Deputy. — What in the name of Christ Almighty is he talking about?

This latest revelation by Brother Scully was met with a further enraged glare from the Deputy.

— Jesus is the son of who? What in the name of Christ are you saying, man, shouted the Deputy.

— Did he just say that Jesus Christ is not the Son of God, gasped Bossman.

— See it all makes sense in a theoretical sorta way, explained Brother Scully. — If you take the gospel at face value, you'll see that it's the story of two families. The Holy Family and the royal family of King Herod ...

— The son of who!

It was too late when Brother Scully realised that once again he had volunteered far too much information. He stood there praying that the ground would open and swallow him up, but the damage was done. It was too late to turn back time and start again. Brother Scully made one last attempt to retrieve the situation.

— Eh? Right? So eh? You didn't call me here to explain my theory about the paternity of Christ either, said Brother Scully.

Bossman Begley slowly got to his feet.

— Christ was the illegitimate son of who, he roared.

— Eh? King Herod, whispered Brother Scully.

— No, said Bossman. — I did not summon you here because you told that young nun that Christ was the illegitimate son of King Herod.

Bossman raised his voice.

— And no! I did not summon you here because you molested that innocent young nun, in the kitchen of this very monastery, in the-heat-of-the-moment...

No, Brother Scully. No!

The reason I summoned you here today is of no consequence in the light of what you have just admitted.

I summoned you here because of some cock-and-bull story you spun about the recently deceased, and saintly I might add, Sister Francesca Of The Birds.

— Sister Francesca Of The Birds?

— Yes, Sister Francesca Of The Birds.

— What's she got to do with anything?

— I might well ask the same question, snapped Bossman. — But for some reason, while you were busy mauling that young nun, or trying to convince her that the Son of God was actually the bastard son of that scut, King Herod, you somehow managed to find the time to inform the young innocent Sister Claire that Sister Francesca Of The Birds had masterminded a betting scam involving racing pigeons back in 1919.

— Oh! Is that all, said Brother Scully. — Sur' it was Sister Claire told me about Dowcha-boy...

— Dowcha-who?

— Dowcha-boy...

— Who the hell is Dowcha-boy!

— The pigeon.

— What pigeon!

— The pigeon that won the race, explained Brother Scully.

— Fuck the pigeon, roared the Deputy, then blessed himself saying, — Pardon my French, Head Brother, but this perverted lunatic has totally overstepped the line, and my patience is at...

With a nod of his head, Bossman instantly absolved the Deputy's passion-fuelled outburst, granting him the freedom to continue with his tirade against Brother Scully.

— Who gives a fuck about some pigeon race back in the year dot, Scully! You have the gall to sit there and admit that you molested that young nun, and then you told her that Jesus is the bastard son of King Herod!

But young Brother Scully was still clutching at straws.

— Eh? If it will make it any better I can meet with Sister Claire and set her straight about the pigeon betting scam. Tell her it was a mistake on my part to suggest that the saintly Sister Francesca Of The Birds would even contemplate such a...

Bossman Begley cut short Brother Scully's mumbling.

— You will do no such thing, he shouted. — You will never see that young nun again! Christ Almighty, man! Not only did you contaminate her pure and innocent mind, but you assaulted her body and soul...

The Deputy lunged at Brother Scully and attempted to tear the collar from his throat.

— 'Tis perverts like you give this Roman collar of Christ a bad name. 'Tis handcuffs you should be wearing! You disgust me! You! You! You pervert! What are ya?

Bossman reached out and managed to deflect the Deputy's wrist just as his fist was about to connect full force down on Brother Scully's jaw.

— No, Deputy Head Brother Lynch! No!
Remember, catchy donkey! Catchy donkey!

— Fuck the donkey!

— There was no donkey, insisted Brother Scully, getting to his feet.

— Shut up, and sit down, roared the Deputy, and pushed him back down onto the chair. — Look, Head Brother, this pervert has the cheek to come in here to this office and tell us that he, he, he assaulted ...

— But I didn't assault her, he pleaded.

— How in the name of God Almighty can you say that on the one hand you embraced and kissed and mauled the breasts of a young novice, and then in the same breath say you didn't assault her.

— It was consensual.
— Cons-what-ual? There is no such thing as the consensual sexual molestation of an impressionable young nun! For Christ's sake, man!
  What sort of a nun would consent to ...
— Honestly, Head Brother ...
— How dare you speak of honesty! You, you, you ...
— Honestly, me and Sister Claire, we only ...
— Oh, it's me and Sister Claire, now is it!
— We only embraced, Head Brother ...
  Honestly, we only embraced and kissed, that's all we did ...
— Oh, is that all? Well, fair enough, so! Fair enough! Forgive me if I'm being a little bit too critical here ...
  Did you hear this, Head Brother? He says he *only* kissed and embraced that young innocent nun! Well, excuse me for suggesting that you did something wrong!
  Kissed and embraced! Kissed and embraced a young nun!
  For fuck's sakes, man! What sort of perverted brain is inside that sick skull of yours? A religious brother kissing and embracing a nun! A nun! She's soon to be a bride of Christ! A bride of Christ! Do I have to spell it out for you? Her body is the temple of the Lord! And you trying to tell me that, that, that, this, this, this sexual violation was of her own volition!
— Yes, Deputy Head Brother ...
— Think about what you're saying now, boy. Think about what you're saying ...
  Think about what you are saying before you damn her soul to the eternal burning flames of Hell! Hell! Do you hear me? Hell!
  What sort of a nun would willingly engage in a sexual act with a brother and she about to vow her life and her virginity to Christ the Almighty? A brother! A brother! Think about what you're saying! I mean if you were a pope, or a bishop or a cardinal, or even a parish priest ... I'd say something, but a brother! Is it the way that you think you are a better catch than Christ the Son of God, is that it! Is it! Is that what you're trying to say? That you, a brother, have more to offer a young nun than the Son of God

and the glorious kingdom of heaven? Is it? Is it?

— Our embrace seemed like the most natural thing at the time, Head Brother.

— Nat-ur-al! Nat-ur-al! There's nothing natural about it! Is there some twist in your brain, Scully? Molestation of a nun is the most vile and unnatural act known to man!

— But I think we're in love, Head Brother. Me and Sister Claire, we love each other.

— Love! Love! For Christ's sake, what's love got to do with anything!

Love is the last refuge of Satan!

Did they teach you nothing in the seminary!

Love is the Devil's trump card!

Brother Scully's persistent denial of guilt only served to further frustrate and infuriate Bossman Begley.

— Look Scully, the choice is yours! We can do this my way or the hard way. Confession and forgiveness is the bedrock of Christianity, and you know that. So my advice to you is to repent and promise never to do it again, and we'll have some hope of resolving this, this, this, this ...this sickening abomination!

— But we did nothing wrong, Head Brother ...

— We, roared the Deputy, then turned on Bossman, — ...this, this, this pervert needs to be taken in hand! But no! Oh no! With you it's always the kid glove approach, always the kid glove. Well the gloves are off now, Bossman!

— Deputy Head Brother Lynch, I insist you leave the office.

— Leave?

— Now, Deputy Head Brother! Now!

As ever, the unresolved animosity since Bossman's appointment as Head Brother was never too far beneath the surface of the Deputy's fury. He stomped across the office, then he turned at the door and snarled like a mad dog, his suppressed self-control released in one final ball of seething vitriol ...

— I warned you about this! On your head be it, Head-Brother-Begley!

I warned you about this, I warned there was a problem weeks ago. I warned you that this lunatic should be locked up. I warned you that this pervert should be booted out of the fuckin' Order! But did you listen to me? No!

And what did you do about it? Nothing!

You did absolutely nothing! In fact you facilitated this whole fuckin' fiasco. You and that bloody colour television, and your blasted Eurovision Song Contest! Wait 'til the Bishop hears about this. Just you wait!

— The Bishop? Hey, hold it there now one minute. I facilitated nothing!

— You did! And I warned you! It's the bloody colour television I blame for all this. I was against it from the start. But no! Oh no! You and your, *in the spirit of Vatican II.* Well by Christ, we'll see what the Vatican has to say about this!

— The Vatican?

— Yes, the Vatican!

— Hold it right there! Before you go any further, Brother Lynch ...

— It's Deputy-Head-Brother-Lynch! If you don't mind!

— Okay! Deputy-Head-Brother-Lynch!

The first question to be asked must be, whose responsibility is it that Brother Scully was permitted to be alone and unsupervised with a young nun in the kitchen on the night in question?

— Well it wasn't my idea, snapped the Deputy.

Like a poker player about to lay down a hand of aces, Bossman stood for a moment or two, his stony face emotionless, and then he said,

— Well it may not have been your idea, Deputy-Head-Brother Lynch. But you are the House Master, so ultimately it is your responsibility. Now I'm not sure, but you might find that this oversight on your part will have serious implications and far-reaching consequences for any career ambitions you may have in the future, Deputy-Head-Brother ...

— But? But? But?

— So before you start pointing the finger of accusation, you should first ...

Young Brother Scully sat there silently, painfully numb. He looked on as the Head Brother and the Deputy exposed their human ambitions from behind the thin veil of the rights and the wrongs of the unfolding crisis. A feeling of hopelessness descended upon his soul as his dreams of ever meeting Sister Claire again faded before his eyes.

Eventually, when stalemate was reached, the Deputy stormed out of the office and slammed the door behind him. Bossman slowly walked back behind his desk and sat down. The seconds stretched to minutes, before Brother Scully broke the silence.

— So, what happens now, Head Brother?

Bossman did not respond.

— Where does this leave me and Sister Claire?

Bossman leaned forward in his chair, and in a cold and controlled voice he said,

- I don't think you've heard a single word that I've said, Brother Scully. There is no you and Sister Claire. Not now! Not then! Not ever! Never!
- And the Combined Schools' Christmas Concert? Is it cancelled, Head Brother?
- Cancelled! Jesus, you'll be lucky if I don't have you thrown out of the Order! Lucky for you we always deal with this sort of depravity internally within the walls of the monastery.
- But me and Sister Claire love each other, Head Brother.
- Christ Almighty, if you carry on with that sort of gibberish, I'll have you thrown bag and baggage out of this monastery! Do you hear me, Scully! Bag and baggage! And let me tell you something for nothing, there's nothing out there beyond the monastery walls for people like you! There's no safety net in Holy Catholic Ireland for religious outcasts! There's no future out there in the big bad world for oddballs and quare-hawks that get flung out of this Order in disgrace ...
- But our embrace was an expression of our love. Surely all love must come from God ...
- Your embrace was an expression of your love? For Christ's sake! Don't you start talking God to me, Scully! D'ya hear me! God is

nowhere to be found in your depravity! You'd want to get yer head in gear, boy! You need to figure out what side yer bread is buttered on, do you hear me!

Now if you were to tell me that it was the voice of Satan tempting and taunting and enticing you into his world of flesh-filled sins, well then maybe, maybe it would go somewhere towards understanding and resolving your vile behaviour. But as long as you continue to deny any wrongdoing, well then we have a problem ... Or should I say, you have a problem.

Bossman Begley allowed Brother Scully a few moments to consider his options, then in a calculating voice he said.

— Brother Scully, maybe this whole thing can be sorted out ...
— But I did nothing wrong, Head Brother.
— Shut up and listen and think about what I'm saying ...
Now listen to me. My advice to you is repent. Confession is the greatest sacrament of them all. Repent, man! Repent! Just admit it was Satan tempting and enticing you into his world of perversion. That's always a good starting place, and we can move forward from there ...

I mean God Almighty, what evil possessed you? Think about it, man! What evil!

Brother Scully blessed himself and, searching the depths of his soul, he examined his conscience. Nowhere could he find any trace of evil in the intimacy he had shared with Sister Claire. There had been nothing corrupt, nothing sordid about their time together in the kitchen. If anything they had shared a beautiful experience of mutual innocence lost, like they had been touched by God and blessed by the Holy Spirit. It had been all beauty, light and love. Brother Scully reasoned that if all love comes from God, then what evil could be found in any aspect of love. But Bossman Begley was relentless in his interrogation.

— What evil possessed you! What evil!

Isolated and vulnerable, Brother Scully's strength of will was crushed beneath the weight of the incessant inquisition. His only escape from Bossman's constant barrage was the path of small compromise.

Brother Scully's mind was cast back to his first confession when he was a child. He remembered the agony of searching his soul for sins that had not been committed, and rather than disappoint the priest in the confessional, he would rattle out a list of imaginary sins, always beginning with,

— *I told lies, Father.*

His opening admission of telling lies would cover the fact that his confession was a total fabrication and devoid of truth. He would then continue with,

— *I stole from my mother's purse, Father.*
— *I was cruel to the cat, Father.*
— *I didn't do my homework, Father.*
— *I was disrespectful to my father, Father.*

Regardless of the gravity of any particular offence, the penance would always be the same. For the simple price of three Hail Marys he could walk away, guilt-free, with his soul cleansed of all misdemeanours and infractions of the laws of God and man.

From a very young age, Brother Scully learned that the confidentiality of the confessional gave him the freedom of conscience to mitch on his homework, steal from his mother's purse, tell a few lies and be cruel to the cat. Confession was the greatest sacrament of them all.

— What evil possessed you, Scully, roared Bossman.

So, in the full knowledge that any admission of guilt would be hollow, empty and untrue, Brother Scully crossed his fingers behind his back in secret denial, and told Bossman what he wanted to hear.

— You are right, Head Brother. I admit it. It was the voice of Satan tempting me, he said.
— Ah-ha! See there, now we're getting places. That wasn't too difficult now was it?
— Eh, no, Head Brother.
— Now tell me in your own words exactly what happened that night. Every precise detail, for you need to know the ways of Satan, so that you may learn his cunning and devious ways...and not fall into temptation again.

Now, go right to the very beginning. How did Satan instruct you to molest the young nun? Was it with his words or did he infect your thoughts?

Brother Scully had confessed himself into a corner of guilt. His only escape was to continue down the path of admitting he had carried out acts of molestation on the young Sister Claire.

— Well, man! How did Satan instruct you?

Bossman's very specific question demanded a very specific answer. Young Brother Scully realised that compromise is a slippery slope, and small compromise was indeed total compromise. So, inspired by the grand temptation of Adam by Eve with the image of the serpent twisting and coiling around the apple tree imprinted in his mind, Brother Scully gave Bossman the full confession he required.

— Satan guided my hand to the forbidden fruit, Head Brother, he said.

— Ah-ha! Just as I suspected.

Once again Bossman's direct and detailed line of enquiry was specific and leading. Suspecting that Bossman's knowledge of the female anatomy and all matters sexual was as limited as his own, Brother Scully decided to imagine what such an encounter might be like, so he proceeded to invent the details of his grand seduction of the young and innocent Sister Claire.

— And did Satan bring any pleasure to the young nun, when he took your hand in his and forced you upon that innocent bride of Christ?

— No, Head Brother…

— What?

— Eh, yes, Head Brother. He did…

— And did she resist in any way?

— Eh? No…

— What!

— Eh? Yes, she did, Head Brother. In the beginning she resisted. But I restrained her. I did. The Devil made me do it, Head Brother. The Devil made me do it…

— And what else did he make you do?

— What else did who make me do?

— Satan, man! Satan!

— What else did Satan make me do?

— Details, man! Details!

Intimidated into compliance, young Brother Scully took his direction and guidance from Bossman's line of questioning. He proceeded to spin a lustful fantasy that wound its way through every wanton debauchery known to mankind. Digging deeper into the darkest depths of his imagination, he described one act of depravity after another. And so through the intercession of Satan and the encouragement of Bossman Begley, Brother Scully proceeded to explore every bump and blemish, every crease and crevice imaginable of the young nun's body.

As afternoon crept towards evening the sound of Bossman's bellowing and desk thumping echoed around the monastery, carrying with it every debased detail of Brother Scully's imagination. Many hours were to pass before Bossman was satisfied he had extracted a full, heartfelt and contrite confession from Brother Scully. He then slowly made his way back to the far side of the desk, and sank down into his leather chair.

Young Brother Scully shifted awkwardly in his seat. It occurred to him that if the sordid details of his false confession were ever reported to Reverend Mother over in St Joseph's Convent it would present severe consequences for Sister Claire. So he broke the deafening silence and said,

— If I may just say one thing, Head Brother?

— I think you've said enough.

— Sister Claire is innocent of any wrongdoing.

— No one is innocent, said Bossman.

— She can't be held responsible for any of my thoughts or actions...

— You think not, do you?

— See my theory about Jesus being the son of King Herod the Great turned her head, and then ...

— Your theory?

— It's only a theory, Head Brother. But when I stumbled on it, I got carried away. Like I felt it had huge implications for the whole of Christianity. And I just had to tell someone. I know now it was wrong of me to impose it on the young, naive Sister Claire. See my theory ...

— Your theory? Bossman repeated.

— My theory on the paternity of Jesus ...

— Your theory, he said it again.

— Yes, Head Brother.

— Here we are, almost two thousand years since the birth of Christianity, and down through the millennia every pope, theologian and intellectual has debated every aspect of the divinity of Jesus. But yet, lo and behold, it took one lowly brother from this very monastery to unearth this earth-shattering theory that Jesus is the son of Herod the Great?

— Well, of course, I spent many the long night researching and cross-referencing the holy texts, Head Brother.

— Maybe, our humble community of brothers should be honoured by the arrival of your deep and enquiring mind to our monastery, Brother Scully ...

Brother Scully didn't detect the overt sarcastic undertones in Bossman's voice.

— Well I wouldn't go so far as to suggest that the monastery should be honoured by my presence. But ...

— Brother Scully?

— Yes, Head Brother?

— You've said enough ...

Bossman reached to the bottom drawer and placed a packet of Sweet Afton cigarettes on the desk. This surprised the young brother. Smoking had always been strictly forbidden in the seminary. It crossed Brother Scully's mind that maybe everyone is entitled to one great secret, and he felt a certain privilege that Bossman had decided to reveal his secret to him there and then that day in the office.

Bossman clumsily held the cigarette between index and middle finger, and then rotated the packet towards Brother Scully.

— No thanks. I don't smoke.

Bossman lit his cigarette, and then, leaning back in his chair, he inhaled long and deep, reddening the tip to a yellow-orange glow tinged with crimson-black, like a pinpoint of the burning inferno of Hell. He then exhaled one billowing cloud of smoke and whispered,

 — Well, maybe you should, Brother Scully. Maybe you should...

Young Brother Scully sat there watching the plaited column of smoke rise towards the ceiling, and an eerie calmness descended on the room. They sat there in silence, in the darkness, with only the cold blue moon-light streaming through the window and the glow of the cigarette picking up the details of their features.

 Bossman closed his eyes, slowly exhaled, and very quietly he began to sing. So soft was his voice that the words could not be heard, more humming than singing, more spoken than sung, each syllable haunt-ingly concealed in its own puff of smoke.

  *It was down by the Sally Gardens, my love and I did meet.*
  *She crossed the Sally Gardens with little snow-white feet.*
  *She bid me take love easy, as the leaves grow on the tree.*
  *But I was young and foolish, and with her did not agree.*

And as young Brother Scully sat there in the semi-darkened room, looking on through the haze of cigarette smoke and listening to the elderly Brother sing, two thoughts crossed his mind: maybe everybody needs a secret, and maybe Bossman Begley was only human after all.

 When the glow of the cigarette had burnt from tip to butt, Bossman stubbed it out, then placed the packet of Sweet Afton back into the bottom drawer.

 — You can go now, he said.

Then, getting to his feet, he escorted Brother Scully to the office door, and placing a fatherly hand on his shoulder he said,

 — I will speak with Reverend Mother. But it's in nobody's interest to open this can of worms, is it? Well is it?

 — Eh? No, Head Brother.

 — I've been around this monastery long enough to know that, in time, this too shall pass and will soon be forgotten. But listen to me, there is to be no communication whatsoever between you and St Joseph's Convent ever again, d'ya hear me? And if you make any attempt to contact that young nun, and I'm not talking about today or next week, I'm talking about for the rest of your living days ...

Any contact whatsoever, I swear! I swear by God Almighty!

Do you hear me? Under no circumstances are you to ...

Don't even think about it!

It was late that Holy Thursday evening when Brother Scully finally left Bossman's office. He made his way along the darkened corridors with only the hollow sound of his own footsteps for company. When he reached the sanctuary of his room he laid down on his bed, and for the first time in his life he felt truly alone.

His mind struggled to unravel the insanity of the previous five days. How could something that began so enchantingly beautiful, end so painfully grotesque? Young Brother Scully turned to his bible for comfort, but found little consolation in the holy texts. He wished he could cry but the tears just would not flow, so he threw back his head and laughed. Right through that night the shrill and mournful sound of Brother Scully's desolate laughter could be heard all around the monastery, like the wailing of a lost soul at the gates of Purgatory.

It was the darkest hour before dawn that Good Friday morn, when young Brother Scully set his bible down. By the pink glow of the rising sun beyond the rooftops along the crest of Patrick's Hill, he knew *The Changing Of The Guard* was about to begin. So he turned his chair eastward, and sat there, eyes clenched tightly shut, praying to God for the strength to resist the temptation to cast a glance towards Sister Claire's bedroom window, yet his mind flooded with thoughts of her.

Those five short days since he first met Sister Claire had stretched to a lifetime. Every second of every minute of every hour he had spent dreaming and planning and scheming, strategy after strategy, to meet her again. It was a dream that had almost become a reality, a dream now lost and gone forever. Like the darkest bereavement, all that remained was an overpowering sense of loneliness and isolation and a hollow pain of loss deep inside. He would never hear the sound of her innocent, carefree, girlish voice again. He would never see her eyes full of life and twinkling bright, or feel the soft touch of her hand. No. He would never meet Sister Claire again as long as he lived, and the pain was crucifying.

It occurred to him that over in St Joseph's Convent, Sister Claire's superiors had probably subjected her to the same gruelling inquisition.

— Oh, Jesus, no, he whispered.

He imagined the anguish she must have felt, when every graphic detail of the web of fantasy he had spun for Bossman was presented to her as evidence of her dance with the Devil. How would she ever forgive him? How would he ever explain? And still the tears just would not flow. He sat there limp and lifeless, quietly giggling to himself, waiting for *The Changing Of The Guard* to bring dawn's first rays of light creeping up over the rooftops.

Then, like a beacon to a floundering ship, a bolt of light shone out bright from Sister Claire's bedroom window, then another, and another and another...

— Flash-flash, Flash Flash. — *Good morning, Brother Scully.*

Scrambling for his light switch, young Brother Scully flicked a frantic response.

— Flash-flash, Flash Flash. — *Good morning, Sister Claire.*

Flash-flash, Flash Flash.

Flash-flash, Flash Flash.

He transmitted his message again and again, but Sister Claire had nothing further to say. Maybe she was afraid? Maybe she was angry? Maybe she felt betrayed? She had every right to be furious when confronted by the sordid details of his expedient confession to Bossman. But after everything he had been through over the previous five days, those four bolts of light from her window connected directly with his soul. It was a confirmation of her love, each flash brought with it a glimmer of hope that fuelled the fire of his determination to go on.

He did not leave his room that weekend. His absence from the refectory on Good Friday was noted, but being a day of black fast it was not commented on. Food sent to his room on Holy Saturday was returned to the kitchen untouched. Concern among the younger brothers regarding Brother Scully's state of mind prompted Bossman and the

Deputy to visit him in his room on Easter Sunday Morning.

    — All you need is time, said Bossman. — Time to rebuild your spirit and fortify your soul. Time to find and welcome the true love of God back into your life.

    — Ah, for Christ's sake, snapped the Deputy. — It's time for you to pull yerself together, man. The Easter break is coming to an end, school reopens and classes begin on Wednesday and you need to put all this nonsense behind you. For Chrisssst's ssssake ...

Then they prayed with Brother Scully, and came away reassured that all would be well.


Young Brother O'Connell visited Brother Scully's room later that night. He was shocked by what he saw. Brother Scully had deteriorated beyond recognition. Unshaven, unwashed, it was as if all life, emotion and enthusiasm had been sucked from his body. He just sat there, a shell of a man, gently rocking forwards and back in his chair, a vacant expression on his face, his eyes dead and staring into space.

    Young Brother O'Connell didn't know what to say, so he said nothing, he just stood at the foot of the bed for a few moments and then left the room. He returned later with a jar of Bovril and an electric kettle, and placed them on Brother Scully's bed.

    — You might need it for times such as this, he said.

* * *

    — *You might need it for times such as this ...*
That's all Brother O'Connell said when he placed the jar of Bovril and electric kettle on the end of the bed. Ever since that Easter Sunday back in 1970, Brother O'Connell still calls to Brother Scully's room every single day, just to look in on him and make sure that all is well.


That was a long time ago, almost fifty years ago, but young Brother O'Connell's act of kindness that night was enough to carry Brother Scully through those darkest of days. Over the years Brother Scully has often turned to Bovril when it became too difficult to face the world beyond his bedroom door.

    — Ah, but that was all a long time ago, a long time ago, alongtimeagoalongtime ...

Brother Scully's crooked fingers grip his mug of Bovril.

— A long time ago, alongtimeagoalongtimeago ...

The Angelus Bell has come and gone this Christmas Eve. Ever since mid-afternoon, when the sun bowed down behind the County Hall and buried itself beneath the western horizon, darkness has cast its cape over the city and taken control of the heavens. Brother Scully is still sitting by his window, staring out over the rooftops, domes and spires, hoping for some sign of life or a flash of light from Sister Claire's window.

His mind wanders back to that Easter all those years ago. He remembers each and every detail as if it only happened yesterday. Four whole days hidden away in his room. Four whole days of isolation. Four whole days, with not one bite of food passing his lips from Holy Thursday night right through to Easter Monday morning. Nothing but Bovril, pills and bolts of light from Sister Claire's bedroom window to keep his body and soul together.

\* \* \*

A strained silence swept the refectory when Brother Scully appeared down for breakfast that Easter Monday morning. He slowly made his way towards the cereal trolley. The tension and anxiety of the previous week was bearing down on him, squeezing and squeezing like a spring coiled tighter and tighter, ready to unwind violently at the slightest touch. All eyes turned to Bossman Begley, hoping for some gesture of reprieve that would somehow relieve the mounting pressure. But no signal came from the Bossman, no nod of acceptance, no wink of forgiveness. He just continued eating his Weetabix, while the Deputy sat there craving conflict, his eyes darting furiously left and right in his head.

Brother Scully inched his way forward, uneasy and unsure, each step intensifying the strain in his brain. That's when his friend, young Brother O'Connell stepped forward and confronted the silent conspiracy of condemnation. He raised his hands in the air and in his most sanctimonious voice he proclaimed,

— Lo and behold! Like Lazarus himself, he is risen!

Jesus we thought you'd never come down outa that room. 'Tis like the Resurrection! And on the third day, as in accordance with the scripture, he rose from the dead! Happy Easter, Brother Scully!

Again, all eyes turned to Bossman. He sat there motionless and emotionless. Young Brother O'Connell then walked the full length of the refectory and, stretching out his hand, he said,

— Good to see you up and about, Brother Scully. We were worried about you. Here, sit next to me.

He then drew a chair from the nearest table, and with the point of his elbow he nudged the two brothers left and right, pushing them aside to make room for Brother Scully to sit down.

Bossman's lips broadened to a smile, and with a nod of his head the message went out loud and clear that all was forgiven and young Brother Scully was to be welcomed back into the fold without further prejudice or sanction. There followed a communal sigh of relief and, with that, all the tension that had been wound so tight just seemed to relax, dissipate and disappear. From that moment forward it was as if the crisis of the previous week had never happened, like it had all been some bad dream, and Brother Scully's life around the monastery returned to normal.

Buffered by chatter and the clatter of cutlery, it was confirmed in Brother Scully's mind that Confession was indeed the most powerful sacrament of all. And though Bossman did not have the ecclesiastical authority to hear confession, or the power to offer absolution it didn't really matter, the process of unburdening a guilty conscience was cleansing. Because no matter what offence, real or imaginary, had been committed, once forgiveness was sought and given, the clock was turned back to zero and the slate wiped clean forever. He sat there next to his friend Brother O'Connell who was busy breaking ice and mending bridges, paving the way for Brother Scully's return back into community life with a constant stream of light-hearted prattle and chatter.

That's when Brother Scully realised that the Brotherhood was a family. It was his family, and maybe it was a dysfunctional family, but it was dysfunctional in a functional sort of way.

\* \* \*

By evening prayer that Easter Monday, the whispers around the cloisters had moved on to the latest scandal sweeping the monastery. It concerned the overfamiliar friendship that had developed between Brother Ambrose, the theology master, and a young Brother Crowley who had recently arrived from the seminary. Rumour had it that Brother Ambrose had been observed coming and going to young Brother Crowley's room late at night. The prevailing opinion laid all the blame on the skittish, younger Brother Crowley.

Once again the Deputy was on the warpath, storming in and out of Bossman's office, ranting and raving, and blaming the television for this latest outbreak of deviant behaviour.

— Don't you tell me that colour television had no hand, act or part in this depravity, Head Brother! I saw it myself with my own two eyes! The filth! Did you see the carry-on of the interval act during the Eurovision Song Contest, dancing and gyrating? Dancing! Dancing and gyrating! Don't tell me that was dancing! I know dancing and that was definitely not dancing!
Homosexuals! Homosexuals, the lot of them. Even the women, homosexuals down to the last man! And you mark my words, we never had homosexuals in Ireland before television! And colour television is a far sight more devious than black and white! I warned you! I warned you this would happen!
But would you listen! No!
And what did you do about it? Nothing!

His rant was cut short by Bossman.

— You're being hysterical, he snapped. — Maybe there is a logical and innocent reason for Brother Ambrose's late-night visits to young Brother Crowley's room ...

— Innocent! Innocent! Has the television infected your brain too? What is innocent about two grown men in a bedroom together? What's innocent about that?

— Look, Deputy Head Brother, said Bossman. — Colour television has nothing to do with it. You know as well as I know, all evil is the work of the Devil. Satan himself!

— And what is colour television, only the Devil's toolbox, shouted the Deputy.

The investigation into the late-night activities of Brother Ambrose and the young Brother Crowley was swift. Brother Ambrose made an impassioned plea for clemency, insisting that it was all just a misunderstanding. He said that the only reason he visited young Brother Crowley's room late at night was to listen to Radio Luxembourg on the transistor radio and eat Marietta biscuits. But his claim was rejected. His appeal for mercy was rebuked with a stiff warning that he might also be sent to the missions.

— Colour television! Radio Luxembourg! Marietta biscuits! What next, roared the Deputy. — What next?

Brother Scully found himself among the whisperers huddled in the cloisters passing judgement on the morality of the two accused. He nodded his head in agreement that young Brother Crowley's flighty and flirty behaviour was at the root of it all. As anticipated, it was decided by the powers that be that the young Brother Crowley would benefit from a few years in the missions.

But in truth, Brother Scully couldn't care less if Brother Crowley was stripped, whipped, or burnt at the stake for his deviant behaviour. He was just relieved that the spotlight of condemnation that had been burning so intensely down on him had shifted focus and had moved on to the latest victim.

Brother Scully appeared to settle back into community life seamlessly, but a dark desperation had taken hold of him as he battled to come to terms with the reality that he would never see Sister Claire again as long as he lived. The cold torment of loneliness infected his mind, body and soul. In the days that followed, the sound of sporadic laughter was heard coming from his room as he grieved for his lost love. But each morning the simple flicker of a light bulb shining out from St Joseph's Convent brought him one step closer towards healing the pain of helplessness.

And so began the love affair between Brother Scully and Sister

Claire, a love affair that survived and thrived down through the decades on nothing more than the flicker of a light bulb over and back between convent and monastery each morning. In the early days Brother Scully attempted to expand the relationship by broadening their vocabulary with the introduction of additional flashes of light,

- Flash-flash-flash-flash-flash-flash, Flash Flash. – *What a beautiful morning, Sister Claire.*

Or,

- Flash-flash-flash-flash, Flash Flash. – *Grey day today, Sister Claire.*

But Sister Claire always chose to keep the message simple,

- Flash-flash, Flash Flash. – *Good morning, Brother Scully.*

Sometimes on special occasions she would say,

- Flash-flash-flash, Flash Flash. – *I love you, Brother Scully.*

To which he always replied,

- Flash-flash-flash-flash. – *I love you too.*

But over the years, when the wild passion of young love had subsided and their relationship settled, their daily communication became less complicated and more simplified.

- Flash-flash, Flash Flash. – *Good morning, Brother Scully.*
- Flash-flash, Flash Flash. – *Good morning, Sister Claire.*

* * *

The hollow sound of the supper bell echoing around the monastery interrupts Brother Scully's thoughts. He sits there at his window, peering out into the sleety darkness and across the city towards St Joseph's Convent. Still no greeting light has shone out from Sister Claire's window today. His concern for her has been escalating since dawn. His mind is haunted by memories, twisting and turning and churning around his tormented brain.

Ever since the darkness of dusk descended on the city earlier this afternoon he has continued to transmit short bursts of light, but still no reply. Gradually his anxiety gives way to acceptance. He laughs at the painful loss of his innocence, and the brutal consequences of a single embrace that set his life trundling off the edge into the big black with no way back.

— Wherediditallgowrong, wherediditallgo...

For almost fifty years Brother Scully has lived with the painful wisdom that hindsight brings. He now accepts that those first few days after he had met Sister Claire were the most traumatic few days of his life.

Looking back on that time, he now knows he was neither mentally nor physically fit to return to his teaching duties while in the depths of such an emotional crisis. It was a mistake he has regretted ever since. He should have listened to his friend Brother O'Connell when he advised against it.

> — Listen to me, said Brother O'Connell. — You've been through the wars this past week. I really don't think you're in any fit state to stand in front of a class. You need to take some time off before facing back into all that ...
>
> No one would think any the worse of you. Just say you've the flu, or somethin'. I'll cover for you. Sur' my classroom is right next to yours. I'll keep an eye on your lot.

He knows he should have stayed in bed that morning, but after all that had happened over the previous few days Brother Scully was determined to be seen to have his life back on track. He knew that missing class on the first day after the Easter break would surely set tongues wagging again. So, against his friend Brother O'Connell's advice and his own better judgement, Brother Scully returned to teaching.

The memory of what happened in the classroom that day has always been confused and hazy in Brother Scully's mind. It was as if something just snapped inside his brain, and ever since, he has not been able to reassemble the exact sequence of events. Over the years he has managed to piece together some of the fragments of what unfolded that morning, but the details are vague. Sometimes Brother Scully does not recognise himself in the painful images that come to life in his mind.

He was late that morning, yet he hesitated outside the classroom, inhaled deeply, closed his eyes and counted to five. He slowly exhaled, and drawing on every ounce of strength and confidence in his body, he crashed the door open and crossed the room in full stride, then slammed his books down on the desk with a bang.

> — Right, lads! Put away the books, he shouted it out. — I have

something to tell ye, and it's important. There has been a change of plan.

It has been decided by the powers that be that our Christmas Concert will not, after all, be in collaboration with Sister Claire's class over in St Joseph's Convent...

A groan of disappointment echoed around the classroom.

— Spell collaboration!

Brother Scully shot out the question in a reflex action.

— Brudder! Brudder! Brudder! Brudder!

And clicking his fingers, he pointed in the general direction of the Parrot.

— Well, Mr Perrott?

— C-O-L-L-A-B-O-R-A-T-I-O-N, Collaboration, Brudder, squawked the Parrot.

— Good man, Mr Perrott. Good man. Now sit down...

Brother Scully remembers the fear and a feeling of panic, his strength seemed to drain from his body. He remembers making his way to the safety of the window, and leaning there against the radiator, he looked out over the city.

The rising sun had yet to burn off the morning mist, and all things familiar seemed lost in a haze of murky fog and shrouded in grey. Even St Joseph's Convent was concealed behind the billowing clouds of brewing malt belching from Murphy's stack. Then slowly he faced the class, gripping the windowsill as he turned. From the corner of his spectacles he saw the faded lyrics of Dana's Eurovision winning song still scrawled across the blackboard since before the Easter break, a painful reminder of his lost hopes and faded dreams.

— Jesus Christ, he whispered.

Not knowing what else to say he just stood there swaying from heel to toe, chewing his lower lip, polishing his spectacles, a tight smile just about hiding his pain. Eventually the silence was broken when the Parrot asked,

— No Christmas concert, Brudder?

— No, he said. — It has been decided that the Combined Schools'

Christmas Concert has been cancelled.

Christmas? What is the point? What is the point?

What-is-the-point...

Then clearing his throat, he said,

> — These past few days I have been forced to think long and hard about everything. I have trawled the depths of my conscience. I have lived through the darkest hours. I have battled with Satan himself, and by Christ, I still carry the scars.
>
> The only conclusion I've come to is ...

Confused glances darted from schoolboy to schoolboy as Brother Scully surveyed the classroom, row-by-row, desk-by-desk. Then in the voice of a broken man he whispered,

> — What-is-the-point?
>
> What-is-the-point, he said it louder.

His eyes were drawn to the plastic holy-water font by the door, starburst silver on garish blue, *Our Lady of Lourdes* on the front and *Made in China* on the back. Then further along the wall, a picture of the founding brothers of the Order, stern and sanctimonious, framed above a yellowing prayer for their beatification. Left and right of him statues and images of long dead Christian icons. And there, staring back at him from the end of the room, the Virgin Mary encased in glass, her feet crushing a serpent's head, golden roses adorning her toes, rosary beads slung between hands clasped in prayer, her compassionate eyes of mercy cast downwards, keeping watch over the banished children of Eve. There nailed to the wall above the clock, her only Son, Jesus Christ, crucified on a cross, blood-drenched and gory in all his glory. There was something vulgar about it all. Suffocating. Unable to breathe. Brother Scully tugged at his collar.

> — What is the point, he said it again. — What is the point, he shouted. — It's all a scam. Christmas is nothing but a scam!
>
> I have something to tell ye, lads. And it's important, probably the most important thing you'll ever learn from me ...
>
> Jesus Christ was not the Son of God!

A gasp of disbelief swept from desk to desk.

— No, he roared. — Jesus Christ was illegitimate ...

— Holy shit, squawked the Parrot.

— Ill-eg-it-im-ate! Brother Scully snapped out each syllable.

And maybe they didn't understand the meaning of the word, but by the deafening silence there was no doubt but they knew it was something bad and most definitely a sin.

— And who can tell me the meaning of ill-eg-it-im-ate?

Brother Scully's question was met by a solid wall of silence.

— Anybody? Mister Perrott? Illegitimate? Meaning of?

But for once the Parrot remained silent.

— Anybody? Anybody? Anybody?

Brother Scully gritted his teeth, as he paced the room, up and down, up and down like a caged wild animal.

— Anybody, he roared, his voice becoming shrill, his face reddening.

Fear crept from desk to desk.

— Ill-eg-it-im-ate! Anybody?

Brother Scully's shadow slowly moved from schoolboy to schoolboy, slinking over shoulders, copybooks and inkwells until a darkness eclipsed Christy Buckley's desk.

— Well Mister Buckley? Ill-eg-it-im-ate! Can you throw any light on the meaning of the word illegitimate?

— Eh, no ...

— No? No, Buckley? No what? No what?

A clatter to the side of Christy Buckley's head lifted him clean out of the desk and onto the floor, crumpled in a heap in the shadow of the Virgin. Brother Scully stood there towering over him, glaring and roaring.

— No, Buckley? No what? No what?

— Eh? No, Brother?

— That's more like it, Buckley!

Then reaching down, he grabbed Christy Buckley by the ear and raised him from the floor to his knees.

— On yer feet, he roared. — On yer feet! When yer addressing me, boy. Show some respect for a man of the cloth! On yer feet!

It was as if by some twisted logic, Brother Scully found relief from his own personal torment by inflicting torture on another. Christy Buckley was the nearest within arm's reach, and so, like a man possessed, Brother Scully began lashing out wildly.

— Illegitimate, Buckley? You telling me you don't know the meaning of illegitimate?

— Eh, yes, Brother?

— But sur' aren't you illegitimate yerself, Buckley?
  Aren't you raised by your mother and your uncle ...
  No father to be seen ...

Then releasing his grip on the young boy's ear, Brother Scully lodged a hail of rapid-fire sharp jabs into his ribs. Struggling to escape Brother Scully's fury, young Buckley became wedged between the desk and the wall.

— And yer mother? Sur' she never knew her father either. Yer mother is illegitimate, Buckley! Isn't she? Isn't she?
  For Christ's sake man, generations of ye Buckleys have come into this world ill-eg-it-im-ate! Isn't that right, Buckley? It's like a family tradition with ye to be born Buckley and without a father! Isn't that right, Buckley ...
  Isn't that right, Buckley? Buckley? Isn't it? Isn't it?

— Eh? I? I don't know, Brother ...

— *I don't know, Brother!* And how in the name of Christ could you know? Spell illegitimate, Buckley! Come on, thick lump! Spell it! Illegitimate!

— I-L-L-I-, he stumbled over each letter.

— No! It's E, man! E! I-L-L-E! E, man! E!

— I-L-L-E-G-E...

— No, Buckley! It's I, man! I!
  I-L-L-E-G-I, I! I!
  I-L-L-E-G-I-T-I-M-A-T-E. Illegitimate!

And a room full of dirty faces flinched as each letter was hammered home with a clenched fist to the back of Christy Buckley's skull.

— Meaning of? Meaning of? Come on, Buckley, meaning of illegit-imate!

But even if Christy Buckley knew the meaning of the word, any attempt

*B-A-S-T-A-R-D, Bastard! Right, lads!*
*Who can tell me one thing that Christy Buckley and Jesus Christ had in common?*

he made to answer was hindered by the continuing cascade of clatters to the back of his head. Then taking him by the ear, Brother Scully hauled Buckley over the desk, and dragged him backwards towards the blackboard. His violent tugging caused the soft connective flesh at his earlobe to tear. Blood began to stream down over the young boy's cheek, chin and neck...

— The word we're looking for is bastard, Buckley! Bastard!

Then raising Christy Buckley to the tips of his toes, he roared into his face.

— B-A-S-T-A-R-D, Bastard!

Right, lads! Who can tell me one thing that Christy Buckley and Jesus Christ had in common?

Anybody? Anybody?

Brother Scully marched up and down between the desks dragging young Buckley behind him by the ear.

— Anybody?

But no one dared to volunteer an answer, even the Parrot kept his beak shut and his arms tight to this side.

— Well I'll tell ye, roared Brother Scully. — Jesus Christ and Christy Buckley share one thing in common. They are both bastards.

No, I lie! They shared two things in common, cause neither of 'em are the Son of God either.

So now ye know! Jesus Christ was not the Son of God! No!

Jesus was the bastard son of King Herod the Great...

And this whole thing is a scam!

\* \* \*

And though the events of that morning are hazy and unclear in Brother Scully's mind, to this very day he is still haunted by fragmented memories. He remembers the young boy stretched to the tips of his toes and dangling by the ear, blood from the ripped flesh seeping down onto his grubby and tattered shirt collar. Sometimes he sees a room full of schoolboys staring back at him with terror in their eyes. Other times he hears the sound of his own voice echoing around inside his cranium, ranting and raving.

— Bastard! Spell it, Buckley! Spell it, man! Spell it!

Sometimes he sees a young boy, crouched defensively, curled up in a foetal position, absorbing the onslaught of full-force manly punches to the neck, head and ribs. Sometimes he sees with more clarity, young Buckley at arm's reach, being wrenched off the ground, suspended by the ear, twisting and turning this way and that.

— On yer feet, boy! On yer feet!

He remembers the squeals of pain, and the blood spurting from the ever-widening gash of torn flesh.

— Spell it, man! Spell it!

And yet, sometimes when Brother Scully looks back on the events of that morning he is unsure if it happened at all. Was it all some insane illusion of his imagination? There has always been something other-worldly about that morning, something that has somehow shielded him from the horrific reality of his own savagery. Like the effigy of the crucified Christ above the clock, sometimes it's as if Brother Scully was a mere spectator looking down on the persecution of Christy Buckley, unable to control the escalation of his own brutality.

Brother Scully has no clear recollection of how it all ended, but sometimes a shiver of fear runs the length of his spine when he considers what might have happened if his friend Brother O'Connell had not intervened.

Young Brother O'Connell was in the next classroom, preparing his choir for the Cór Fhéile. They were belting out *Trasna na dTonnta* as one voice in full harmony. Brother O'Connell was all hands in the air, swaying this way and that with all the passionate staccato movements of a maestro conducting a symphony orchestra.

> *Trasna na dtonnta, dul siar, dul siar,*
> *Slán leis an uaigneas 'is slán leis an gcian.*
> *Geal é mo chroí, agus geal í an ghrian,*
> *Geal bheith ag filleadh go hÉirinn!*
> *Chonaic mo dhóthain de Thíortha i gcéin,*
> *Ór agus airgead, saibhreas an tsaoil,*

*Éiríonn an croí 'nam le breacadh gach lae,*
*'S mé druidim le dúthaigh mo mhuintir!*

The first thing Brother O'Connell noticed was the sound of a few random stray notes filtering through the high-harmony section. There was nothing out of the ordinary in that, young boys' voices often broke without warning, especially when their vocal cords were being stretched to the limits that singing demands. He cocked his ear to one side as he attempted to identify the source. Then, flicking his finger he muted individual voices one by one, but still the offending sounds persisted. With broad gestures of his hand, Brother O'Connell proceeded to shut down whole sections of the choir, beginning with the base, then the harmony, followed by the melody section. It soon became apparent that the source of the discord was not coming from the choir at all.

— Fan nóiméad, lads! Fan nóiméad!

Hold it, lads! Hold it there lads one minute ...

Tapping his baton on the desk, Brother O'Connell called his choir to order. He stood there for a moment confused by the sound of the escalating commotion. Then a chill of concern caused his heart to stop momentarily when he realised that the interference to his harmony was in fact squeals of pain seeping through from Brother Scully's classroom next door.

— Jesus, he whispered, and hurried to investigate.

He barged into Brother Scully's classroom without knocking. The first thing that struck him was the cold, sharp atmosphere of fear that filled the room. Row after row of terror-struck, ashen-faced schoolboys. Brother Scully was on his knees, slumped on the floor by the desk crying uncontrollably, his arms hanging limp with hands outstretched like he was begging forgiveness.

That's when Brother O'Connell saw what he thought was just a heap of clothes, or an old overcoat bundled beneath the desk. But no, it was a child coiled up into a ball, cowering, whimpering, blood streaming from his ear, trickling down his neck, and smeared all over his face and clothes. A crimson stream streaked all the way across the floor in a trail of guilt that led directly to Brother Scully's bloodstained hands. Brother O'Connell asked no questions. He helped young Christy Buckley to his feet and instructed the Parrot to run to the office and get the nurse. Then he took Brother Scully by the arm and escorted him from the classroom.

* * *

The first up to the monastery that afternoon was an old man, his face tightened, his knuckles whitened.

— Bring that fucker out here, he roared. — Bring him out now!

Brother Ambrose opened the door as far as the security chain would allow.

— Brother Scully is unwell, he said. — He's in no fit condition to see visitors.

— I'm no fuckin' visitor! I'm Christy Buckley's grandfather! Bring that fucker Scully out here now!

Then he picked up a stone and sent it crashing through the common room window.

— Bring him out here or I'll break every fuckin' window in this monastery! I'll say this only one more time and one time only! Bring that fucker out here now!

A second stone shattered the library window.

— Or by Christ, I'll go in there and drag him out by the fuckin' neck, meself!

Brother Ambrose hurried into the common room and returned with a dazed Brother Scully by his side. Young Brother O'Connell was next to appear on the scene, clutching Brother Scully by the soutane he said,

— Where do you think you're taking him ...

— We must hand him over, whispered Ambrose.

— This is a monastery, a place of refuge, argued young Brother O'Connell. — We can't just hand Brother Scully over to that lunatic out there.

A third stone rattled the fanlight above the door, sending shards of coloured glass crashing in the hallway.

- Look! If we don't hand him over, he'll smash every window in the place ...
- To hell with the windows, shouted Brother O'Connell. — He can burn the place to the ground for all I care! This is a monastery! This is a sanctuary! Handing Brother Scully over would be against everything we stand for! Brother Scully is unwell, for Christ's sake ...

That's when the Deputy came storming out of the common room.

- What in the name of Christ is going on here!
- There was a problem between Brother Scully and one of the lads earlier, Deputy Head Brother, said Brother O'Connell.
- Scully? Jesus Christ what are you after doing now, Scully!

Brother Scully did not reply, he just stood there stunned and staring into space. Then another crash of glass as a stone came hurtling through the side panel.

- Jesus, shouted the Deputy.
- That's the lad's grandfather, said Ambrose, pointing in the general direction of the escalating fury outside the door.
- Bring that fucker Scully out here! I'm warning ye! Or I'll go in there and ...

The Deputy went to open the door.

- No, shouted Brother O'Connell, and he pressed the full weight of his slight frame against the door.
- Get a grip, man!
- But you can't send Brother Scully out there! He'll get the head beaten off him!
- There will be no one beating the head off no one!
  Now get out of my way, Brother O'Connell, if you know what's good for you ...
- Thanks be to God, whispered Ambrose. — At last, a voice of reason.
- You can't do this, Deputy Head Brother, pleaded Brother O'Connell, and again he attempted to block the door. — Can't

you see Scully's unwell! He'll be a lamb to the slaughter! No! Stop! No! Don't do it...

The Deputy pushed Brother O'Connell to one side, then reaching towards the door, he unhooked the security chain. He took the dazed Brother Scully by the arm and led him out onto the monastery steps. Young Brother O'Connell set off at a sprint down the corridor searching for the higher authority of Bossman Begley.

Brother Scully stood there, like a soulless corpse, his eyes glazed and vacant, his face expressionless. The Deputy stepped forward to challenge Christy Buckley's grandfather.

— What's all this commotion about, he said. — Can't you see, Brother Scully is unwell? Now I have no idea what has you so riled up, but if we all just calm down, we can sort out this problem whatever it is, in a calm and reasonable manner...

The old man's response was swift and brutal. A full-forced fist into the bridge of the Deputy's nose stretched him out flat onto the gravel.

– Get outa me way, he roared as he lunged at young Brother Scully.


Bossman Begley was having a late lunch that day. Brother O'Connell burst into the refectory, and found him still sitting there, reading the morning paper.

— Head Brother! Head Brother! Come quick! He's going to kill him!
— Who's going to kill who?
— Brother Scully!
— Brother Scully's gonna kill who!
— No! Not Brother Scully! A man outside screaming blue murder.
— Outside where?
— Outside the monastery!
— Outside this monastery?
— Yes, Head Brother. And he's gonna kill Brother Scully!
— Kill Scully? Jesus, what's that screwball after doing this time...

Bossman got to his feet, then wiping his mouth he threw his napkin down onto his plate and stormed out of the refectory muttering.

— Monastic life, me hole! A man can't have his lunch in peace in this place!

Brother O'Connell followed hot on Bossman's heels. He managed to overtake him in the corridor by the library.

— Hurry, Head Brother! Hurry! Before it's too late...

As Bossman approached the monastery door, he was surprised to find the Deputy with his hands to his face and staggering backwards in the hallway. In the confusion, it took a moment or two before Bossman noticed the blood pumping from the Deputy's nose, streaming through his shielding fingers. Red rivulets rippled across the back of his hands and soaked into the tight weave of his soutane, only to resurface at the leather-trimmed cuffs, and drop in puddle-sized crimson pools onto the terrazzo.

— Jesus, whispered Bossman, and stepped toward the door.

Outside he found young Brother Scully stretched out on the ground, his eye puffing up and changing colour to varying shades of reds and hues of purples and blues. A stream of blood ran along his stark white roman collar from the gash that had opened along the back of his skull at the point where his head connected with the cast-iron urn as he collapsed to the ground. The old man was standing over him roaring,

— ...and if I ever have to come up here to you again, I swear by
  Christ Almighty, I won't be responsible for what I'll do.

He delivered a crushing boot into the lifeless Brother Scully's ribs and cast a warning glare in the direction of Bossman. Then he shrugged his shoulders to the cold and turned and walked away.

Though still unsure of what had unfolded earlier that morning in Brother Scully's classroom, Bossman knew a storm was brewing, and it would only be a matter of time before it came crashing down on the monastery.

A call came through from the Bishop's Palace.

— The phone is hopping off the hook all morning! Nip this thing in
  the bud, the Bishop roared down the phone. — Do you hear me,
  Begley? In the bud!
  If wind of this gets into the newspapers, I swear, I swear to God
  Almighty, I'll come over there to that monastery to you and I'll,

I'll...

D'ya hear me! By Christ, I'll come over there to you and I'll, I'll...

By mid-afternoon a mob of mothers had assembled at the gates and marched on the monastery. Like a pack of hounds, they were baying for blood, Brother Scully's blood. The Deputy was confined to sickbay with a fractured cheekbone, broken nose and black eye, so Ambrose joined Bossman on the front steps.

Following the initial chaotic scenes of recrimination, and the hurling of verbal abuse, the Parrot's mother stepped forward as the self-appointed spokesperson. She told how over the previous few weeks the parents had become increasingly alarmed at the tales the boys were bringing home from school...

— ...but what happened in that classroom this morning is beyond belief!

Bad enough the children witnessing the brutal beating of young Christy Buckley...

But to be told that Jesus Christ is not the Son of God...

To be told that Jesus Christ is the bastard son of King Herod! What sort of a school are ye running up here? This is the last straw. The last straw! D'ya hear me, she shouted. — Next ye'll be teaching devil worship instead of religion! What sort of a Christian education is it at all, at all?

And what's more...

She struggled to catch her breath,

— What's more, she gasped. — This past two weeks my boy Jimmy is after getting it into his head that he is Dana. Dana! Dana, if you don't mind! The boy is only nine years of age, and he's walking around the house acting like a girl, putting slides in his hair, trying on his sister's clothes, spends half his time looking at himself in the mirror...

Singin' into a hairbrush...

— Your son thinks he's Dana, questioned Ambrose.

— Yes, she shouted. — It's not natural!

— Well I empathise with your predicament, Mrs Perrott. It sounds like a classic case of a teenage fixation with fame. It's quite a common phenomenon these days. But surely you don't believe that your son thinking he's Dana has anything to do with us here in the monastery?

— It was that lunatic Screwball Scully put the notion into his head. It's not healthy! Not healthy to be having a nine-year-old boy thinking he's a girl, even if the girl is Dana! It's not healthy! Ever since that madman Scully put them notions into my Jimmy's head, he's not been right! If his father was alive to see this ...

I found Jimmy in my bedroom on Easter Sunday morning. In my own bedroom I found him! And do you know what he was doing? Do you? Do you? Well, he was ...

She hesitated when she noticed an inquisitive silence had descended on the other mothers as they cocked a nosy ear in her direction, intrigued by what young Jimmy Perrott had been up to in his mother's bedroom the previous Easter Sunday morning.

— He was ...he was ...eh ...Well it doesn't matter what he was doing. But take my word for it, it wasn't healthy! I sent my son up here to the brothers to make a man of him, and ye're sending him back to me as a little girl! What sort of depraved education are ye giving the future men of this country?

Bossman attempted to bring calm to the situation.

— Please! Please! This I promise you. I will not stand idly by, and no stone shall remain unturned until we get to the bottom of this, he announced in his most authoritative voice. — I can assure you it's all just a big misunderstanding. We will get to the bottom of this, and it will all be explained and set to right in due course.

— *Due course*, came a voice from the crowd. — *Due course* usually means cover-up!

— Or whitewash, roared another.

— Or sweet fuck all!

There followed another chorus of roaring and shouting.

— We'll report this to the Department of Education!

— And the Guards!

— Don't mind the Guards, call the fuckin' Bishop!

The very mention of the Bishop was enough to stir Bossman into action, so there and then on the steps of the monastery he hastily organised a special meeting for parents and concerned members of the public to be convened later that very evening.

A larger than expected crowd packed into the gym that night. The cold, stark, flickering fluorescent lights set the tone for what was about to unfold. They had gathered for some straight talking. Wishy-washy beating around the bush and empty promises would not be tolerated. Bossman climbed onto the stage and immediately set about calming the fears of all those assembled. He began by reassuring them that young Brother Scully's comments regarding the paternity of Jesus had no official authorisation from the Vatican. Then he was joined by Ambrose who, in a grand display of compassion, stated categorically that there was no excuse for the brutality unleashed by Brother Scully on young Christy Buckley, and insisted that all avenues would be explored to find an agreeable way to make amends to the Buckley family. He then explained that Brother Scully had been under much strain preparing for the Schools' Christmas Concert.

— ... and young Brother Scully will be stepping down from his teaching duties immediately until further notice, he said.

Ambrose's compassionate words, backed up by his promise of action, had the desired effect. Gradually the anger abated, the storm subsided, tea and biscuits were served, order was restored and the crisis was averted.

Later that night Bossman phoned the Bishop's Palace.

— It's all under control, Your Excellency, he said. — I've managed to put a lid back on that particular can of worms. I explained the situation to the parents, and after tea and biscuits they all went home happy and reassured that it was all just one big misunderstanding.

— Good, good, said the Bishop. — By the way, I must confess I was a little hot under the collar when we spoke on the phone this morning. You'll appreciate I was worried that the Vatican would get wind of it. I mean, the last thing I need is the Papal Nuncio screaming down the phone at the Cardinal, and the Cardinal giving it to me in the neck ...

So please accept my apology and forgive my outburst...
— Of course, Your Excellency, said Bossman.

That night Bossman lay his head on the pillow and fell into a deep sleep. He slept well. In his dreams the Bishop came to the monastery, head bowed, begging forgiveness and asking Bossman if he would hear his confession. In the darkness of the confessional an endless list of venial sins were whispered, and after the Bishop's deep and heartfelt Act of Contrition, Bossman absolved him of all his sins. Then from a diamond-encrusted golden chalice, Bossman took a holy host and, raising it above his head, he uttered the words,
— Corpus Christi.
— Amen, whispered the Bishop with eyes closed and opened mouth.
A vile odour of stale wine, putrefying meat and vegetation gushed from deep in the Bishop's bowels up past his throat, and out over his mouthful of rotting teeth. A solid black line ran the full length of the Bishop's tongue from tip to tonsils. Bossman wondered if maybe the Bishop also harboured one great lie.
Bossman Begley slept well that night. His dreams were those of a righteous man.

* * *

But all that was a long time ago, and as this Christmas Eve stretches towards night, old Brother Scully becomes increasingly agitated. He continues flicking his light switch, hoping for some glimmer of life from Sister Claire's bedroom window, but still no reply. Deep in his heart and soul he knows all is not right, but rather than accept the inevitable, his mind is firmly set and locked in denial. Still clutching at straws, he attempts to control his anxiety by imagining logical and almost plausible reasons why no light shone out from St Joseph's Convent this morning. He has a vague recollection that Brother O'Connell mentioned something during the week about plans for a special Midnight Mass to be celebrated in the convent this Christmas Eve.
— Jesus, maybe that's it?
Over the years he learned not to trust his memory, but he is almost

certain that Brother O'Connell did say something about Midnight Mass in the convent. It had something to do with the newly appointed Bishop of the diocese and some news about some saint or other.

— Was there some hullabaloo about news from the Vatican? There was. I think there was. He did. I think Brother O'Connell did say somethin' about somethin'. He said something about Midnight Mass, so he did. Or did he?

But once again he doubts his memory and questions that maybe it's just a deceit of his imagination. But still he seems to have a vivid and clear memory of Brother O'Connell standing at the bedroom door a day or two ago, saying something about something...

— Maybe that's it. That could be it! Midnight Mass for the new Bishop? That must be it! That's it...

He is now convinced that Sister Claire did not flash her light this morning because she had been too preoccupied preparing for the Midnight Mass.

— That's it, he says. — And Christmas can be a funny time of the year, a funny time of the year, afunnytimeoftheyearafunny- timeofthey...

Over and over again he continues to transmit short bursts of light into the darkness. He laughs as the fear festering deep inside oozes to the surface like an open, gaping wound.


The supper bell fades to silence. Brother Scully closes his eyes and prays for peace of mind...

— Poor ol' Ambrose, poor ol' Ambrose, poorolambrosepoo...

And just like that, his mind drifts to the free-falling chaos that engulfed the monastery all those decades ago in the days following his announce- ment to the class that Jesus Christ was the bastard son of King Herod the Great.

* * *

Maybe Bossman and Ambrose had managed to reassure the parents that it had all been some misunderstanding. Maybe the Bishop was satisfied that everything was in order again, but the genie was out of the bottle and there was a growing unease among the younger members of the community.

When Brother Scully was eventually released from the mental hospital, Deputy Head Brother Lynch was still furious and stomping around the monastery. The pinched face on him, a patch concealing his swollen eye, he was venting to anyone who'd listen about Bossman's blundering. With renewed conviction he took every opportunity to barge into Bossman's office to spew more bile...

— Well I think we were lucky, argued Bossman.
— Lucky? Lucky? What's so lucky about having a mob of angry parents screaming blue murder at the monastery gates? What's so lucky about the Bishop roaring down the phone? What's so lucky about having our windows smashed? And look at my face! Just take one look at it! A black eye, broken nose and fractured cheek? What's so lucky about that?
— Well, we were lucky we managed to nip it just in the nick of time, said Bossman.
— Well Jesus if that's what you call lucky! You won't be so lucky next time!
— Next time?
— Yes! The next time! I warned you about this ever since you brought that colour television into this monastery...
— For God's sake! Would you ever give over? This has nothing to do with the colour television. Clearly young Brother Scully is going through a crisis of faith. And we didn't intervene soon enough.
— Crisis of faith! I'll give him crisis of faith!
— Well I think it'd be more in your line to show compassion, Deputy Head Brother...
— Compassion?
  You've your head buried so deep in the sand, Head Brother, you can't see what's happening! There's a revolution going on!
— A revolution? I think you're being a bit dramatic...
— Can't you see, ever since television, the sleeping giant that is the masses has woken up right across the world and they're overthrowing the Old Order.

— What are you talking about...
— It's true, there's a New World Order coming! And if television has anything to do with it, there'll be no place for people like us in it...
— Get a grip, Deputy Head Brother. The Church is two thousand years old. It would take more than a magic lantern with a few electric wires sticking out the back to destabilise the Church.
— But don't you see, Head Brother, television is a product of the masses, for the masses? It speaks directly to the masses.
  For the first time in the history of mankind, God has been cut out of mass communication! Television sidesteps the Church. It sidesteps God. And the message it's spouting all day every day is, — *God is dead!*
  Believe me, Head Brother, the time will come, maybe even in our lifetime, when the churches will be empty, and baptism, communion, confirmation and confession will become things of the past. Shops will be open on Sundays. And Good Friday will be a day of drunken debauchery. It'll be like St Patrick's Day except worse!
— Nonsense! Children will still have to go to school...
— Schools will be godless places, without even as much as a prayer!
— For God's sake. People will still have to bury their dead!
— Mark my words, Bossman. The time will come when they'll be throwing the dead into a hole in the ground without a priest to bless their eternal souls. We will all be redundant! The Church will be redundant!
— You need to calm down, Deputy Head Brother! You're speaking pure hysterical nonsense!
— But it's true! It's true! The Church as we know it is over. Finished, unless we step in and do something about it. Television will be the new God. Mark my words, by the turn of the century, the world will have turned its back on the Church to face their television sets. Can't you see it, Head Brother? Television is the anti-Christ we have all been warned about!
— Look, Deputy-Head-Brother-Lynch, we will all be dead and

buried by the turn of the new century. I can only deal with the present.

— The present! The present! This is exactly what I'm saying. For thousands of years we have been watching, waiting, guarding against a cloven-footed Satan with two horns protruding from his skull. We're living in the past, Head Brother. Satan stalks the land. He walks among us. Television! Television with its two-pronged rabbit-eared aerial, like the horns of Satan perched on top! Television is Lucifer himself.

— Ah for Christ's sake, there'll be plenty of time to deal with Satan! But right now we need to worry about young Brother Scully. We need to determine if he is having a crisis of faith, or if it's all just some emotional crisis ...

— Next you'll be giving him a medal! A medal for madness! I think he should have his arse kicked out of the Order, or at least sent to the missions for a few years. Might help him refocus...

— Maybe you are right, Deputy Head Brother. Maybe you're right. But I still have hope and faith in Brother Scully's potential, so I have decided that Ambrose should speak with him, before we take any further action.

— Ambrose? Radio Luxembourg and Marietta biscuits Ambrose? For Christ's sake, Head Brother! Would you ever just wake up! This is a crisis, much larger than a row with an angry parent outside the monastery door. This is a crisis of global proportion! What we are experiencing is only the sprinkle of a rain shower before the lightning storm ...

— Just give over, will you? Just give over! I would like Ambrose to speak with young Brother Scully and that's my final word on the matter.

— Sure Ambrose is as bad as the other fella, with his late-night bedroom visits to the new vocations. Radio Luxembourg and Marietta biscuits me hole!

— Look Ambrose is a master of theology, and his expertise will be invaluable in dealing with the crisis of faith facing Brother Scully.

— Jesus! That lunatic Scully needs to be locked up in a madhouse, not a monastery!

Bossman chose to ignore the Deputy's blatant disregard for his authority, and asked,

— Where is Ambrose now?

— I don't know, he snapped, and turned to leave the office.

But Bossman was not about to tolerate any further disrespect, so he reined the Deputy in.

— Eh? Deputy Head Brother Lynch?

— Yes, Head Brother!

The Deputy stood by the door rigid with anger.

— Eh? Deputy Head Brother Lynch? Would you please find Brother Ambrose and ask him to come and see me. I wish to speak with him ...

Now, Deputy Head Brother! Now ...

— Theology? Codology, he muttered and slammed the door behind him.

He found Ambrose in the herb garden, and proceeded to rant for a full fifteen minutes about Bossman's botched handling of the Brother Scully crisis.

— Compassion! Compassion! What that lunatic Scully needs is a good boot up the hole!

And, as if as an afterthought, he mentioned to Ambrose that Bossman wished to speak with him.

— What! Bossman wants to speak to me?

— Yes, he's in his office.

— Oh, Jesus! Why didn't you tell me ...

— I'm telling you now, amn't I!

Ambrose's bulbous body waddled off at a trot, through the green house for a short cut, in the direction of the monastery. By the time he reached Bossman's office he was flustered, red-faced, and on the defensive.

— I know what you're going to ask of me, Head Brother, so I just want to put it on record, that I am not the right man for the job, he stated his position clearly.

— You've been talking to Deputy Head Brother Lynch, I see?

— So what if I have, he said. — I have two eyes and ears of my own. I can see what's going on around the monastery. Look, I have championed young Brother Scully since his days in the seminary. Without doubt he was my brightest student. I even suggested he might make Superior General of the Order one day. But something has flipped in his mind.

So for the record, I wish to state my position clearly. I believe Brother Scully has become a dangerous and destructive force in the monastery. His presence here is detrimental to the very survival of our community. I don't think you fully appreciate the level of unease his behaviour is causing, especially among the younger brothers.

Bossman sat there listening attentively, absorbing the heat from Ambrose's concerns.

— You can rest assured, Head Brother, he continued, — I am fully aware of my role as counsellor to members of this community who find themselves in a crisis of faith and those experiencing difficulty with their vocation, but Brother Scully has gone beyond any help that I have to offer. There comes a time when enough is enough, and tough decisions must be made, Head Brother.

When Brother Ambrose said all he had to say, Bossman stretched out his hand and pointing to the chair he calmly said,

— Please, Brother Ambrose, take a seat ...

Look, I know, Brother Scully's recent behaviour has been, how should I put it, eh? Somewhat odd ...

— It is more than odd behaviour, argued Ambrose. — I've been a member of this community all of my life, and I've seen many odd things in those years. And believe me, this is not a simple case of Brother Scully going through a crisis of faith! No! No! No! This is something far more insidious and sinister.

I mean, what about his mad demonic laughter in the chapel during the reading of the gospel the other night? I mean the Wedding Feast Of Cana was the Lord's first miracle, probably his most significant miracle, and there's Brother Scully howling his head off like a possessed hyena! In all my days I've never known a situation where a fellow brother had to be manhandled from the chapel...

— Please, Ambrose, he said softly. — I only ask that you go and speak with Brother Scully. If anyone can get to the root of his problem, you can...

— Are you commanding me to do this, Head Brother?

— No, I'm not commanding you. I am appealing to your compassionate nature. Because I believe young Brother Scully deserves our compassion...

Ambrose got to his feet and stood there for a moment, his mind weighing up his options. After due consideration, he came to the conclusion that his responsibilities outweighed his opinions, leaving him with little choice but to go and speak with young Brother Scully.

— Fair enough, he said. — I'll give it my best shot. But I'm promising nothing.

He found young Brother Scully down in the library, his presence there only detectable by the low green glow of a reading lamp from behind a stack of books. As Ambrose approached the table, Brother Scully raised his head.

— Ah, Ambrose, he said. — I suppose you were sent here to try and talk some sense into me...

— Well actually no. I have no intention of talking sense into you, as you put it. But maybe you'd like to talk to me?

— Talk to you?

— Yes, talk to me. Maybe you have some concerns or questions regarding your vocation?

— A bit late now, don't you think, Ambrose?
A few years ago when I was in the seminary, you were always the first person I went to whenever I had difficulty with the holy texts. But back then you told me I was on my own. You told me to keep my thoughts to myself! And now, after all this time, you say you want to listen to me?

Too little, too late! Don't you think?
— It's never too late, maybe I can help you ...
— Help me? Brother Scully laughed. — Help me?
And what makes you think I need your help, Ambrose?
— I won't beat around the bush ...
But when you announced to the children in that classroom that
Jesus was the bastard son of King Herod the Great, you were way
out of order.
— Out of order! Look Ambrose, we recite the Nicene Creed every
single day, and in that we are told without ambiguity that Jesus
was *begotten not made.*
I mean it's there plain and simple for all to see, he was begotten
not made. The word beget means only one thing. Look it up in
the dictionary, it means to procreate, copulate or to sire by a
man. There's nothing divine about it. And when Jesus speaks
about his father, the King of heaven, that could just as easily
have applied to King Herod the Great, who was dead at that time
and, by Jesus' reckoning, was in heaven.
— Look Brother Scully, there is a time and a place for theological
debate, but God Almighty, man, the classroom is not the place.
They are only children for Christ's sake! Innocent young children! Your actions were reckless in the extreme ...
— Is that so? Well I think it is far more reckless for us grown men
to be telling those same innocent young children that there is an
all-knowing, all-powerful God up in the sky, watching them,
judging them.
And if that isn't bad enough, we are telling those children that
every Sunday they must eat the body and blood of a man who
was brutally crucified? Sound like cannibalism to me, Ambrose.
— Ah give over will you.
— Not to mind telling those same young children that they must go
into a dark confession box every Saturday night and confess
their sins and impure thoughts to a man who in turn will pass
them on to this all knowing, all-powerful God up in the sky ...
For Christ's sake, Ambrose! Children should be encouraged to

talk to their parents, not some celibate man in a blacked-out box!
— We're Christian, we're Catholic. This is all fundamental Catholic culture ...
— Did you ever stop and think that in every classroom in this school we have an effigy of a mutilated body of a man crucified on a cross who died two thousand years ago? What sort of message are we sending out to those children? Christ Almighty, Ambrose! It's obscene! Obscene and perverse!

Did you ever stop to think that the first thing we teach every Christian child on their first day at school is, — *Who made the world? God made the world!*

Think about it ...

It's the first undisputed fact we teach them. A Christian God created this world from nothing in seven days. It's presented as an undisputed fact without fear of contradiction. Just think about it, Ambrose ...
— You need to get a grip, Brother Scully!
— So, I was right. You did come here to talk sense to me.
— No, Brother Scully. Obviously you're unhappy, and if you want to know my honest opinion? I think you are unwell.
— Unhappy? Unwell? Damned right I'm unhappy and unwell! Why wouldn't I be unhappy and unwell? I've recently realised that I've committed my life, my mind, my body, my soul, to a bloody fairy tale!

I may as well pledge a vow of poverty and celibacy to the Easter Bunny! The whole thing is a sham, a scam and a fraud. Dress it up anyway you like, Ambrose, but as a doctor of theology you know better than anyone. It's all one big conspiracy, a fairy tale that just about conceals a fascist regime at its core ...
— Look, Brother Scully. If you are going through some sort of crisis of faith ...
— Crisis? Faith? Christ's sake ...

Papal infallibility sounds more like the rule of Josef Stalin than Jesus Christ. What was it Goebbels said?

— Josef Goebbels? The Nazi? What's he got to do with anything?
Young Brother Scully picked out a book from the stack on the desk and, thumbing through the pages, he said,

> — Here, I have it here. Ah yes, let me see. Yes here it is...Goebbels, the great Nazi propagandist said, — *If you tell a big enough lie and keep repeating it, people will eventually come to believe it.*
> That's what Goebbels said. He could well have been talking about the Catholic Church. I mean, what is the church but a state built on a lie?

— For God's sake, Brother Scully! Pull yourself together man! Since when did we Christians start taking direction from the Nazis?

> — And what's more, Goebbels goes on to say, let me see? Where is it now? Here it is, here it is ...
> Goebbels goes on to say, — *It thus becomes vitally important for the State to use all of its powers to repress dissent, for the truth is the mortal enemy of the lie, and thus by extension, the truth is the greatest enemy of the State.*
> Does that sound familiar, Ambrose?
> Basically he's saying that anybody who questions the great lie must be stamped out. We call them blasphemers and then excommunicate them. In earlier times we burned them at the stake as heretics, but these days we have more subtle, but no less effective ways of shutting them up. Isn't that right, Ambrose?

— Shutting who up?

> — Questioning and dissenting voices. That's who?
> Shove them into mental homes, laundries, correctional schools. Take your pick Ambrose ...

— For Christ's sake, Brother Scully, smarten up will you? Maybe those institutions are managed by the Church, but it's society puts them there.

— And who are the guardians of all society's morality? Only the Church.

— Your head is twisted, Scully. It falls to the Church to perform duties demanded of us by society.

— Ah right, I get it. We're just acting under orders. Where did I hear that before?

— Jesus, you're not back to the Nazis again? Look Nazism was a cult! A cult that caused much pain and death to millions of people through indescribable acts of genocide. Thankfully it was a cult that failed, and failed miserably!

— Yeah well, the last time I looked at the history book, Christianity caused a fair amount of pain too you know. And as for genocide and the death of millions of people, remember the Crusades, the colonisation of the New World?

Go ask the native peoples of Africa? South America? North America? Australia? They'll tell you all about our Christian God of love. The extermination of indigenous cultures and belief systems in every continent of the world is the stock-in-trade of Christianity, for Christ's sake!

What compassionate God of creation would want us to go out and butcher, slaughter and wipe out whole cultures in his name? Especially as we're supposed to believe that our God actually created those very same cultures.

For God's sake! Wake up, Ambrose!

— Well, granted the Church has had its troubles, Brother Scully. But those were the dark old days. The world was a different place, a far more violent place. That's all ancient history ...

— All I'm saying is that the idealism of Christianity has been lost over the past two thousand years. Somewhere along the line we have moved away from helping the less fortunate, and now the main focus of Christianity is all about protecting the organisation at all costs. And when it comes to protecting the organisation, we Christians are ruthless, hell bent on world domination, even if it means destroying mankind itself. The only thing that justifies all our butchery, slaughter and oppression is that we have God on our side!

— I think you need to be careful of what you're saying, Brother Scully!

— Where do you think all our wealth and Cathedrals of gold came from? Donations from the poor? Vow of poverty, me arse!

Christ's sake, Ambrose! Wake up and smell the roses, will ya?

Christianity is a cult, but unfortunately it's a cult that succeeded! But put all that aside, I'm asking you to be honest with me, Ambrose. Tell me the truth. Do you really truthfully believe that Jesus was the Son of God?

— Without a shadow of doubt. Jesus was the Son of God, snapped Ambrose. — If you weren't so pathetic, Brother Scully, I would charge you with blasphemy.

— Blasphemy? Here we go again! Because I dared to question the great lie? Here we go again!
Jesus himself was accused of blasphemy! So when did the blasphemers become recognised as the one true faith? I'll tell you when! When, as our old friend Josef Goebbels put it, we told the lie long enough and enough people came to believe in it, that's when!

— Look Brother Scully, I think you are being deliberately provocative. Jesus is the Son of God, and no more about it! If he's not the Son of God, there'd be no point to Christianity. And if there was no Christianity, what in the name of Christ have we been doing for the past two thousand years!

— So now we're getting to the kernel of the issue!

— No, Brother Scully, we're getting nowhere.

— All I'm saying is that the question of the paternity of Jesus must be fundamental to any theological debate. Look-it, in the book of Numbers, chapter 23, verse 19, it clearly states,
    — *God is not man, nor a son of man …*

— So what's your point, Scully?

— My point is that Jesus himself stated categorically over and over again, that he is the *son of man.* The son of man! That's the very thing that the Book of Numbers insists that God would not be! And where in the New Testament does Jesus say that he is the Son of God. Nowhere! Imagine that, the four gospels tell the story of Jesus, often quoting the man himself in his own words. It tells his story, his life, his times, his philosophies, and yet not once in the four gospels does Jesus come out and plainly say, — *I Jesus am the Son of God.*
End of story! I rest my case!

— It's inferred in the gospel.
— Inferred? Inferred!
— Yes inferred. In John's gospel, Jesus says, — *I am the way, the truth, and the life. No one comes to the Father except through me.*
— What the hell does that mean? The way, the truth and the life? For God's sake, Ambrose? Where does he say that God is his father?
— Well he says, — *Don't you believe that I am in the Father, and that the Father is in me?*
— Sur' that could just as easily refer to his father King Herod the Great!

If Jesus wants me to devote my life to the belief of something as outrageous as he's the Son of God the creator of heaven and earth, he should at least have come straight out and said that he is the Son of God, and no more about it!
— Are you just pretending to be stupid, Scully? Sur' if Jesus went around publicly saying he was the Son of God, he'd have been stoned to death.
— But I thought that was God's plan in the first place. Jesus would show mankind he was God by dying for us.

Look, all I'm saying is he didn't have to say publicly he was God's Son. But the least he could have done was to say it privately to his disciples. But no, it was all that cryptic stuff. All this, go figure it out yourself lark, is only a load of aul' bollocks! And you know it!

Brother Scully closed the book with a thud.
— I would expect better from an educated man, Brother Scully. Educated by the brothers I might add, and there is no need to resort to such vulgar language.

I really haven't the time or the patience for that sort of talk, or your juvenile, round-the-garden, half-baked, ad-hoc grasp of theology. Your argument is simplistic and trite, bordering on immature and childish word play...
— Word play? Look, when Jesus was asked under oath if he was the Messiah, the Son of God, with the threat of his own crucifixion hanging over him, that was the perfect opportunity for him to

come clean and say it out straight to the city and to the world that he was the Son of God. But no! He dodged the question ...

— Jesus is the Son of God, and no more about it, Scully!

It's the cornerstone of our belief. This question has been discussed and debated by the greatest theological minds and biblical scholars for centuries. In fact, this very question almost tore the Christian Church asunder back in the fourth century, so it did. It took the Council of Nicaea to sort it out.

— The Council of Nicaea?

— Yes the Council of Nicaea, look it up, snapped Ambrose. — Constantine the Great and Alexander gathered the most scholarly, intellectual and theological minds together to resolve the issue of Jesus Christ's divinity and relationship to God the Father once and for all, and they confirmed beyond a shadow of doubt that Christ is the one true God in deity with the Father ...

— Council of Nicaea? The fourth century, Constantine and Alexander, you say?

— Look it up, Brother Scully, whispered Ambrose. — The Council of Nicaea, in the year 325 AD. Christ's sake, man. The divinity of Jesus was discussed and debated and confirmed over fifteen hundred years ago ...

So really, you need to get a grip on reality, and move on from this madness ...

Ambrose stood up to walk away, but Brother Scully reached out and, grabbing the sleeve of his soutane, he drew him close, and said in a very low but determined voice,

— If the gospel was more straightforward in its declaration of the divinity of Jesus, there would have been no need for the Council of Nicaea in the first place. You don't have to tell me about the Council of Nicaea, Ambrose. I know all about the Council of Nicaea, thank you very much.

— Well sometimes a little knowledge can be a dangerous thing.

— Look Ambrose, why do we blindly take our belief system at face value, a belief system that was defined back in the fourth century? Sur' Christ Almighty, back then they believed the sun moved around the earth! They didn't even know that America existed! Over one and a half thousand years were to pass before the bloody bicycle was invented, not to mention the magic of electricity ...

For God's sake, Ambrose, this is 1970. This is a modern world. The Russians have put a dog in space. The Americans put a man on the moon. This is the atomic age. The Americans dropped the bomb a quarter of a century ago, and here we are still taking our spiritual guidance and fundamental beliefs from a civilisation whose greatest scholars and intellectuals believed the earth was flat.

I mean, look at the state of us, for Christ's sake! Just take one look at us? Going around dressed like bloody druids. Just take one look at us, the priests, bishops, cardinals, even the pope, dressed like the ancients, with our capes and cloaks and soutanes, and funny hats, and crowns! We're going around dressed like we're from a different age! And maybe that's the problem! We are from a different age, living in the past! Dinosaurs long past our extinction date!

The whole thing is as farcical as it is blindly ritualistic. It just doesn't hold water any more, not in this modern world of travel and television. For crying out loud, Ambrose, but with the greatest respect ...

Brother Ambrose stood back, then coldly said,

— One thing I've learned over the years is when anyone says, — *with the greatest respect*, it usually means they have no respect at all.

And just for the record, Brother Scully, the term, *son of man*, does not mean *son of man*, as we understand it. The term actually refers specifically to the Messiah. And Jesus is that Messiah ... Look it up, the book of Daniel chapter 7, verse 13.

— I know all about Daniel 7:13, Ambrose. But if you took the time to read the next verse, Daniel 7:14, you will find that it says that the *son of man* would have *authority, glory and sovereign power* ...

— So what! So bloody well what, shouted Ambrose.

— Did Jesus Christ seek authority, glory or sovereign power?

— What's your point, Brother Scully!

— My point? My point is that the description of the Messiah, or the son of man, having authority, glory and sovereign power is more fitting of Adolf Hitler than Jesus Christ.

— Oh we're back to National Socialism again, are we? Next you'll be saying that Hitler is the Son of God ...

— Look, Ambrose, I couldn't give a rattling fuck if Hitler was the son of John Balls the Ragman! But if you start quoting the bible at me, I'll start quoting the bible at you!

— You're the one who's been trawling through the bible this past couple of years looking for contradictions, Brother Scully.

— All I'm asking is for you to use your brain. Just think without prejudice, Ambrose. Open your mind. Use your mind like a free-born, freethinking human being. Think with the God-given freedom of your conscience, and not with the blinkers imposed on you by some man-made religion. All I ask is for your own personal, fair, honest and informed assessment. I'm not asking you for some bloody lecture on ancient texts and theological dogma. I mean, surely be to Christ, the very fundamental basis of Christianity hinges on the divinity of Jesus. Was Jesus' father God, or was he man? And as brothers of the Christian faith, it is vital that we address this question, and not take it at face value just because a few Romans, Greeks or Turks or whatever they were, back in the year dot said so. What would they know! Back then they had a God for every change in the bloody weather!

Ambrose was not prepared for such an aggressive stance, but there was something enticing in Brother Scully's appeal to think without prejudice. His invitation to tease out the anomalies in the scripture was irresistible. Ambrose had devoted his life to teaching underprivileged boys, yet his true vocation had always been the study of the ancient holy texts. In his heart of hearts he craved the challenge of theological debate. So, like a dog gnawing on a bone, he gradually found himself being drawn ever closer to the marrow ...

Ambrose pulled a chair up to the table and sat down.

— Well, he said. — I must admit, your theory that King Herod the

*One thing I've learned over the years is when anyone says, — with the greatest respect,*
*it usually means they have no respect at all.*

Great was the father of Jesus Christ did come as a bit of a surprise. It is both interesting and challenging to say the least. Maybe you would expand on how you formed this opinion?
— It is not an opinion, said Brother Scully. — As far as I'm concerned it is a fact.
— Well in that case, maybe you'd enlighten me as to the source of your facts?
— It's all in the Testament, the New Testament.
— Really?

Young Brother Scully hesitated. This was the moment he had been waiting for ever since he had set out on his quest to discover the living Christ. For years he had hungered for an opportunity to present all the conflicting evidence he had uncovered in a no-holds-barred debate with a fully informed and respected theologian. Ambrose was that theologian, and there he was sitting across the table, ready and willing to rise to the challenge. And so the debate began.

— Well, at its very basic level, the New Testament tells the story of Jesus, his mother, Mary and his stepfather, Joseph.
— Okay, nothing new in that, said Ambrose.
— Well the gospel also tells the story of a second family ...
— A second family?
— It tells the story of the royal family of Herod.
— Go on ...
— Well the gospels begin with King Herod the Great and how he set out to kill an illegitimate child called Jesus, and so commenced a game of cat and mouse between the Herod family and the Holy Family. Jesus and his cousin, John the Baptist, were hounded by the Herod family at every turn, right throughout their lives. The story ends thirty years later when John the Baptist has his head chopped off, and not long after that his cousin, Jesus Christ, was captured and executed, killed by Herod the Great's son, Herod Antipas ...
Now the question I put to you, Ambrose, is why do you think that the almighty royal family of Herod the Great, King of Judea,

had any interest in those two misfortunate cousins?

— I can see where this is leading, said Ambrose. — But your opening presupposition is flawed. After all, Jesus and John the Baptist were not your ordinary, every-day, run-of-the-mill misfortunate cousins ...

They were divinely incarnate.

— Okay, said Brother Scully. — I would like to pose this one very simple and much neglected question.

— I'm listening, said Ambrose.

— Jesus and John the Baptist were cousins because their mothers, Elizabeth and Mary, were cousins.

— So what's your question?

— Jesus and John's paternity was said to have been facilitated by an intervention of the Holy Spirit. The question I'd like to ask is, were Jesus and John also half-brothers in the Holy Spirit?

— Interesting thesis, said Ambrose. — But you are imposing earthly parameters on a divine situation ...

— Were they half-brothers, Ambrose?

— Well, I suppose if Elizabeth became pregnant due to divine intervention of the Holy Spirit, and Mary was also conceived by the Holy Spirit, then I suppose there could be an argument to be made that John the Baptist and Jesus were half-brothers in the Holy Spirit, but really you're imposing human familial terminology on a heavenly intervention. You're just attempting to confuse the issue with your semantic hair-splitting ...

— Ah, ha, interrupted Brother Scully. — Half-brothers in the Holy Spirit? And the Holy Spirit is a fundamental part of the Holy Trinity that is God?

— Well? Eh? Yes ...

— So I ask you, Ambrose. By simple deduction, that means that John the Baptist is also a Son of God?

— I can't stand over a wild speculation such as that, Brother Scully. There are fundamental doctrinal flaws in your thesis. After all, Elizabeth was not a virgin, neither was she conceived without sin ...

— Christ's sake, Ambrose! Conceived without sin! Conceived without sin! Would you ever just listen to yourself!

What in the name of God does conceived without sin mean? What sin? The sin of conception? Since when did God deem conception a sin?

— Since the fall of man, when Adam and Eve lost their innocence in the Garden of...

— Garden of Eden? Adam and Eve! The snake! The apple! Next you'll be telling me about Goldilocks and The Three Bears. Spare me please, Ambrose...

— There is an axiom of Christian tradition that supports the point that...

— An axiom of Christian tradition? Me hole!

For God's sake, Ambrose, my suggestion that John the Baptist is also the Son of God must be a valid consideration, and you're just sidestepping it.

Is it too much of a stretch of the imagination for us to believe that God might have sent not one, but two of his Sons down to earth? One of them spent his days dressed in a camel skin loincloth, ranting around the desert like a madman, while the other half-brother was like some sort of sideshow, magic act, pulling loaves and fishes out of a basket, turning water into wine, and walking on water. Or, or, or like some snake oil charlatan curing the blind, the crippled and the insane! Think about it, Brother Ambrose?

— Are you quite finished, Scully?

— No I'm not!

Just think about it! We're supposed to believe that, for no apparent reason, after millions of years, God, the all-powerful creator of heaven and earth, suddenly felt the need to communicate directly with mankind by making two cousins, Elizabeth and Mary, pregnant...

Stop the fuckin' lights, Ambrose!

Is this what we've devoted our lives to? Christ's sake, it has got more holes in it than a sieve. Lift it up to the light and you can see right through it.

— Look, I concede that everything about the Christian faith is a stretch of the imagination, reasoned Ambrose. — But Christianity is all about believing the unbelievable. I mean if you didn't believe the unbelievable, you've no business believing in Christianity...

— You know and I know that the priests and the bishops and the archbishops and the cardinals and the popes are only human beings like you and me, Ambrose.

— Of course they are...

— And like us they are plagued with the curse of human failings, cursed by greed, vanity, lust, envy...

Think about it, Ambrose? What are these men, but high-ranking civil servants in a global empire we call the Church, it's a non-democratic, global dictatorship.

— Well I suppose it is true to say that ambition is part and parcel of being human, otherwise we'd still be living in caves...

— But here's the thing, the most powerful men in the church are among the most powerful men on this earth, and when we start believing some prehistoric notion that they are in direct communication with some all-powerful God of creation, it becomes pure farcical! But when they themselves start believing they are in direct communication with the all-powerful God of creation, well then it stops becoming farcical and becomes downright dangerous!

This is 1970 for God's sake! And our leaders are dressing like they're living in the Dark Ages, acting like witch doctors with their hellfire and brimstone, magic potions, miraculous relics, rattling bones, voodoo, burning fires of Hell, mumbo-jumbo, gobbledegook! Perched up on their magnificent, man-made altars, dripping in gold and paved in marble, their arms outstretched, ringing bells and waving incense in the air, calling out to the heavens, to some all-powerful invisible deity up in the sky, offering body and blood sacrifices to please the Gods.

For Christ's sake!

It's prehistoric, Ambrose! I mean, come on, like...

— Hold it there now one second, Brother Scully! The ritual, the faith and the practice are three quite distinct aspects of any religion. You seem to be totally hung up on the ritual...

— No, you hold it there! Look Ambrose, think about this. Last year the Pope requested that Christians throughout the world should pray for an end to the famine in Biafra.

— And what's your problem with that, Brother Scully?

— Well if God is all-knowing, and the Pope is God's man on earth and has a direct line of communication to God, well, surely be to the Lord God Almighty, one good, well-directed prayer to God from the Papal Office in the Vatican would sort the whole thing out!

— It's not for us the question the ways of God, said Ambrose.

— That's a load of rubbish, Ambrose! And you know it! I'm not questioning the ways of God! I'm questioning the ways of man!

— Before you say another word, I'd just like to point out that...

But Brother Scully reached out and, clutching Ambrose by the hand, he spoke in a cold, clipped whisper.

— Look, he said. — All I ask is that later, when you are alone, alone in your bed, or out walking in the garden, that you search for that place where your conscience is morally free from the constraints of perceived right and wrong. Free from the millennia of brain-numbing belief. Find that place where the only truth you are answerable to is your own private and personal truth, and the only honesty you rely on is the honesty of your own conscience...

Then, and only then, I beg you to question your beliefs without prejudice, search your heart and ask yourself what you really believe.

Brother Scully paused to give Ambrose time to digest and understand the challenge he had set him, and then continued.

— ...maybe we rattle off the Nicene Creed every day as a statement and endorsement of our faith, but therein you might find the great lie...

Ambrose pulled his chair close to Brother Scully.

— Ah, Jesus, we're not back to, *begotten not made,* again ... Let's get one thing straight, he said. — As a theologian, I question my belief every day of my life.

— Well maybe you should stop questioning your belief as a theologian, Ambrose. And start questioning it as a man ...

And so, once again the elder theologian and the young brother fell to battle on all aspects of God. They questioned the essence of the Holy Trinity: God the Father, God the Son and God the Holy Spirit.

— So God created the universe?

— Yes!

— And God is a composite of the Holy Trinity: Father, Son and the Holy Spirit?

— Correct!

— One God, comprising a Trinity of equals?

— That's right, said Ambrose.

— And the Holy Trinity is eternal?

— Right!

— And God created the Earth?

— Where are you going with this, Scully? God created the earth, the universe. He created everything!

— So here's the question I'd like to ask. Did the Holy Trinity of God exist before creation?

— Of course it did.

— But the Earth was created millions of years before the birth of Jesus. Yet Jesus is a fundamental part of the Holy Trinity we call God. So how could the Holy Trinity exist before the birth of Jesus? After all, Jesus was only born two thousand years ago. Or put it this way, if Jesus, God the Son, is a fundamental part of the Trinity, how could God the Son exist before the birth of the Son of God?

— Because God the Son or Jesus or whatever you want to call him is eternal, he came down to earth bringing with him the word of God.

— So, Jesus, the Son of God, existed before he was born to Mary?

— Eh? As part of the Holy Trinity, yes!
— Are you saying that God the Father always had a Son, even before the birth of Jesus? Like did Jesus have a mother in heaven before he was born on earth? If so, who was the Son of God's heavenly mother before Mary his earthly mother? Like up there in heaven is there a maternal deity, God the Mother, that we've heard nothing about? Or did Jesus Christ, the Son of Mary, just pop into existence as a brand new, fully formed deity two thousand years ago, a few billion years after creation?
— Mary wasn't just any ordinary maiden! Mary was born without sin! You've heard of the Immaculate Conception?
— Are you implying that Mary was also a God, Ambrose? Because if she was a God, you have to ask why she was surprised when the angel came and announced to her that she would be giving birth to the Son of God?
— Look, said Ambrose. – It's as simple as this. Mary was conceived without sin. And through the power of the Holy Spirit she gave birth to Jesus Christ, the Son of God, in a process that has become known as the virgin birth. That is our belief as Christians. It's as simple as that!
— Belief? For Christ's sake, would you ever just listen to yourself, Ambrose?

Let me tell you about belief! Long before Christ was even born, it was believed that Romulus, the first King of Rome, was born of a virgin and was the Son of God. And what about the Persian God Mithra? He was also supposed to have been born to a virgin mother ...
— For Christ's sake, they are pagan myths, Scully!
— For some reason you think it's fine to dismiss all pagan belief of virgin birth as mere myth and, yet, without fear of contradiction, you blindly believe the Christian myth ...

And so the debate intensified. They argued back and forth about the origins of Jesus Christ and his deity in God. When Brother Scully insisted that the details of Jesus' early life were undeniably similar to the ancient Egyptian God, Horus, Ambrose conceded to the possibility that the origins of the Virgin Mary may have been influenced by some echo of a folk memory of the cult of Isis, Horus' mother. But when Brother Scully quoted from the work of Arius, Ambrose dismissed it out of hand, claiming that Arius had been excommunicated from Christianity by Bishop Peter of Alexandria, and insisted there was nothing further to be said on that matter.

   — God took his vengeance on Arius!

   — God had nothing to do with his death, snapped Brother Scully.
     — Poisoned by Bishop Alexander is more like it!

Then Brother Scully launched a new offensive when he stated that some Jews believed that the true Son of God was Ezra, a man who walked the earth three hundred years before Jesus.

   — That's a load of rubbish, countered Ambrose. — Read the texts! Ezra never made any claim that he was the Son of God!

   — Ah, ha! My very point! Neither did Jesus! Check and mate!

   — The old trick of switching texts to win an argument might work in a first year students' debate, Brother Scully. But you're in the big league now.

Like duelling swordsmen, the two lunged at one another, thrilling in the cut and thrust of theological debate. They teased out disputed details that reached far into the past, back through the mists of time, back to the reassertion of the New Covenant of Moses, and beyond. They clashed angrily on the identity of Yeshua Bar Abba, Yeshua Ben Stada and Yeshua Ben Panthera. And when Brother Scully suggested that the Holy Trinity was no more than a concession by the monotheists to keep the polytheists on side, Brother Ambrose just shrugged his shoulders and dismissed him saying,

   — Is that the best you've got, Scully? You can do better than that...

They fell to battle once again. They argued the relevance of a God in a time before the origins of man, and teased out the essence and existence of a creator in a time before creation. They probed the existence of the universe in a time when there was nothing, just an enormous endless black emptiness that would neatly fit on a head of a pin. Eventually they found their way to the fundamental question of all.

— Was there a creator before the creation?
— If you're asking, did God exist before creation? The answer is yes. How could there be creation without a creator?
— So there was a creator in the nothingness of pre-creation.
— You are just trying to confuse the matter, Brother Scully.
— Well, did God create man in his image, or was it the other way around, did man create God in our image?
— Ah, not that old chestnut, dismissed Ambrose. — Don't insult my intelligence with that sort of trite, clichéd, amateur-night one-upmanship...

They continued late into the night, neither claiming victory nor conceding defeat. Many more hours of convoluted theological and word-contorting debate were to pass, but as night crept towards morning, the conversation drifted away from the existence of God and the divinity of Jesus and towards the fundamental essence of human nature. Gradually the elder theologian and the young brother stepped out from behind the facade of clerical catechism and spoke as men...

— ...joining the monastery was the biggest and yet the easiest decision I ever made, said Brother Scully. — To be totally honest, I'm not sure if I even knew what a vocation was. But at fourteen years of age, monastic life offered more than this boy from Barrack Buildings could ever have dreamt of...
Things like a television in the sitting room, snooker in the common room, table tennis in the games room, hurling and football every evening after school, four hot meals a day, a biscuit box that was always full, a bedroom of my own. I'm telling you, religious life sounded like Butlin's to me. It was a heaven on earth.
I mean, the house I grew up in seemed to be getting smaller every year. And me and my dad? We were never going to see eye-to-eye. I just had to get out of there. So I guess, the writing was on the wall. As I say, joining the brothers was the easiest decision I ever made.
And as for celibacy? What is celibacy to a fourteen-year-old? I

didn't even know what the word meant. Funny, but at that age, a vow to give up sweets would have been a far more difficult decision than a vow of celibacy, Brother Scully laughed.

— Interesting that you say that, said Ambrose. — I find many aspects of religious orders difficult, but celibacy has never been an issue for me. I never quite understood the big fascination about women, don't get me wrong, some of the nicest and most important people in my life have been women. Y'know, women like my mother, and my sisters. But hand on heart, I've never been tempted by women, never been drawn to them, not in that way, if you know what I mean?

And as for my vocation, I came to the conclusion a long time ago that a vocation is like a marriage, you go through your rocky patches, but you've just got to work at it. And I'm still working on mine. But to be honest, my road to religious orders was written in the stars long before I was born.

— You're saying, your vocation was preordained by God?

— God? Ambrose laughed. — God had nothing to do with my vocation. Naw, naw, naw. My vocation was preordained by my mother.

And he laughed again.

As Ambrose proceeded to share of his path to religious life, Brother Scully caught a glimpse of the man behind the soutane. Ambrose's story was a familiar one. From a small farming background, he grew up an ordinary, dirt-under-the-fingernails lad who worked the land with his family. As the second son, his birthright dictated that there would be no land for him when he came of age. Like every second son on every smallholding up and down the country, the farm would be inherited by his older brother. Ambrose was a landless country boy who became a religious brother, a country boy now concealed and encased behind a social respectability of piety and theology.

— My vocation was a lot less divinely inspired than you might expect, explained Ambrose. — It's the age-old story, my eldest brother Mick took over the farm, my younger sister Mairead moved to Dublin with her job in the civil service, got married and settled down. And my sister Julia stayed at home and looked after my parents until they died. So, like so many other second sons, it was religious orders for me, or else the boat to England. That's the way it was back in the '50s.

I often think about my sister Julia. Often wondered maybe she'd have been better off if she joined a convent?

Not been easy for Julia since my parents passed away, not easy for her at all. Living in the same house as my brother Mick and his wife and children. Y'know, two women under the one roof, two women in the one kitchen? That can't be easy for Julia. No, not easy for Julia at all, at all. She'd probably have been better off in the nuns.

Then again, sometimes I wonder if I had taken the boat to England instead of the Roman collar, would it have been a different story altogether? Ah but, my mother was praying for my vocation since before I was born, and I suppose her prayers were answered.

— Her prayers were answered? Doesn't sound like you had much of a choice, said Brother Scully.

— My mother was delighted. Proud as punch she was. Whenever I'd go home, she always insisted I wear the collar around the village.

But you know a funny thing? I always had a feeling that she was a little disappointed in me?

— Disappointed?

— Well, disappointed that I was only a brother and not a priest...

— Really, said Brother Scully.

— I suppose there's far more status in having a son a priest rather than a brother. Y'know, like when we'd be down the village and she'd be talking to the neighbours, she'd never say that I joined the brothers. Instead she used to say that I had taken Religious Orders, or she'd say something like,

— *My son the theologian.*

Funny isn't it? Something about being just a brother that didn't quite measure up? Strange thing, the vanity of pride?

I suppose it was never on the cards for me to become a priest.

— Ah well, I can see where yer mother was coming from, Brother Scully laughed. — The brothers are fairly limited when calling in favours from the Almighty ...

I suppose when it boils down to it, the brothers are the poor relations of the Catholic family ...

— The poor relation? The poor relation, laughed Ambrose. — You hit the nail bang on the head there, he said. — That's all we are, the poor relations of the Catholic family ...

Ambrose chuckled and repeated the words, poor relation, a few more times.

— What was your baptismal name before you took Ambrose as your religious name?

— You'll only laugh.

— Go on, try me, said Brother Scully.

— Right so. But you will laugh. I was christened Pius.

— Pius? You're joking?

— No seriously, I was called Pius after Pope Pius the twelfth, said Ambrose. — Like I said, preordained by my mother, and boy was she disappointed ...

And just as Ambrose predicted, Brother Scully blurted out a laugh.

— Pius? Jesus, your destiny was well and truly written on the wall long before you were born ...

They talked into the early hours, sharing their dreams and disappointments. They laughed and they sighed, and maybe tears did well up in their eyes, but not enough to say that they actually cried. It was coming close to the dawn of morn when they decided to call it a night.

As they walked along the hallways, Brother Scully suggested that Ambrose might like to join him to watch *The Changing Of The Guard*.

— ... and welcome the new dawn, he said. — It's something I do every morning. We can watch it from my bedroom window, if you like?

— I don't think that's a very good idea, said Ambrose. — Especially after the recent hullabaloo about me visiting young Brother Crowley's bedroom.

— Oh the Great Radio Luxembourg and Marietta Biscuit Scandal, Brother Scully laughed.

— The Radio Luxembourg and Marietta Biscuit Scandal? Is that what they're calling it? The Radio Luxembourg and Marietta Biscuit Scandal? Well b'the hokey ...

Ambrose's rosy cheeks broadened to a smile.

They continued their way along the corridors in darkness, the sound of their footsteps on the teak block flooring beating out a rhythm in perfect unison.

— *The Changing Of The Guard*, said Brother Scully. — That's what I call it. I watch it every single morning. Something spiritual about the rotation of the planets, don't you think? It's like each morning the slate is wiped clean, and then with the first ray of a new dawn it begins all over again ...

— You're starting to sound more like a pagan than a Christian, Ambrose smiled.

— And how bad? God knows, the pagans have been around a damned sight longer than us Christians ...

— Ah, now! Let's not go there again, said Ambrose. — But if you'll take some advice from an aul' fella, Brother Scully? It's all about belief, and sometimes you just got to believe.
I'll tell you one thing about belief. You should always question your own belief, but think twice before you go questioning another man's belief. D'you know what I'm saying ...

They stopped outside Brother Scully's room.

— You sure now you won't come in to watch *The Changing Of The Guard*? I have a jar of Bovril inside under the sink if you'd like a warmer ...

— I don't think so, Ambrose smiled. — The two of us watching the sunrise and sharing a mug of Bovril? The Deputy would have a field day. We'd both end up in the missions.

275

— ...could always blame it on the colour television, I suppose?
Again they laughed, for there's something about the stillness of night
that can bring out the silliness in men.

Ambrose reached out and placed his hands gently on Brother
Scully's arms.

> — You know, Brother Scully, you might be as mad as a box of frogs,
> but you're not as mad as they think you are ...

> — I suppose that's some sort of a back-handed compliment ...

Ambrose smiled and continued,

> — ...I enjoyed our chat. I enjoyed your company. This has been a
> very special night, Brother Scully. A very memorable night. I
> think I shall cherish the memory of this evening 'til my dying
> day ...

He then embraced Brother Scully. It seemed like the most natural
thing to do. There's something about the darkness before the dawn that
can intensify the feeling of warmth and comfort in mankind, something
about one lonely human reaching out to another in a caring embrace.
As they released, Brother Scully sensed the moist warmth of Ambrose's
lips gently brush against his cheek. They stood at arm's length, hands
clasped in a firm, manly grip.

> — You know, said Ambrose. — I remember you in the seminary. I
> knew then that you were a special one, always knew it. I always
> knew it. Good night, Brother Scully.

> — Good night, Ambrose.

Ambrose's soft chalky fingers released their grip on Brother Scully's
hand,

> — Enjoy *The Changing Of The Guard*, he said.

Then he turned and walked off into the darkness. Young Brother
Scully stood at his bedroom door and waited for the sound of the footsteps to fade into the distance.

Brother Scully sat at his window waiting for *The Changing Of The
Guard,* his thoughts were of Ambrose.

Brother Ambrose had been through the wars in recent days. The allegation of making improper advances towards the novice, Brother Crowley was a most grievous charge. Maybe Ambrose's defence, that he had only visited young Brother Crowley's room to listen to Radio Luxembourg and eat Marietta biscuits, was as futile as it was false. But seniority comes with its own privilege. It was the young Brother Crowley who would pay the ultimate price and be banished to the missions. Brother Scully wondered if Brother Crowley was just an innocent victim of an older man's infatuation? But who cared?

Who cared if young Brother Crowley was a sacrificial lamb? Did anyone really care if Ambrose and Brother Crowley had found comfort in each other's arms? Surely no all-powerful God, creator of heaven and earth could take offence in an expression of love between two lonely creatures, even if they were created in his own likeness. Could a God who had borne indifferent witness, over countless millennia, to death, war, starvation, disease, torture, injustice, inequality and all the horrific tragedies that play out each day across the globe, really care one iota about an expression of affection between two men? And maybe theirs was a love denied, a love that dared not speak its name, but surely the Christian God of love had greater concerns than to castigate two men, then cast them, body and soul, down into the burning fires of Hell for eternity just because they craved the heaven-sent need for human intimacy.

It was as if the mark of Cain had been placed on young Brother Crowley in the days leading up to his extradition to the missions. As if fearing contamination by association, he was shunned by his community of brothers. But on the morning he was to leave the monastery, young Brother Crowley took an unprecedented step. He challenged his superiors.

Brother Crowley entered the refectory, head held high. He walked with confidence towards the top table and stopped directly in front of Bossman and the Deputy. He stood there for a moment with a gaze of utter contempt until an uncomfortable silence filled the room. Then he began,

— You call this a house of God.

I ask myself what God is worshipped here?

I ask myself what is God?

Call It the sun. Call It the stars. Call It the moon.

Call It Vishnu. Call It Allah. Call It Jehovah.

Call It nature. Call It everlasting life.

Call It whatever you like. After all what is in a name?

There is only one true God with a humility that knows no bounds.

Call It what you like, It will always answer as long as you call It with respect ...

It is the responsibility of each and every one of us to find our God.

Well my God is a God of love, a God of unconditional love.

Yet all I have found in this monastery is a God of conditional love.

My God does not live within these walls,

for a love with conditions is no love at all ...

Young Brother Crowley unbuttoned and removed his soutane, then folded it carefully and placed it on the table. He turned and walked from the refectory. Brother Crowley walked out of the monastery that morning, never to return again.

For most of those present, it was the first time they had witnessed a brother just walk away from religious life. That night the whisperers in the cloisters agreed that there was something seriously defective, if not evil, in Brother Crowley. They concurred as one voice that not only his soul, but the souls of generations of his family would be damned to the blazing inferno of Hell.

That night, young Brother Scully considered his own love for Sister Claire, a love forbidden. He wondered how a God of love could set so many conditions on love. But he took comfort in the knowledge that after all the trials and upset of the previous week, he was not alone in his loneliness. He had found an understanding friend in Ambrose, a friend he could turn to in the future, a friend he could turn to in times of need. Brother Scully looked out across the city from his window and waited for *The Changing Of The Guard* to begin.

* * *

— Poor ol'Ambrose, poor ol'Ambrose, poorolambrosepoorol...
Brother Scully says it over and over again.

He looks back on that night all those years ago with the bittersweet pain that memories often bring. He remembers the disturbance the following morning, the shrill screams of young Brother O'Connell, the sound of doors opening and doors slamming shut, the whispering voices becoming loud and frantic. Then, like a cannibalising knot of cancerous cells, the expanding commotion seemed to converge in a cluster outside Deputy Head Brother Lynch's bedroom door.

— Brother Lynch! Brother Lynch! Brother Lynch!
— What? What is it, he snapped. — And it's Deputy-Head-Brother Lynch! Deputy-Head-Brother, he repeated. — Now what's your problem, Brother O'Connell?
— Ambrose! Ambrose, gasped Brother O'Connell.
— Pull yerself together, Man! What about Ambrose?
— He's ...well he's ...
— Come on, man! Spit it out! He's what!
— He's dead! Ambrose is dead ...
    Poor ol' Ambrose, he whimpered. — Poor ol' Ambrose ...
Young Brother O'Connell began to cry.

Brother O'Connell had found Ambrose in the chapel earlier that morning, hanging by the neck from the sash of his soutane. For weeks after that he would just break down and cry. Over and over he would retell the details of what happened.

— ...the chapel was in darkness. The vestibule door was locked. So I went in through the transept, and made my way down along the chapel towards the light switch. Pitch black. I was feeling my way along in the darkness from pew to pew. I could hear a soft gurgling sound. Thought it was an air lock in the old plumbing. I didn't see him in the blackness. I didn't see him hanging there. It was only when I bumped into his dangling body. Jesus God Almighty. Swear to Christ he was still alive. His legs still twitching, his fingers clutching the sash where it cut into his

279

throat, like he'd changed his mind at the last minute, and didn't want to die after all.

Couldn't find the light switch. I tried to save him. Lifted him up by the legs trying to take the pressure off his throat.

— *Don't die, Ambrose*, I was saying. — *Christ's sake! Don't die* ...

Too late. Too late. Too late. The gurgling stopped. Managed to loosen the sash from his neck. He collapsed, a dead weight down on top of me, pinning me to the ground. His eyes! Jesus his eyes! Never forget his eyes.

Bulging out of their sockets, like they were ready to pop. Whispered an Act of Contrition into his ear ...

An Act of Contrition?

An Act of bloody Contrition?

But sur' what harm could come of an Act of Contrition. What harm ...

Brother Ambrose had left a note on the altar, written in his distinctive, beautifully formed, broad sweeping strokes of penmanship. It was addressed by name to every brother in the monastery. In it Ambrose apologised for the inconvenience and distress his imminent death would cause. He explained that life with the brothers was the only life he knew, and he could not have wished to share his life with a better family of human beings.

But he had arrived at a crossroads in his vocation. He had lost his faith in the existence of a God of conditional love, so he had come to the conclusion that religious life was no longer an option for him.

He finished by saying that he was convinced that the afterlife was a man-made conceit fuelled by mankind's egotistical desire to live for-ever, and in all probability he would never see any of them again. Brother Ambrose then listed the names of every brother in the monas-tery, and signed off with a postscript,

*P.S. Please give my watch to my sister, Julia.*

When young Brother O'Connell was asked what he was doing in the chapel at that ungodly time of the morning, he explained that he often met Ambrose there before dawn to pray.

    — ...we had a special friendship, me and Ambrose, ever since my days in the seminary. He always said I was a special one...
Poor ol' Ambrose. Poor ol' Ambrose...
If only I had been a few minutes earlier...

Then young Brother O'Connell just broke down in tears again.

* * *

Old Brother Scully sips his cold Bovril, looks out over the darkened silhouette of the city and whispers,

    — Poor ol'Ambrose, poor ol'Ambrose, poorolambrosepoorol...

He has often wondered why Ambrose ended his days in such a brutal and violent way. Ambrose was a gentle soul, he could have just walked away. But then again, that was a long time ago, and life beyond the monastery gates may have been a life not worth living.

    — A long time ago, a long time ago, alongtimeagoalongtimeagoalon...

Brother Ambrose's death had a profound effect on Brother Scully; suicide is always toughest on those left behind. He was the last person to speak with Ambrose, they talked for hours that night. He remembers the last words Ambrose said, before he walked away.

    — *...I enjoyed our chat. I enjoyed your company. This has been a very special night, Brother Scully. A very memorable night. Yes, I shall cherish the memory of this evening 'til my dying day...*

Brother Scully wondered if there was anything he could have said or done that would have changed the savage brutality of Ambrose's decision to take his own life. Maybe Ambrose was trapped in a world that had no understanding of men like him, trapped in a community where he didn't fit in. Or maybe Ambrose saw the light and realised for the first time that his vocation was to the illegitimate son of a carpenter and not some divine intervention from God Almighty. Whatever the reason, with no way out, there was only one way to go.

    Later that morning at breakfast, silence filled the refectory. Inspired by young Brother Crowley when he walked out of the monastery a day or two earlier, young Brother Scully decided it was time for him to speak up and be heard. He walked all the way to the top table. He stood there for a moment unsure what to say or do. Deputy Head Brother Lynch paid him no heed and just continued eating. Eventually he raised his head from his bowl of Rice Krispies.

— Something to say, Brother Scully?

— I do, he said. — I have a lot to say.

    But today I have only one thing to say to you. The blood of Brother Ambrose is on your hands, Brother Lynch. You are a disgrace! Shame on you!

Brother Scully just stood there and repeated the words,

— Shame on you!

    Shame on you!

    Shame on you!

— Sit down, Brother Scully!

Brother Scully continued saying the words over and over, in a very quiet, measured voice.

— Shame on you!

    Shame on you!

    Shame on you!

— I said sit down, Scully!

— Shame on you!

— Sit down you mad man! Sit down!

— Shame on you!

    Shame on you!

— Sit down you lunatic! I'm warning you Scully!

But Brother Scully did not sit down. He stood there, his cold stare locked on Deputy Head Brother Lynch, repeating the words over and over and over again. That's when young Brother O'Connell got to his feet and joined Brother Scully in his chant.

— Shame on you!

    Shame on you!

He clapped his hands to the beat.

    The rhythm was picked up by the drumming of cutlery from the novices' table at the back of the refectory. Slowly the sound travelled from table to table, building in force, echoing from stone walls and vaulted ceiling.

— Sit down, Scully! I order you to sit down! I said sit, you fucking lunatic! Sit!

But the chanting became louder and louder. Deputy Head Brother Lynch got to his feet and stormed out.

Early the following morning young Brother Scully was whisked away and, once again, committed to the local mental hospital. He has no recollection of how long he was held there, nor does he remember the treatment he received, except he knows it was not a pleasant experience nor was it a happy time. Over the years he found himself incarcerated in that institution on a number of occasions, usually following some act of belligerence or an episode of heightened emotion when he'd get it into his head that he needed to see Sister Claire again. His behaviour was always interpreted as a sign of his deteriorating mental state, his anxiety always subdued by increasingly complex cocktails of medication.

\* \* \*

But all that was a long time ago. Brother Scully now lives the life of a reclusive hermit, institutionalised behind monastic walls. He seldom leaves his room, and on those rare occasions when he does, he moves about the monastery like a ghost unseen, except when he meets his old friend, Brother O'Connell, who always stops and attempts to engage.

For many years now, Brother Scully's only meaningful contact with another human being has been the flickering of lights over and back between convent and monastery each morning. Brother Scully lives for that moment when Sister Claire greets him with,

— Flash-flash, Flash Flash. — *Good morning, Brother Scully.*

But for the first time in almost fifty years, no light has shone out from her bedroom window this Christmas Eve.

A knock on the bedroom door distracts Brother Scully from his thoughts. His arthritic fingers release their grip on the cold mug of

Bovril as he places it on his bedside locker.

    — Brother Scully? You in there, Brother Scully?

He recognises the voice of his old friend Brother O'Connell, but chooses not to reply.

    — You in there, Brother Scully?

With much huffing and puffing and shuffling and fumbling, Brother O'Connell prises the door open with his zimmer frame. His spine is stooped and shoulders hunched, his footing unsure and his movement cautious. And though only a few silver-flecked strands of hair remain of his once wild shock of ginger curls, in many ways Brother O'Connell has not changed over the years. He still has that boyish sparkle of excitement in his eyes, just like he had all those years ago when he came barging into the kitchen shouting that the Belgian jury had awarded Ireland nine votes.

    Brother O'Connell's humanity has remained unchanged over the decades. He is still the caring and considerate man he has always been, for the human spirit is as constant as time itself, and kindness has a beauty all of its own that shines through the ravages of time.

    — Evening, Brother Scully, he says. — Just said I'd call in to see how you're getting on?

Down through the years Brother O'Connell has always been a loyal friend. Ever since the darkest of times, when it seemed like the whole world had turned its back, Brother O'Connell has called to Brother Scully's room every single day. He usually just stands at the door and asks a few simple questions like, — *How are you today, Brother Scully? Or, did you hear the rain last night, Brother Scully? Or, will you be coming down for dinner, Brother Scully?* Simple questions like that. Other times he relays some vital piece of breaking news, like the latest score in the county final, or the death of some Pope or other.

    Brother Scully lost all interest in small talk many years ago, so he usually just sits there smiling, saying nothing, sometimes on a good day he will engage and share a few words, but most often he just sits there repeating some jumbled gibberish.

— Funny ol' time of year is Christmas, funny ol' time, funnyoltime-
funnyoltime. Yes a funny ol' time a' the year ...

Brother O'Connell interrupts his mumbling and says,

— Shocking weather out there?

Brother Scully raises his head and smiles. He then turns his back to
Brother O'Connell and looks out into the darkness.

— Will you be coming down to join us, Brother Scully? Should be
a bit of fun this evening. The Past Pupils' Union will be down
below in the common room for a few Christmas carols. Bit of
a party. Maybe you'll come down and join us? Should be a bit
of fun ...

— I might, I might, I might, I might, mightmightmightmight-
might ...

I might do that alright ...

— Just before I came up to see you, I was talking to the new presi-
dent of the Past Pupils' Union. He was asking for you.

Brother Scully turns in his seat, his eyes widen as if to say, — *Asking
for me?*

— Yes, asking for you, so he was. Wondering how you were getting
on? He was tellin' me that you were his teacher when he was a
young lad.

James Perrott, his name? Do you remember him? Big man in the
Civil Service now so he is? Perrott? Do you remember him? Jim
Perrott? Jimmy Perrott?

Brother Scully does not reply, he sits there, his eyes vacant and expressionless.

— Anyway, he was asking for you, so he was. So, maybe you'll come
down and join us? Should be a bit of fun ...

Brother O'Connell notices the jar of Bovril on the bedside locker. It is
a little telltale sign that all may not be well with Brother Scully this
Christmas Eve.

— Can I do anything for you, he asks. — Or is there anything that
you want?

But Brother Scully just gently rocks from side to side and smiles.

Brother O'Connell stands there for a few moments, and then he says,

— Can I send up anything from the kitchen? Maybe a ham sandwich and a cup of tea or something...

Again Brother Scully just raises his eyes and smiles, then turns towards the window.

— Right-e-oh, says Brother O'Connell. — Sur' you might come down and join us below later. Should be a bit of fun. Ah, it will be a bit of fun right enough, so it will.

Brother O'Connell struggles to turn his zimmer frame in the doorway then adjusts his centre of balance.

— Merry Christmas, Brother Scully, he says. — Merry Christmas...

He shuffles off as quickly as he arrived.

Out there in the sleet-strewn darkness, Brother Scully can just about make out the familiar silhouettes of spires, domes and belfries. His eyes find focus on St Joseph's Convent. It has been a long day, and still no greeting light has shone out from Sister Claire's window. His anxiety has given way to painful acceptance, yet he continues flicking his switch, beaming bolts of light out into the night, in the hope that maybe she will reply.

With each flash he catches a glimpse of his own reflection in the window. It's a face he barely recognises. It's like the face of death looking back at him. It is old, gaunt and grey, skin stretched tight over a skull-like frame, cheeks sunken into the void of missing teeth and shrunken gums, and trenched wrinkles gathered and draped at the corners of his mouth.

— Jesus Christ, he whispers. — Tempus fugit...

It occurs to him that over all the decades, the image of Sister Claire in his mind has remained intact like the uncorrupted remains of some long dead saint, unblemished, untarnished by the curse of time. But time is a funny beast and a lot can change in fifty years.

He wonders what she might look like now? The beauty of that young novice he met in the kitchen all those years ago must be well tainted by time. He wonders if he would even recognise her. Maybe not? When he thinks of her, all he sees is the image imprinted in his brain, the youthful beauty of her veil-framed face. Tears of pained laughter stream down his cheeks when he realises that all these years he has been in love with nothing but a memory, a memory of a beauty that has long since faded.

And what about Sister Claire? What does she see when she thinks of him when she reaches for her light switch each morning? In her mind's eye is Brother Scully also forever young, in his prime, eternally fit and enthusiastic? Does she see him as she remembers him, spouting wild theories and sparking with plans and ideas? Is that what she sees when she thinks of him?

Brother Scully smiles at the painful realisation that he has lived his life physically and emotionally removed, isolated from the woman he loves. He now concedes that all the flashing light bulbs in all the world would never amount to the power of a single human touch. And all those bolts of light that had been beamed over and back between St Joseph's Convent and the monastery could never say as much as three simple words spoken.

— I love you, he whispers.
— I love you, he says it out loud.
— I love you, he shouts.

For some reason the story told to him by Sister Claire all those years ago comes to his mind again. He thinks of the tragedy of unspoken feelings that existed between Mossie The Gardener and Sister Francesca Of The Birds, and how they had shared a lifetime in love in the convent garden, yet Mossie The Gardener waited until the last possible moment, when she was on her deathbed, to hold her in his arms and tell her he loved her.

Maybe that was enough? Maybe throughout their lives they had expressed their love in so many other ways, a brush of a hand, a glance, a smile, a shared experience and wonderment at the marvels of nature? Maybe something as simple as a bee laden down with bulging nectar sacks on his way back to the hive, or the sight of a gormless springtime rabbit bounding along the lawn full of the joys of life? Maybe their love had been expressed in so many ways that Mossie The Gardener had never felt the need to utter the words, — I love you.

Yet when all that was to be seen had been seen, and all that was to be said had been said, the old gardener had the overpowering need to hold the dying nun in his arms as she breathed her last. And just at that moment before death did them part, there was nothing left to say except, — I love you.

Maybe that was enough, because sometimes, things of great importance need only to be said once, and once only.

Brother Scully sits there looking out over the city, his mind is tortured with the pain of regret. He regrets the things he said to Sister Claire that night in the kitchen all those years ago, but most of all he regrets the words that remained unspoken. He knows now that he should have told Sister Claire that he loved her.

That night when they sat beneath the mottled shade of the old cherry blossom tree, she pleaded with him to say it, but the words just did not come. He could have walked over to St Joseph's Convent the following morning, or any morning down through the decades and told Sister Claire straight to her face that he loved her. But he didn't. It was like he had been paralysed by fear. In his mind he had made that short journey across to St Joseph's Convent over and over again. He knew exactly what he would say to Sister Claire if he ever came face-to-face with her. The words have been revolving around and around inside his brain for almost fifty years.

He should have taken her by the hand and, looking deeply into her eyes, he would have told her that he loved God, but he loved her more. He could have promised to trade his soul for eternity, just to be able to share a lifetime with her. He should have reached out to her and just carried her away.

— ...would have, could have, should have ...

And it crosses his mind that the monastery was not a place of incarceration. It was not a prison. It was a place of sanctuary. No chains, no bars, no barbed wire restrained him. He had been free to walk out the gate and over to Sister Claire at any time on any day down through the decades. And for the first time in his life, Brother Scully now realises that all his plotting and scheming to meet with Sister Claire had only been a smokescreen behind which he hid from his true feelings.

— What have I done? What could I have done? What should I have done?

He sits by his window tormented by his one great regret.

But it is never too late for love, and he must do now what he should have done a long time ago. As if enlightened by the Holy Spirit, he knows he must leave his room and go over to St Joseph's Convent this very night. He must meet with Sister Claire and tell her once and for all what he should have told her all those years ago. Maybe she will ridicule him and laugh in his face. Maybe she will dismiss what he has to say as the meanderings of a senile old man, but that is the risk he must take. It is the risk he should have taken a lifetime ago.

He stretches his knee-buckling arthritis and gets to his feet. Then, leaning towards the mirror above the sink, his beady eyes study the creases and crevices of his timeworn features. His bony fingers rub against the grain of his bristled chin. A splash of cold water brings a blood-rush blush of rosy life to his cheeks. Then, dragging his old rust-encrusted razor across his face, he nicks skelps off every bump and blemish, sending streams of blood trickling down his neck. He wets back the few remaining wisps of hair on his head and, rummaging in the wardrobe, he pulls out his best soutane, the one he keeps for special occasions. It is still wrapped in dry-cleaner's cellophane, worn only once, but for the life of him he can't remember when. Then, with a spit and buff, he kicks new life into his old battered boots, bringing them to a sterling shine. Brother Scully sits on the edge of his bed for a moment of contemplation. Then slowly, with certainty, his sense of self shifts into full focus.

Gradually the truth dawns that only he alone is responsible for his own happiness. He smiles when he remembers the words of Deputy Head Brother Lynch all those years ago.

— *Life is all about happiness. And what is happiness, but a state of mind. So, if you act happy, you will be happy, it's as simple as that. It's all about denial. Denial is the most highly evolved coping mechanism known to the human mind. It's what separates man from the beasts of the field. Sur' Christ Almighty, if we didn't have denial to*

*turn to, most of us would go and throw ourselves into the flamin'*
*river!*

And it occurs to Brother Scully that Deputy Head Brother Lynch, despite all his mad fury, blind rage, bluff and bluster, may have been right about many things. Brother Scully now knows that happiness is something he has to reach deep inside himself to find. For the first time he realises that the monastery was a prison of his own making. He had lived his life locked behind the walls in his own mind, imprisoned behind the cold steel bars of his own fear. The chains that restrained him had been forged, link by link, by his own hand, and the only lies that truly deceived him were the lies he told himself. The realisation brings a pained smile to his face. But no, no more regrets. He slowly gets to his feet and moves towards his bedroom door. The fear that has always been lurking deep inside dissipates and fades with every step.

The monastery is in darkness. Brother Scully tiptoes his way towards the landing. He looks left, he looks right and, then, peeping over the banister, the only visible sign of life is the flashing of lights on the Christmas tree, four flights down. He takes the stairs, step-by-step, all the way to the ground floor.

At the far end of the corridor by the front door, a single shaft of light from the common room pierces the darkness. Brother Scully slowly makes his way towards the sound of clinking glasses, laughter and singing.

*He's making a list, Checking it twice.*
*Gonna find out who's naughty or nice.*
*Santa Claus is coming to town*

*He sees you when you're sleeping.*
*He knows when you're awake.*
*He knows if you've been bad or good.*
*So be good for goodness sake!*

*You better watch out. You better not cry.*
*You better not pout. I'm telling you why.*
*Santa Claus is coming...*

Brother Scully hesitates. He has a vague recollection of Brother O'Connell saying something earlier about a Christmas party hosted by the Past Pupils' Union. From the safety of the shadows he peers into the common room, and there's something about Christmas carols that puts his head spinning and his mind doing somersaults. He sees the glitter and tinsel, plastic trees, holly boughs, garlands of coloured paper strung up along the walls, polystyrene polar bears, cardboard penguins, an inflatable Santa with distinctly Asian features and flashing fairy lights strung up along every hook, nail and picture rail.

There, in the middle of it all, he recognises Jimmy Perrott. No longer a schoolboy, but he's still the Parrot, flapping his arms in the air and driving on the feeble voices of a handful of geriatric brothers with choice words of encouragement squawking from his beak.

— All together now!
Ohhhhhhhh!
*You better watch out. You better not cry.*
*You better not pout. I'm telling you why.*
*Santa Claus is coming to town.*

— Everybody now, chirps the Parrot. — One more time!
*He sees you when you're sleeping.*
*He knows when you're awake.*
*He knows if you've been bad or good.*
*So be good for goodness sake.*

— All together now!
Soooooo!
*You better watch out*
*You better not pout...*

The aromatic blending of mince pies, eggnog, port and brandy fill Brother Scully's senses. This symphony of sight, sound and scent, coming together seamlessly, so seasonally seductive, like some satanic serpent enticing him out of the darkness and into the warm glow of the common room. But Brother Scully will not be led into temptation. He hugs the shadow of the doorway, content to be on the outside looking in.

He sees them all gathered around a giant television screen, singing along to a You Tube Christmas Mix download. There is something predictably comforting about the sight of the Parrot, now a man on the far side of midlife, leaping around the room, shouting out the lyrics of verses so obscure that nobody else seems to know the words. It crosses Brother Scully's mind that Jimmy Perrot has changed so very little over the years.

> *With little tin horns and little toy drums.*
> *Rooty toot toots and rummy tum tums.*
> *Santa Claus is coming to town.*
> *Santa Claus is coming to town.*
> *Santa Claus is coming to town...*

— All together now, squawks the Parrot.
> *He knows if you've been bad or good,*
> *so be good for goodness sake!*
>
> *Oh! You better not pout!*
> *You better not cry,*
> *You better watch out!*
> *I'm tellin' you why...*
> *Santa Claus is comin' to town...*

At the far side of the common room Brother Scully spies his old friend Brother O'Connell, rosy-cheeked and smiling, struggling to keep time. And it's difficult not to be moved by the tragic figure of Deputy Head Brother Lynch, slouched there in the corner, still bitterly disappointed not to have been appointed Head Brother of the monastery. It had been his greatest ambition. And maybe he was a difficult man, prone to outbursts of self-righteousness in his younger days, but Deputy Head Brother Lynch had devoted his life and his loyalty to this monastery. Without doubt he would have been next in line for the post when Bossman died. But destiny dealt him a treacherous blow. There he is propped up in his wheelchair, saliva seeping from the side of his mouth, locked in suspended animation, crippled by a stroke almost thirty years ago. This man, who had always battled the evils of television, is now forced by the imbalanced scales of injustice to live out the rest of his living days in an earthbound purgatory, impotently immobile, in front of a giant television screen. Yet they all seem so happy, sing-songing along and clapping their hands. Brother Scully smiles, there is something about it all that makes him so sad.

This monastery, once a powerhouse of the city, is now no more than a waiting room at death's door. This band of brothers, who had lived in the service of God, shared everything in life, now face the certainty of death, together for eternity and yet so very much alone. Brother Scully struggles to make sense of the pointlessness of it all. He battles to hold back the laughter of melancholy that is once again threatening to take hold of him.

— Here's another one you all know, squawks the Parrot, and without missing a beat he's off in full flight.
*Dashing through the snow,*
*In a one horse open sleigh,*
*O'er the fields we go,*
*Laughing all the way.*
— Ha! Ha! Ha!
*Bells on bob tails ring.*
*Making spirits bright.*
*What fun it is to laugh and sing,*
*A sleighing song tonight...*

No one notices the flicker of Brother Scully's shadow across the golden shaft of light on the terrazzo as he scurries past the common room. He heads towards the main door, slinking from shadow to shadow as he goes. In the distance he hears the Parrot belting out the chorus as enthusiastically as ever.
— All to-get-her now! Ohhhhhhhhhhhh!
*Oh, jingle bells, jingle bells.*
*Jingle all the way.*
*Oh, what fun it is to ride,*
*In a one horse open sleigh.*
*Jingle bells, jingle bells,*

*Jingle all the way.*
*Oh, what fun it is to ride,*
*In a one horse open sleigh...*

Brother Scully steps out into the cold night and closes the monastery door behind him. Then, hunching his shoulders against the driving frozen rain, he leans into the wind and sets off down the avenue, each footstep sending a pulse of blood pumping through his veins. He's striding along, picking up speed as he goes, each step covering more ground than the previous, quarter iron heels knocking sparks off the stones. For the first time in a long time, Brother Scully is truly alive, like he's young again, like he's free, like he's driven on by life, driven on by love, driven on to hold Sister Claire in his arms once more.

At the main gate he hesitates, then, tempting fate, he casts a glance behind him to the monastery. Once a hub of power, now it stands there in all its faded glory, proud yet pointless like the barking of a toothless dog. Something about that vast house of shadows reminds him of an Edgar Allan Poe story he once read. The memory sends a shiver along his spine. There is a coldness in his heart, not the chill of anxiety but rather the icy bitterness that resentment brings. Yet, with each passing moment, all the pain and confusion and torment of the past fades, as if washed away by the clarity of the present.

The monastery gate creaks shut behind him and he hurries off across the deserted street towards St Joseph's Convent, darting from doorway to doorway as he goes.

* * *

Over in St Joseph's Convent it has been the busiest Christmas Eve in living memory. Since dawn the sisters have been frantically preparing for the big event scheduled for later this evening. It all began earlier in the week when the new Bishop phoned Reverend Mother.

— White smoke, Reverend Mother! White smoke, he said. — I have just come off the phone from the Vatican, and it's official. Yes it is official!
Sister Francesca Of The Birds has been declared Venerable by Rome.

— What? Really?

— Yes, Reverend Mother, it's true! Sister Francesca Of The Birds has been venerated by the Pope. Can you believe it? From now on she will be officially known to the world as the Venerable Sister Francesca Of The Birds.

— I can't believe it! After all these years! That's absolutely wonderful news, Your Excellency, absolutely wonderful! It's been such a long campaign...

— Almost half a century, he says.

— Almost half a century, she repeats. — My God, and how time flies...

— Well, our endeavours have paid off, says the Bishop.

— And just think of the long line of reverend mothers and bishops that went before the two of us, all those who championed Sister Francesca's cause down through the years. Pity they're not still around to enjoy the fruits of their labours, they'd be so proud of this moment...

— Thanks to the efforts of all those who went before us, Sister Francesca Of The Birds is well on her way to full sainthood, he said. — We can start printing prayer cards now, fire up the local faithful for the next phase in the campaign. Next stop beatification, then all the way to canonisation...

— After all these years, I just can't believe it...

— There's no stopping us now, Reverend Mother. No stopping us now...

Ever since Sister Francesca Of The Birds died back in 1970, each successive Reverend Mother of the convent worked hand-in-hand with each new bishop appointed to the diocese in a relentless campaign for her canonisation. Much of the credit for the latest announcement from the Vatican is due to the efforts of the recently appointed bishop. Ever since he took office a little over a year ago he has been a determined advocate for Sister Francesca's case. Like a breath of fresh air to the campaign, he has even travelled to Rome twice in the past six months to further the cause. So when he phoned St Joseph's Convent two days ago and told Reverend Mother that the Vatican had venerated Sister

Francesca Of The Birds, it came as no surprise when he suggested that he would like to mark the occasion by celebrating midnight mass on Christmas Eve in St Joseph's Convent.

— It would be our great honour, Your Excellency.
— No, Reverend Mother. It would be my privilege, said the Bishop. — Mark my words, Sister Francesca will be a saint one day ...
— Do you really think so, Your Excellency?
— Absolutely, he said. — It will take time. Maybe another fifty or sixty years, who knows, maybe a hundred years, but the ball is rolling and gathering momentum, nothing can stop us now ...
   And by the way, I think we can dispense with formality, so please, from now on there's no need to address me as, Your Excellency. Bishop will do just fine ...
— Thank you, Your Ex ...er? Bishop ...
— Now I have one further request, he said.
— Request?
— Well here's the thing, I would like to celebrate Midnight Mass this Christmas Eve in the actual room in which Sister Francesca Of The Birds died ...
— In her bedroom?
— Yes, said the Bishop. — In the room that Saint Joseph appeared. Is there a problem with that?
— Eh? No. Eh? No. No problem at all, Your Ex ...? Bishop.

Reverend Mother's reticence concealed a concern. Struck silent in a sudden surge of panic, she was gripped by the realisation of the mammoth task that lay ahead. The old accommodation wing had been abandoned decades ago.

Almost fifty years had passed since Sister Francesca Of The Birds died, and Reverend Mother was not sure if she could even identify her bedroom. And even if by some miracle she did manage to find the right room, it would be next to impossible to have it prepared within two days, in time for Midnight Mass on Christmas Eve.

The rooms in that wing had fallen to dereliction. What began as a temporary storage area had become crammed full with all sorts of junk, everything from half-used pots of paint, to broken statues, old photocopiers, overhead projectors and obsolete school machinery, bits of furniture and general odds and ends from around the convent.

Over the past thirty years the community of sisters had been in decline. The flow of new vocations had been reduced to a trickle. It was as if some greater power had just reached down from the heavens and turned the tap off. Convent life had become stagnant, strangled for want of youth, new blood and vitality. These days, all that remains of this once vibrant community is a handful of elderly nuns, most too feeble for the demands of the repetitive daily routine and rituals of religious life. It crossed Reverend Mother's mind that the remaining few sisters in the convent were far too infirm to be of any practical assistance with the transformation of Sister Francesca's old bedroom in time for Midnight Mass on Christmas Eve.

> — After all, the Bishop continued. — Now that the Vatican has offi-
> cially venerated Sister Francesca Of The Birds, her bedroom
> must be preserved intact as a sacred shrine for future genera-
> tions. When she is canonised, and trust me, she will be canon-
> ised one day, her bedroom will be renowned throughout the
> world as the site of all her miraculous cures. And the crowning
> glory, her humble little bedroom, the location of the magnificent
> and miraculous apparition by Saint Joseph.
> Sister Francesca's bedroom will become a place of great pilgrim-
> age for future generations ...

But there was no turning back the clock. The sisters of St Joseph's were the last of a dying breed. Reverend Mother wondered who would open the convent gates to welcome the pilgrims of the future. She considered a convent without nuns, and questioned if the sacred room would become a site of religious devotion, or some quirky tourist sideshow, with the chapel converted into an exhibition centre with coffee shop attached and trinkets for sale ...

> — Roll up! Roll up! Pay yer money, Take yer photograph! Buy your
> holy relic! Next stop the Blarney Stone, she whispers.
> — Pardon, said the Bishop. — Did you say something, Reverend
> Mother?
> — Eh? No. Sorry, my apologies, Bishop. I said nothing at all, just

thinking out loud ...
— Well just imagine, he said. — Midnight Mass in Venerable Sister
Francesca Of The Birds' bedroom. In the very room where Saint
Joseph appeared? It'll be magical!
I can see it now. Christmas Eve night. Darkness. A candlelit procession of sisters carrying the wine and the holy host through
the darkened halls of the convent. Then, right on the stroke of
midnight, we will unlock the door and file into the small stark
bedroom. This room of mystical power that has remained locked
and sealed for decades, now opened for the first time after all
these years, like a time capsule, revealing the true life and times
of the Venerable Sister Francesca Of The Birds.
Can you see it, Reverend Mother? The austerity of the 1970s.
Flaking paint, condensation running down the walls ...
Just imagine it? So evocative ...
A bare room, sparsely furnished. A small hard bed with a coarse
horsehair mattress and a porcelain commode underneath. A
basic wardrobe of rough-hewn wood, a bedside locker, a wash-
stand in the corner. It will look like a place of miracles. Can you
see it, Reverend Mother? Can you? A place of miracles ...
— Eh? I think so, she said.

Reverend Mother closed her eyes in silent prayer when she remem-
bered that all the old furniture had been broken up and burnt a long
time ago. But the Bishop was still busy visualising.
— A cross over the bed, her only decoration. A well-thumbed bible
on the side locker, her only diversion. Can you see it, Reverend
Mother?
Mass by candlelight, on the stroke of midnight on Christmas
Eve. What a magnificent setting. Just imagine it, a site-specific
Mass in memory of the Venerable Sister Francesca Of The Birds,
celebrated in her very own bedroom.
— Site-Specific Mass, she echoed faintly.
— Maybe we could even have a podcast.
— A what-cast?
— Podcast, Reverend Mother! A podcast!

When the Bishop finished visualising, Reverend Mother hung up the phone and went directly to investigate the condition of the old accommodation wing. What she found there was worse than she had anticipated. Room after room was in varying degrees of decay, ceilings collapsed, doors hanging off hinges, windows cracked and curtains frayed. And as for identifying which room was Sister Francesca's bedroom? Reverend Mother was at a total loss, all the rooms looked the same. So there and then, she took the executive decision to select a room that was most structurally sound, a room with the ceiling and window intact and, keeping in mind that it may become a place of pilgrimage in the future, she chose a room nearest the toilet block. Then, as if staking her claim, she whispered to herself,

 — This is Sister Francesca's bedroom, and no more about it. There's nothing wrong here that a bit of elbow grease wouldn't put right.


With only two days to Christmas Eve, Reverend Mother began phoning junk shops and auction rooms around the town in search of sufficiently distressed old bedroom furniture of the right vintage.

She then called a general assembly of the sisters. Her concerns were confirmed. Maybe Sister Mary Michael, at the ripe old age of eighty-nine, was feisty enough and could be relied upon for some of the lighter tasks, and Sister Thomasina, a lay-nun who had attached herself to the convent many years ago, was still fit, active and willing, but Reverend Mother realised the job that faced them required young blood. So she sent out an urgent but discreet call for assistance to a select few of the senior girls, to come and help convert the old storage room back into Sister Francesca's bedroom in time for the special Mass. Six young volunteers arrived up to the convent that very afternoon.

The set designer from the local theatre company joined them the following day.

 — So, he said. — You want '70s. Well you've come to the right place, Sister! I am the '70s queen of this town. May I suggest a base colour scheme of orange and black. Formica topped tables, maybe a swath of orange flecked shag pile carpet...
 — What pile carpet?
 — Shag, Sister. Shag...

— There'll be no shaggin' carpet in this room, she snapped. — The
    Bishop wants frugality, starkness, restraint...
— But the '70s is all about excess, Sister.
— Well not in this convent it's not!

And though it took a considerable amount of convincing to talk him
away from the shag pile, furry dice, mirror ball and glitter of the 1970s,
eventually, under Reverend Mother's cajoling, he was guided on track.
With a few dabs of rag roll paint and distressing of timbers with lime
and a few other tricks of his trade, he created the authentic look of
austerity as envisioned by the Bishop.

* * *

It has been two frantic days but, as the clock strikes eight this Christmas
Eve night, the Venerable Sister Francesca Of The Birds' bedroom is
repaired, revamped and ready for Midnight Mass. Reverend Mother
sits down on the bed exhausted but relieved. She gathers her helpers
around her.

— Well girls, she says. — This has been the busiest Christmas Eve
    in living memory here at the convent. You've done a marvellous
    job. We couldn't have done it without you. Thank you all for your
    hard work over the past two days, and thank you for giving up
    your Christmas Eve.
    The Bishop isn't due here until half-past-ten or eleven o'clock
    this evening, so maybe you'd all like to join me in the visitors'
    room for some lemonade and biscuits...

They beam with delight at Reverend Mother's invitation.

— Right so, girls. Follow me...

As Reverend Mother gets to her feet, one of the helpers asks,

— Reverend Mother? Did you ever meet Sister Francesca Of The
    Birds when she was alive?
— That was a long time ago. But yes, I'm privileged to say that I did
    know Sister Francesca Of The Birds before she passed on to her
    eternal rest.

As the reality filters from one to the other that Reverend Mother had
actually been in the presence of a living saint, a surge of excitement fills
the room.

— What? You actually met Sister Francesca Of The Birds, Reverend
  Mother?
— Yes I did, she said.
This sets off an avalanche of questions.
— What is it like to meet a saint?
— Was she very holy, Reverend Mother?
— Like, would I know a saint if I met one?
— Did you know she was a saint while she was alive? Or did you
  only realise she was a saint after she died?
Reverend Mother stretches out her hand.
— Well first things first, she says. — Let's not count chickens before
  they're hatched. Sister Francesca Of The Birds is not a saint yet.
  She has been honoured by the Vatican with the title Venerable.
  But I'm confident that she will be a saint some day.
  In answer to your questions, Sister Francesca Of The Birds was
  a very special person. I was very young at the time, and she was
  nearing the end of her life, so I didn't know her very well personally. Put it this way, back then I wasn't much older than you girls
  are, and Sister Francesca was a little older than I am now ...
  Time is a funny old thing, says Reverend Mother. — Like a conveyor belt, so it is.
The senior girls raise eyebrows and shrug shoulders as they mentally
grapple with the concept of time as a conveyor belt.
— Tell us about Sister Francesca, Reverend Mother?
Reverend Mother re-settles herself on the bed, her young helpers like
a clutch of chicks to a mother hen.
— Well, as I explained, I was very young at that time. But back then
  we had a Sister Agnes The History Teacher, and she was a close
  friend of Sister Francesca Of The Birds throughout her life. They
  both joined the convent around the same time, back before
  World War One, and Sister Agnes The History Teacher told us
  all about the amazing cures that had been performed by Sister
  Francesca Of The Birds when she was a young nun ...

Maybe it is the passage of time that caused the facts to fade? Maybe it
is because the story of Sister Francesca had been retold so many times

and had become so highly polished that the fine detail had been wiped clean from popular memory. Or maybe, the awkward edges of Sister Francesca's early life had been streamlined to fit the requirements of the various petitions submitted to the Vatican down through the decades. Whatever the reason, Reverend Mother neglects to mention Sister Francesca's lifelong special friend, Mossie The Gardener. Neither does she tell of the heroic exploits of Dowcha-boy, the bravest and most magnificent pigeon ever to have hatched on the Northside and all trace of the epic pigeon race that had the people dancing for a week seemed to have disappeared, like it was airbrushed from the pages of history.

    — Reverend Mother?

    — Yes, child?

    — Were you here in the convent on the night Saint Joseph appeared to Sister Francesca Of The Birds?

    — I was, she says.

    — Really! Tell us what happened.

    — Well I remember that night like it was only yesterday. The whole convent was awoken ...

Reverend Mother hesitates for a moment as if attempting to align her facts. Then she continues.

    — The convent was filled with the Holy Spirit that night ...

But once again the boundary between fact and fiction seems to have blurred with time. For some reason she does not tell how the elderly Sister Francesca Of The Birds came running along the corridors in nothing but her nightgown, deranged and screaming that Saint Joseph had been in her bedroom. Neither does she mention that Sister Francesca's lifelong friend, Mossie The Gardener, had retired from his duties earlier that week, and he had been seen wandering around the garden that very day. Various other minor yet complicating details seem to have vanished from the story, such as the half bottle of wine that had been reported missing from the sacristy, and how it had been widely speculated at the time that a half bottle of wine was probably all the courage Mossie The Gardener needed to do something as daft as to visit the senile Sister Francesca's bedroom that night ...

    — Yes, she says. — It was such a special time. Sister Francesca died very soon after that. And on the night she died, a saintly presence descended on the room.

— This room, Reverend Mother?

And maybe Reverend Mother chooses to omit certain details from the life and times of Sister Francesca Of The Birds, but she is genuinely unsure if this room is, in fact, the saintly nun's bedroom so, rather than tell a blatant untruth, she just nods her head and says,

— Yes, there was a saintly presence in her room that night...

* * *

Brother Scully is breathless. He steps into a doorway across the street from the convent to shelter from watchful eyes and the cold driving sleet. For almost fifty years he has viewed Sister Claire's bedroom window from his safe and distant perch high up in the monastery. But here and now, standing in the shadow of the towering convent walls, it all looks so very different. Viewed at such close quarters it seems so strangely unfamiliar. Brother Scully is disorientated. He is unsure which window is Sister Claire's bedroom. Stepping closer, he examines every crack, crevice and crumbling grain of mortar in the old weather-pitted sandstone.

He paces the length of the convent wall searching for some recognisable detail. Then, turning the corner, it all looks like sandstone trimmed with limestone to him, he wonders if he is even standing at the right face of the building. He retreats to the relative safety of the doorway, confused, unsure what he should do next. Then, taking his bearings from Shandon steeple, the stack of Murphy's brewery and his own bedroom up in the monastery, he attempts to calculate the location of Sister Claire's window through a crude process of triangulation.

— That must be it. It must be it, must be, must be...

He stands there starry-eyed, looking for a sign of life.

Still etched in his memory is the beautiful vision of her face from all those years ago, and though Brother Scully concedes that Sister Claire's youthful beauty will have faded with the passage of time, his love for her remains steadfast and unchanged. He reminds himself that a love such as theirs could not have endured if it only relied on something as superficial as the fleeting beauty of youth. His love for her is not some nostalgia-fuelled flirtation of memory. No. Brother Scully loves Sister Claire with all his heart, with all his mind, with all his soul. It is a love that has grown stronger with each and every flash of light that has been beamed out from her window, every single morning for almost fifty years.

He leans from the doorway and calls out her name in a forced whisper.

— Sister Claire! Psssst! Sister Claire!

Then, picking up a pebble, he lofts it gently towards her window. It falls short.

— Pssst! Sister Claire! Sister Claire, he says it a little louder.

He throws another larger stone, sending it rattling off the small glass pane. He thinks he sees a slight movement of the curtain. Could it be just a gust of wind as it slips through the old breezy window frame, or maybe it is the stone causing the glass to shudder so, stepping out from the shadows, he calls out her name.

— Sister Claire!

Then a little louder,

— Sister Claire!

Again he throws a stone, this time sending it crashing through the window, shattering the glass.

— Oh Jesus...

He ducks back into the safety of the doorway.

\* \* \*

Reverend Mother is still seated on the bed, her young helpers are held spellbound at her feet. She is relating the miraculous events that took place around the time of Sister Francesca Of The Birds' death.

— ...it was indeed a very special night, she says. — I remember all the sisters praying at her bedside, our Reverend Mother at that time was leading the Salve Regina. Then a saintly calmness came over Sister Francesca. It was a long time ago and I was very young, but it was one of those moments I will never forget...

Just close your eyes and imagine what it was like here in this

room, almost fifty years ago. Try to experience the closeness to
God...

Reverend Mother's ethereal voice fades as she conjures up the past.
She remains silent. One by one they close their eyes and their minds
drift from the present towards a deep meditation and the total calmness of being.

She inhales deeply and is about to describe the final moments of
Sister Francesca's life, when the sound of breaking glass shatters the
serenity.

   — Jesus! What's that, she says.

Tilting her head to one side, then left and then right, she listens for a
second or two.

   — Shhhh! Anyone hear that, she asks.

She waits for a moment then continues with her tale of the elderly
nun's death.

   — ...well as I was saying, Sister Francesca Of The Birds had a saintly
   countenance, like a heavenly glow emanating from her bed.
   Then she raised her head from the pillow, her eyes fixed in a
   glazed stare towards the door, and she calmly whispered,

   — *He's here. He's here among us. I knew he would come...*

Reverend Mother neglects to mention how sister after sister stepped
aside, forming an avenue of nuns that gradually made its way from the
end of Sister Francesca's death-bed all the way to the door, and when
the last sister stepped aside, standing there in the hallway was her old
friend Mossie The Gardener, cap in hand, crying inconsolably. Reverend
Mother does not describe how the elderly gardener inched his way into
the room, and asked to be alone with the dying nun. No. She does not
tell how Mossie The Gardener held Sister Francesca in his arms. The
elderly couple spoke in hushed tones of the gentility of death, the
brutality of life and the many wonders of nature they had witnessed
during a lifetime shared in that little walled convent garden. And no,
Reverend Mother does not describe how the elderly gardener and
dying nun cuddled in each other's arms and giggled like young lovers,
and how they spoke in hushed tones for over an hour, and the last
words from Sister Francesca's lips were,

   — *And I love you too, Mossie.*

Maybe sometimes it is easier to believe the unbelievable, than to understand the miracle of a love that exists between two mere mortals.

— Hers was the death of a saint. The light of God emanated from Sister Francesca as she breathed her last, and the calm of the Holy Spirit descended upon the room, says Reverend Mother. — And then there was silence, a silence that remained intact until the mournful sound of a lone harrier hound cried out in the distance. Then, one by one, every dog right across the Northside began to howl, from doorway to doorway and street to street, from the Northside across two rivers to the Southside, they howled out a lament that echoed round the five hills, like they were saying goodbye to a dear friend. Goodbye to one of their own...

Once again Reverend Mother is interrupted, when one of her young helpers is drawn to the window by the sound of wild howling outside down on the street.

— What's going on out there, she asks.
— It's the Mad Monk.
— Who?

The girls jostle for a better view. Reverend Mother elbows her way through.

— Please girls, stay away from the window.
  Now, what's going on down there?
— It's Screwball Scully!
— Who?
— You know the one, Reverend Mother? The Mad Monk!
— What mad monk?
— The one that spends his days looking out from his window...
— What window?
— The monastery window. You know, the brother with the yellow face, always looking out the window...

Then rotating her index finger towards her temple she says,

— Screwball Scully, Reverend Mother? The Mad Monk...
— What are you talking about, child? Here, out of my way! Let me

through to the window! Out of my way.

Screwball Scully? Brother Scully from the monastery?

— Yes, Reverend Mother. That's him down there ...

Reverend Mother leans towards the window.

    — Where?

    — There?

    — Where?

    — There, he's just stepped into that doorway, Reverend Mother.

    — Jesus! This is all I need! Stay back from the window, girls!

They watch as the elderly brother peeps out from the shadows of the doorway, then steps from his hide and moves into the middle of the street. Once again he begins calling out for Sister Claire. Reverend Mother manoeuvres herself between the girls and the window, shielding them from the escalating insanity down below.

    — But he's shouting and roaring and throwing stones at the windows, Reverend Mother!

    — Like a madman ...

    — He is a madman, says another.

    — That must have been him breaking one of the windows a few minutes ago, Reverend Mother!

    — Please, girls. Please! Stay back from the window.

Brother Scully is standing there in the middle of the street, his arms outstretched, skin soaked by the driving sleet. Streams of blood from the shaving scars trickle down over his chin and onto his stark white collar. He is bellowing like a wild animal and laughing hysterically.

    — Sister Claire! Sister Claire! Sister Claire!

    — Jesus, Mary and Joseph! This is all I need! Christmas Eve! The Bishop on the way ...

The window is sealed shut by decades of layered paint, but she manages to prise it open just a few inches, then, tapping at the glass with her rosary beads to get his attention, she leans towards the small gap and shouts down to the street.

    — Hey! What do you think you're at down there!

Brother Scully is drawn towards the sound of Reverend Mother's voice.

— Sister Claire! Sister Claire! Is that you, Sister Claire?
— No, she shouts. — There is no Sister Claire in this convent. Now clear off, or I'll call the Guards!
— Sister Claire! Sister Claire?

Brother Scully is confused, his eyes dart from window to window as he attempts to pinpoint the source of her voice.

— Sister Claire! Sister Claire!
— Go on! Clear off! she shouts again.


That's when he sees Reverend Mother's silhouette up on the third floor. Again she crouches sideways towards the gap at the bottom of the window and shouts,

— Go on! Go home! Clear off!
— Sister Claire! I need to speak with Sister Claire, he says it louder. — Sister Claire!
— There is no Sister Claire here!

Worried that the commotion outside the convent might draw the attention of the police, Reverend Mother calls Sister Mary Michael and Sister Thomasina to her side.

— Right, she says. — Sister Mary Michael, you take the girls to the visitors' room and give them lemonade and biscuits. Then phone the monastery and tell them that Brother Scully is here outside the convent and needs to be collected and brought home. Immediately!

Now, Sister Mary Michael! Now!

Reverend Mother claps her hands.

— Okay, girls. Follow Sister Mary Michael down to the visitors' room. I have a few things to sort out here. I will join you as soon as I can, and I will tell you all about Sister Francesca Of The Birds then.

Reverend Mother smiles at the sight of old Sister Mary Michael, shuffling off in a mad blustering dash, her right hand hitching her habit above her ankles, left hand holding her veil firmly in place.

— Sister Thomasina, she says. — You come with me.

She leads the way, her veil billowing as she glides silently along the

*Sister Claire! Sister Claire! Sister Claire!*

corridor and down the stairs, followed close on her heels by Sister Thomasina. By the time they reach the main convent door they are winded and gasping for breath.

Reverend Mother leans back against the wall for a moment until she regains her composure. Beyond the convent wall she can hear the demented roaring of Brother Scully outside in the street.

    — Sister Claire! Sister Claire! Sister Claire! Sister Claire!
Reverend Mother attempts to catch her breath.

    — Jesus, she gasps in a hushed voice. — We don't need this, Thomasina, and we definitely don't need this tonight with the Bishop on his way over. We don't need this at all.
    Look, I'll go out and speak to him. See if I can put a stop to all this madness.
    — I'll go with you, Reverend Mother.
    — No, Sister Thomasina. You stay here, she instructed. — The less fuss out there, the better. I'll keep him distracted until reinforcements arrive from the monastery. You stay here in case we need a Plan B.
    — Plan B, Reverend Mother? What's our Plan B?
    — I'm not sure yet, I'll think about it after I figure out Plan A.

* * *

    *Then one foggy Christmas Eve,*
    *Santa came to say,*
    *Rudolph with your nose so bright,*
    *Won't you guide my sleigh tonight?*
    — Hold it! Hold it! Stop! Hold it! Stop!
The Parrot is fluttering and spluttering and waving hands in the air.
    — Okay, hold it! Stop!
But the combination of eggnog and senility has *Rudolph The Red Nosed Reindeer* off at a gallop and proving difficult to control.
    *Then how the reindeer loved him,*
    *As they shouted out with glee,*
    — Hold it! Please! Hold it!

*Rudolph the red nosed reindeer,*
*you'll go down in...*
— Ah, please! Hold it! Enough! Stop!
The Parrot is still waving his hands frantically above his head.
   — Stop, he roars. — Stop! Will ye stop! Will ye!
   *His-toor-eee...*
   *You'll go down in*
   *his-tooor-eeee...*
One by one the choir of voices disintegrates to silence.
   — Hold it! Hold it just for a second there! Thank you! One moment...
     My apologies, but I eh, have an announcement to make, says the
     Parrot. — Eh? We have just received a telephone call from St
     Joseph's Convent. It appears that Brother Scully has escaped
     and is...
   — Escaped, old Brother O'Connell shouts. — Escaped? Escaped?
     How do you mean he escaped?
Brother O'Connell grapples with his zimmer frame and gets to his feet.
   — How dare you! What do you think this is? A prison! This is a
     monastery, a place of refuge! Not a place of incarceration!
     Brother Scully is free to come and go as he pleases.
   — Sorry! My sincerest apologies, Brother O'Connell, says the
     Parrott. — Eh? I didn't mean he escaped...
     But we have received an urgent call from a distraught nun over
     in the convent, saying that Brother Scully is over there causing
     a disturbance. They are concerned that he may be a danger to
     himself. They have asked that we go over and bring him back
     before someone calls the police, and the whole thing gets blown
     out of all proportion.
     But please don't let this interrupt the party. So if you will excuse
     me, I'll just pop over to St Joseph's and bring Brother Scully
     back...
   — Not without me, you won't, says Brother O'Connell. — I'm his
     oldest friend, and it's at times like this he needs a friend.
   — Certainly! By all means, Brother O'Connell. You're more than
     welcome to accompany me, says the Parrott. — My car is parked
     out in front...

With much puffing and huffing and clearing of the way and moving of footstools and coffee tables, Brother O'Connell manoeuvres his zimmer frame around the various obstacles and slowly makes his way to the door of the common room.

— Take your time, Brother O'Connell.

Easy, now, easy.

Steady, steady!

Mind the table there, good man.

No rush.

Plenty of time.

Careful now, careful...

Easy, easy...

\* \* \*

Brother Scully is distracted by the snap of the bolt and the click of the latch at the far side of the rusting ironclad door. It takes all of Reverend Mother and Sister Thomasina's combined strength just to swing it on its hinges. Slowly it creaks open. From the relative safety of the doorway, Reverend Mother announces in her most forceful voice,

— What in the name of God is going on here!

Brother Scully stands there in swirling sleet, like he's lost in the middle of the street.

— Pull yourself together, man, she says. — What is wrong with you!

He does not respond, as his mind struggles to construct a sentence.

— I need, speak, Sister Claire, he stumbles over the words.

— No, she snaps. — You need to calm down! That's what you need!

Reverend Mother's instruction to calm down sends a surge of rage coursing through his mind. All his life he has been told to calm down. All his life he has been calmed by rules, and when the rules didn't work they calmed him with pills, and when the pills didn't work they attached electrodes to his head and electrocuted short, sharp jolts of calm into his brain. All his life he has been...

Brother Scully opens his mouth to respond but the only words to make it past his lips are,

— I need to speak to Sister Claire...

And pointing towards the sky, he says,
  — Her bedroom...
He attempts to gather the words storming around inside his brain into some sort of a logical grouping.
  — Speak with Sister Claire, he says in a quieter more controlled voice. — I need to tell her...
Brother Scully has not engaged in a coherent conversation for many years, and though his words strengthen in confidence, the logic of what he is attempting to say is lost in the swirling maelstrom of emotions.
  — Dana...
  Eurovision Song Contest...
Then, pointing over his shoulder in the direction of Shandon steeple,
  — Changing of the Guard. Bounced off the fish, he says.
  — Fish? What fish, she says it again as she struggles to make some sense of what he is saying.
He turns and with an outstretched finger he points in the general direction of the grand houses up on Patrick's Hill. Then slowly he retraces the exceptional journey of this morning's first ray of dawn's light. He tracks how it cut across the sky and connected with the golden fish weathervane on Shandon steeple, and was reflected all the way to the second floor of St Joseph's Convent. Brother Scully then places his hands to his face as if protecting his eyes from the glare, and says,
  — Sister Claire's bedroom window. Dazzling gold.
Reverend Mother is more confused than ever.
  — I want to speak with Sister Claire, he says.
For the first time his words are distinct and clear. But yet again the words echoing around inside his head revert to a chaotic tangle of nonsense as they find their way past his lips.
  — Up there!
  Up there, he shouts. — Up there every morning.
  Since Dana! Dana won the Eurovision!
  Flash-flash, Flash Flash!
  Good morning, Brother Scully!
  Every morning!

Flash-flash, Flash Flash!

Good morning, Sister Claire!

Brother Scully is pointing vigorously towards the twelve-pane window, third from the left on the second floor.

— Up there! Up there! Every morning. Flash-flash, Flash Flash!

Then with arms outstretched and looking skywards, he shouts out her name, becoming more and more agitated.

— Sister Claire! Sister Claire! Sister Claire!

— Shhhh! Shhh! Please, calm down. You are creating a disturbance, and frightening the sisters. Please, just calm down...

Now, take your time and tell me calmly what's on your mind?

Brother Scully inhales deeply as he tries to put a structure on the stream of sound from his lips. Gradually the syllables align themselves into words, and the words form a logical sequence.

— I need to speak with Sister Claire...

She's up there! Up there!

Her bedroom window up there.

She flashes her light.

Every single morning since Dana and the colour television.

Flash-flash, Flash Flash! Good morning, Brother Scully.

And I always reply,

Flash-flash, Flash Flash! Good morning, Sister Claire.

No flash this morning...

Please! Please!

I need to speak with Sister Claire.

Each word he utters inspires confidence, and gradually his conversation becomes more lucid and fluid.

— I really need...

...to speak with Sister Claire.

— Sister Claire, repeats Reverend Mother.

Brother Scully closes his eyes, and drawing on all his innermost strength he says,

— Please listen to me.

I met Sister Claire many, many years ago. The night of the colour television.

— Colour television?

— The night Dana won the Eurovision ...

— Sister Claire?

— That's right, he says. — Long time ago. We have not spoken in all these years. Every morning for almost fifty years, she flickers her light to me, and I flicker my light to her. This morning no flash of light. I am worried.

I need to speak with Sister Claire ...

— Sister Claire? Reverend Mother repeats the name as if some long forgotten memory is stirring in her brain. — Sister Claire, she says it again.

— Yes, he says.

— Well there was a young novice in this convent, a Sister Claire.

— That's her, he says. — I need to speak to her.

— That was a long time ago. Forty or fifty years ago or so ...

— That's her, he says. — I need to talk to her. I need to tell her ...

There is a desperation in his voice. So to avoid any confusion, Reverend Mother speaks with clarity as if talking to a child.

— Do you hear me, Brother Scully? That was a long time ago.

— I only want to speak with her.

— But that Sister Claire is not here any more.

— She is here, he insists.

— There is no Sister Claire in this convent.

— She's up there!

Again Brother Scully points towards the second floor, a surge of anxiety rises up from inside him.

— Her bedroom!

She flashes her light every morning...

Flash-flash, Flash Flash!

Up there! Sister Claire's bedroom. Every single morning! She flashes her light.

Flash-flash, Flash Flash!

Sister Claire, he shouts. — Sister Claire! Sister Claire!

Reverend Mother steps out from the convent doorway and moves onto the street. She attempts to ease Brother Scully's distress and asks,

— Show me the window you think is Sister Claire's bedroom, Brother Scully?

Then staring upwards at the towering convent wall she says,

— Just point it out to me. From which window do you see the flashing light each morning?

Brother Scully hesitates, then points his finger feebly towards the second floor, and slowly he begins to count the windows.

— One, two, three. That's Sister Claire's bedroom there, he says.

— The third window from left on second floor, is it?

— Yes, he says quietly. — That's it.

Reverend Mother looks Brother Scully directly into his eyes and shaking her head she says,

— That is not a bedroom.

— It is, he insists. — It's Sister Claire's Bedroom. Every morning. She flashes her light bulb.

— Look, clearly you are confused and upset. I really don't wish to cause you you any further distress, but that room, third from the left on the second floor is not a bedroom.

— Not a bedroom?

— No. There are no bedrooms on that floor.

— No bedrooms on that floor?

— We never had bedrooms on that floor, she says.

— Never had?

— No, she says.

— It is Sister Claire's bedroom, he insists. — She flashes her light bulb every single morning.

— No, she says. — You're not listening to me. There are no bedrooms on that floor. That floor has the kitchen, dining room, utility room and the laundry room. Believe me, there are no bedrooms on the second floor.

— No bedrooms, he echoes her words.

— I'm sorry, she says it again. — But there's obviously some mistake here. That window you are pointing at is actually the pantry window.

— The pantry?

— Yes, Brother Scully. That is the pantry window, the little room just off the kitchen.
— But, her light? She flashes her light!
 Flash-flash, Flash Flash!
 Every single morning since Dana won the Eurovision ...
Reverend Mother interrupts him and, placing a comforting hand on Brother Scully's arm, she gently says,
— No, Brother Scully. Listen to me ...
 The flashing light bulb you've observed every morning is just the flickering of the fluorescent light in the pantry. That's all ...
 The pantry is one of the first lights turned on in the convent every morning.
— Flickering fluorescent light?
— Yes, she says. — The kitchen staff are first to start work in the convent, preparing for the breakfast in the pantry. And that is the flashing light you've been observing all these years. It's just the flicker of a fluorescent tube. That's all ...
— A fluorescent tube?
— Yes, she says. — It's always been like that.
 One of the old type ...
 It always flickers when we switch it on ...
Crushed under the burden of truth, Brother Scully's knees give way beneath him. He staggers backwards. His mind is plunged into turmoil with the realisation that for almost fifty years his devotion to Sister Claire has been squandered on a fluorescent bulb.

Reverend Mother is still chuntering on in the background. She's saying that ever since she can remember the light in the pantry has been like that.
— Sometimes we have to tap the white thingy on the side of the light fitting with a broom handle to get it to work, she says. — I think it's called a starter? A faulty starter ...
She's saying that fixing the light in the pantry has been on her list of jobs for years,
— ...but other more pressing things always seem to push it to the back burner.

317

— The light in the pantry?

— Yes, she says. — That's right...

Brother Scully becomes distressed as the reality sinks in that for almost fifty years, he has beamed out his undying love and devotion to nothing but a faulty starter in a fluorescent light fitting.

— A faulty starter?

— Yes.

— Jesus Christ, no...

All his life he has straddled the fine line of madness. Insanity has always been his refuge from the pain of sanity. His rare moments of sanity were only made bearable by the flickering light of love that beamed out from Sister Claire's bedroom window each morning. But now, after all those years, Brother Scully finds himself standing in the middle of the street this Christmas Eve, with nowhere to hide from the pain of reality; nowhere to hide from the questions spinning around in his brain.

How could he have been so naive? How could he have been such a fool? He had always been the cynical one, the one with the enquiring mind, the one who questioned everything, the one who took nothing at face value, the one who dismissed all belief without proof, the one who had boldly held blind faith up to the light and had seen right through it.

— Oh, Jesus Christ, he says it again.

From the intellectual high ground of his deep and enquiring mind he has always ridiculed true believers and scorned the sheepish innocence of the faithful...

— No, Jesus, no.

How could he have been so deluded? How could he have been so gullible? For almost five decades he has been blinded by his own unquestioning belief that behind every flash beamed out from St Joseph's Convent was the hand of a beautiful woman, flicking a light switch sending her secret and undying love to him.

— Jesus Christ Almighty...

How could he have been so blinkered? A gentle moan of pain passes his lips as he hangs his head in shame.

— No, no, no, no ...

Painful memories of that night in the monastery kitchen all those years ago flash before his mind. The conceit of youth, the swagger, the chest puffed out, the high notions and grand theories. The big man himself, with all the answers, pontificating to the young nun, proclaiming statement after statement, as he ridiculed the nonsense of her blind belief without proof. His words come back to haunt him.

— *Belief? What is belief? Belief is but the acceptance of something that on the face of it is blatantly untrue ...*
*There are none who believe like those who need to believe.*

How quickly he had dismissed the beliefs of others without once stopping to question his own beliefs. And now, after all these years he must confront the painful truth that all his life he too has been a believer. How could he have been so shamelessly smug, to imagine that a young beautiful woman would faithfully and exclusively surrender her life's love to him? How could he have been so pathetically vain to think that a flash of light from his bedroom each morning was all she required for her to put her whole life on hold?

— No, no, no ...

The truth is too painful to contemplate. He stands there in the middle of the street, soaked to the skin, his Warfarin-thinned blood still streaming from his razor-scarred chin, his arms outstretched, and in one final act of desperation he calls out her name.

— Sister Claire!

As the full realisation of the futility of his life comes crashing down on him he just whispers,

— Sister Claire ...

And there in the middle of the street he crumples to his knees, and for the first time in almost fifty years, Brother Scully begins to weep. Tears of painful self-pity trickle down over his cheeks. He is grieving a love lost to denial, and a life lost to fear. He sheds tears that have been locked away inside his frozen heart for decades, for there is nothing more painful than to mourn the loss of something you never had. And so the elderly Brother Scully cries out loud, lamenting the love of his life, a love he never knew.

Seeing the depth of his despair, Reverend Mother steps closer and places her hand on his shoulder, there is something in the human touch that can soothe the deepest pain. She stands there in silence. Brother Scully looks up, his once piercing blue eyes now milky with encroaching cataracts, glowing translucent in the light of the street lamp. His stare has the intensity of a blind man. Slowly he begins to speak,

— You pity me, he says. — You think I'm just a foolish old man, and maybe you're right. Maybe I am mad, like they say I am. But this I know is true …

I was young once, a long time ago.

I was young once and I met a young novice. Her name was Sister Claire. It was forty, fifty years ago or so. A long time ago.

There are things I should have said back then. Maybe my life would have taken a very different path if I had. But I didn't come over here to the convent this night to change my life. It's too late for that. I came here just to tell Sister Claire what I should have told her all those years ago. Maybe some would say I am a mad man? And maybe they'd be right.

Reverend Mother comfortingly says,

— Please, no …

Her hand squeezes his shoulder gently.

— Jesus. I should have told her all those years ago, he continues.
— It's been bottled up, burning a hole in my soul and festering inside me ever since.

She asked me to tell her.

She pleaded with me to tell her.

She begged me to tell her.

The last words on her lips as she walked away from the monastery gate that night were,

— *Just say it. Please say it* …

But I being young and foolish, I just didn't have the courage, I didn't say what I should have said. I didn't tell her what was on my mind. And by Christ, I have lived with the pain of regret ever since.

There is something about the hopelessness and anguish in the elderly brother's eyes that recalls Christ's agony in the garden of Gethsemane.

— Love? What is love, he says. — Look at me? Just take one look at me. Christ's sake, just look at what love has done to me. Maybe Bossman Begley was right all those years ago. Maybe love is Satan's trump card.

In the distance, Reverend Mother sees the headlights of a car winding its way down the avenue from the monastery. It will only be a matter of minutes before they come to take Brother Scully home.

There is calmness in the air as the wind subsides and the driving sleet turns to gently falling snow. The elderly nun helps Brother Scully to his feet, there is something magical about this moment, a long-forgotten tinder of tender intimacy is rekindled.

— Maybe you should tell me, she says.
— Tell you? Tell you what?
— Yes, she says. — Why don't you tell me what you would say to Sister Claire, if she were standing here in front of you?
— You think I should tell you what I would say to her?
— Yes, she says. — Fifty years is a long time to have something bottled up inside.

It crosses his mind that her request may be just another patronising gesture to calm a foolish old man, but there is a glimmer of sincerity in her eyes.

— Please, she says. — Please, tell me. We don't have much time ... Just say it ...

And maybe it's the moonlight, or the stillness of the night, or the urgency in her voice, but Brother Scully is at ease and comfortable in the elderly nun's company. It seems so familiar, as if he has been here before.

— Please, she says it again. — Please, tell me what you would say ...
— What I would say to her, he asks.
— Yes, what would you say to Sister Claire if she were standing here in front of you? Do you know what you would tell her?
— Do I know, he says. — I know exactly what I would say to her.

— Well say it now, or say it never…
— I have thought about nothing else for the past fifty years, he says.
  — All my life I have been tortured by the words I didn't say that night. Ever since that night, they've been churning and turning and twisting around and around in my brain.
  It's like all these years I have been trapped in the spell that was cast that night and, ever since, regret has devoured me like cancer of the soul…

Brother Scully closes his eyes.
— You can tell me. Please, tell me now, she whispers.

Her words connect with the deepest of Brother Scully's emotions. He stands there, snowflakes blending with tears as they melt and stream down his cheeks and gather at the corners of his lips.
— Please, she says.
— You really want to know what I would have said to that young nun all those years ago?
— Yes, she pleads in a hushed voice. — Yes…
— What I would say?
— For God's sake! Yes! Say it now or say it never…

He breathes in deeply and, reaching out, he gently holds the elderly nun's fingertips, then, drawing her close, the words begin to flow,
— I would say to her…

He stops to regroup his thoughts.
— I would say, I would say…
  I would say. I love Jesus Christ. But I love you more.

Brother Scully hesitates for a moment. He sees a flash of recognition in the elderly nun's eyes like a faint echo from the past.
— What else, she whispers.
— I would say I don't know the meaning of love, but I know I can't live without you. I would sell my soul for eternity, just to spend the rest of my living days with you.
  That's what I would say…

They stand there in the moonlight, hand in hand, face-to-face, snow-flakes gently falling all around, like they are encased in their own private snow globe, living in a dream, sheltered from the cold, the pain and the harsh realities of life.

   — Is that all you would say, she asks?

Brother Scully leans closer and, looking into her eyes, he says,

   — Take my hand. Trust that love is a Godly thing and heaven sent. Trust that God in all his wisdom will provide.

Again Brother Scully hesitates. The sparkle in her eyes, the soft touch of her fingertips, the sensation of her hand on his transports him to another time.

   — There are a thousand things I would say, he says.

   — Could have, would have, should have.

   — But there is really only one thing I regret, that I did not say.

   — Say it now...

The elderly nun holds him closer, her eyes pleading.

   — Please, just say it.

But he stands there mute.

   — Believe me, Brother Scully, she says. — Regret may be the deepest pain. But the regret of words unheard cuts just as deep as the regret of words unspoken.

And, standing there in the middle of the street, they hold each other close.

   — Please just say it. I beg you, Brother Scully.

   Tell me what you should have told me all those years ago.

Her words resound around Brother Scully's head, as he attempts to unravel what she has just said.

   — *You*, he says. — You were there?

   — Yes, she says. — Yes! For Christ's sake, Brother Scully! Have I changed so much! I was there that night. I was there in the library garden. We sat beneath the shadow of that cherry blossom tree.

Brother Scully's lips tremble as he says her name,

   — Sister Claire?

   — It's Sister Bernadette. Remember! Remember, I told you. I would take the name Bernadette as my religious name. Remember I

told you that I had seen the film *Song For Bernadette*. Saint
Bernadette inspired me to choose the religious life. Do you
remember, she says it softly.

— Sister Bernadette?

— That's right, she says. — This is me. So please say now what you
should have said all those years ago. I have waited almost fifty
years to hear the words ...

Just say it...

There is something about the mottled moonlight and how it filters and
flitters through the falling snow that casts him right back to that night
when they sat in the shade of the cherry blossom tree. Brother Scully
looks into the elderly nun's eyes, then, studying her features, her face
becomes the most beautiful vision he has ever seen. Tears begin to
flow ...

— I love you, Sister Claire. I always have and I always will ...

Wrapping his arms around her, his hands cradle the curve of her spine
beneath the coarse weave of her robe. They stand there for an eternity.
The two lovers are transported to another time, another place, transported to a place of possibilities, where all is young and fresh and
bright in the world. They stand there in the middle of the street, holding
each other tight and, once again, like Adam and Eve in the Garden of
Eden, their true emotions are stripped bare in the eyes of God.


The car screeches to a halt, headlights pick up the falling snowflakes.
The sound of the doors opening and Brother O'Connell grappling and
battling his zimmer frame out of the back seat cuts through the stillness of the night. Then in the distance the Parrot calls out,

— Brudder Scully? You're safe now, Brudder Scully.
We're here to bring you home ...

— Home?

Brother Scully echoes the word quietly. He acknowledges his full
understanding of all that is past and present, and whispers,

— It is finished.

Gently releasing his warm hold on her, he bows his head, resigning
himself to the destiny of his fate. He gives up the ghost of the future and

returns to his past. He turns and walks away. The elderly nun stands there in the falling snow, alone in the middle of the street. Caught in the high beams like shadow puppets, the silhouettes of the Parrot and old Brother O'Connell reach out and escort Brother Scully away. The stillness of the night is interrupted by the huffing and puffing and racket as Brother O'Connell struggles back into the car.

She sees the Parrot open the passenger door and hears him say something like,

— Maybe you'd like to sit in the front, Brudder Scully?
— Thank you, Mister Perrott, he says. — You were always a good lad, a mannerly lad…

Brother Scully straightens his shoulders, stretches his back and stands erect. Through the snowflakes he sees her, still standing there in the middle of the street, ankle deep in a blanket of white snow, the tears on her cheeks glinting like streams of silver in the glow of the street lamp. And maybe it's a trick of the light and how the falling snow casts a shadow on her face, but he swears he sees her lips move. Or maybe it is just the whispering of the wind, but he hears her say,

— I love you too, Brother Scully…

# Epilogue

It's the darkness before dawn this Christmas morn, and all the world is at peace. Not a soul scurrying through the streets, no movement along the quays, nothing stirring. The only sign of life is the odd flicker of light from the houses away up on the Northside.

In a convent towering above the town, an elderly nun sits at her window staring into the darkness. She removes her veil, leans forward in her chair and examines her reflection in the glass.

Her skin is soft and supple. In a fleeting moment of vanity, she cradles her face between thumb and index finger and, gently caressing her chin, she tightens the slack, revealing her once youthful bone structure and taut jawline. But she is under no illusion, she will be seventy next birthday and the reflection she sees is the face of an old woman.

— Have I changed so much? Have I changed at all ...

It's been the busiest Christmas Eve in living memory, but now that the Bishop has come and gone, peace and calm have been restored to the convent once more.

Looking out over the city, her eyes travel across Brewery Valley, through a forest of TV aerials, past darkened silhouettes of twisted slate clad buckled beams, half-cocked chimney pots, spires and towers, before finally fixing on the monastery. She sets her gaze on a six-pane window on the top floor, Brother Scully's bedroom. It is a private and secret ritual she has observed every single morning for almost half a century, this Christmas morning is no different.

She sits there pondering the life she has lived, decisions made, opportunities lost, opportunities gained. She wonders what if? What if she had said what she should have said? What if she had done what she could have done? What if? Yet deep in her heart and soul she knows she would not change one moment of the life she has lived, even if that means living with the pain of, *what if?*

And, just as the faint glow of dawn begins to gather on the horizon, she reaches towards the switch of her table lamp. She strays from the usual greeting and beams out the words,

— Flash-flash-flash, Flash Flash.

She waits a few moments.

— Flash-flash-flash-flash.

Is his reply.

THE END

# Biography

Cónal Creedon is a novelist, playwright and documentary filmmaker.

Adjunct Professor of Creative Writing at University College Cork [2016-2020).

His published books include: *Pancho and Lefty Ride Out* (1995), *Passion Play* (1999), *Second City Trilogy* (2007), *The Immortal Deed Of Michael O'Leary* (2015), *Cornerstone,* an anthology of student writing. (ed.) UCC/Cork City Libraries (2017).

His prose has been translated into German, Bulgarian, Italian, with English extracts published in China.

Cónal's stage plays include: *The Trial Of Jesus* (2000), *Glory Be To The Father* (2002), *After Luke* (2005), *When I Was God* (2005), *The Cure* (2005). His plays received critical acclaim in Shanghai, China, when they featured at World Expo Shanghai (2010) and The JUE International Arts Festival Shanghai (2011). The USA premieres were produced at The Irish Repertory Theatre, New York (2009) and the Green Room Theatre, New York (2013). The New York productions were critically acclaimed. Productions of his work have been awarded two Irish National Business2Arts Awards (2000), Best Director at The 1st Irish Theatre Awards New York (2009), Best Actor at The 1st Irish Theatre Awards New York (2013) — with nominations for the Irish Times Theatre Awards (2000), Best Playwright at The 1st Irish Theatre Awards New York (2013).

Creedon has written over 60 hours of original radio drama — broadcast on RTÉ, Lyric FM, BBC, BBC Radio 4 and BBC World Service. His short fiction has achieved recognition in the One Voice Monologue Awards (BBC), The Francis McManus Awards (RTÉ), The PJ O'Connor Awards (RTÉ) and has represented Ireland in the BBC World Service World Play Radio Drama Competition. Critical reviews of Cónal's radio work include commendations in the Irish Times radio critics list of Best Radio of the Year for 1994 and 1997.

Cónal has produced, written and directed a number of film documentaries: *The Burning of Cork* (2005), *Why the Guns Remained Silent in Rebel Cork* (2006), *If it's Spiced Beef* (2007), *The Boys of Fairhill* (2009). His documentary, *Flynnie: The Man Who Walked Like Shakespeare* (2008) was shortlisted for Focal International Documentary Awards UK London. Creedon's documentaries were broadcast by RTÉ TV — and were presented at numerous public screenings including at the Irish Pavilion in Shanghai China, during World Expo 2010.

## *Second City Trilogy* [three stage plays]

*1st Irish New York Theatre Awards 2009, 2013*
   Awarded: Best Director & Best Actor
   Nominated: Best Playwright

*ICA Wicklow Federation Drama Festival 2014*
   Awarded: Best Actor & Best Supporting Actor

*Commissioned by European Capital of Culture 2005*
   First production Cork Opera House 2005

*Production History*
   New York — Plays Upstairs 2008
   New York — New York 1st Irish Theatre Festival 2009
   Irish Repertory Theatre 2009
   Shanghai — World Expo 2010
   Shanghai — Jue International Arts Festival 2011
   New York — New York 1st Irish Theatre Festival 2013
   Green Room Theatre — Ryan's Daughter 2013
   New York — Beal Bocht 2013
   New York — Irish Arts Centre Queens 2016

As written by Cónal Creedon, such moments resound with wince-inducing authenticity before they are eclipsed by an inspirational twist — words, inflected with the faintly Scandinavian accent of Munster, soar like a bracing breeze off the River Lee.
   *Andy Webster, New York Times, 2013.*

Fathers and sons and the damage done: this is the theme, with variations, of the Cork writer Cónal Creedon's fine plays "After Luke" and "When I Was God," which can be seen in a nearly pitch-perfect production. Mr Creedon's words are enough to create a world that is at once comic and dramatic, poetic and musical.
   *Rachel Saltz, New York Times, 2009.*

Irish playwrights (from Yeats and Wilde and Synge and Shaw on down to now) are always good going on great, and the latest in that endless chain is the all but unknown in America, Cónal Creedon. Unknown no longer, Creedon's short, idiosyncratic "After Luke," and even shorter, punchier "When I Was God," comprise a disturbing two-hour double-bill. Idiosyncratic? Bite off any hunk of either work; it's all as chewy as leather yet weirdly digestible. None of this would be unfamiliar to, let's say, D.H. Lawrence, or, for that matter, George Orwell. What hasn't been heard before is the thorny voice of 48-year-old Cónal Creedon of County Cork, Ireland, who, from all reports, is a lot gentler in the flesh than on paper.

*Jerry Tallmer, New York Villager, 2009.*

At times it feels Beckett-like, you might think the people are too unusual to exist but they actually do.

*Gwen Orel, New York City Arts, 2009.*

...the highlight of last year's theatre in Shanghai came all the way from Cork in Irish playwright's Cónal Creedon's double-header of short plays — powerful, yet punctuated with humour, lyrical and richly colloquial. They were terrific!

*That's Shanghai Magazine [China], March 2011.*

They were discussing what should go into the Irish Millennium Time-Capsule. If they are looking for something to represent Ireland, how about Cónal Creedon's *Under the Goldie Fish*? It's so off the wall, that it shouldn't ring true, but the most frightening fact is that it does...

*Eilís O'Hanlon, Sunday Independent, 2008.*

*The Cure* is a dramatic creation that straddles what we once were and what we have become. It examines closely the fracture at the heart of our contemporary experience — scavenging the thesaurus for sufficient superlatives for this fine piece of writing — yes we liked it. We liked it a lot.

*Irish Examiner, 2005.*

Everyone loves the Irish. It's just a fact. Creedon's script is a rich fusion of melancholy poetry and affable banter. Aidan O'Hare and 'The Cure' are a match made in monologue heaven. Its potency lies in the profound ability of the playwright and the actor to connect directly with people. 'The Cure' is a truly fine piece of theatre, one that is Irish to its core but anything but provincial in its scope. You couldn't ask for anything more than this.

*Smart Shanghai Magazine, March 2011.*

This is contemporary theater that plays like the works of a past master. The work of Irish playwright Cónal Creedon, are quite simply a delight, [but] not in an all sunshine and light way. On a sparse stage on which the characters can only live or die, it lives. Underlying all is a love of language and a keen observance of detail — Creedon is lyrical, and uses rhyme and rhythm, without being showy, and enriches with the Cork colloquial without alienating — Come back soon, you are always welcome on the Shanghai stage.

*Arts Editor, Talk Shanghai.*

A one-man show at the Ke Center proves that you don't need a huge cast to produce a hit — their recent collaboration with Irishtown Productions proves that they are on top of their game. Cork playwright Cónal Creedon's gritty soliloquy 'The Cure' saw Irish actor Aidan O'Hare command the stage as a man left behind by a racing economy and changing city. Creedon's use of language is dizzyingly attractive. He manipulates repetition to great effect, bringing the opening lines back several times in chilling sonata form. As for the staging, the Ke Center's stark space was the perfect backdrop for a bleak but redemptive piece of drama.

*Asiacity Network, Shanghai, China, 2011.*

A pair of tenderly drawn plays by Conal Creedon, set in Creedon's native Cork, probe the tough love and tough hurt — exchanged by men in Irish Families. Both plays — are intimately conceived and performed, tracing in chiaroscuro, the intersection between kinship and machismo.

*New Yorker Magazine.*

The Cure is the bittersweet tale of a man who has emotionally lost his way. As with the previous two plays, Creedon explores the frustrations of average lives, to the backdrop of historical happenings in the play-wright›s hometown. And as with the previous two, the script is lyrical and rich with colloquialism, the melancholy lifted with moments of delightful amusement. ("When the chemistry goes in a relationship,» he reflects on marriage and drink, "There's nothing for it but to take more chemicals –A fine piece of theatre...

*That's Shanghai Magazine, Urbanatomy Shanghai, March 2011.*

A complex enthralling piece of theatre that boasts the dual achieve-ment of entertaining and educating — a testament to Creedon's shrewd writing skill.

*Irish Independent, 2005.*

Vigorously sustained by stylish performances and an ingenious script which marries comedy and pathos with a sure hand. They'll love it. It's impossible not to.

*Sunday Times, 2001.*

# Passion Play

## Critical Review

*Passion Play — Book of the Year*
*Saturday Review, BBC Radio 4, 2000.*

The novel's interior is much indebted to Joyce. The way Creedon combines the child-centred perspective of *Paddy Clarke Ha! Ha! Ha!* with the tough teenage world of *The Commitments* and the domestic cruelty of *The Woman Who Walked Into Doors* is ambitious and effective. His exposition of his characters' thought processes owes much to Flann O'Brien's skewed sophistication and Patrick McCabe's scabrous vision as to an earlier prototype of Seán O'Casey's Joxer. Creedon has found a form all of his own.

C.L. Dallat, *Times Literary Review [TLS, London]*.

Creedon can create characters, not just mouthing amusing philosophical meanderings, not just cold abstractions, these are creations of Creedon's great humanity. It is essential that I tell you here that you must finish this book. A wonderful inventive comedy.

Tom Widger, *Sunday Tribune*.

It's one of those books where it often feels inappropriate to either laugh or cry, at times surreal, frequently hilarious, often poignant but never, ever dull — the reader enters the twilight zone.

*U Magazine*.

In my opinion one of the finest novelists to emerge in Ireland. Passion Play is terrific. Do yourself a favour — go out and buy a copy of this book.

*First Edition, Chorus TV*.

I thought so much of this was so good. I haven't been as impressed by a book in a long time, Irish or otherwise. The sheer vitality of *Passion Play* is wonderful.

*Declan Lynch, Imprint, RTÉ TV.*

I think he's fantastically skilled as a writer, a wonderful read — it came as a huge surprise. The whole thing worked amazingly well.

*Kathy Sheridan, Imprint, RTÉ TV.*

The characters blend into a technical stew and keep you laughing, even though you know unfolding events are desperately sad. The people stay with you, their situations desperately real, so implausible they are possible and probable; you are invited to suspend disbelief and follow, an invitation worth having.

*Tatler Magazine.*

*Passion Play Translation History*
> Italian: Le Lettre Publishing House, Florence, Italy
> Bulgarian: Zoltar Publishing House, Sofia, Bulgaria

*Extracts Published*
> Germany: Verlag Die Werkstatt Publishing, Berlin
> Australia: Kunappi Press, Australia
> China: Irish Network Beijing, Millennium with extracts published in various literary periodicals.

*Reaction to Book*
> Best Seller List, Eason [Irish Bookseller]
> Book of the Week, W.H. Smith [UK Bookseller]
> Book of the Week, *Irish Examiner*
> Book on One, RTÉ [Irish National Broadcaster]
> Book of the Week, RAI [Italy National Broadcaster]

*Academic Appraisal of Passion Play*

*Passion Play* was translated into Italian by Dr Fiorenzo Fantaccini, Florence University in 2001.

Two papers delivered by Dr Gioia Gamerra and Dr Conci Mazzullo at the International Association of the Study of Irish Literature (IASIL):

Dr Gioia Gamerra, Universita degli Studi di Firenze, *Memories [as] a mixture of stories, truths, untruths and other people's memories: Narrative and cinematographic strategies in* Passion Play *by Cónal Creedon.*

Dr Conci Mazzullo.
*Station Ireland:* Passion Play *According to Cónal Creedon.*

Made in the USA
Columbia, SC
16 August 2022

65422061R00205